THE CARDINAL'S CURSE

LYNDEE WALKER

BRUCE ROBERT COFFIN

SEVERN RIVER

PUBLISHING

Severn River Publishing
www.SevernRiverBooks.com

This is a work of fiction. Names, characters, businesses, places, events and incidents are either the products of the author's imagination or used in a fictitious manner. Any resemblance to actual persons, living or dead, or actual events is purely coincidental.

ISBN: 978-1-64875-595-8 (Paperback)

ALSO BY THE AUTHORS

The Turner and Mosley Files

The General's Gold

The Cardinal's Curse

The Pirate's Secret

The Pharaoh's Tomb

BY LYNDEE WALKER

The Faith McClellan Series

The Nichelle Clarke Series

Never miss a new release!

To find out more about the authors and their books, visit

severnriverbooks.com

To our loyal readers, thank you for accompanying us on yet another wonderful adventure.

"The greatest adventure is what lies ahead." — J.R.R. Tolkien

PROLOGUE

Lierre
November 1537

Cardinal Olav Engelbrektsson knelt beside an open crate and reached inside, lifting the heavy jewel-encrusted golden crown from its bed of hay. The weight of the crown was nothing, he realized, not when compared to the weight of actual rule. For thirteen years Olav had presided over Norway. Absent a king, and floundering through the Black Death, the country's leadership had fallen on Olav as the Archbishop of Nidaros. It was a role he had fully embraced, even fought to defend. For seven months in exile, he'd prepared to fight anew for the crown he nestled back into the hay now.

"Soon," he murmured.

Following the accession of Christian III to the throne of Denmark and the Danish claim of Norway as a dependency, Olav had been forced to flee his home in Steinvikholm Castle for Nidarholm Abbey on the isle of Munkholmen. Accompanied by one hundred of his most loyal followers, including his cousin and trusted confidant, Admiral Trondson, Olav spent a long cold winter on the remote island, plotting his return to Norway, intent on seizing control of his country and securing its independence once again from Danish rule.

Olav's gaze returned to the crate and the ceremonial sword contained within, his thoughts wandering to the idealistic young priest who had tried to prevent him from taking the crown—one the Danish king would never deserve—and the shocked expression on the boy's face as Olav ran him through with the sword. Dark streaks of dried blood still stained the quillon and blade. Ruthlessness and power came at a price Olav's followers would never know.

"Is something wrong, my lord?" Trondson asked, appearing in the doorway, the buzz of low conversation among his trusted soldiers barely audible outside.

Pulled from his reverie, Olav turned his head to respond to his cousin.

The admiral was a burly, bearded man with a fierce gaze. But his eyes also carried within them a darkness. *His own burden*, Olav thought. The heavy weight and cost of battle.

"No, Kristoffer," Olav said. "All is as it should be, save for one thing."

"Norway," Trondson said, as if reading Olav's very thoughts.

"Home," Olav said, his attention returning to the crown.

"When we have completed this journey and forced the Danes out, you will once again be restored as the rightful leader of our country," Trondson said, then beckoned for two of his men to come forward.

"There will be obstacles, Kristoffer," Olav said. "Men who will stand in our way."

"We have faced obstacles before, my lord."

Indeed, they had. Ruthless men like Vincens Lunge, the Rikshovmeister of Norway. But Kristoffer had personally seen to that problem for Olav, slaying the lord high steward in defiance of the Danish Privy Council. Lunge's murder had been tantamount to treason, forcing Olav to flee to exile.

"There are scores who will stand and fight for you," the admiral continued. "This I know. You will see. Besides, we still have God on our side."

Olav fixed his cousin with a weary half smile. "Yes, God." Kristoffer's confidence and unwavering faith had provided Olav with strength, but his heart was heavy once again as his gaze returned to the distant mountains of Denmark. "I pray you are correct, cousin."

But which of God's teachings was precisely the problem. The struggle for power and control of Norway extended far beyond the Danish monarchy and was now infecting the House of God as the Protestant Church attempted to replace Catholicism by force. Olav had already learned a painful and expensive lesson regarding the fragility of alliances. He had foolishly mistaken what another man saw as an opportunity for loyalty. It was a mistake he would not make a second time.

Two broad-shouldered young men approached, both loyal subordinates of Trondson's.

"We are nearly loaded, Admiral," the taller of the two men said as he gestured between the wagons and crate at Olav's feet.

"Shall we go, my lord?" Trondson said.

"It is time," Olav said, settling the lid over the wooden box and sealing the crown out of sight. As he watched Trondson's men carry the load toward the wagons, he couldn't help but wonder if he would live long enough to wear the precious headdress again.

1

***

Present Day

Avery Turner peered through the scuba mask at her diving partner, Carter Mosley. Though he was less than ten feet away, she struggled to make out the details of his form. She wished her diving light was brighter—or that the chilly water of the Hudson Bay was a bit less disgusting and more transparent. She hadn't expected this much sediment, nor the dangerous tangle of debris protruding from the ocean floor reaching up toward them like gnarled hands. The Caribbean, this was not.

Strapped to her wrist was the prototype for TreasureTech's DiveNav. Constructed from a lightweight and extremely strong alloy, the high-tech, waterproof navigational computer was state of the art in every conceivable way. Avery herself had written the software code in hopes the device would assist them in their future treasure hunting adventures. Fresh off a major historical find, one that had her speaking publicly at a handful of museums, Avery wanted to build on the momentum and success she and Carter had already achieved.

The seaward current was strong, bordering on a dangerous underwater riptide. Avery felt its pull and wondered what effect it was having on Carter. The DiveNav flashed, indicating they should retreat toward a narrow shelf at the edge of what was known as the Hudson Canyon. With less than twenty minutes left before they would need to begin their ascent to the surface, she was torn between Carter's well-tuned internal compass and her own programming prowess. As if in answer to her thoughts, Carter signaled for her to follow, the water pushing her harder away from him. When the DiveNav flashed again, Avery saw a beacon locator return for the Fiji islands and shook her head and her wrist. The device switched back to the nearby shelf, and she swam after Carter, searching her vicinity for anything that might have interfered with its ability to locate the most likely resting place of the yacht *Moneymaker*—if it really was in Fiji, the New York City DA was about to be sorely disappointed.

Avery's mother had been working a lead involving the *Moneymaker* before she died. So when her former partner and Avery's right-hand man, Harrison, had gotten a call from NYPD Homicide Commander Roger Antonin asking for Avery's help searching for the wreck, Avery cleared her schedule.

"What are we looking for?" she'd asked.

"Less a what and more of a who," Harrison replied grimly. The body of a Broadway showgirl named Melody Fisher was possibly down there—she was last seen boarding the *Moneymaker* with Randolph Maggio, playboy son of famed Wall Street trader Bennie Maggio, who was long-rumored to have ties to organized crime. "No cop in New York can hear Maggio's name without asking if Wall Street or the mob makes him more of a criminal," Harrison had said when he explained the urgency of the search to Avery. "Randolph is about to go to trial on conspiracy charges associated with an online Ponzi scam, but he has an army of powerful lawyers and the DA's case is thin. If we can find Melody's body, there are deals to be made that could take down more than just his crook of an old man."

Avery had read the entire case file: the yacht had left the New Moon Bay marina on a summer night with calm seas, and never returned. The coast guard picked up a drunk and blubbering Randolph Maggio from a lifeboat around dawn the next day, and her mother had thought he killed the girl— possibly by accident, possibly not—and then scuttled the yacht with her body on board on his father's orders. Several coast guard and NYPD dive crews had failed to find the wreck, working from the coordinates of where

Randolph was found. Using the DiveNav's current-and-tidal-analysis software along with sonar and video records from other ships that night, Avery had placed the wreck several miles from the location earlier divers had used—at least, assuming Fiji was a glitch and not a guess.

Avery looked up from the DiveNav, intending to signal Carter, but he had vanished. Her breath quickened. She looked left, then right, but he was nowhere to be found. Nothing but the murky depths of the bay and the sound of her own breathing. With no means of communication beyond the visual, she was completely helpless. She had the required skills to surface safely, but she couldn't—wouldn't—abandon Carter. What if he was in trouble?

She rechecked the gauge on her air tank, struggling to keep her anxiety at bay. There was still plenty of time, but nothing would deplete her air faster than panic. She drew her dive knife and tapped it against the side of the tank as Carter had taught her. The sharp ping of metal on metal was a nearly foolproof method of underwater communication whenever a diver needed to get the attention of another. She tensed, waiting to hear a response. Nothing. Avery repeated the maneuver, striking the tank harder this time. At last came Carter's acknowledgment. He was close. She swam toward the edge of the underwater canyon, scanning left and right as she moved forward and downward. Fighting the pull of the current was like struggling to stand in a gale-force wind.

There it was again. Another loud ping. Avery knew she had to be right on top of Carter, but where was he? At last, she saw him. He appeared to be caught on something protruding from the wall of the drop-off. Avery moved in close and quickly identified the problem. He was hung up on a rusted length of rebar. The metal rod had torn his wet suit and was now entangled in his dive harness. Carter pantomimed a cutting motion with his knife. Avery nodded her understanding and swam around behind him. Carefully, she sliced through the harness at several points until he was free of the construction debris.

Avery checked her gauges: fifteen minutes of air remained; after that she would need her emergency reserve. They had to get on with the search if they wanted any chance of locating the yacht. She sheathed her knife, then gave Carter an okay sign. He returned the gesture and Avery pointed to the screen on the DiveNav, waving for him to follow her. As they swam along the canyon rim, peering into a long crevasse created by one wide shelf jutting out over another, a familiar shape loomed into view. Until this moment Avery had only seen photographs, but she recognized it instantly. It was the wreck of the *Moneymaker*.

2

Present Day

Harrison stood in the bright sunshine on the gray deck of the United States Coast Guard Cutter *Penobscot Bay*. Beside him stood NYPD Lieutenant Roger Antonin, the current commander of homicide, or as Harrison liked to call him, the chief of Ds. Standing with one foot up on the wide black railing, Harrison squinted at the spot where he'd seen Avery and Carter enter the water.

The USCGC *Penobscot Bay* was based out of Bayonne, New Jersey. At 140 feet in length, the large black-and-white bay class cutter was one of only nine coast guard ice breakers in the nation's fleet. When she wasn't breaking ice, *Penobscot Bay* was responsible for waterside security and search and rescue in the Port of New York and the surrounding areas, including the New England coast.

"Think we'll get lucky this time?" Antonin said. "I know what this collar meant to Val—and to you."

"I'm thinking I shouldn't have dragged them into this mess," Harrison said. "Guess I didn't totally understand how dangerous this area is. Something about the word *canyon* might've clued me in."

"Hell, Harry, isn't every dive dangerous?" Antonin chuckled.

"Not helpful, Rog."

Their attention was pulled away from the water as the captain announced the approach of another vessel—a bigger one.

Harrison turned to Roger Antonin. "You expecting company?"

"I am not," the commander said.

As the ship drew nearer it became clear that the approaching craft was not another coast guard vessel but something else entirely. White from stem to stern, it looked like a small cruise ship. The only distinguishing marks were a purple-and-aqua logo and the letters NOAA. The National Oceanic and Atmospheric Administration?

"Why do I get the feeling this is bad news?" Harrison said.

"Maybe because Bennie Maggio is wired into the top half of New York City government. Must have heard what we were up to through the grapevine."

"But we're all cleared to be here, right?"

"Officially?" Antonin said.

"Rog," Harrison said, dragging out the nickname.

"Okay, not officially," Antonin said. "More like the captain owed me a rather large favor."

"Great," Harrison growled.

It took several minutes for the other ship to take up a fixed position about two hundred yards off *Penobscot Bay*'s port side. Harrison knew the other captain would maintain a safe distance, as *Penobscot Bay* was flying the red-and-white diver down flag. Shortly thereafter, a small inflatable boat, occupied by two people, sped toward the cutter. Holding their positions, Harrison and Antonin observed as a clearly agitated woman wearing a tailored navy pantsuit marched onto the ship and animatedly engaged the first mate, her eyes flashing, hands gesturing as fast as her mouth moved.

"She seems nice," Antonin said as he turned and fixed Harrison with a knowing smirk.

"Pissed is the word I think you're looking for," Harrison said.

"Twenty bucks she's a fed," Antonin said.

As they continued to monitor the show, the first mate was joined by the captain of *Penobscot Bay*. After a moment the captain turned and pointed toward Harrison and Antonin.

Harrison groaned.

"Looks like she made us," Antonin said. "Whatever this is, Harry, I'll take the heat. Come on. Let's go get better acquainted."

Avery was barely able to contain her excitement as their diving lights illuminated the cream-colored hull of the *Moneymaker*. Perched in the shadow of an overhang upon a crescent-shaped shelf about as long as two football fields at the very edge of the canyon drop-off, it looked like someone had positioned a boat on the edge of a roof.

And the DiveNav found it, a last-ditch effort by Avery's mother's former boss to close Valerie Turner's last case. Avery and Carter had spent a great deal of time researching the area before uploading historical underwater mapping data to the DiveNav computer to calculate their best odds at locating the yacht. But there was a vast difference between projecting a high degree of location probability and finding the vessel. Up until this very moment both felt they were searching for the proverbial needle in an Atlantic-sized haystack. But there would be time for champagne and hooting over a successful field test later. This boat could be the key to closing her mom's last case. While she wasn't exactly excited about looking for a dead body, Avery could almost feel her mom alongside her as she kicked harder toward the hull.

Several of the letters from the port side were missing, due mostly to some very large holes in the fiberglass. The holes made it look as though the yacht had been named the *MO AKER*. They moved closer as Carter began videotaping the damage to the hull. Avery swam around the stern to the opposite side. The shelf itself, only about twenty feet wide, was slanted downward at what appeared to be about a thirty-degree angle. A quick examination of the underside revealed the boat's transom was hung up on a perch of twisted metal embedded in the continental slope of the underwater canyon. The rusted debris appeared very similar to the rebar she had freed

Carter from only moments before. These few entanglements appeared to be the only thing preventing the large yacht from plummeting nearly two thousand feet into the depths of the Hudson Fan Valley. Avery turned her head and peered down into the darkness. She was grateful she was unable to see to the bottom of the chasm. All she could think of was the movie *The Abyss*, which made her wonder what might be looking back at her.

Before she could scare herself any worse, Carter appeared beside her, drawing her back to the task at hand. Avery pointed to the yacht's underpinnings and the precarious nature of their mission. Carter nodded understanding. They would need to take great care as they searched the interior of the boat. The vessel's unstable grounding, coupled with a strong underwater current, meant even the slightest jostle might send the *Moneymaker* tumbling into the crushing depths below, taking them with it.

Carter tapped his dive watch, reminding Avery to check the time. She flashed the fingers of her right hand twice, indicating they had only ten minutes left before they would need to begin their ascent. Carter signaled for her to lead the way. Avery rolled her eyes, unsure if he was being chivalrous or if he was simply trying to sex up his video with shots of her swimming in the frame. He'd told her just last week that the analytics company his agent hired said only 40 percent of his followers were men ages seventeen to thirty-four, which was a hot target market for Carter's paid sponsors, so . . . she wouldn't be surprised. Carefully, Avery skirted the stern, swimming just above the aft deck of the yacht and into the forward cabin, laying a line secured to a bit of broken railing as she went.

Even aside from the decompression considerations and gas mixtures, everything about diving this deep was an entirely different experience for Avery. Sunlight only managed to penetrate through the first two hundred feet of underwater depth. According to the gauge on Avery's watch, they were now at 265 feet, the deepest she had ever dived. The only available light emanated from their headlamps and the light on Carter's video camera.

The opulent furnishings scattered about didn't surprise her. It was clear Randolph Maggio had inherited his father's expensive tastes and spared no expense on the *Moneymaker*, nor any of the other facets of his life. A newly minted billionaire herself, Avery enjoyed having money but saw no sense in rampant spending: she could put a Starbucks in her kitchen complete with a full-time employee and never miss the cost, but she loved everything about getting a two-dollar coffee at the convenience store up the street and taking it to walk on the beach. Her house was a splurge, sure, but the furniture that hadn't come with her from New York was soft and comfortable—and reasonably priced.

The floor of the yacht's living area was littered with items that appeared to have fallen free from cabinets and/or toppled off shelves. Her headlamp caught the smooth surface of a ruby-colored egg peeking out from under a couch cushion. Upon closer examination she could see the egg looked very much like the Fabergé eggs she had seen displayed in a Virginia museum during a speech she had given about the General's Gold. She pointed out the egg to Carter before swimming onward into the lower forward cabin.

Off the main hallway, Avery located the bathroom. It was every bit as luxurious as the ones in her beachfront mansion in the Keys. She searched the tub, the cupboards, and the under-sink vanity. Finding nothing, she exited the room. Carter was still filming at the far end of the hallway. After exchanging a quick okay with him, Avery moved on down the hall.

She located a large master stateroom at the end of the hallway. The sleeping quarters occupied most of the boat's forward compartment. A waterlogged and torn king-size mattress sat askew and upside down on the frame, trapping the bedclothes beneath it. Avery considered the possibility that the yacht might have sunk bow-first. As Avery looked around the suite, she couldn't help wondering how much time the late Ms. Fisher had spent here before meeting her demise.

Twin night tables, bolted to the floor on either side of the bed, were partially obscured by the mattress and box spring. Intending to search under the bed, Avery grabbed onto the mattress and began to slide it out of the way when a coal-black moray eel wriggled out from beneath it and startled her. Avery punched out instinctively, scoring a direct hit on the creature's nose. Surprised, the eel retreated slightly, and Avery did the same, allowing it space to depart. Its sleek form shot through the water and down the hallway, leaving Avery shuddering. Not all marine life is wonderful and glorious.

Avery rummaged through the mattress, box spring, and underbed area, not finding so much as a finger bone. Next, she searched the closet, wary of any other underwater critters that might have sought refuge there. Finding none, Avery tossed the entire space, using her dive knife to sweep the shelving. Again, she was unable to locate any sign of Melody's remains.

She scanned the room until her eyes paused on a piece of wall art that had been knocked off-kilter by the mattress. Peeking out from behind the painting was the gunmetal gray corner of a wall safe. Would a body fit in there? No. But a skull might.

Avery called up from memory the combination supplied by Maggio's lawyers to the Manhattan district attorney. She wasn't the least bit surprised to find that after trying the combination twice, the lock would not disengage. She turned to find Carter gliding into the stateroom. Avery pantomimed twisting the dial, then shook her head. Carter gestured to her to try again. She humored him but got the same result on her third try.

Carter pointed to himself before handing the camera to Avery. Reluctantly, she moved back and kept filming. She couldn't wait until they were topside again so she could have her "I told you so" moment. As she zoomed in on the safe, Carter spun the combination through the same numbers she had tried, but instead of reversing direction after hitting each mark he gave the dial an extra full spin between numbers. After completing the sequence, Carter pulled down on the release lever, but nothing happened. Carter braced himself by placing his knees against the hull and his feet on the floor, then tugged on the handle with both hands. The latch disengaged and the door to the safe swung open.

And Avery grabbed the edge of the headboard and blew a string of bubbles out on a shriek when a groaning noise came from somewhere beneath the hull as the yacht shifted to starboard.

3

Back aboard *Penobscot Bay*, the captain introduced Harrison and Antonin to Agent Allison Miranda from the NOAA. Harrison dropped his hand after realizing Miranda had no intention of shaking it.

"It's nice to meet you, ma'am," Antonin said.

"Do you have any idea how dangerous it is to dive here without the proper permits or authority?" Miranda's words dripped disdain. So much for pleasantries.

"Well, we are with the coast guard," Antonin said, grinning as he cocked a thumb at the captain.

"Is that supposed to be funny?" Miranda shot back.

"Humor isn't exactly Roger's strong suit," Harrison said, attempting to defuse whatever was happening here. He'd been around enough diving with Avery and Carter to know this woman was madder than logic dictated she should be. "Look, nobody wants to step on your toes, okay? We are out here acting on a tip that might just help us put away a murderer."

"Who is we?"

"In addition to the two of us, and an able crew of coasties, we've got Avery Turner and Carter Mosley conducting the underwater search," Harrison said proudly.

"That's just great," Miranda said as her hands went to her hips. "The newly anointed dynamic duo of the treasure hunting scene. Seems like exactly the wrong way to conduct a police investigation."

Harrison's jaw loosened. He had to be missing something—dropping Avery's and Carter's names would have calmed most people down with as much as they'd been on the news lately, but somehow she was just madder.

Antonin stepped up to the plate for another swing. "Look, the dive and recovery were my idea, okay? We needed someone trustworthy and skilled enough to dive this deep. None of our certified divers can go to three hundred feet."

"That's another thing," Miranda snapped. "You do realize I could have their certificates pulled for diving so deep. Recreational diving is limited to two hundred feet."

Swing and a miss. Harrison sighed. "They're experienced divers. And this isn't recreational. They've got rebreathers and mixed gas tanks made for exactly this type of dive."

"Not to mention, this is an NYPD matter, which has absolutely nothing to do with you, or, for that matter, your agency," Antonin said, his temper leaking through his polite tone.

"Um, the Hudson Canyon Marine Sanctuary makes it my business, Detective."

"It's Commander. And tell me again why no one notified us you were coming here today? Your arrival could have put our divers in danger and potentially compromised an active criminal investigation."

"It couldn't be helped," Miranda said as she gestured to the surrounding water. "I only learned of your intent to dive here thirty-six hours ago. This is a protected zone, hence the word *sanctuary*. The ocean floor is vitally important to the environment and to the sea life inhabiting the canyon. God knows what kind of laws your divers are probably breaking at this very moment. How long have they been below?"

Harrison blinked, checking his watch and eyeing the still water around the boat, suddenly not at all worried about Agent Miranda and her dramatic accusations. Going on a half hour into the deepest dive Avery had ever done, Harrison hoped a few fractured marine preservation laws would be the worst of their problems.

After inhabiting her throat for thirty or so seconds, Avery's stomach finally settled back to its normal location. Her heart rate was still racing, eyes still wide, as she and Carter waited to see if the yacht might shift further.

It didn't.

First a close encounter with an eel, then nearly plunging to an early death—Avery'd had actual nightmares that went better than this. She checked her air gauge, then held up her watch for Carter. It was nearly time to head back.

He nodded, then held up an index finger as his attention returned to the safe. Avery caught sight of a length of wire running just inside the safe. She grabbed onto his arm to prevent him from reaching inside. Neither had been sure what to expect, but a brick of C-4 and a waterproof detonator were most definitely not on the list. Avery's pulse went into overdrive as she studied the multicolored wires running between the latch and the explosive. She was trying to figure out why they hadn't already been blown to smithereens when Carter pointed to a corroded and broken connector. The system wasn't waterproof after all.

Carter reached inside, past the explosive, to the back of the safe. Carefully, he withdrew a fat bundle wrapped in several layers of plastic and held it up for Avery to see. She couldn't tell what was inside but knew it must have been important to cause a Mafia boss to wire his own boat. Avery opened the red neoprene bag clipped to her dive belt, allowing Carter to slip the bundle inside.

Carter reached back into the safe again, coming up empty-handed. Avery turned, her eye falling on a rip in the fabric of the sofa that she hadn't noticed before because she'd been focused on the glittering ruby egg. She pulled the cushion free and saw that it ran the length of the seam under the cushions, the waterlogged fabric loose in places. She took her knife and sliced easily through it, pulling the cover back to find a long, bulky object wrapped in plastic, tarps, and . . . was that a . . . tablecloth?

Turning, she waved Carter over. He pumped a fist in the air and then put his palms up in a "what now?" signal. Avery put her gloved hands under one end of the bundle and gestured for him to do the same, unsure and a little afraid of what might happen—or leak—when they moved it. Perhaps the only good thing about the darkness and the murky water was that if anything came from the package, Avery couldn't see it.

Carter flashed a thumbs-up. They needed to head back. Avery nodded, balancing the bundle on her shoulder and swimming for the exit.

4

Avery and Carter had barely returned to the cutter before Agent Miranda pounced. Still clad in their dive gear and dripping onto the aft deck, they listened as she read them the riot act, Avery's eyebrows inching closer to her hairline with every sentence.

"Do you have any idea how much danger you put yourselves in today?" Miranda said with the last of the breath she'd used to lecture them.

"You're telling me," Carter said, pointing to his damaged gear. "It's like a junkyard down there."

"Well, it is New York," Harrison said, earning a hearty laugh from the coast guard skipper.

"I don't think any of you are taking this very seriously," Agent Miranda said. "You have likely violated a dozen or more federal laws today. I want to see the video you shot. And I want to inspect anything you recovered."

Carter exchanged a nervous glance with Avery at the mention of the recovery. They'd slid the bundle onto the dive deck below while Miranda was still yelling at Harrison and his cop friend, so no one really knew they'd located it or anything else. Avery gave a nearly imperceptible shake of her head.

"And I want a look at that DiveNav device you've got," Miranda continued.

Avery stepped in front of Carter. "I'm afraid none of that is going to happen, Agent Miranda."

"Excuse me?"

"DiveNav is a proprietary holding of my company, TreasureTech Designs, powered by software I developed. Software which you have no legal cause to examine. Not unless you have a warrant. You don't have a warrant, do you?"

"And his video?" Miranda ignored the question, pointing at Carter's diving camera.

"Also protected," Avery said. "The camera and footage are the property of Carter Mosley Incorporated. Any evidence contained in the footage, should such footage exist, will be provided voluntarily to the New York Police Department expressly for the purpose of charging and convicting a murder suspect."

Miranda's eyes narrowed. "Do you have any idea what kind of fines could be levied against all of you?"

"Just tell me who I should make the check out to." Now *that* was a nice thing about having money.

"Are you really sure you want to test me, Miss Turner?"

"I could ask you the same question, Agent Miranda. I'm not sure how you found out about us being here, but, if you'll pardon the obvious pun, it feels like you're on a fishing expedition."

"Or she's bigfooting the NYPD's case," Carter said, earning a curious look from Harrison.

"Look," Antonin said. "They were down there at my request, okay? This whole operation was authorized by the chief of Ds at One Police Plaza. Her name is Patricia Fielding. Feel free to call her."

"Don't worry, I will," Miranda said.

They all watched as Agent Miranda climbed down into the rigid-hulled inflatable where her pilot awaited.

Miranda untethered her craft from the cutter, and the pilot motored toward the NOAA research ship. Miranda turned back and hollered, "You haven't heard the last of me."

"Somehow I believe that," Avery said.

"Is it just me, or does she sound like a bad movie villain?" Carter asked as he began to shed his wetsuit.

Harrison turned his attention to Carter. "Bigfooting? How do you even know that word, Junior?"

"Don't you watch *Bosch*?"

Harrison rolled his eyes.

"Hey, that's a pretty good show," Antonin said.

Harrison waved him off, turning to Avery. "Tell me you found something."

A silly grin spread across Avery's face as she opened her dive bag and removed the bundle, pointing down at the deck with her other hand. "We hit the jackpot, Harry. At least, if I'm right about what's under all this plastic, we did."

"Seriously?" Harrison put up a hand for a high five.

"Oh yeah. But before I forget, Carter's gonna need a tetanus shot."

"He's probably not afraid of needles," Harrison said.

Antonin tipped his head to one side and gave Carter a once-over. "Hard to tell how much actual nerve is under the pretty-boy bravado."

"Ha, ha," Carter said as the second mate clipped a lock of blonde hair back into her ponytail and brandished a first aid kit.

"Some guys have all the luck," Antonin muttered, giving the captain an all clear to head back to land.

With the wind whipping through her hair, Avery stood outside on an upper platform as the USCGC *Penobscot Bay* sped toward its New Jersey homeport, the coastline just beginning to materialize in the distance. Avery watched Harrison and Captain Antonin pace the deck below while simultaneously talking into their respective cell phones, both men clearly giddy with excitement over having possibly located Melody. Not that anyone had investigated past the roughly person-sized bundle yet, but there was supposed to be a coroner's van meeting them at the dock. Carter sat cross-legged on a nearby bulkhead, hunched over his laptop, replaying the underwater video they had just shot.

Avery felt surprisingly well considering this had been her deepest dive to date. The number and length of the decompression stops would take some getting used to, but overall, it had been a smooth trip. And with the sole exception of Agent Miranda, it had been a good day.

She looked down as her cell phone vibrated with an incoming call from a New York number she didn't recognize. Before she could decide whether to take the call, Avery felt a tap on her shoulder. She turned to find Harrison wrapped in a worried expression.

"When were you going to mention the C-4, Ave?"

"I didn't want to worry you unnecessarily."

"Too late," he said as he stepped closer and draped a protective arm across her shoulders.

She wrapped her arms around Harrison's burly torso and squeezed. "You think Mom would be proud?"

"She is, Ave. I know it. You just helped solve one of her cold cases."

"One of your cold cases, too, Harry."

"Yup," he said, hugging her back. "And I am proud of you too."

5

Lierre
24 December 1537

A light snow drifted down from the heavens. The sky was dark, the night air cold and still. Cardinal Olav stood beside his horse just inside the empty wooden barn, awaiting two of his most trusted apostles.

During summer months the large barn was used to store and sell fruit. The air inside the structure was still ripe with the scents of the previous harvest of apples, cherries, pears, currants, and straw. Olav breathed deeply of the pleasing aromatic medley, then watched as the cold transformed his own exhaled breath to a lacy cloud of frost.

The silence was broken by the sound of approaching horses and a wagon. With one hand tight around the handle of his sword, Olav cinched the fur cloak tighter around his neck, then receded into the shadows. A gleaming lamp hung upon the wagon distorted the features of the drivers' faces until they were close enough for Olav to recognize. It was Eryk and Wilhelm.

"Good evening, my lord," they greeted in unison.

"I trust you were not followed?" Olav said.

"We were not," Wilhelm said as he and Eryk climbed down from the bench seat and retrieved two long-handled spades from the back. Eryk unhooked the lantern from the carriage and passed it to Olav.

"Good," Olav said. "We haven't much time. Follow me."

He guided them to the back of the barn at the far-left corner where a large hatch hidden beneath a layer of hay led down to a cooling cellar under the barn. After prying the heavy wooden lid out of the floor, Eryk and Wilhelm descended the stone steps while Olav followed with the lantern.

"You will dig there," Olav said, pointing to a spot that looked like any other on the basement floor.

The two men toiled for the better part of a half hour before all the debris was removed and two large wooden trunks were unearthed and lifted from the ground. Taking one trunk at a time, they struggled up the steps and carried them to the waiting carriage.

Olav was pleased. Their nighttime mission had been a success. The trunks contained dozens of priceless artifacts he had methodically looted from Nidaros Cathedral during his tenure as cardinal. Among the valuables were not only the Norwegian king's crown and sword of state but also solid gold and silver bars, heavy crosses, chalices, and other assorted bejeweled regalia.

Olav kept watch as they refilled the hole in the floor then replaced the trap door to the cellar. He followed them back to the carriage. Once seated, he handed Wilhelm a leather satchel.

"Your orders are inside," Olav said. "Guard this treasure with your very lives if needs must. You will deliver this precious cargo straight to Italy. There is a Catholic nobleman I have made an agreement with who will purchase these artifacts now in your charge. His name and location are contained within the satchel. Once you have made the exchange for the agreed-upon amount, you will ride without delay to meet with Admiral Trondson. He will be waiting. Do you understand what I have told you?"

Both men nodded their understanding.

"This money is to be used to build a secret army of mercenary soldiers loyal to the Catholic Church, of which you will both be a part. The money will persuade the men to turn against the new king. You, Eryk and Wilhelm, will help Admiral Trondson lead a surprise attack against the castle guard during a state visit in the spring. King Christian's death should provide a swift and complete transfer of power. Once I have been coronated as the rightful king, wearing the ancient Norwegian crown, Norway will once again be sovereign, powerful, and blessed."

"My lord," both men said with a nod.

"The last and most important part of your orders is you must remove two items from these trunks before the nobleman takes possession. The crown and the sword must be hidden within the tunnels being constructed under the Nidaros Cathedral. Do you both understand?"

"Yes, my lord," Eryk said.

"Yes, my lord," Wilhelm echoed.

"Godspeed to you both."

6

New York City
Present Day

It was nearly seven by the time Avery, Harrison, and Carter approached the Park Avenue lobby doors of New York City's Waldorf Astoria Hotel.

"Welcome back, Ms. Turner," a dapperly dressed doorman greeted as he pulled open one of the gleaming glass doors.

"Good evening, Rudy," Avery said.

"I trust you all had an eventful day?"

"You can say that again," Carter said. "Tonight, we celebrate."

"With steak," Harrison added. "I. Am. Famished."

"They prepare a marvelous aged filet mignon in the Champagne Bar. I could call up and have them reserve a table for you?"

"Thank you, Rudy," Avery said, "but that won't be necessary. I think these two strapping young lads can handle that. At least I hope they can."

"Call? What's that? Can't I just click a button on my phone?" Carter laughed at Avery's eye roll.

"Very good, Ms. Turner." Rudy winked, tipping his cap.

Harrison and Carter headed directly toward the restaurant while Avery walked to the front desk.

"Good evening," the balding middle-aged male concierge greeted. "May I help you, miss?"

"Good evening to you. My name is Avery Turner. I received a voice mail message from the hotel on my cell phone—I believe you have a package for me?"

"Ah, yes, Ms. Turner. Three packages. And one is rather large."

The concierge waved over a valet standing across the lobby and asked him to retrieve the packages.

Avery was intrigued. Aside from Carter and Harrison, there weren't many people who even knew she was staying at the hotel, and she wasn't expecting anything to be delivered. A moment later the valet returned with three boxes stacked on a luggage cart. "Here we are."

Avery leaned in to study the labels. Each box was simply addressed to TreasureTech, care of Avery Turner and Carter Mosley. Neither a mailing address nor return address were listed on any of the packages. This had all the makings of a secret admirer. Had Harry bought them a gift? Had Lieutenant Antonin?

"Would you like assistance getting these to your room?" the valet asked.

"Are they heavy?" Avery said, lifting the top package.

"Surprisingly, no. Just bulky."

Just then Avery's stomach grumbled. She decided the packages could wait. "Honestly, I'm just headed to dinner. I'd be grateful if you could deliver them safely to my room."

"As you wish, ma'am."

After tipping the valet, Avery hurried straight to the Champagne Bar. Harrison was right. It was time for a strong drink and a great meal.

Following a marvelous five-course meal, the three of them stood in the center of the living room inside Avery's suite, studying the stack of boxes. Sitting directly on the carpet was the largest of the three packages, easily big enough to contain an old tube-style television. Two smaller boxes sat atop the glass coffee table. The larger of the two was longer and thinner and looked like it would be perfect for holding a boogie surfboard.

Rounding out the pile was the box she had picked up earlier, the smallest of the three, a cube-shaped container about twelve inches square.

There was nothing unusual about any of the packages save for the lack of sender information and origin. The boxes were numbered in ascending order by size.

"Who sent them?" Carter asked.

"Not a clue. I asked after dinner and the valet told me they were delivered by a private courier driving an unmarked black Cadillac SUV. Which is weird because almost nobody knows we're here. Harry, did you splurge on some presents?"

"No, and I don't like it, Ave. Not after what you guys found today."

"The C-4?" Carter asked. "Why would that have anything to do with this? No one knows we have it but us."

"Maybe, maybe not. Bennie Maggio has ears and eyes all over the city. How do we know he isn't behind these mystery boxes? Maybe they're rigged. I have no doubt he knows what you found, and he also knows it could be the key to putting junior away for a long time."

"You said it yourself, Harry, even if that is Melody's body, their lawyers will argue that no one saw him with her, and it was recovered years after the boat sank. The DA still has work to do here."

"Yup, and part of that work is that you and the boy wonder here will be required to testify as to where you found that wad of plastic and the condition of the shipwreck. With both of you out of the equation, the case gets a lot harder here."

Carter pointed to the packages. "So how do we tell if they're wired?"

"I was a homicide detective, not a bomb guy. We'd have to call One PP."

Avery pulled out her cell and punched in a speed dial number.

"Don't use a cell!" Harry shouted. "That could be what sets them off."

"Relax, Harry. No one blew up."

"You're not really calling the bomb squad, are you?" Carter asked.

"Of course not. I'm calling my housekeeper. If the boxes came by private courier, this may not have been the first place they looked for us. Let's see if she knows anything about these."

Avery put the phone on speaker, then held it up for everyone to hear.

"Good to hear your voices, Ms. Avery," Dorothy said. "How is New York?"

"It's nothing like the Keys, Dorothy," Harrison said.

"Listen, Dorothy," Avery said. "I was wondering if there had been any deliveries to the house since we've been away?"

"Nearly, Miss Avery. A private courier attempted to deliver some packages yesterday morning."

"Attempted?"

"Yes. They wanted you to sign for them, but they left when they found out you weren't here."

Harrison raised his eyebrows in an *I told you so* gesture.

"Did you happen to mention where I was?"

"Oh no, Ms. Avery. I would never do that."

"Do you remember how many packages there were?" Harrison asked.

"The man driving the black SUV said three."

"How likely is it a delivery service is going to truck package bombs from Florida to New York and risk blowing up a hotel, Harry?" Avery asked. "You really think someone would bring them from there to here? Who is signing up to drive that truck?"

"I'll admit it is unlikely, but—"

"Besides, yesterday we hadn't located the *Moneymaker* yet," Avery interrupted.

"I'd still feel better if you would wait until we get someone to check these out."

Shaking her head, Avery snatched an ornamental brass letter opener off an end table and sliced through the tape on the midsized box.

"Jesus, Ave." Harrison grabbed his chest. "I wasn't ready."

"And yet we're all still here."

7

"I don't get it," Carter said. "Why would someone send us snowshoes?"

"Maybe they're trying to tell you something," Harrison said.

"Like what?"

"They want you to take a hike?"

"Then it's definitely not from a woman, so that narrows it down by half the population already."

"If that's the case, our secret Santa must want to get rid of me too." Avery held up her own snowshoes. "Are you sure these aren't from you, Harry?"

"I am full of surprises, but I can't take credit for any of this."

"This is top-of-the-line gear." Carter examined the snowshoes.

"Wrong season though." Avery reached for another box. "It's almost springtime."

The largest box contained two of the thickest cold-weather jackets Avery had ever seen. According to the tags, they were made to withstand nature's worst weather, constructed using all the latest technology.

"Look at all the buzz words," Harrison said. "Gore-Tex, Polar Tech, PrimaLoft . . . All we need now is that Weather Channel guy."

"Jim Cantore?"

"That's the one."

"These coats are ridiculously expensive," Carter said.

"And how would you know that, Mr. Fashion Plate?" Harrison said. "I thought you were all about scuba and skydiving. Don't tell me you're a hiker too."

"Hiking, climbing, skiing, you name it. Outdoor gear is kind of my sweet tooth, Harry. These babies set someone back almost two thousand bucks each. They're rated to sixty below."

"Zero?" Harrison asked, wide-eyed. "Why would anyone want to go outside when it's sixty below zero?"

Avery slipped into one of the jackets. "Exactly my size."

"Mine too." Carter followed her lead.

"You two aren't planning to enter the Iditarod, are you?"

"Hardly," Avery said with a laugh as she slipped out of the jacket and laid it atop the bed.

"Sounds like we've got a secret admirer, Avery," Carter said.

"Tracking you guys down to New York? Sounds more like a secret stalker."

"What's inside the last one?" Carter asked.

"Let's see," Avery said, making quick work of the tape.

The third box, the smallest of the three, contained two pairs of goggles and a beige envelope. Using the letter opener, Avery removed the matching embossed stationery from inside.

"Cool," Carter said as he picked up one pair of goggles and turned to Harrison. "VR. Want to try them?"

"No thanks. Tried those damn things once. Some kind of video game. Made me seasick as all get out."

"What does the note say?" Carter asked.

"It's an invitation." Avery read, "Dear Ms. Turner and Mr. Mosley. Please accept these gifts as a small token of friendship."

"Your new 'friend' wants something," Harrison said.

"An invitation to where?" Carter said.

"They want us to join a group of climate scientists hunting a shipwreck called the *Fortitude*." Avery's voice betrayed her excitement, rising with each word.

"Where is this ship?" Harrison said as he pointed to their jackets. "The North Pole?"

"Wrong end of the earth, Harry," Avery said. "The note says it's in the seas surrounding the Antarctic."

"How exciting." Harrison made no attempt to hide his sarcasm.

"So, who is the invitation from?" Carter asked.

"Doesn't say." Avery flipped the invitation over to check the back side. "It's simply signed with the letter *N*."

Avery and Carter each slipped a pair of goggles over their heads, then adjusted the straps. The devices activated as soon as they were in place, transforming the hotel suite into a stark arctic plain.

"Are you seeing what I'm seeing?" Avery marveled at the detail.

"It's incredible," Carter said. "I feel like I'm really there. Did it just get colder in here?"

"Would someone mind telling me what's so incredible?" Harrison asked.

"You had your chance," Carter said.

"It's the South Pole, Harry," Avery said as she turned slowly to take in her virtual surroundings. "Everything looks so real."

"Mystery gifts, an unsigned invitation, and two alleged adults spinning about blindly in a hotel room." Harrison shook his head. "Who else could use a drink?"

8

Harrison poured each of them a nightcap as Carter continued to play with the VR and Avery scoured the internet for information pertaining to the *Fortitude*.

"So, was this ship supposed to have been lost in the ice or what?" Harrison said as he handed Avery her drink.

"Something like that—it looks like the *Fortitude* has a fascinating history, Harry. It was a Norwegian sailing ship built in the early 1900s for the express purpose of transporting the wealthy to polar adventures."

"Wealthy and bored, you mean," Harrison said, carefully placing a drink in Carter's hand. "Here, AI Guy. I made yours neat. Figured you wouldn't need real ice."

"Thanks." Carter chuckled. "Honestly, Harry, you've gotta try this."

"No, I honestly don't," Harrison said as he settled back onto the plush couch. "Tell us more about this ship, Ave."

"Well, it looks like it was repurposed at the start of World War I. Its owner and captain offered it up to the Royal British Navy, who gladly put it into service. Constructed as it was, the *Fortitude*'s strength was her ability to navigate ice-strewn waters. Ultimately, the navy wanted it for exploration to see if there was a way to traverse Antarctica by ship, which could have proven useful to the navy during wartime."

"This is starting to sound familiar, Ave," Harry said. "I feel like I may have read a history book about this ship. Didn't she become mired in ice or something?"

"Indeed," Avery said. "In fact, the crew survived on the vessel trapped in the ice of the Weddell Sea for months before the captain finally deemed her too damaged to save and gave the order to abandon ship. The last of the crew was rescued more than a year after they'd begun their mission."

"Hey, cool." Carter pointed as he wandered about the room. "Penguins."

Harrison rolled his eyes. "What about the ship itself? Surely, someone must know where it is?"

"Not according to this," Avery said. "Despite crew journals that purported to note the exact final location, the *Fortitude* has never been found."

"How big of an area can it be?" Harrison said.

"Antarctica?" Avery said. "Oh, only about five and a half million square miles. We probably don't need to search it all."

"And someone thinks *you* might be able to find this thing." Harrison's words dripped pride.

"Me or the DiveNav?"

"You are a package deal, right?"

"I'm part of the package too." Carter continued to reach for things in his invisible world.

"Hey, Max Headroom, any chance you could take that thing off your head and tell us what you think?" Harrison said.

"Sure." Carter returned to reality and plopped down next to Harrison on the couch. "Man, this thing is crazy cool."

"It is," Avery agreed. "Your thoughts on joining an expedition to search for this lost ship?"

"Well, unlike our normal dives, the cold water at the ninetieth parallel would have preserved a wooden shipwreck like no other. It would be a fantastic opportunity. But there are a multitude of dangers surrounding an expedition like this. Navigating hostile terrain, the unpredictability of the environment, the weather, ice in the water, the depth of the wreck, assuming we can even find it, and water temperature. Any one of those things alone would be capable of killing us; put them together and we'd be just plain crazy to try."

"Then you wouldn't do it?" Avery's face fell.

"The world has gone wonky when the boy wonder is the voice of reason." Harrison looked relieved.

"I'm not saying that at all." Carter drained the last of his whiskey. "I'm just saying all that stuff is completely outside of my wheelhouse and comfort zone. But put up against a chance to be the first to locate and explore a perfectly preserved wooden ship over a century old? Hell yeah, count me in. Water is water. If it's where we can reach it, with the right gear, I can figure it out."

Harrison crossed his arms over his chest. "You can't go if we don't have any way of contacting whoever sent this stuff."

Avery reached back inside the envelope that had held the invitation and produced a plain white business card with gilded edges. Printed in the center of the card was the name Noah Wyndham, PhD. followed by a telephone number.

"Dr. Wyndham I presume." Avery waggled her eyebrows. "Looks like he's expecting our call."

"Why do I get the feeling this is an incredibly bad idea?" Harrison scowled.

Carter handed Avery her phone. "No guts, no glory."

Avery activated the phone's speaker, then keyed in the number on the card.

"Good evening, Ms. Turner," a computerized voice greeted. "I am saving your number to our database."

"At least it's honest artificial intelligence," Harrison said. "Not like the shyster who sold me a timeshare, five minutes before he sold my contact info."

The automated staccato voice continued. "To accept the invitation, press one. To decline, press two."

"And if I want to speak to a human?" Avery said.

"This is how it ends." Carter nodded. "Did you see the movie *Terminator*?"

"Hit two, Ave."

"I'd rather you punched one. On the off chance I only received an invitation because of you."

"I'm choosing my own option." Avery pressed zero.

After a series of clicks, the call switched to another extension and a voice that might've belonged to a real-life female came on the line.

"I'm so glad you called, Ms. Turner. My name is Giselle. Is Mr. Mosley there with you?"

"He is. We have you to thank for these gifts?"

"They were sent by Dr. Wyndham. I am his personal assistant."

Avery looked over at Carter, who mouthed the word *Terminator*.

The voice was polite and professional with a bizarre sort of non-accent Avery couldn't quite identify—like Giselle wasn't really from anywhere. But her diction was flawless and her tone warm.

"Have you made a decision, Ms. Turner?" Giselle said. "Do you have any questions?"

"I have many questions, Giselle. I guess the obvious one is, assuming we decide to accept your offer, when does the expedition leave for Antarctica?"

"Four months ago, Miss Turner. They are waiting for you."

9

Avery and Carter leaned into the laptop screen on the coffee table, while Harrison opted to sit across the room out of view of the camera. It had taken a bit of finagling on Avery's part to get the satellite link application up and running, but it looked as though they had made a connection to the Antarctic substation at last, unstable as it was. The image came and went, and the voice was partially garbled and entirely British, but they were linked.

"Can you hear me okay, mates?" Noah Wyndham asked.

"We can hear you, Dr. Wyndham," Avery said.

"Good. I was afraid you might not be able to understand me. The sat link can be a bit wonky in this part of the globe. Magnetic fields."

"It's great to meet you, Doctor," Carter said.

"Likewise, Mr. Mosley. I see you received our gifts."

"Thank you so much," Avery and Carter said in unison.

"Not at all. It was the least we could do. So, have you given any th—"

The feed became grainy, and the audio cut out completely, before Wyndham returned on-screen.

"—my invitation?"

Avery glanced at Carter. He nodded for her to take the lead.

"Indeed, we have, Dr. Wyndham."

"Please, call me Noah."

"As you might imagine, we have many questions, Noah," Avery said.

"As one would. I suspect that is the scientist within you, Ms. Turner. Where would you like me to begin?"

"Maybe a simple overview of your project and how it is being funded."

"Of course. Well, you already know my name, and I imagine you've checked me out online, but I can give you a thumbnail of my qualifications if you wish."

"If you wouldn't mind," Avery said.

She had in fact spent the last twenty minutes doing precisely that. A deep dive into Wyndham's credentials and history had revealed that he was a noted environmental scientist and marine archaeologist. Dr. Wyndham had worked on shipwrecks big and small, and on environmental conservation projects with world-altering potential. From interning as a college student on the *Titanic* expedition in the nineties to serving as a vital part of a team that developed a device for siphoning carbon from rainforest trees to allow the trees to absorb more from the atmosphere, this guy was the real deal. She listened as he hit the highlights of the resume she'd turned up online.

"I've held posts at the British Museum, the Smithsonian, Oceana, the Stockholm Environment Institute, and Greenpeace, among other, lesser-known organizations and think tanks," he finished.

"Greenpeace?" Carter blurted.

"Are you surprised, Mr. Mosley?"

"Well, no. I mean—I always pictured Greenpeace people as . . ."

"Hippies?" Dr. Wyndham laughed. "It's okay. It was during my younger, more impetuous years. And I was in love."

Carter nodded like that last bit explained everything.

"Anyway, all this brings me to my current research," Wyndham said. "We are running out of time and money, and looking for a miracle. I think it might be you."

"Running out of money?" Avery asked. "From what I can gather online, it looks like there are dozens of countries who have research facilities in Antarctica. Aren't they there largely to conduct climate research?"

"A most astute question, Ms. Turner. The truth of the matter is there are dozens of countries here, and each one brings with them their own geopolitical baggage. I'm not sure if you have much experience dealing with governments, but let's just say if one is searching for answers and a quick result, the government is the last place you'd look for help. Besides, the research we're doing here on rebuilding the Antarctic shelf by artificially mimicking the process by which winter sea ice forms here is pretty far outside the standard scientific box and doesn't fit neatly in a sound byte. Which means most politicians aren't interested."

Harrison nodded enthusiastically from across the room.

"There's someone here who agrees with you," Avery said.

"That would be Mr. Harrison, I presume."

Avery raised one eyebrow. "It is indeed. May I ask how you know so much about us, Noah?"

"I've done a little research of my own, Ms. Turner. I know all about you, Mr. Mosley, Mr. Harrison, and TreasureTech. I've been following your exploits pertaining to the General's Gold and, not to put too fine a point on it, I am quite impressed. The truth of the matter is I think you can assist us with our current venture."

"I'm afraid we don't know very much about making an extension of a polar ice shelf," Avery said.

Wyndham laughed. "No worries. That isn't what you'd be doing. You'd be helping us with our secondary research in locating the *Fortitude*."

"That's more our speed, but I don't follow what the *Fortitude* has to do with climate research," Carter said.

"Absolutely nothing, Mr. Mosley. The *Fortitude* has little to do with science but a lot to do with legend and—hopefully—with money. I'm hoping that finding the wreck will galvanize enough interest in what we're doing here to keep us funded long enough to complete our climate work."

"How? And if it's not government funded, who is bankrolling this project?" Avery asked.

"Like any project of our size today, we have dozens of grants and sources of funding, most of them think tanks and corporations with a monetary interest in what we're doing."

"But you think you might not be able to renew your grants."

"Correct. The world has less of an attention span today than thirty years ago, I'm afraid, thanks to social media. I'd like to find a way to use that to my advantage if I can, and Mr. Mosley's audience is part of the reason we'd like to have you aboard here. A lost legendary shipwreck is a much more interesting story to the masses than a crazy old Englishman who thinks he can save the planet. I'm hoping that Mr. Mosley's internet followers will get excited enough about the search for the *Fortitude* to get us enough funding to extend our research work here after the ship is recovered. We are scientists first, Miss Turner, and I assure you this offer is on the up and up."

Harrison shook his head and mouthed the words, *Sure it is.*

"And safe?" Carter said.

"You'd have nothing to fear, Mr. Mosley."

"Something I still don't understand," Avery said. "If your team is as experienced as you portray them, why would you need us at all?"

"Truthfully? We believe your DiveNav device might be just the thing that takes our search for the *Fortitude* to its logical conclusion. Antarctica's winter is approaching quickly, and we need to be able to generate a result if we hope to continue to receive funding. So, what do you say, Ms. Turner? Will you and Mr. Mosley join our team?"

Avery twisted her lips to one side. So this brilliant scientist who was trying to save the planet was backed into a corner: if he didn't find the ship, he would lose the funding for what sounded like important environmental research that could have far-reaching implications, and he was running out of time. Which meant she and Carter might be the only people who could save the research project. She looked across the room to Harrison, who only shook his head. She glanced at Carter, who gave an enthusiastic thumbs-up.

"If we decide to accept your offer, I will want to get started immediately on my own research for updating the DiveNav."

"I can send everything you'd need to get started."

"And Harrison?" Avery asked.

"Mr. Harrison is more than welcome to join our merry band of researchers. We'll make sure he is outfitted as well."

"How would we find you?"

"I'll provide location information as well. Does this mean you're in?" Avery took one last look at Carter and Harrison before answering. "Count us in, Noah."

10

They checked out of the hotel early the next morning. Avery had been up half the night researching anything and everything to do with Antarctica and the HMS *Fortitude*. She had also called the best information hawk south of the Mason-Dixon, MaryAnn, directly after ending the call with Dr. Wyndham to provide a heads-up about the expedition and the incoming maps.

MaryAnn, who'd left her post as a museum director and gone to work full-time for Avery and Carter at TreasureTech a few months back, was beyond excited about the new assignment. It beat the heck out of the mundane acquisition and digital capture of historical maps that had comprised the lion's share of her new job to date.

"How soon before you get the maps?" MaryAnn said.

"Don't know but I'll send them to you as soon as I do," Avery said.

"This is going to be so exciting," MaryAnn said. "The missing wreck of the *Fortitude* is something of a legend in maritime lore, Avery. Even though the crew members' journals listed coordinates for where it went down, there's no trace of it."

"So I've heard." Avery nodded when Harrison signaled that the car was there. "We're headed your way, MaryAnn—anything you can turn up about any of this would be helpful."

Their driver took them directly from the hotel to the airport, where Marco, Avery's personal pilot, was waiting to fly them back to Florida so they could prepare to head to Antarctica.

It wasn't until Marco balked at her plans that Avery realized traveling to Antarctica would not be like traveling to Boston or London. One of the best perks of Avery's vast resources was travel: usually, all she needed to do was reach out to Marco and he would whisk them anywhere her heart desired on her Gulfstream jet.

"Flying to the South Pole is complicated, Ms. Avery," Marco said.

"I thought you could fly anything?"

Marco grinned at her attempt at reverse psychology. "I can fly any*thing*, but not any*where*. There are magnetic fields around the poles that can affect instruments and flight paths. Only a pilot experienced with that part of the world would know how to navigate it. It requires equipment and knowledge that's beyond my scope, I'm afraid."

"But doesn't my Gulfstream have everything?"

"It is a fine craft, Ms. Avery, but it is not equipped for that type of travel. I could fly you all as close as Buenos Aires, but you will need another pilot and a different plane to get you to the Antarctic expedition."

"See?" Harrison said. "I knew this was a bad idea."

"Relax, Harry," Avery said. "I'll figure it out. Besides, Argentina is right on the way." She turned to Marco. "I don't suppose you'd know any pilots who could make such a trip?"

"It just so happens I do, Ms. Avery," Marco said with a wink.

"Let me guess—he lives in Buenos Aires?"

"Indeed, he does."

"You are the best, Marco."

"I keep telling you, Ms. Avery."

"Take us home, then, please. We gotta get packed."

They'd only been in the air for about thirty minutes, but the excitement surrounding the trip was palpable. Avery was seated in one of the plush leather recliners, studying the mapping information Noah had sent, when she looked up from her laptop to find Carter making calculations on a notepad across the aisle.

"Whatcha doin'?" she asked.

"Just trying to figure our chances of finding this thing in water we might actually be able to get in. This part of the world has some pretty deep seas."

"Didn't we just make a deep-water dive? Successfully, I might add."

"Deeper than that. Deeper and colder."

Harrison weighed in from one row back. "Not that anyone cares, but I'd like to reiterate my vote against this whole thing."

"Duly noted, Harry. Aren't you at all excited about visiting Antarctica? Not many people get to do that."

"There are no words to adequately describe my excitement."

Avery laughed, and Carter joined her.

"Actually, I was just thinking about the body you guys recovered."

"Any word from Lieutenant Antonin?" Avery said.

"Other than the fact that there was indeed a body in there? Nothing yet," Harrison said. "Those lab guys are always out straight. I'd be surprised if we hear anything before next week."

"The important thing is we found the body though, right, Harry?" Carter asked.

"As long as they can prove it's Melody. And you two don't freeze to death before you can testify."

"We'll do our best, Harry." Avery turned to Carter. "I've been thinking about our underwater communication—I'm thinking of a couple signals we could add to our own version of sign language."

Communication was always essential when diving. In addition to the universal dive signals, Carter had also taught Avery the baseball signals he and his old diving partner Jeff had used underwater.

Harrison appeared above Avery's seat. "That's a good idea, Ave. Your mom and I had signals in case one of us got into trouble on the mean streets of the Big Apple. Like a hostage kind of thing."

Carter put down the notepad. "Okay, let's hear them."

"Well, I'm thinking that if I wave my arm behind my back while we're inside a wreck, it means for you to move on to the next area."

Carter laughed. "How am I supposed to tell the difference between that or your back itches? Or maybe you're just dismissing me."

"All right, fine," Avery said. "What if I touch my nose, then pull an earlobe."

"I thought we were using that for approaching shark, because my little league coach used that for a runner about to steal a base?"

Harrison rolled his eyes and returned to his seat. "You guys are too much."

Avery sighed. "What does it mean if I give you the finger?"

Carter grinned. "Means I'd have to tag the video as explicit, and I'd get way fewer views."

The intercontinental trip was known for being anything but easy, and the DC-3 shook and shuddered from the moment the wheels left the ground. Avery had debated telling Harrison about the likelihood of severe turbulence as they flew from South America to Antarctica over Drake Passage—infamous for being one of the roughest ocean crossings on the planet—but as she looked across the aisle of their private charter, it was apparent that he'd already figured it out. Harrison's eyes were clamped shut while his hands were clasped tightly to the ends of each armrest, his knuckles white.

She reached across the aisle and placed a hand on his forearm. "You okay, Harry?"

"Just ducky," he said without opening his eyes. "Tell me again how much fun this is going to be."

"I can't tell if you could use a drink or if that would make you puke," Carter said. "But either way, I'm afraid our luxury flight here is suspending beverage service."

"Ha-ha," Harrison said through gritted teeth as he gave his seatbelt a yank, cinching it tighter. "Just let me know when it's over, Ave."

Their pilot was everything Marco had said he would be. A combat veteran of the wars in Afghanistan and Iraq, Rollie "Fingers" Jenkins had flown pretty much anything and everything the military possessed, including the B-2 Stealth Bomber. The stripped-down and retrofitted DC-3

Basler was his private moneymaker. Primarily used to transport people to remote destinations like Antarctica where conditions were far less than favorable, Rollie had named the plane *White Out*. He proudly referred to himself as the "Uber driver of the skies."

"I've made this trip more times than I can count," Rollie had told them when they first met at a dive bar in a seedy part of Buenos Aires. "Landing on an ice shelf can be a bit tricky, but trust me, it's a piece of cake when compared to dodging anti-aircraft rounds." Upon hearing this, Harrison groaned audibly before ordering another round.

"What would you say is the toughest thing about flying to Antarctica?" Avery had asked Rollie.

"You mean besides a runway made of ice and the crazy weather?" Rollie had said with a chuckle. "Well, for the uninitiated I guess it would be the magnetic fields. They can get really wonky at the poles."

"Exactly what Marco told us," Carter said.

"And he's right," Rollie said. "Wreaks havoc on the gauges and equipment."

"What do you do if that happens?" Harrison asked, clearly alarmed.

"I just sit back and fly by feel," Rollie had said before downing the rest of his drink, then signaling for another.

Avery tightened the seatbelt on her own seat as the DC-3 continued to bounce around, trying not to worry about how Rollie's gauges were behaving just then.

11

Their touchdown on the runway in Antarctica was as smooth as any Avery could remember, a blessing after such a turbulent ocean crossing. Marco had been right about Rollie. He really was the best.

Avery looked out the window, hoping to get her bearings, but there was nothing but snow and ice as far as she could see.

"We're here, Harry," Avery said as she felt the plane come to a stop and the prop engines powering down.

"If only *here* wasn't in the middle of frozen nowhere."

"You'll feel better once we get something to eat," Carter said.

"As long as they have something besides Tang and freeze-dried ice cream." Harrison groused. "This place looks like the moon."

After taxiing the DC-3 to the unloading point, Rollie lowered the ramp, letting in a blast of frigid air.

"My God, our lungs are going to freeze before we get off this plane." Harrison pulled his scarf up and his hood strings tighter.

"Refreshing," Avery said.

"Antarctic air," Rollie said with a smile. "Nothing like it."

"There's a reason humans never settled here," Harrison said.

Rollie helped them unload their gear. As they descended the ramp, two bright orange vehicles that looked like snowmobiles cross-bred with ski lift gondolas, glass boxes sitting atop long, tank-track wheels, rolled toward the plane. The drivers, decked out in ski goggles and bright orange hooded arctic gear, identical to the jackets Noah had sent to New York, stopped near the bottom of the ramp and climbed out of their vehicles.

The man closest to the steps gave a wave, then lifted his goggles. "Welcome to Halley VI Research Station."

Avery recognized Noah immediately.

"I trust you had an uneventful trip," he continued.

Harrison spoke up before anyone else could answer. "It was everything I thought it would be."

"Thank you, Doctor," Avery said, ignoring Harrison. "It wasn't bad at all."

"Well?" Noah said as he gestured to the station and surrounding landscape. "What do you think of our home?"

Avery and Harrison were speechless.

"Wow," Carter said.

At first glance the station looked more like a giant freight train than a research facility. Eight modules mounted atop legs connected to form a long chain. There were seven similar-sized blue modules and one oversized red module Avery took to be a gathering place. She had viewed online information about the station but seeing it up close and personal provided an entirely different perspective. It looked more like a space outpost from some science fiction story than anything found here on earth. *Harry was right*, Avery thought. This was truly like being on the moon. She looked back toward the runway as Rollie's plane left it, most of the concrete already re-covered in snow.

They were alone with strangers in the most isolated place on the planet. While she had no reason to expect anything to be amiss, the feeling of control over her surroundings and situation slipping away with Rollie was disconcerting—at best.

From reading online, Avery knew Halley Station was one of only twenty year-round research stations in Antarctica. Run by the government of the United Kingdom, it had seen more than its share of financial ups and downs.

"If the government isn't funding your research, how is it that you came to be here at Halley?" Avery asked as Noah's assistants grabbed their bags and loaded them into the Sno-Cats.

"Fluctuations in the British economy made it possible for us to lease space here at a reduced rate," Noah said, ushering everyone toward the vehicles as a sharp wind sliced right through their polar outerwear. "They get to show publicly that the station is still supporting important research, yet they're at least breaking even on the operational cost."

"Like a billion-dollar Airbnb?" Carter asked.

"I suppose you could say that."

Located approximately 1500 miles from Cape Horn, the Halley Research Station sat squarely on the seventy-fifth parallel at the edge of the Weddell Sea.

"Does the ground look like it's wavering slightly to anyone else?" Harrison asked as the vehicles lumbered toward the station.

"You're not imagining it, Mr. Harrison," Noah said. "We're on a floating ice shelf—stable, I assure you, but floating all the same. You know, Halley Station has the distinction of being the first scientific research center to discover the hole in the ozone layer of Earth's atmosphere in 1975."

"And fifty years later, here we are using gas generators right underneath it to try to reverse its effects," Harry muttered as Noah parked out front. "Seems a little counterproductive when you think about it."

Noah glanced back at Harry before he opened the door and nodded but didn't speak.

They were led inside one of the blue end modules, which functioned as an equipment room. The heated space was warm and inviting, a sharp contrast to the bitter sting of the outside air. A row of helmets lined a counter along one wall, the shelves beneath stuffed with additional harsh-weather gear and plastic storage containers. On the same wall, to the right of a set of dual glass fire doors, was another long counter, more shelving, and a wall-mounted corkboard with typed notices pinned to it. A quick glance at the postings told Avery they were duty rosters.

"Everybody has assignments here," Noah said as he followed her gaze.

"Even us?" Harrison said.

"You're a guest, Mr. Harrison," Noah said. "Though I'm quite sure we'll be able to find something for Ms. Turner and Mr. Mosley to do."

"I don't remember anything about signing up for chores," Carter said.

"Neither do I," came a voice from behind them, and Avery and Carter spun around to find a woman in a thick sweater and ski pants, nearly a foot shorter than both of them. "But there's a lot here I didn't know to consider before I arrived, and we push through."

"Dr. Courtney Abbott, meet Avery Turner, Carter Mosley, and Mr. Harrison," Noah said. "Dr. Abbott is our resident climatologist. She holds multiple postgraduate degrees from Oxford and is a leading mind in her field. She's been here longer than anyone else, so even I ask her questions about the station from time to time."

"How long is that?" Avery asked, putting a hand out for the curvy, blue-eyed woman to shake. Dr. Abbott didn't wear a speck of makeup, her round wire-rimmed glasses sitting high on her pink nose.

"Coming up on two years," she said, shoving the sleeve of her sweater back to reveal her hand and shake Avery's. "But I'm finally going home next week." She smiled weakly, but Avery didn't think it reached her eyes, which were hooded and tired.

"What's the most interesting thing you've learned in all that time here?" Avery asked.

"Aside from the limits of human psychological and physical endurance?" Courtney asked without a trace of irony. "That this place is beautiful if you can get past it being too bright and too big and too much and really see it." She spoke faster with each word, excitement seeping into her voice. "The climate here is a miracle in action—the effects of slight changes in Antarctic conditions have repercussions that are felt around the world like no other environment on Earth. Our collective human climate relies on this place being balanced, which is why Dr. Wyndham's vision is so important."

"I can hear your passion for your work in your voice," Avery said, seeing a parallel between herself and the middle-aged scientist with the spiky graying hair. "Thank you for lending your expertise to this project. I'm excited to be here."

"Ms. Turner has a master's in Information Science from Columbia," Noah offered.

"I can't believe how cold it is here," Carter said. "It makes me wonder if the climate situation is really as dire as people say. Dr. Abbott, it seems like you'd be the person to ask."

Courtney kept her eyes on Avery. "Things aren't as bad as people say they are." She looked between them. "They're worse. If we don't figure this thing out with the ice, the whole damn planet is on a crash course with disaster that will happen sooner rather than later."

She reached into a box and retrieved a pair of thick socks and some gloves. "The heat is trying to go out in my lab. Nice to meet you folks." She bustled out through the fire doors.

"Dr. Abbott isn't quite the finishing school social type," Noah said. "But she is brilliant and very passionate about her work."

"Her work, or her disdain for this place?" Carter asked, twisting his lips to one side in a move Avery recognized as meaning he was uneasy.

"You'll find that a few of our staff are on edge," Noah said blandly. "It's not unusual for a group that's spent so much time here, especially as we near Antarctic winter and the sunset. Please, if you hear anything that bothers you, come ask me. I'm happy to explain. Now. Who's hungry?"

"I'm starving," Carter said.

"I could eat a horse," Harrison said.

Noah chuckled. "Well, I don't know about equine provisions, but our chef prepares a delicious porterhouse."

"Now you're talking," Harrison said.

"Chef?" Avery said.

"Why certainly. Just because we're sharing a zip code with the South Pole doesn't mean we can't enjoy some of the creature comforts of home. Come on. I'll show you to the dining hall. You can stow your belongings in your rooms along the way. By the way, don't bother to unpack."

"Why not?" Carter asked.

"We'll be taking the last leg of your trip tomorrow."

12

They took a late dinner in front of picture windows overlooking the barren Antarctic landscape. The snow almost glowed in the low light, the sun still hovering just above the horizon despite the late hour.

"What time does the sun set here?" Harrison asked as he sliced off another healthy chunk of his steak.

"Next week," Noah said.

Harrison's fork paused halfway to his mouth. "Seriously?"

"Yes. It rises in September and doesn't go below the horizon again until March. We are watching the sunset."

"That's incredible," Harrison said.

"Does that mean that when it sets it doesn't come up again until September?" Carter asked.

Noah nodded. "Antarctica's winter."

"The aurora australis must be incredible," Avery said.

"It is," Noah said.

"Don't you mean borealis?" Harrison said.

"No, Avery's correct, Mr. Harrison—"

"Harry, please."

"Well, Harry, the aurora borealis is the northern lights, which of course we can't see from here. The same anomaly exists here, only it's called the southern lights or aurora australis."

"Whatever it's called, I'm sure it's beautiful," Harrison said.

"It truly is."

"Is that why you invited us on such short notice?" Avery said. "Because the Antarctic summer is ending?"

"Precisely. I fear the clock is ticking on our project."

"How so?" Carter said.

"If we aren't able to locate the *Fortitude* soon, the search will end until September."

"Why not simply resume the search for the ship then?" Avery said.

Noah picked up his napkin and wiped his mouth before answering. "I'm not convinced we'll be able to afford to come back."

Avery and Carter nodded understanding, Carter looking around.

"Why is the station called Halley VI?" Carter said.

"Improved versions, I would imagine," Avery said.

"Quite right," Noah said. "We kept losing the others."

"Losing?" Harrison nearly choked on a bite of steak. "What exactly does that mean?"

"The previous iterations sank into the ice. Engineers eventually figured out a way to move the modules."

"Move? As in, the whole place?" Carter asked.

"The fix was telescoping legs. We simply raise them up and drag them to a new location with our Sno-Cats."

"But I thought this place was permanent," Carter said.

"Heavens no," Noah said. "This is only an ice shelf we're sitting on. Much like one of your American ice-fishing shacks, if you don't move the structure occasionally, it will become embedded in the ice, slowly sinking down until eventually it's lost to the Antarctic."

"But that can't happen with this one, right?" Harrison asked.

"Haven't lost her yet," Noah said with a wink.

"Tell us a little bit about the station itself," Avery said.

"Well, we are currently on the first level of the red module, or what we call the leisure and dining center."

"I like the sound of that," Harrison said as he reached over to the platter at the center of the table and carved off another hunk of meat.

"Additionally, we have a command module, several accommodation modules, where your private rooms are located, a generator and sewerage-treatment module, science module, and weather module. And, as you've likely noticed, reenforced fire doors separate each module."

"Fire?" Harrison said.

"This station is designed to withstand any wind and weather Antarctica can throw at us, and we guard against the danger we bring on ourselves as well. You noted the generators outside as we arrived, Harry. Using them for our power means fire is always a risk."

After dinner Harrison retired to his room, while Noah wandered off to "see to other tasks." Avery and Carter, too excited to even think about sleep, retrieved their laptops from their gear bags and returned to the lounge for some more research.

Avery was lost in reading more about the history of the *Fortitude* when Carter interrupted her focus.

"Do you know what the temperature is this time of year in the Weddell Sea?"

"I'm guessing really cold," Avery said.

"Try minus twenty to minus thirty degrees Fahrenheit."

"And?" Avery said, not entirely understanding the point.

"That would in theory perfectly preserve a wooden wreck like the *Fortitude*. Like it sank yesterday."

"That's our hope," a voice said from behind him. "Though we haven't found so much as a stray plank yet."

Carter and Avery turned to find a tall, thin-faced man wearing a cream-colored Irish fisherman's sweater and cap.

"Hello," Avery said.

"Good evening, miss. I'm Owen. Owen Fisher, Noah's chief research assistant. You must be Avery Turner and Carter Mosley."

"Guilty as charged," Carter said.

"I apologize for missing your arrival," Owen said.

"I imagine everyone here stays quite busy," Avery said.

"Indeed, we do."

"We're excited to learn more about the research here," Avery said.

"I assume Noah filled you in on his theories? He loves to talk to new people about his theories."

"Not yet," Avery confessed. "He said he'd bring us up to speed when we get the full tour tomorrow."

"Then I mustn't spoil it. I'll leave you both to your work."

"It was nice to meet you, Owen," Avery said.

"Yes," Carter said. "Great meeting you."

"Likewise. Have a pleasant evening." With a tip of his cap, Owen was gone.

13

They reassembled in the dining room at eight o'clock the next morning. Avery, dressed in jeans and a sweater, was pleasantly surprised to see Harrison seemed fully recovered from his turbulent arrival-flight jitters. Looking bright-eyed and bushy-tailed, Harrison slurped noisily from an oversized mug of coffee while listening to Noah and Carter chattering about sea depths and drone visibility.

"Morning, all," Avery said.

"Morning, Ave," Harrison said.

"Good morning," Carter and Noah said in unison.

Avery fetched herself a cup of strong java from a station set up near the dining table. She felt surprisingly good herself, despite having been up until near midnight conducting research. Maybe it was the constant sunlight, a disturbance in her circadian rhythm, or maybe it was plain old adrenaline, but she wasn't that tired. She returned to the table with her coffee and sat down beside Noah.

"How did you sleep?" Noah said.

"Amazingly well," Avery said. "Must be the cold air."

"You folks need some room-darkening shades," Harrison said. "The sunshine made sleep almost impossible."

"The shape of the windows makes it hard to outfit them with proper shades. It takes some a while to adapt to the sun, but I barely notice it anymore," Noah said. "I thought we might start with a tour of the facility as soon as your bellies are full, if that works."

"Works for me," Harrison said. "The chef is whipping up some blueberry pancakes and a side of bacon for me."

"And you?" Avery asked Carter.

"Western omelet with a side of hash."

"Nope, nothing wrong with their appetites," Avery said.

"They can drum up almost anything your heart desires, Avery," Noah said.

"Caffeine is good for now," Avery said.

"Understand you met Owen last night," Noah said.

"We did," Carter said. "He said you like to tell new people about your research."

Noah winked. "All in good time."

When breakfast was finished, Noah led them to the command module.

"This is the heart of Halley Station," Noah said. "All of our communication links and environmental controls are remotely run from here. And this is our keeper of the controls, Lennie Hodgdon."

"Pleased to make your acquaintance," Lennie said.

"Likewise," Avery said as she stared through the surrounding windows across the frozen expanse. "I'd dare say you've got the best view in the world, Lennie."

"This end of it, anyway. We call this the crow's nest."

"Too bad you can't see under the water from up here," Avery said. "It would make things easier."

Lennie raised one eyebrow like he wasn't sure what she meant as Carter pointed to the panel of gauges and buttons he'd been studying since they walked in.

"Does that control the interior temperature here?" he asked. "What happens if, say, your environmental controls fail? I mean, it must be, what, thirty below outside?"

"Thirty-seven below, actually," Lennie said. "These controls can be over-ridden of course, at the source module, but normally everything is controlled from up here."

"Redundancy is the answer to your question," Noah said. "The previous five versions of this station provided the opportunity to work out all the bugs, which tend to accompany such a remote research facility. Funding for the type of research this place was built for may rise and fall, but the safety of all our researchers is first and foremost. The equipment and hardware we depend upon to sustain life—generators, fuel, food stuff, water, transportation, satellite links—all have redundancy backup units. There are only twenty year-round stations in all of Antarctica. Being one of them means we must plan for every possible eventuality."

"Last night when we spoke, you mentioned that the end of the summer season is almost here," Avery said. "How difficult is it to travel back and forth to South America during Antarctica's winter?"

"It does present its own unique challenges, the most obvious being the lack of sunlight and the occasional blizzard associated with the winter months, but we make sure we always have enough on hand to allow us to hunker down in safety during the worst weather."

"That's a relief," Harrison said. "This place does feel a little bit like the Overlook Hotel."

Noah's brow creased in confusion.

"You'll have to forgive Harry," Avery said. "It was an obscure reference to a Stephen King novel."

"And movie," Carter said.

"Ah, bravo, Harry," Noah said. "I'm a big fan of the horror genre."

Harrison raised and lowered his eyebrows mischievously.

"How many people are stationed here at any one time?" Avery said, attempting to return to the topic at hand.

"Halley Station was constructed to comfortably house fifty researchers at any one time. We have thirty-one researchers residing here currently."

"Including us?" Carter said.

"I stand corrected. Thirty-four. Well, there's much more to see. Shall we push on?"

"Catch you later, Lennie," Avery said.

"I look forward to it."

Their next stop was the science module.

"This is where all of the research data is stored and analyzed," Noah said. "Anything and everything to do with climatology is studied here. We collect data hourly from more than two hundred different sources. Everything from wind speed to solar activity to air and ocean temperatures."

"Man, this is so cool," Carter said. "I feel like I may have missed the bus when choosing a career path."

"That's not the only bus you've missed," Harrison teased.

"Yeah," Avery said. "Because being a social media celebrity is such a burden."

"You have no idea," Carter said.

Noah and Harrison laughed.

"We're hoping to make sure Halley is not only the place where the ozone hole was discovered but the place we figured out how to reverse its catastrophic effects," Noah said. "Credit yet another scientific achievement to the United Kingdom."

"We've still got the moon landing," Harrison replied.

"Touché," Noah said.

A tinny-sounding voice emanated from a wall-mounted intercom speaker panel. "Doctor, we're ready anytime you are."

Noah pressed the talk button. "Thank you, Sergey. Be there shortly." Noah turned back to face them. "Well, it appears we've come to the end of our tour. Time to gather up your belongings and dress for the out of doors."

"But you haven't told us anything about the hunt for the *Fortitude*," Avery said.

"That's because I've saved the best for last. Now, if you will kindly follow me."

"Where are we going?" Harrison said.

Noah's lips spread into a grin. "I thought we'd take a little ride."

14

Gear for walking around Antarctica, even in the "summer," included a full set of thermals, pants, sweaters, outer wear, boots, gloves, face coverings, and goggles.

"I feel like I've done a day's work just getting ready to step outside," Carter said.

They exited by way of the blue end pod through which they had arrived the previous evening. Parked and idling near the base of the ramp were two blaze-orange Sno-Cats, engines running.

"Avery, why don't you jump in with me," Noah said. "Carter, you and Harry can ride in the other transport with Sergey."

Avery, who'd been hunting an opportunity to talk one-on-one with the expedition leader, readily agreed.

Harrison shouted to be heard above the Sno-Cat engines. "Where exactly are we going?"

Noah turned. "You'll love it, I promise."

"Does it really look brighter out here than it did last night?" Avery asked, scanning the brilliant-white horizon ahead of their Sno-Cat, which was leading the one with Carter and Harrison inside. The belted track vehicle moved across the ice surprisingly smoothly for such a large conveyance. "I feel like there's so much light everywhere I look."

"You're not wrong," Noah said. "The sun does rise slightly higher during the day, and the way it hits the ice and snow makes for quite a show, doesn't it?"

"I'll say." Avery stared out the window.

"You must have been wondering how we would search for a sunken ship in the middle of a frozen tundra," Noah said.

"It had crossed my mind," Avery said. "I figured perhaps you had a giant ice auger stowed away somewhere."

Noah laughed. "If it were only that easy, Ms. Turner. No, we're headed to a second research facility."

"You have two Halley Stations?" Avery said.

Noah laughed again. "It's not quite as complex or large as Halley VI, but it is infinitely more mobile, and it accommodates our needs quite nicely. It's a research ship. An ice breaker that, contrary to its intended purpose perhaps, allows us to study the forming sea ice in real time, and activity in that area is picking up every day with winter approaching."

"Will we get to see how your invention works while we're here?" Avery asked. "I'd love to have a look."

"I knew you'd be up to the task, Ms. Turner," Noah said.

"Please call me Avery, and I am more than up to just about any task, Doctor."

"Noah, if you please."

"Okay, Noah, you've done a fair bit of talking about funding, and it's got me wondering, from the philanthropic standpoint of someone with a bit of money who enjoys going to the beach and not boiling like a lobster—how much money does something like this cost?"

"Our total grants to date come to just over seven hundred twenty-six million dollars."

Avery whistled. "That's more than the GDP of many small countries."

Noah yanked the controls much faster than the Sno-Cat was capable of swerving as he prepared to circumnavigate a large rock outcropping. The machine bucked slightly as they crossed over refrozen tracks from a previous trip, missing the rock by inches.

"How often do you make the trip between stations?" Avery asked.

"As often as we need to," Noah said. "Now, I have a question: Would you be so kind as to tell me a bit more about this DiveNav device you've developed?"

"It's cutting edge, if I do say so myself."

As they neared the edge of the ice cap, Avery stared with wide eyes at a sea of ice floes and the ocean beyond. The *Weddell* began to materialize in the distance as if it were an oceanic mirage.

"I assume you must enjoy having a research facility that moves more easily than Halley Station," Avery said.

"It is quite convenient but also necessary. A so-called fixed station at water's edge would need to be relocated much more frequently than Halley," Noah said.

"Why?"

"The changing seasons drastically alter the shoreline, for lack of a better term, of the ice cap. As the ocean water refreezes, or thaws, the expanding or receding shoreline can force us to move literally miles away. The ship makes perfect sense. It also puts us right in the thick of the sea ice formation, which has been invaluable in recent weeks to fine-tuning the method I'm hoping to use to rebuild the melting shelf."

"How much progress have you made toward locating the *Fortitude*?"

"Very little, I'm afraid. It has been frustrating to say the least. But I hope our luck is about to turn," Noah said. "The future of the planet may depend on it."

"Surely you have other investor possibilities," Avery said.

"I'm afraid you wouldn't be here if I did, Miss Turner."

"And if we manage to locate the ship?"

Noah shrugged. "Who knows? It is my sincere wish that such a discovery would guarantee the continued benevolence of our current supporters and possibly dangle a publicity carrot to increase our support from the British government, or if not, perhaps it will ignite enough public interest to drum up funding I haven't even thought of."

"I have already uploaded the information you provided to the DiveNav, but I'd like the coordinates from the original crew journals to enter as a starting point."

"I'm afraid they'd be of little use. We have already conducted an exhaustive search of that area. It was a complete waste of time."

Avery nodded politely, reminded of their recent search for the *Money-maker* and how they had been told the exact same thing. The DiveNav, with its built-in analytics and artificial intelligence software, was designed to outthink every conceivable human scenario at mind-bending speed, using decades of tidal, weather, and earthquake records along with last-known locations to calculate the most likely whereabouts of a lost object.

The *Moneymaker* had been a flawless trial run. Well . . . except for the whole Fiji thing, but Avery had gotten the device right back on track and would work out whatever bug had caused the glitch as soon as she had some spare time. The important thing was that using the DiveNav, she and Carter had managed to locate the missing yacht in less than an hour when the NYPD had wasted months searching for it.

"I'm sure you're right, Noah," Avery said, "but you invited us to assist you in the search and I'd like to see them all the same."

Noah fixed her with a look she couldn't quite interpret. "You're quite right, Avery. I'll see that you get them just as soon as we're aboard the *Weddell*."

15

The red-and-white research vessel was significantly larger than Avery had imagined. Size-wise the *Weddell* was a cross between a fishing trawler and the coast guard cutter *Penobscot Bay* they had utilized while searching for the *Moneymaker*. Glancing around as she stepped out of the Sno-Cat, she shivered, not from the frigid wind coming off the water but from the stark remote feel of the landscape. Harry's comparison to the isolation in *The Shining* wasn't invalid—the ship was the only man-made thing as far as Avery could see in any direction, snow stretching one way and ice-riddled water the other. In the book, the isolation hadn't ended well.

Shaking off the jitters, she followed Noah and Carter into the ship, Harry on her heels. The interior layout reminded her of Halley Station, as if the same designer had visited both vessels.

"How many people do you have in this crew?" Carter asked as they moved through the bridge to an interior hallway. "Do they overlap with the Halley crew?"

"Only myself and my research assistant go between the stations regularly. Here on the ship—including you and the two of us—we have a crew of twenty-three. Not big, but we keep things moving forward."

Belowdecks they were shown a science lab, environmental lab, main gathering area, and individual quarters for the onboard researchers. The array of technical research equipment was downright mind-boggling. The one additional space, not seen on Halley, located at the ship's center, was dedicated entirely to underwater drones, cameras, and all manner of sea condition monitoring. The space even featured its own moon pool for diving and lowering equipment from within the safe confines of the ship regardless of weather.

The ship had fewer staterooms than there were quarters at Halley Station, as the *Weddell* was designed only to house up to thirty people. Avery noticed there seemed to be far less instrumentation and climate study equipment than she had seen in the crow's nest at Halley Station.

According to Noah, satellite communications were available to the ship only through a relay to Halley Station. It was quickly apparent to Avery that the *Weddell* was far less self-sufficient than the research facility from which they had just departed.

"Now I want to show you something really special," Noah said as he led them back out onto the deck. "This is our secret project."

Avery stared at the large stainless-steel contraption mounted directly onto the deck.

"It looks like a giant cocktail shaker," Carter said.

"I guess it does at that." Noah laughed.

"You could throw a heck of a party, Doc," Harrison said.

"Indeed, we could. Actually, this one is our miniature prototype of what will eventually be an enormous ship-mounted rig, which will create amorphous ice from sea ice that can then be packed onto the existing shelf. If successful, we will literally be able to reconstruct the melting polar caps. This, lady and gentlemen, is why we need your help."

"Cool," Carter said as he poked at one of the softball-sized metal spheres contained inside the device.

"Amorphous ice?" Avery asked. "What's the difference between it and regular ice, aside from the hundreds of millions of dollars and this cool gizmo?"

"Amorphous ice is the prevalent form on other planets, whereas crystalline ice is unique to Earth. I have spent years trying to find a way to create it here in the hopes it would be pliable enough to bond to the natural shelf."

"That's amazing," Avery said. "Have you been able to field test it yet?"

Noah smiled as he pointed to the nearby ice shelf. "You couldn't tell the difference just yet, but we've managed to add a three-foot section to that stretch of shelf using our giant cocktail shaker here. The next test is whether or not it lasts through the winter. And then, on how large a scale could we manage it?"

"I'm impressed, Doc," Harrison said. "Though a little sad there isn't a game room on board here," Harrison said, making no attempt to conceal his disappointment as they followed Noah back into the ship.

"I'm afraid the *Weddell*'s sole purpose is research, Harry," Noah said. "No time for fun, at least not according to the people footing the bills. We do have an extensive scientific library, if you find yourself in need of reading to fill downtime." He pointed down a side hallway.

Harry wrinkled his nose but nodded.

"Was it your idea to keep the two research stations completely separate?" Carter said.

"Each area of research requires its own skill and expertise. All our researchers here on the ship were handpicked specifically for their underwater knowledge and abilities. I'd like you to meet our marine geologist, Reggie Marston," Noah said as they entered the ship's meeting room.

Reggie looked to Avery to be in his late thirties to early forties. He was ruggedly handsome with thick, wavy blond hair and a ruddy complexion that came from spending a lot of time outdoors.

"Reggie, these are our shipwreck experts from the States. Avery Turner, Carter Mosley, and Mr. Harrison."

"I'm not sure about experts," Avery said. "But I appreciate the compliment. It's a pleasure to meet you, Reggie. Or is it Captain?"

"It's Reggie, and the pleasure is all mine," he said as he stepped forward and shook Avery's hand, holding on a bit longer than necessary.

Avery glanced at Carter, whose eyes were on Reggie's fingers still wrapped around hers.

Carter stepped in and offered his own hand.

"Great to meet you, Carter," Reggie said, both men locking eyes as if in a showdown. "I've really enjoyed your entertaining dive videos. I'm a certified dive master myself." When at last they released each other's hand, Reggie moved on to Harrison.

"Happy to meet you, Harrison."

"Likewise, Reggie. My friends call me Harry."

"Harry it is then. I hope you'll consider me a friend."

Avery gazed around the space. Hung on every square inch of available wall space were maps and underwater survey scans of search areas, each one marked up with various scribbled codes, which meant nothing to Avery.

"Looks like you've done quite a bit of searching already," Avery said.

"Indeed, we have," Reggie said. "Nothing to show for it yet, I'm afraid. I know Noah's been hoping you folks might be able to offer a fresh perspective to our search before we run out of time."

"We'll certainly do our best," Avery said. "What's the biggest obstacle you've found in your search to date?"

"Besides the extreme temperatures? It's the sheer vastness of the unexplored area here and the depth of the water. We can't piggyback on what others have done because no one really comes here to search for . . . well, anything really. Not deep enough for it to be useful to us. In the six months we've been at this, we've conducted hundreds of underwater drone explorations and sonar mapping, but we've just scratched the surface of what's possible."

"Wow," Avery said.

"But you have all of the necessary equipment to do deep cold-water video and sonar searches?" Carter asked.

Reggie nodded. "Everything we need, including a few toys that haven't become available on the open market yet, though we've had a few untimely glitches lately that have caused us some setbacks, but new equipment always has glitches, right?"

Avery laughed. "My DiveNav had a hiccup the other day and told me a yacht that sank in the Hudson was in Fiji." She glanced between Noah and Reggie. "Not to worry though, I'm working out every kink as I go, too."

"Yes, you might say we've been conducting some live field tests while we search here," Reggie said. "Nothing better for advertising new products than being able to say they were instrumental in the shipwreck discovery of the century, am I right?"

"It makes for a heck of a marketing push," Carter agreed.

"Very happy to have you here," Reggie said as he looked Avery up and down before turning his attention to Carter. "Both of you."

16

After stowing their gear in the cramped holds inside each of their adjoining cabins and changing into more suitable clothing, they met back at Avery's room. Avery and Carter wore turtlenecks and sweaters over jeans, while Harrison had opted for the more traditional untucked long-sleeved plaid chamois. Harrison had started growing a beard, and combined with the plaid shirt, Avery couldn't help but see the resemblance between the barrel-chested ex-cop and the mythical lumberjack Paul Bunyan.

Avery was busy uploading information from the crew journals Noah had hand-delivered to her when she happened to look up and see Harrison searching her cabin.

"What are you doing, Harry?"

"Looking for bugs."

"Isn't it a little cold for cockroaches, Harry?" Carter raised his eyebrows.

"Not insects, Junior G-man," Harrison said. "Little microphones."

"Seriously?" Avery's voice went up half an octave. "You honestly think Noah would invite us here and then bug our rooms?"

"I'm a homicide detective with twenty years of experience dealing with the worst of mankind, Ave. We're in unfamiliar surroundings, in a hostile environment, cut off from the outside world, and we're under someone else's control—haven't you ever read an Agatha Christie or Dennis Lehane book? Spoiler alert: this kind of scenario never ends well."

"Come on, Harry," Avery said. "Don't you think you're being just a bit overly dramatic?"

"Wouldn't you rather me be overanxious and wrong than too laid-back and wrong?"

"Fair point," Avery said. "I suppose it's better to be safe, right? I'm just so excited to be part of something this important—I can't believe how much it took to fund this, let alone that they still need more."

"The equipment they've got is crazy expensive to rent," Carter offered. "I can't even begin to imagine what it costs to own."

"I can't believe more governments aren't investing in his research, though," Avery said. "Climate change affects every nation, and while three-quarters of a billion dollars is a lot even for me, doesn't the Pentagon spend that much on like, a box of hammers? Why isn't this already getting attention?" She eyed Harry. "Don't say it's because there's something nefarious afoot, either."

"All I'm saying is it doesn't hurt to be careful." Harrison softened his tone. "We don't know any of these people, Ave. If I'm wrong, I'll be the first to admit it, and gladly."

"It is a little weird they knew right where to deliver the packages in New York," Carter conceded.

Avery shot him a look. "You didn't notice that before we left?"

"They had to have been checking up on us, Ave," Harrison said. "I mean, how else would they have known about our trip to New York? Or our hotel?"

"Or our coat sizes," Carter said.

"Dorothy said she didn't tell them," Harrison said.

"Suppose you're right," Avery said. "But haven't we been checking up on them too? I could probably write a reasonable biography on Dr. Wyndham if pressed at this point."

"But we didn't do any of that until we got invited to this little soirée," Carter said.

"It's possible that he didn't read up on us until he decided to consider inviting us here," Avery said, not really sure why she sounded so defensive.

She sighed and tapped the stack of papers Noah had handed her on his way up to the bridge. "None of this will matter anyway if the *Fortitude* has either already been located or rotted into the ocean floor."

"Both of those things are highly unlikely," Carter said. "I study this stuff constantly, Avery. If a wreck as significant as the *Fortitude* had been discovered, I'd know about it. And the frigid water here wouldn't allow for rot."

"I've been thinking about Noah's funding and his request to have the discovery videos posted to my Insta: GoFundMe is a powerful tool, but there are still ways to maximize it. I should find out if there's marine life we can get in the drone shots and include information on. People love animals. They'll definitely get us more shares and him more money. Particularly if the animals are cute."

"Why are you so sure the thing hasn't just rotted into the dirt?" Harrison asked. "The shipwrecks in all those Caribbean dives you do are nothing more than mushy boards buried in sand and coral. You said so yourself."

"This is different, Harry," Carter said. "The cold water and lack of sunlight would both help preserve a wooden ship. It's one of the reasons I wanted to come on this trip. The only complete shipwrecks I've seen to date were constructed either from steel or fiberglass, and none of them were anywhere near as old as this one. The *Fortitude* is older than the *Titanic*."

"So, are we all in or not?" Avery said. "If you'll pardon the obvious pun, I don't want anyone getting cold feet."

"I'm all in," Carter said, raising his hand. "There's no way I'm going to chance someone else finding this ship before we do when we've been given an invite to first dibs."

"What about you, Harry?" Avery said. "If you're not comfortable with this, now's the time to say so. I'll just tell Noah we've reconsidered and decided not to be a part of the search."

Harrison shook his head. "Nah, I'm not quitting. I know how important this is to both of you. Besides, I feel better about being here with you than if I went back to the States."

"And I feel better with a big scary experienced detective protecting my six," Avery said.

"Big scary experienced former detective," Harrison corrected.

"As long as we're all agreed," Avery said.

"Just promise me you'll both be careful, okay?" Harrison said. "What do I always say?"

"Trust but verify," Carter said dutifully.

"There's hope for this guy yet." Harrison grinned.

17

Lazio, Italy
February 1538

Eryk and Wilhelm stood staring in silence at Orsini, unable to believe their own ears. One of the horses whinnied and stomped his hooves on the ground, the sounds echoing inside the walls of the nobleman's stable.

"Cardinal Olav is dead?" Eryk repeated, as if hearing the words through his own voice would somehow make the statement more believable.

"I only recently received word from Norway," Orsini said.

"But how?"

"Apparently he took ill during the last month. I am sorry to be the one to break the news of his death. I know Olav trusted you both highly."

"Thank you for saying so, my lord," Wilhelm said.

Eryk's gaze shifted to the wagon and the trunks hidden at the bottom of a load. "But we have been tasked with delivering these trunks and their valued contents to you."

Orsini's expression was one of pity, but he remained firm.

"I am sorry to have to decline my previous offer. But in the absence of a Vatican representative to Norway, I can see no path forward."

"But we have traveled very far to deliver these treasures to you," Eryk implored.

"Hear me now," Orsini said. "Know that I sympathize with your plight, but I believe that a curse has now set upon this stolen treasure. Anyone foolish enough to try to acquire these religious artifacts may well face a similar fate to that of Cardinal Olav."

Eryk and Wilhelm exchanged an uneasy glance.

"My advice is to take these back to the cathedral from whence they came. If they are cursed, it is by God himself."

Months later Eryk and Wilhelm stood tired and defeated in the twilight at the edge of a lake a day's ride south of Skagens Odde, Denmark. With no way of contacting Admiral Trondson, or even knowing whether he was still alive, they had run out of options.

"We have failed to complete our mission, Wilhelm," Eryk said. "Failed Cardinal Olav."

"The cardinal is dead, brother. You heard as well as I. Orsini was right, God has placed a curse on these treasures. If we keep them for ourselves, we will be cursed and our families will suffer greatly."

"We could still try to smuggle them back into Nidaros Cathedral," Eryk said.

"And if we should be caught?" Wilhelm said. "They will kill us for certain."

Both men looked out into the deep water of the unnamed lake. Uninhabited and remote, the area seemed perfect.

"Then we sink the treasure," Eryk said. "Bury the curse forever and escape this place."

The sun had set completely as the two men loaded the trunks onto a makeshift raft they found abandoned on the shore. They rowed out to the center of the lake. When they were sure the dark water was deep enough to keep the trunks hidden, they pushed the locked trunks overboard, then threw in the key.

Relieved at having unloaded their secret burden, Eryk and Wilhelm sat down on the raft, breathless, and stared out into the darkness. Within minutes a strange thing happened to the lake beneath them: the water began to glow from within as if full of starlight.

They quickly rose and paddled back to the shore. Mounting the wagon, they raced away from the lake, never to return.

18

They had less than an hour before they planned to meet up with Noah again. Carter pulled out his cell phone to text MaryAnn but found he had no signal. Poking his head into Avery's room, he asked if her phone was working.

"Noah said the only comms link here was a satellite connection relay through Halley, remember? You could try using that." Avery pointed to the sat phone on her room's tiny desk.

"That's right," Carter said. "I'm calling from the land the internet forgot. I'll try the one in my own cabin so I don't bother you two."

Back in his own cabin, he dialed MaryAnn's home number on the boxy desk phone.

"Hello?" a sleepy, familiar voice said.

"Hey, Brady." Carter shook his head at the image of his brother in Mary-Ann's bed. "What's happening?"

"Oh, you know. Little bit of this and a whole lot of that."

Gross. Carter did know, and that was the problem: the fact that his brother was currently seeing a woman he himself had previously slept with felt a little icky and a lot weird, and it didn't matter that he'd been trying to distance himself from her. Carter picked at a loose thread on his sweater, trying to focus on something else before the Two Degrees of Kevin Bacon lack of separation between him and MaryAnn and Brady made him nauseous.

"Don't suppose MaryAnn is around?"

"She's in the shower, bro. Want to leave a message?"

Pacing the cabin, looking for anything else he could focus on, Carter's gaze fell upon a data port in the wall just above his desk. Trusting Brady with something this important was not an option. "Just tell her to check her email. I'll be sending something to her shortly. I hope, anyway."

"No problem. Anything else?"

"Nope. That's it. Thanks."

Carter hung up and plugged his laptop into the sat port on the wall, two-finger typing an email to his former girlfriend and current employee —another recent development that felt squicky to him, but he was getting better at seeing her as a colleague. He asked for any data she could find about the *Fortitude* and its general perceived location, as well as listing the names of the principal players here and asking for background checks, Harrison's comment about Agatha Christie novels and extra caution rattling around the back of his head. Carter had never been much of a reader, but he knew people tended to die in Agatha Christie books and he wanted everyone to make it home safely. Trying to downplay Harrison's fear of danger, he added a line asking if she knew of any climate research funding sources Noah might not have considered. In her former career as a museum director, MaryAnn had been an expert fundraiser—and it sounded like Noah could use some of her magic touch.

Besides, Harrison was probably paranoid.

As Carter clicked Send, a soft rapping rattled his cabin door. He answered it and found Reggie standing there.

"Hey, Reggie."

"Am I interrupting anything?"

"Not at all. Just making a call home. What's up?"

"Don't suppose you'd be interested in seeing what we've done so far with our search for the *Fortitude*, would you?"

"And a look at some of that crazy gear?"

"By all means."

Carter followed Reggie from the room as an error message popped up at the top of his computer screen.

Reggie ushered Carter back to the moon pool bay where most of the gear was stored, his eyes popping wide at all the high-tech gadgetry.

"Man, this stuff is totally cutting-edge," Carter said. "I would think with all this state-of-the-art equipment, you would have located the *Fortitude* already."

"You would think, wouldn't you? The truth is technology has its limits, and we are finding all of them here. We have had to modify almost every piece of equipment in one way or another to make it operate to spec in these conditions. And changes and upgrades take time, especially with prototypes. Not to mention the fact that more of our toys are failing us every day as winter nears and the temperatures plummet further. Even the ice has become a problem."

"But you're on an ice breaker," Carter said.

"That's true, but with winter approaching, the sea ice forms faster than we can keep our search areas cleared. It slows everything down."

"What about the technical gear? I thought they were providing you with stuff meant for this environment?"

"In theory. But it's not like there's a big market for fancy gear that withstands the weather conditions here, you know? Lab simulations might get a sticker on the box, but here in the field it's just too harsh for most of the gear. Cameras, drones, even sonar scanners. We've either had to retrofit the equipment, tweak the way we use it, or abandon things altogether."

"Mind if I take a look at what you have so far?"

"Not at all."

Reggie led him up a flight of stairs, back to the meeting area they had been in earlier. As they entered the room, an auburn-haired woman Carter had not met greeted him with a bright smile.

"Carter Mosley, meet Erin Corliss."

"Hello, Carter," she said, blushing.

"Erin is our tech specialist. If she can't engineer it or fix it, then it likely can't be fixed."

"I'm such a big fan," Erin confessed. "I've watched all of your videos."

"Thanks," Carter said. "They pay the rent."

"So, Carter, which area were you looking to see specifically?" Reggie asked.

"How about we start with the sonar scans from the location mentioned in the *Fortitude* journals?"

"Erin, would you mind grabbing the printed maps?" Reggie asked.

"Not at all." She scampered off.

"I'll warn you in advance, we haven't been able to use the ship's high-definition side-scan sonar for weeks now. The ice makes it too unreliable. We've been using a robotic relay unit, which is more than an order of magnitude lower in range and accuracy than the ship's more sophisticated system."

"I'm familiar with that problem," Carter said. "It's the same with my gear. The higher tech a gadget is, the more prone it is to breakdown."

Erin returned and handed Reggie a large cardboard tube. Reggie unrolled a printout that covered half of the table surface. The map reminded Carter of a building blueprint, only there was nothing remotely man-made about the shape of the underwater topography.

"You can see we've managed to capture quite a lot of detail despite the malfunctioning equipment. But there's nothing here resembling a sunken ship."

Carter studied the image, looking for anything out of the ordinary. He noticed several dark splotches in the far reaches of the sepia-toned side-scan image. Pointing to them he said, "What are these?"

"Likely interference from the depth and water temperature. You can see three more smaller spots here, here, and here. I've got a 3D model that might help you visualize it better."

Carter waited while he retrieved the model from a nearby cabinet.

"Here we go," Reggie said, setting it in the center of the conference table.

The model was about three feet long by a foot wide. Casting it in cobalt-colored plastic gave it an underwater feel. Carter ran his fingers gently across the uneven surface. Nothing beyond the smallest of irregularities popped up from the surface.

"You can feel those little anomalies," Reggie said. "They could be anything from sand piles, to stone, to debris. Anything but a 145-foot sailing ship."

Carter nodded his agreement. "Have you tried sending a camera to the area of these blotches?"

"We're waiting for some temperature modifications to be made to our new underwater camera. The previous one malfunctioned when we tried for that depth."

Erin chimed in. "The refit on the camera should be finished tomorrow."

"What are the chances you could deploy the camera tomorrow?" Carter said. "I'd like to see the footage live."

"Well, I was going to ask Avery to suggest areas to explore with the sonar after she'd had a chance to look with the data I provided for the Dive-Nav," Reggie said. "But I'm sure if the camera is ready, we can send it out with the drone, too."

"Looking forward to it."

"Sometimes I feel like we should bypass all this tech and just dive for the damn thing," Reggie said. "If we could, I'd be tempted."

Carter glanced back at the legend on the sonar map. "Just out of curiosity, how many experienced divers on board?"

"None with enough experience to attempt such a depth. Most of these people are scientists. The area you're looking at right there is about four hundred fifty feet below the surface."

Carter whistled. "That would be one hell of a dive."

"Something tells me you're already considering it, aren't you?"

Carter shrugged. "I'll say this: more information wouldn't disappoint me."

Erin looked at Carter with wide eyes. "Would there be a video?"

"Oh, I don't have to get in the water for there to be a video," Carter said. "How'd you like to be in this one?"

"Would I ever," Erin said.

"What about you?" Carter said, turning his attention back to Reggie.

Reggie stared at the sonar map. "You've developed a bit of a reputation as a deep-water guy, haven't you?"

"It depends on who you ask. How about you?"

"I've completed a few at more than a hundred meters. I know enough to know I couldn't pull it off here. Diving here is like nothing you've ever done, I guarantee it. And it really isn't advisable this close to winter. There's moving ice and frigid temperatures."

"And crystal-clear water," Carter said. "Or so I've been told."

"That's true, but the sunlight won't penetrate past two hundred feet. It's near total darkness down there. Like being buried alive."

Carter leaned his elbows on the table, the familiar pull of the impossible queuing his adrenaline. "Tell me more."

19

"Tell me again how that thing works?" Harrison said as he watched Avery input data from a *Fortitude* crewman's journal into her computer, which was directly linked to the DiveNav by a cable.

"It's simple, at least in theory. We've uploaded as much information as we can. Current maps and landmarks, along with historical mapping and known weather disturbance and tidal data, which allows the DiveNav to arrive at the most probable location of whatever it is we might be searching for."

"Like when you found the lost treasure with the computer."

"Precisely. And the *Moneymaker* with this."

"I know it works, but I still don't understand how."

Avery laughed. "The final piece of the puzzle is the artificial intelligence software the DiveNav uses to calculate probabilities."

"Yeah, you lost me at AI."

"The best thing about it today is that I followed Carter's suggestion to make it a self-contained unit, so the DiveNav doesn't rely on a cell signal or a fixed internet connection or even Bluetooth to function. I can plug it into my laptop, and the onboard GPS can ping off any satellite and plot a location."

"Is it just me, or does that sound a trifle illegal?"

"What the CIA doesn't know won't hurt anyone."

"And by anyone you mean you and Carter. You're the apparent hooligans who developed the thing."

"Relax, it's not like we've got state secrets embedded in the prototype. Carter keeps telling me sooner or later we'll have to switch it over to some other off-the-grid non-satellite capability. Or find a partner willing to give us our own."

"Satellite?"

"Why not?" Avery said.

"Sure, doesn't everyone need one of those? I can't quite believe I'm saying this, but I'm with Carter on this one. Let's make it sooner and keep you out of federal prison, okay?"

"We haven't gotten in a jam yet, Harry."

"*Yet* is the operative word. Besides, I made a promise to your mother I'd like to be able to keep."

"She was worried I might go to prison?" Avery raised one eyebrow.

"More of a concern for your general well-being. Prison has a tendency to negatively impact that."

After a few more keystrokes from the encrypted app on Avery's laptop, she disconnected the DiveNav and waited for it to calculate a location.

"What's that dot on the screen?" Harrison said.

"That is the DiveNav's best guess at the *Fortitude*'s current location." She frowned. "Which should not be off the coast of Denmark." She plugged it back into the computer and opened a small window with a black background that quickly filled with code. "Where are you, glitch? Show yourself."

Harrison stayed quiet while she worked, well acquainted with her habit of talking to herself.

She muttered and poked keys for another ten minutes before she unplugged the DiveNav and pushed the green button again. "Much better," she said, watching the screen.

"A computerized guess?" Harrison asked. "Heck, I can guess. How accurate can that possibility be?"

Avery checked the display. "Ninety-seven-point-eight-five percent accurate."

"You're serious?"

"Yup. Looks like it's about a mile to the west of our current location. Which makes sense if the British were looking to navigate the channel that would have taken the *Fortitude* across the continent."

Harrison shook his head in disbelief. "You do know, assuming that thing is correct, there are people who would kill to get their hands on it?"

"I suppose there probably are."

"No probably about it, Ave. They might even be aboard this ship. There's a lot of money and a lot of prestige riding on what's happening here."

"You still think we're being monitored?"

"I'm trying not to, but I can't shake it. I've just got to find it."

"You checked and didn't find anything in here, though."

"Maybe we poke around the control rooms on the lower level."

"Do you even know what we're looking for, Harry?"

"I'll know it when I see it. Come on."

Avery and Harrison descended the steps from the crew quarter level to the control and engine rooms. Everything at this location of the ship was noisy and mechanical sounding, perfect for masking any noise they made.

They checked the first few unsecured doors along the walkway but only found storage rooms stuffed with broken furniture and crates of provisions. At the last door on the right, Avery jerked her hand back from the handle like she'd been burned.

"What?" Harrison reached for her hand to inspect her palm, which was red.

"It's freezing." Avery leaned down to look at the knob, which was covered with frost on closer inspection. Covering her hand with her sweater sleeve, she tried the knob again and found the door was locked.

"Maybe there's a hole in there?" Harrison mused.

"Pretty sure we're below the water line here," Avery said, laying a wool-covered hand on the door and finding it more frigid than the knob. "Weird."

Moving to the left side of the hall, they hit pay dirt with a large mechanical room.

"Here we go," Harrison said. "The control room is where I'd hide something I didn't want detected."

They entered the room, then closed the heavy steel door behind them.

"Assuming you're right about us being monitored, what are we looking for exactly?"

"If there is something to find, it will need a power source. Something to help it receive and send data out to someone at the other end."

"Makes sense," Avery said. "Hey, Harry, what if they're using the same method of communication as the DiveNav?"

"A satellite link?"

"Why not? You said this would be a clandestine operation."

They each searched half of the space. Avery found gauges, pressure valves, and electronics, but each one seemed to correspond to something that would control a necessary function on a ship.

After a few minutes Avery whispered loudly, "Anything, Harry?"

"I think I may have found something, Ave."

She walked around to the far side of the room, where she found Harrison kneeling atop a metal bulkhead. The space was cramped, and Harrison was forced to lean over in an awkward position.

"What is it?" Avery said.

"I don't know, but it doesn't appear to control anything. There are zero markings, and it is hardwired into the ship. If I didn't know better, I'd say it was some kind of transmitter, like a modem."

"Let me see," Avery said.

Harrison climbed down from the bulkhead to give Avery room.

"Well?"

"I think you're right, Harry."

"Think you can snap a few pictures of that with your phone?"

"Great minds," she said as she snapped one last shot, this one with a flash.

The loud squeal of metal hinges came from the far end of the control room. Someone was opening the door.

"Someone's coming, Harry," Avery whispered. "Hide."

"What about you?"

"I'm already hidden. Go!"

Harrison scuttled out of sight as Avery listened to rapid footsteps tick across the steel floor.

20

Sandefjord, Norway
November 1910

Following countless years of struggle under alternating Danish and Swedish rule, Norway finally enjoyed a newfound stability and independence under a new house governed by a freshly crowned prince.

Sweaty and tired, Bjorn, a young shipwright's apprentice, labored with hammer and chisel on the framework of a massive three-masted pleasure ship, designed with a low bow and wide bottom to traverse the icy seas of the farthest ends of the earth. To be christened the *Fortitude*, the ship was designed by a famous adventurer who wanted to take Europe's rich and privileged on tours of the south pole. Bjorn was thankful for the steady work of building the ship, letting his mind wander to the lives he imagined for the people who would one day board it with heavy trunks of fine clothing and furs to keep them warm in the polar climate.

He wielded the chisel with precision, standing up straighter as a pair of well-dressed older men approached. After months of working on the vessel, he recognized them as the principal financiers of the project. If they were pleased with his work, he might be hired again for their next build.

"She will be an impressive Norwegian passenger vessel once complete," the younger of the two men declared. "Transportation for those of means who wish to see the most exotic parts of the world by way of the seven seas."

The elder man, named Johann, followed closely by his silent young manservant, nodded in agreement.

"And only fitting it should be built under Danish rule," the young man continued.

"I'm afraid on that point we must disagree," Johann said. "While I am a proponent of an independent Norway, the rightful heir to the throne should hail from Sweden."

"You don't honestly believe that?" the young man said.

"Wholeheartedly, I do. The rightful heir to this country's throne must be a direct descendant of King Magnus Erlingsson. And I believe my recent discovery of the kingdom's lost crown jewels to be a sign. Jewels the current Prince of Norway is wholly unfit to wear."

Bjorn's ears perked up upon hearing the mention of the jewels. The tale of Norway's lost crown jewels and the curse put upon them by the cardinal, told to him by his father and grandfather, had captured the imaginations of generations of young men. Bjorn strained to hear their words above the din of construction.

As the three men passed, the younger man dismissed Johann's comments with a haughty laugh and a wave of his hand.

"Do you doubt my claim?" Johann said, clearly offended.

The apprentice lowered his tools, his focus now entirely on the conversation between two men.

"If what you say is true, how have I heard nothing of this?"

"Because I have not spoken of it until now," Johann said.

The younger man continued to scoff at the notion. "Given your proclivity for gossip, Johann, it is highly unlikely. If you had located the lost treasure, you would be unable to keep such a thing a secret for more than two seconds."

Johann stopped and whirled on the other man, but before he could utter as much as a single word in his defense, a loud crack and the sound of men shouting erupted from above. The apprentice watched in horror as a massive support timber fell to the wharf, crushing Johann where he stood.

The sound was sickening, and if he lived a hundred years, Bjorn wouldn't forget the cracking crash laced with a squishy, liquid undercurrent.

Dropping his tools, Bjorn pushed through the throng of men that had quickly surrounded the gruesome scene. As he reached the front of the crowd, Bjorn could clearly see the lifeless, broken body of the man who claimed to have found the lost jewels protruding from beneath the heavy beam. The manservant knelt, helpless beside his employer's mangled form, a puddle of crimson still flowing from where Johann's head had once been. Afraid that merely having overheard their conversation had put him in peril, Bjorn fled in terror.

21

Avery held her breath until her lungs burned, and for an experienced diver, that takes a bit of time. The footsteps didn't slow as they crossed the room, but they didn't come near her either. Tucked into the bulkhead, she didn't dare try to look and see who it was—she just prayed Harrison had found a good enough hiding place.

Three beats passed before she heard metal screeching on metal so loud the fillings in her teeth hurt. It stopped just as abruptly as it had started, and the steps clicked back out of the room, the door opening and closing in a matter of seconds.

Avery gave it a count of thirty before she poked her head up. "Harry?" she whisper-shouted.

"All clear," he replied.

Avery climbed down and met him in the middle of the floor. "What the heck was that noise?"

"I didn't dare look out, but it sounded like a stuck metal door opening."

They looked around as thoroughly as they dared and found nothing resembling a door, scooting out after voices in the hallway gave them a second scare.

A few paces toward the steps, Harrison shook his head. "I don't like the atmosphere here, Ave. But I do like the food. Time for dinner?"

Avery started up the steps. "Carter's meeting us in ten minutes."

The dining space was a wide, plain room with a ten-foot-high ceiling, directly off the galley, with a scattering of circular tables and enough seating to accommodate everyone on board the *Weddell*. The clattering of silverware and murmuring of conversation echoed throughout the hall.

"Jeez, I've seen more cheerful ambiance in hospital cafeterias," Harrison muttered as he sat down beside Avery.

A tall, thin woman at the next table looked up from her soup. "You stay here for six months taking care of frostbite and colds and stomach bugs and heart conditions brought on by weather God never intended people to thrive in and we'll see how chipper you are."

"I'm so sorry," Avery said quickly.

"No disrespect intended, ma'am," Harrison said.

"I'm Avery, and this is Harry."

"Dr. Jillian Contamopolis. Everyone here calls me Dr. Jill." The woman offered a ghost of a smile. "I haven't had cause to see you two . . . at all." She furrowed her brow. "Have I? I don't even know anymore. I think the last time I slept well was before Christmas. I didn't fully understand the toll the constant light would take on me when I signed up for this, I'm afraid."

"We've only recently arrived here," Avery said.

"Why'd you come?" The question was flat, like Dr. Jill couldn't imagine anyone wanting to join the expedition. Had she forgotten why she'd come herself?

"Dr. Wyndham invited us to help locate the *Fortitude*," Avery said.

"A fool's errand," Dr. Jillian said. "And probably one that will cost lives before he gives up." She put headphones on and went back to her soup without another word, and Avery glanced at Harrison.

Warm welcome, she thought, and he nodded like he'd heard her. Avery could tell he was thinking the same thing she was: maybe they'd better not stay terribly long.

"At least the food smells good," Avery said as she scooped up a spoonful of thick brown stew. "I'm starving."

They both glanced over to the serving line, where Carter was busy chatting up a young redheaded woman.

"C Dawg certainly seems to have hit it off with that young lady," Harrison said as he sopped up some of his stew with a piece of bread.

"I hadn't noticed," Avery said. "And since when do you talk that way?"

"I can be hip," Harrison said. "She certainly is a looker. Can't remember her name though. Edith or Emma maybe."

"It's Erin," Avery snapped.

"That's it," Harrison said with a smirk as Carter and Erin approached their table.

"Good evening," Erin said. "Would either of you mind terribly if I joined you?"

"Of course they wouldn't," Carter said.

"Not at all," Avery said, gesturing to an empty seat.

"Erin, this is Avery and Harrison," Carter said. "Erin is one of Dr. Wyndham's research assistants."

"It's a pleasure to meet you," Avery said with a polite nod.

"We were just saying how nice it is you two seem to have hit it off," Harrison said. "Weren't we, Ave?"

Avery responded by grinding her heel into Harrison's foot under the table. "So, Erin, tell us a little bit about your work," she said, forcing a smile.

Avery feigned interest as Erin chattered on about every single thing she had ever done during her time on board the *Weddell*.

"Are you also a diver?" Harrison asked, mercifully stopping Erin in what had appeared would be a never-ending story.

"I'm not a serious diver," Erin said with a giggle. "Not like Carter here. I did take a class at a resort in Cabo once. But I was hungover at the time, so I don't know if that even counts."

"I'd be happy to teach you sometime," Carter said. "In warmer water, that is."

Avery decided to pull the conversation back from the brink of nauseous. "Harry and I saw some interesting sights below deck, Carter."

"Oh?" Carter said.

"Yeah," Harrison said. "Some pretty high-tech stuff."

Carter nodded, indicating he understood the vague reference, before moving on to safer topics in front of Erin. "Noah wants to know what you and the DiveNav think about where they should search next. My gut says there's a black hole on the sonar map that's as good a place as any."

"Black hole?" Avery asked.

"The unit malfunctioned over one area," Erin explained.

"They think," Carter countered.

"It is weird that the sonar wouldn't register anything at one location, when it did at others," Avery said.

"It's not weird at all," Erin said. "The sonar is in less-than-perfect condition because of the damage sustained when the whales attacked the ship."

"The what attacked the huh?" Avery said, her mouth falling open.

"Orcas," Erin said. "There were four of them slamming themselves into the ship multiple times while we were traversing the channel and running sonar."

"Orcas aren't aggressive mammals," Carter said.

"Well, these sure were," Erin said.

"How do you account for such unusual behavior?" Avery looked around. "And how do we know it won't happen again?"

"Dr. Wyndham didn't have an explanation, but I do."

"Care to share?" Avery said.

"It's a curse."

"Come again?" Harrison said.

"We were running sonar looking for the *Fortitude* when the whales attacked," Erin said. "That night I overheard the cook talking to someone on the sat phone about the *Fortitude* being cursed."

"You don't really believe in curses, do you?" Avery asked Erin. "I mean, you are a scientist."

"Six months ago? No. Today? Not entirely," Erin said. "I've seen enough weird things over the past few months that I can understand why some people think they exist."

"For instance?" Carter said.

"In addition to the behavior of the whales, which, as you said, is more than strange—it's practically unheard of—we've had a lot of equipment breaking down."

"I thought that was due to the cold," Harrison said matter-of-factly.

"Sure, the outside stuff," Erin said. "But we've had inside issues as well. A rare bacillus overgrowth in the food supply sickened the whole ship for days and decimated our provisions."

Avery's eyes slid to Dr. Jill, her comment about treating a stomach bug running through her head. Was it bacteria or a virus? And how much did it really matter if there was a string of bad things happening on this ship already?

"Well, that could have just been a refrigeration problem, right? Or even a virus," Avery said.

"Except there was nothing wrong with the units when we checked, and it affected our non-refrigerated foods too. We were down to nothing but mayonnaise, peanut butter, and sardines before an airlift brought in more supplies."

Harrison wrinkled his nose. "Peanut butter and mayonnaise certainly explains all these dour faces."

"I think those are owed more to constant stress and worry and months away from our families," Erin said. "I know this has been less of a dream than it seemed at first for a lot of the people here."

"Has anything else gone wrong?" Carter asked.

"Then there was the freak wind that knocked Noah right off the deck of the ship down onto the ice. He's lucky he wasn't killed."

"Did you see that happen?" Harrison asked before taking a sip of coffee from his mug.

"No one saw, but Noah told us about it afterward. He needed help getting back on board. He could have died out there. Good thing he wasn't knocked unconscious, and darn lucky Seamus saw him."

"Who's Seamus?" Avery said.

"The chief mechanical engineer." Erin half stood and searched around the mess hall for a moment before spotting him. "He's right over there."

"What does he do, exactly?" Harrison said.

"He keeps the ship running."

Avery decided to change up the subject matter before they got any further into the weeds.

"Did Carter tell you he's a social media star?"

"He didn't have to tell me." Erin turned to Carter and batted her lashes. "I'm one of his biggest fans."

Harrison rolled his eyes.

"It's nothing, really," Carter said.

"Don't be so modest," Avery said. "How many followers do you have now? Six or seven million?"

"I'm not sure," Carter said, shooting her a *knock it off* look. "I keep telling Avery she needs to get on social media."

Erin's eyes widened again. "You're not on social media? Why not?"

Avery shrugged. "It's not really my thing."

"I'm totally addicted to it," Erin said. "Besides, Avery, I would think your treasure hunting thingy would be huge."

"Honestly, I try and stay off the internet unless I'm researching something. I think the internet might just end up being the worst invention of all time."

"But aren't you a programmer?"

"I am. And I know it probably sounds like a weird thing for a programmer to say, but the social media thing is all just so fake. I have no interest in spending time in the virtual land of filters and faux perfection."

"That's weird for anyone to say," Erin said before her attention returned to Carter. "Have you ever met anyone famous?"

"As a matter of fact, I dove a wreck off the coast of Jamaica with Sandra Bullock just last year."

"Seriously?" Erin couldn't have looked more enamored if she was giving Carter a lap dance.

"Oh yeah," Carter said, glancing over at Avery as he grabbed his tray and stood.

Erin let out a squeal of delight before rising from her chair and begging for details.

"Come on," Carter said. "I'll tell you all about it."

Avery looked over at Harrison, then stuffed a large hunk of bread in her mouth to keep from saying what she was thinking. She rose to return her dishes, leaving Harrison by himself at the table.

"Where are you going?" Harrison said.

"I want a word with the cook."

22

Avery and Harrison made their way to the ship's kitchen, where a middle-aged woman was working alone on a large ball of biscuit dough for the next day's breakfast. The woman was fair skinned with striking hazel eyes. Her light brown hair, pulled back into a tight ponytail, was dusted with flour, giving her a flustered appearance.

"Can I help you?" the woman said in a barely detectable Scandinavian accent. Wariness creased her forehead.

"We just wanted to thank you for a fabulous supper," Avery said, delivering a bright smile.

"Thank you, but beef stew and bread are hardly extravagant. I'm a much better chef if given half a chance and the right resources."

A younger woman walked out of the refrigerator with a flat of eggs and a giant steel bowl and began cracking them at the next counter. Avery smiled at her, but the younger chef wasn't looking at them. Harrison stayed focused on the head chef.

"Well, it was excellent just the same," he said, patting his belly. "And I do love to eat."

Avery watched the angst depart from the woman's expression as Harrison smoothly slid into the role of lead investigator. He had always been able to put people at ease. Avery imagined her own mother had possessed the same skill, though she'd never seen her in action. Sadly, she never would.

"Thank you, Mr.... ?"

"Harrison, but my friends call me Harry. And this is my best friend in the whole world, Avery Turner."

"Pleased to meet you both, Harry. I'm Tuva."

"Yes, you are," Harrison said, making her blush.

Avery fixed them with an inquisitive look.

"Tuva means beautiful," Harrison explained.

"And how would you know that, Harry?" Avery said.

"Hey, I read."

Tuva laughed at the exchange, then used her forearm to wipe a strand of hair off her brow, leaving a streak of flour behind. "You are the ones who have come to help find the sunken ship?"

"We are," Avery said, surprised that someone so far removed from the research knew that. Maybe it was just the team at Halley that didn't know Noah was searching for the ship?

"I have heard the others talk about you," Tuva said.

"Hopefully, they only said nice things," Harrison said.

Tuva gestured to a pair of glass carafes sitting on a Bunn warmer. "Help yourself to another coffee, Harry."

"Don't mind if I do." Harrison strutted toward the counter.

"Have you worked here long?" Avery asked.

"A few months. I needed a break from reality, and this seemed to be as far from that as I could get."

"What did you do before this?" Harrison asked.

"I was the head chef for several five-star restaurants, from New York to Miami."

"Stressful?" Avery asked.

"You have no idea," Tuva said as she began rolling out the dough onto the heavily floured stainless-steel counter.

"And this?" Harrison asked.

"This is a sabbatical."

"You may be the first person we've met who doesn't mind being here after a while," Avery said. "Everyone else seems to love their work, but the place . . . not so much. Though maybe that explains why you've taken a sabbatical here and not on a high-end cruise ship with your culinary talent."

Tuva opened her mouth, hesitated, then closed it again.

"I didn't mean to pry," Avery said.

"No, it's okay. I don't mind being here because I came for a reason. You see, my great-grandfather, Johann, was a Danish shipbuilder. He was killed during construction of the *Fortitude*. The story goes that he was inspecting the construction when a heavy staging timber broke loose and crushed him."

"I'm so sorry," Avery said. "That's a horrible tragedy."

"It's okay," Tuva said. "You couldn't have known. So, I grew up hearing tales of his exploits from my great-grandmother, Gigi. She always said he was a remarkable man who couldn't stand sitting still and loathed boredom."

"Sounds a lot like someone I know," Harrison said, angling his head toward Avery.

"Is that why he got into shipbuilding?" Avery said.

"According to Gigi, it was. It filled his life, and that of his family, with nonstop adventure. My Gigi wasn't always entirely there in her later years, but her eyes always lit up when she talked about Johann."

"How awful, to lose someone you loved that much in an accident," Avery said.

"It was no accident," Tuva snapped. "And it was never investigated. If it had been, someone would have been charged with his murder."

Harrison lowered his mug to the counter, his eyebrows shooting up. "That's a hefty accusation. How do you know it's warranted?"

"My Gigi died convinced Johann was murdered for something he had found. And after years of my own research, I have arrived at the same conclusion. That is why I am here. An old friend who knows my connection to the *Fortitude* cooks for Dr. Wyndham when he is in London and told me he had developed a fascination with the ship. I came for answers."

"And you think if Dr. Wyndham finds the *Fortitude*, you'll get them?" Avery said.

"Dr. Wyndham is a smart man with big ideas, but my Gigi would say he couldn't find his own backside with two hands and a flashlight. If *you* find the *Fortitude*, I will find what I came here for."

Avery exchanged a glance with Harrison. "So you're here to try and solve a century-old murder?"

"I came here to honor my Gigi's memory of Johann and to allow my ancestors to rest in peace." Tuva shrugged. "So . . . yes. I suppose I am."

Before Tuva could say more, Seamus entered the galley and gave them the once-over as he headed toward the refrigerator. Avery could sense Tuva's unease at the man's presence as she continued cutting out the biscuit rounds.

Tuva waited until Seamus was gone before speaking again. In hushed tones she said, "Meet me tomorrow morning, after breakfast."

"Is there something we should know about Seamus?" Avery asked, glancing at the younger cook, who was whisking the eggs as if she hadn't heard a word.

"Tomorrow. Now go. Both of you."

"That was weird," Harrison said as they walked down the hall toward their rooms.

Avery couldn't disagree.

"You think she's on the up and up?"

"I don't know," Avery said. "But I know who might be able to tell us."

"MaryAnn?"

"Exactly."

Avery stepped inside her stateroom and closed the door. After changing into her sweatpants and hoodie, she plugged her laptop into the sat phone and tried to open her email.

Connection failed flashed in the center of the screen. She jiggled the wire in the port on the wall just as the wind howled and the lights flickered.

Remembering Noah's comment about the uplink relay through Halley Station and the effects of the weather, she sighed. Technology makes life easy—until it doesn't work. Especially when you're at the ends of the Earth and the lack of function means you're cut off from communicating with the outside world.

23

Avery bit into a buttery, flaky, yet dense biscuit that rivaled the best she'd had at some of the South's premier restaurants, chewing slowly before she swallowed the bite. "Harry, if you make friends with Tuva, Dorothy needs this recipe."

Harry hadn't had a chance to reply when a disheveled Carter walked into the dining room with Erin clinging to his arm. The smug, satisfied look on Erin's face made Avery's flush.

"I don't get it," Harrison said. "What is it about him that gets women so worked up?"

"Well, he is good-looking, Harry," Avery said. "And charming. At least when he wants to be."

"Hell, you just described me to a tee."

Avery reached over and wiped a dab of syrup from Harrison's chin. "Sure."

"Thanks," Harrison said.

"I don't know, Harry." Avery's eyes were still on Carter. "Maybe it's the excitement of being with someone famous."

"I guess. Fame never did a thing for me."

"Probably one of the many things my mom loved about you, Harry."

Carter approached the table alone, with a coffee mug in his hand.

"Where's your groupie?" Harrison asked.

"Her name is Erin, and she's gone to check in with Noah," Carter said as he pulled out a chair and sat down.

Harrison looked over at Avery. "Is it me or did you detect a bit of defensiveness?"

Avery grinned. "It certainly sounded like defensiveness to me. Good morning, Carter. Sleep well?"

Carter ignored the comments and pointed at Harrison's biscuits, practically floating in a bowl of maple syrup. "Are you trying to drown—whatever those are?"

"They're homemade biscuits, hotshot. Tuva made them and they're awesome."

"Who's Tuva?"

"The chef," Harrison said as he sopped up the remaining syrup from the bowl.

"I'm trying to make him get the recipe," Avery said as Carter picked up his own biscuit.

Avery gestured to the room. "You're behind the times this morning, but the entire ship is buzzing about deploying the drone with the temperature-fortified camera. Everyone's hoping to get a better look at the anomaly you found on the sonar image."

Amid the clatter of dishes and silverware came the unmistakable sound of excitement. Compared to the previous evening's dinner, the enthusiasm was palpable.

"Either of you want anything?" Harrison stood. "I'm going back for seconds."

"I'm good, Harry," Carter said.

"Ave?"

"Maybe another coffee."

"You got it."

"Can we get serious for a minute?" Carter asked as soon as Harrison departed.

"About?"

"The *Fortitude*. I have a theory I want to run by you."

"Shoot," Avery said, intrigued.

"I'm thinking the *Fortitude* might have slid into a canyon. Like the *Moneymaker* nearly did."

"Go on."

"Maybe that dark spot on the sonar isn't interference, but a canyon so deep the sonar is incapable of detecting the bottom."

"From what I've read, that would make the canyon impossibly deep."

"How deep is impossibly deep?"

"Like miles. Twelve thousand feet at least. I've studied all the area maps, including those from Noah, and there is absolutely no mention of an underwater canyon here."

"Maybe it's not on a map. I mean, they are still discovering things here. Remember the Five Deeps Expedition in 2019? They recorded a depth of over four miles at the sixtieth parallel."

"You're talking about the Factorian Deep, and that is nowhere near here."

"I wouldn't say nowhere near, Ave. We flew over it on the way here from South America."

Avery said nothing as she gave him a *don't be stupid* look.

"Are you angry at me for something?" Carter said.

"Why would you think that?"

"'Cause you're sitting there with your arms crossed like you do when you're mad at someone."

Before either could say another word about it, Erin ran up to their table and made an announcement to the entire room.

"Hey, you guys, they're about to launch the drone with the new camera setup. If you want to see the live feed, come to the bridge."

24

Twenty people jammed shoulder to shoulder into the bridge, everyone holding their breath as the first images fed in from the newly upgraded underwater camera to the high-definition monitors on the center console.

Avery was amazed at both the quality of the feed and the clarity of the Antarctic Ocean. The water was every bit as clear as Noah had described, but there was also abundant sea life captured on screen. Seals, dolphins, and in the distance, orcas—which made Avery shudder after what Erin had told them about the attacks on the *Weddell*.

A sleek silver dolphin nosed at the housing on the drone, the image shaking on the screen.

"I'm surprised the mammals will follow a drone down that far," Carter said.

"It's marvelous," Erin said. "There haven't been enough humans in this part of the world to teach them to be afraid. They're simply curious."

"But that's over a hundred feet down," Harrison said as he checked the monitor.

"That's nothing, Harry," Noah said. "Whales and dolphins will hang around to a depth of around four hundred feet, and the seals have been tracked as far as five thousand."

"Feet?" Harrison said, clearly shocked. "I would think that kind of depth would crush them like a soda can."

"Normally, you'd be correct," Owen, the research assistant, said. "But the Weddell seals have evolved a unique biological ability to collapse their lungs as they descend, allowing them to achieve depths greater than most other sea creatures." Avery liked the way his long face became animated as he talked about the wildlife.

"Really?" Carter's head swiveled like it was mounted on ball bearings.

Owen nodded, his eyes on the monitors like everyone else's.

"Has there been much research into this?" Avery asked. "I would think something like that would revolutionize diving science."

"Thus far nothing that anyone has been able to apply to humans," Noah said. "If we could figure out how to harness that ability, imagine how much more of the ocean we could explore."

"Does this dot correspond to the drone's current location?" Carter said as he gestured to one of the monitors.

"Yes," Owen said.

"We'd like to search in a different area, if you don't mind," Carter said to Noah.

"Where are you thinking?" Noah said.

"Here," Avery said as she approached a wall-mounted grid map, pointing to the area that Carter had noticed as dark on the sonar map—which happened to be right where the DiveNav thought the ship should be.

Noah shook his head. "We've already covered that area with the sonar, and we didn't find anything. Besides, it's over four kilometers from where the drone is presently. It will take us hours to reposition the ship and the drone."

Reggie piped in, taking Noah's side. "Our research indicates it's unlikely the *Fortitude* could have drifted that far due to the tidal currents in this area. We've been following a very precise and calculated grid search pattern from the very beginning. It doesn't make sense to change now."

"And what have you found so far?" Carter said.

Reggie gave Carter a look that didn't need comment.

"I'm afraid I must concur with Reggie," Noah said. "We've approached this search in a logical manner so we wouldn't overlook anything, assuming the ship is still out there."

Avery weighed in. "With all due respect to you and your team, Dr. Wyndham, you invited us here to help you find the ship because you're running out of time and money. I have compiled over one hundred fifty years of weather data, ocean current data, and mapping information, including what you provided to us, and painstakingly entered all of it into the DiveNav. Our device has pinpointed an area outside of your search zone as the most likely location of the *Fortitude*."

"How accurate could that thing be?" Reggie scoffed. "It's just a fancy computer's best guess, using information you dumped into it."

Avery grinned. "The DiveNav also calculates the precise probability of the location given."

"And?" Reggie said.

"And it calculated a 97.85 percent likelihood that the *Fortitude* is located right here," Avery said as she pointed to the map again, this time with confidence.

Noah sighed while everyone in the room stared in silence, awaiting his decision. After several moments Noah turned to Reggie. "Recall the drone. We're moving the ship."

"But I think—" Reggie began.

"Miss Turner is right," Noah said, cutting him off. "We invited them here to help us locate the *Fortitude*."

Avery nodded her appreciation.

"If she believes they've located the wreck and we have working video feed, then by all means, let's go see."

25

Recalling the oversized drone and moving the ship through the ice toward the location Avery had indicated on the map took longer than she and Carter had anticipated.

Avery passed the first hour in her room, double-checking her coordinates. If the DiveNav was glitching, she could still backtrack.

Looking for a coordinate she couldn't find on her laptop, Avery ducked into Carter's room and woke his laptop, intending to go to the notes file. The screen lit to an email that said it failed to send. She read his note to MaryAnn, and the request for background information on the crew here, nodding her head to every word. Picking up the laptop, she took it back to her room and plugged it into the sat port, sending the note to MaryAnn herself.

Finding the numbers she needed in Carter's notes, she was just about to unplug his laptop from the sat link in favor of her own when an email alert flashed up: MaryAnn had replied already, and the subject read *READ ME*, all in caps. Avery knew MaryAnn well enough to know she never shouted in her messages, or even in person. Whatever this was had to be important.

Carter,

I was just about to message you when I received your questions, and I'm so glad to know you're all okay. I spoke with an old friend in London yesterday who was out of town when I tried to call him before you left. He wasn't as enamored with Noah Wyndham as my other contacts, which inspired me to look into your leader there and his staff. This is one of the most tangled webs I've ever researched, but I found out some very interesting things about Dr. Noah Wyndham. The first is he has three aliases. He was born in London to a wealthy family named Karlsson. His father appears to be a direct descendant of the captain of the Fortitude. *I was unable to obtain Noah's financials, but I was able to find out through my unofficial connections that he is in dire straits financially. Flat broke. He has amassed the kind of debt that drives people to fall in with sketchy characters out of desperation.*

The last paragraph of MaryAnn's message made Avery's heart skip a beat.

After learning of Noah's connection to the Fortitude, *I took it upon myself to do a little online digging in some treasure hunting message groups, looking specifically for anything connected to the* Fortitude. *I managed to locate a small group of anonymous users who spend a great deal of time speculating about an exiled cardinal, a curse, and the lost crown jewels of Norway. Some of these people seem highly committed to recovering this treasure. Please be careful, all of you.*

M

Avery slammed the computer shut and ran for the bridge.

The ship shuddered and screeched—cutting through the ice with a steel-hulled ship was unlike anything she could have imagined. The constant vibration and scraping conjured up images of what the doomed passengers on the *Titanic* must have felt and heard before the mighty ocean liner sank. Avery worked hard to push the uncomfortable thought out of her mind as she stepped back onto the bridge, her eyes skimming the crowd for Noah. She didn't want to say anything to anyone until she'd had a chance to speak to him alone. She didn't see him, though.

"Pretty cool, huh?" Harrison said as he sidled up beside her on the bridge.

"It's amazing," Avery said. "It doesn't seem possible, and yet here we are doing it."

"All I can think about is how my mom used to scold me for chewing ice," Harrison said. "Maybe I really am lucky I didn't break a tooth."

Avery glanced to the far side of the bridge, where Carter and Erin were speaking in hushed tones about something.

Harrison followed her gaze. "What do you think those two are jawing about?"

"Nothing that interests me," Avery said as she turned her attention back to the ice off the ship's bow.

Twenty minutes later, Noah returned to the bridge. "Well, we've got a problem. One of the engines is overheating, we have no choice but to shut them down."

"What does that mean?" Carter asked.

"It means this is as close as we're going to get to your magical coordinates," Reggie said, following Noah into the room.

"But you're still sending the drone out to do a visual check, right?" Avery asked, studying Noah. If MaryAnn was right, he wouldn't give up easily.

Noah nodded. "We'll take a peek. It may just take a bit longer to get there. I had hoped we wouldn't have to push our luck with the signal strength on the drone's newly reconfigured camera, but here we are."

"How far are we from the coordinates we gave you?" Carter said.

"Just under a kilometer."

Noah pointed at Avery. "Would you like to help me launch the drone?"

Avery, Carter, and Harrison stood beside the moon pool, shivering from excitement as much as the icy air coming off the water. Staying out of the way, they watched as a team of technicians hoisted the bulky orange drone into place above the large rectangular opening in the *Weddell*'s hull that allowed access to the sea below.

"I'm still fuzzy on how this thing isn't sinking us, but it's sure pretty," Harrison said, pointing at the edge of a dolphin's tail gliding by as the drone broke the surface of the water. This rig bore little resemblance to the ones Carter had used during previous dives. The twin smoked-glass bubbles at the front and the overall shape made it resemble a large dragon-fly. It appeared nearly big enough to be manned from the inside, but according to Noah the only things contained within were state-of-the-art electronics.

"What's the range on this thing?" Carter said.

"That depends upon underwater conditions and the depth of the search," Noah said. "But hypothetically, with a fully charged main battery and a half-sized backup, she can operate for about ninety minutes at up to two kilometers away."

"She?" Avery said. "Does she have a name?"

One of the technicians moved to the side and pointed to the name stenciled on the nose of the drone. Bertha.

"Perfect," Avery said with a chuckle.

"Ninety minutes is plenty of time to get to the search area and locate the ship, right?" Harrison said. "I mean, you said it was less than a kilometer from here."

One of the technicians prepping the drone addressed Harrison. "There are always variables to consider, which can greatly affect time and distance."

"Like what?" Harrison said.

"Depth," Noah said. "Even assuming the *Fortitude* is where you think it might be, we still have no idea how far below the surface she may have come to rest."

"Or if it's even still whole," the technician said, holding up one hand. "The conditions here are brutal. I lost two fingers last month to frostbite because I grabbed the wrong gloves on an excursion and a small wind-storm popped up. Thank God for Dr. Jill."

"Jesus, it's like this place is trying to kill us all," Harrison said.

"Isn't it?" Noah mused, staring into the water.

Avery stared at him, biting her tongue to keep from asking what he wasn't telling them.

The other technician checked a fitting on the lowering mechanism. "Additionally, she's got to be able to get back to the ship. Think of it like diving. Most scuba divers have plenty of air for whatever they are diving, but they still must account for the return trip to the surface."

"Gotcha," Harrison said as he nodded his understanding.

"Like most of the drones amateur enthusiasts like to fly around their neighborhoods, Bertha has a built-in return program. An onboard computer keeps track of battery life and rate of usage, as well as the distance the drone has traveled from its home base. As soon as Bertha nears the halfway point on the main battery charge, the computer will order the drone to return to her point of origin, regardless of any remote commands she may receive from us."

"Sounds a bit like that movie *2001: A Space Odyssey*," Harrison said.

"Harry's not a big fan of technology," Avery said.

"Not to worry, Harry," Noah said. "Unlike the spaceship's computer in that movie—"

"HAL 9000," Harrison said proudly.

"Right. Well, unlike HAL, Bertha can't kill you." Noah paused for a moment, side-eyeing the drone. "At least I don't think she can."

After lowering Bertha into the ocean, the group returned to the bridge, where Noah took over control of the drone. As before, Avery and the others fixed their attention on the high-definition underwater images being broadcast back onto the monitors. The video was so clear Avery could almost feel the cold water pressing in on her, like she was swimming alongside Bertha.

Noah leaned in close to Avery. "There is one nice thing about this part of the planet."

"What's that?" Avery asked.

"No matter how long we delay a search, daylight doesn't change much. Not for a few more days, anyway."

As Bertha neared the coordinates Avery had provided, the clear water dropped into sudden darkness. The change was both unexpected and dramatic.

"Why did everything go dark?" Harrison asked.

"Looks like Bertha may have found a canyon." Noah leaned closer to the monitor as a light on the drone activated.

Carter raised an eyebrow at Avery. *Told you so.*

"But there isn't a mapped canyon anywhere near here," Avery said. "I triple-checked."

"That isn't all that surprising," Noah said. "Thousands of earthquakes happen every day, all over the globe. Tectonic plates shift, lift, and separate, creating fissures and an entirely new planet surface right under us, and we often don't notice. The ocean floor is no different, and ever-changing."

"Not comforting, Doc," Harrison said.

"What, Harry?" Carter said. "Didn't you know the earth is nothing more than a thin candy shell wrapped around a delicious center of molten rock?"

"Whatever, Willy Wonka," Harrison said.

"Carter is right," Noah said. "As unnerving as that concept might seem."

As Noah sent the drone into the abyss, Avery and Carter continued to monitor the depth.

"I can't believe it," Avery said. "Bertha's more than three hundred feet down."

"Three twenty-five," Noah agreed. "And counting."

As the drone passed the four-hundred-foot mark, the image appeared to go fuzzy, though it was difficult to tell due to the limited light. At 417 feet, something flashed across the screen, caught momentarily in the beams of the drone's headlamps before it was gone.

"What was that?" Carter's whole body exuded tension, from his raised shoulders to the coiled muscles in his legs to his unusually tight voice. He grabbed Avery's hand and squeezed so tight it would've hurt if she'd had any attention to give it.

She squeezed back, staring at the screen. She was floating, yet her chest was so heavy with anticipation she couldn't breathe.

"Hang on while I circle back," Noah mumbled, concentrating on the controls under his fingers. "One moment please . . . There we are."

Avery risked a fleeting glance around the bridge, at the faces of people who'd spent months in one of the world's most unforgiving places, hoping to find something no one had seen in more than a century.

Erin clasped her hands under her chin like a child in a Christmas pageant choir. Owen clapped a hand over his mouth, a shine in his eyes that looked a lot like tears. Reggie stopped blinking for far too long as he stared at the screen.

Noah bit his bottom lip as he brought Bertha around slower on the second pass, the headlamps brightening the field just enough to send a collective gasp through the crowd on the *Weddell*'s bridge as the image feed snapped into sharp focus, a completely intact, perfectly preserved crow's nest from a wooden sailing ship filling the monitors.

For two seconds, Avery could've heard a flea sneeze, and then the bridge erupted into the kind of hoots and whistles most people reserved for sporting events.

Carter raised their clasped hands in the air and wolf-whistled, neither of them able to take their eyes off the structure gently swaying in the icy water on the screens. They had found the long-lost wreck of the HMS *Fortitude*.

26

We did it. The DiveNav was a success. Fiji and Norway notwithstanding.

Avery's head spun, the first three words repeating on a loop as she watched the drone pass slowly around the outside of the legendary ship. She and Carter had just made their third successful discovery on another long shot. First the General's Gold, then the *Moneymaker*, and now, maybe the biggest find yet in terms of historical and scientific significance: the *Fortitude*. Along with whatever secrets she still carried on board.

She barely noticed when Erin nearly knocked her down, launching herself at Carter with a whoop.

Noah steered the drone carefully down between the masts, and Avery marveled at the condition of the ship. Everything was so well preserved, exactly as Carter had predicted. It was as if time had stopped the moment the *Fortitude* sank over one hundred years ago.

"Oh my God, Carter," Erin shrieked. "You did it. You found the *Fortitude*."

"It wasn't just me," Carter said as he nodded toward Avery. "Avery—"

"Stop being so modest," Erin cut him off. "This may be the biggest find of the century. Two biggest finds if we throw in the canyon. And it's all thanks to you."

"Six hundred feet and counting," Carter said. "In water that cold, the range is seriously impressive. Did you modify this drone, Erin?"

"I tinkered," she said. "It was nothing."

Avery turned away to find Noah standing at the far end of the bridge, apart from the crowd. He had his cell phone out and appeared to be furiously typing. She wondered how Noah managed to find a signal when none of them had been able to—and why he wasn't more forthcoming about it. And what was he typing? Was it a message to his principal donors? That made sense. If she were bankrolling this project, she would expect—demand—to be the first to know. After all, how long would it take before one of the crew members figured out a way to post a selfie with a still from the video showing the entire world that the *Fortitude* had been found? Noah might have been the only person on board with a functioning cell, but the sky-link and sat internet were still available.

She shifted her gaze when Noah looked up, then quickly pocketed his phone. He placed two fingers at the corners of his mouth and gave a loud whistle.

"I know you're all as excited about this discovery as I am," Noah said. "We've spent a great deal of time and resources reaching this point. But it's important that word of this discovery not leak out until I give the all clear. Understood?"

Avery nodded along with everyone else, watching as Noah pushed through the crowd toward her when the rest of the group went back to congratulating each other. Drawing close, Noah signaled to her and Carter.

"We need to talk in private," Noah said.

"What about?" Carter asked.

"Follow me."

Avery and Carter fell in behind Noah as he hurried from the bridge. Harrison, watching from the end of the center console, followed hot on their heels.

"Finding it isn't enough," Noah said as they stood beside the moon pool a few minutes later. "We have to bring people into it, up close and personal." He held Carter's gaze without blinking.

"You want to dive this wreck?" Carter rubbed his chin, his eyebrows furrowing.

"That's more than a little nuts, isn't it?" Harrison said.

"I've researched deep cold-water diving extensively," Noah said as he began to pace the cavernous room. "And I believe it can be done safely."

"With all due respect, there's a big difference between researching something and actually putting it into practice, Dr. Wyndham," Avery said. "You're talking about diving in over six hundred feet of water. Correction: you're talking about *Carter* diving in six hundred feet of water. There's no risk to you or any of your personnel."

"That can't be done, can it?" Harrison looked back and forth for an ally.

Noah stopped pacing and turned to face Carter. "You can do it. I know you can."

"Even if I could, I don't have the equipment for that kind of dive with me," Carter said.

"We have all the equipment you'd need. For Avery, too, if she's interested."

"Now, hold on a minute," Harrison said. "Don't think for one second that—"

Avery raised one hand, her narrowed eyes on Noah. "This is the real reason you invited us, isn't it?" Avery said. "You assumed we'd find the ship, and you needed Carter for more than just feeding his Instagram following a drone video."

"And you did find it," Noah said. "Just as I knew you would. Diving the *Fortitude* to uncover her secrets is simply the next step."

"I don't know. The deepest dive I've ever read about was nine hundred feet," Carter said. "And that guy got really sick even with a year of training and a whole team helping him."

"Did he live?" Noah said.

"I think so," Carter said.

"The Guinness world record is eleven hundred feet, and the man who did that is definitely still among us," Noah said. "I've investigated your background. You live for this stuff, Carter. You're this generation's Evel bloody Knievel. If some no-name git can make eleven hundred feet and live to tell the tale, you can take the whole world into the *Fortitude*. This is bigger than just a shipwreck. This is history." Noah paused. "And as such, has tremendous capacity to increase your follower count and reach with one single video."

Carter pinched his lips between his teeth the way he did when he was thinking.

"You're not seriously considering going down there, are you?" Harrison gaped.

Avery knew Carter was considering it as she watched his gaze drop to the pool.

"Pardon the pun," Noah continued. "But this is your chance to make a big splash, Mr. Mosley."

Harrison exchanged a glance with Avery and shook his head in disbelief. "Nope. I don't want any part of this." He turned on his heel and left.

"Carter, you have no idea what could happen down there," Avery said. "The conditions here are so severe that their equipment keeps breaking down. A dozen things could go wrong. A hundred things could go wrong. You could bleed into your lungs at that much pressure or drop your heart rate far enough to send you into fibrillation, you could lose consciousness from the body's forcible transference of blood from the brain and limbs to your heart and lungs. And that's just the pressure, not the temperature." She waved at the drone tech on the other side of the large window. "Ask him how much fun frostbite is. What if you have a storm pop up, too?"

Noah shook his head. "Conditions below the surface are extremely stable. Weather wouldn't be an issue. Even the water temperature would remain fairly constant."

Avery swallowed a *shut up* and stayed focused on Carter. "Carter, we only have limited visibility of the site from today's drone video. You have no idea what else might be down there. The site itself is nearly three-quarters of a mile from the ship."

"We have Sno-Cats and boats to carry us out to the dive site and back," Noah said.

"This is nearly twice as deep as anything you've done before," Avery said.

Carter grinned. "That you know of."

Avery let out a frustrated sigh as she locked eyes with Carter. He'd already made up his mind—at least mostly—to attempt the dive. Nothing she said would stop him now.

"Fine," she said.

"My concern right now is what else we don't know, Dr. Wyndham." Carter crossed his arms and turned back to Noah, the exact words Avery was thinking coming out of his mouth. "What exactly are you hoping we'll find down there?"

27

Noah glanced about the room before answering. The technicians who were preparing to retrieve Bertha had slipped back in, but otherwise they were alone. Noah still motioned Avery and Carter to follow him away from the moon pool.

"What I am hoping to find down there is quite literally the billion-dollar question."

"A treasure hunt." Avery wanted to shake the world-renowned scientist. "I gotta hand it to you, saving the planet is good cover for a get-rich-quick scheme."

"I don't suppose you see the hypocrisy in the two of you criticizing someone wanting to better their finances," Noah said.

"Then why not just tell us the truth up front?" Carter asked. "It's not like we weren't going to find out before you got what you wanted. We know about the curse."

"And the treasure," Avery added, poking Carter to smooth his furrowed brow. "We also know you're in some pretty serious debt."

"How dare you look into my personal finances!" Noah shot back.

"I'm quite sure you've looked into ours." Avery struggled to keep her voice civil. "And I'd bet my house in the Keys you're not actually here for anything so noble as science or humanity."

Noah waved a dismissive hand. "I'm afraid you'd find yourself homeless making that bet, Miss Turner. Mr. Mosley, curses are for smaller and less-informed minds than mine. I could do a lot of good with this money. As for keeping things from you—would you have come if I'd mentioned treasure on our call?"

Ignoring his question, Avery plowed on. "You need to start telling us the truth, and I mean right now."

"I'm afraid there are some things better left unsaid," Noah said, his eyes never leaving the water.

"Then we're leaving."

"You wouldn't," Noah said.

"Try me," Avery said. "I won't just go home, I'll go straight back to New York and announce this find on the *Today* show and to every other camera I can get in front of at 30 Rock. No more games, Dr. Wyndham."

Defeated, Noah sat down on a nearby bulkhead. "Fine, fine. I may have inadvertently led you here under somewhat false pretenses. While I am a true scientist and my passion is indeed reversing the disastrous effects of global warming, I'm afraid any meaningful progress in that arena takes money, Ms. Turner. I came here to do it all: save the planet and locate the *Fortitude* and retrieve the lost crown jewels of Norway."

"What makes you think there is any treasure to find on the ship?" Carter said.

"Because Rigby Weymouth, captain of the *Fortitude*, was my great-grandfather. I probably know more about that ship than anyone alive."

Avery nodded, giving him points for owning up to the family connection without being told she already knew.

"Did Rigby smuggle the treasure aboard the ship?" she asked.

Noah shook his head. "No, but someone did. Rigby believed the Cardinal's Curse sank the *Fortitude*."

"Smaller minds, something something—you do remember saying that just a minute ago, don't you?" Avery asked.

"I believe people make their own destinies, Ms. Turner. You are right about me. I haven't been honest with you. The truth is I've spent years quietly researching the wreck of the *Fortitude* and the lost treasure of Nidaros. The treasure is believed to have been stolen by a corrupt cardinal from the Norwegian royal family and the Catholic Church centuries ago. This expedition has cost me time and money that I didn't have."

"Were the corporate benefactors a lie, too?"

"The amount I led you to believe they gave me was." Noah massaged his temples. "I did come here primarily to test my amorphous ice theory. The planet has always been my first love: I spent two years scrounging for grant money before I got desperate enough to sell every square inch of property I had. The shelf is melting at an increasingly alarming rate every year—we can't wait until the world catches up and decides to take this research seriously. I looted my trusts and savings and used my family's name and a couple of others, too, borrowing from every bank in England, and I was still a hundred million short."

It's always all about the money, Avery thought. Her mom had often said following the money could solve most murder cases.

"So, who made up the difference?" Carter said. "Because . . . here we are."

"A wealthy collector who believed me when I said I was a scientist who is also a master scuba diver and a descendant of Rigby Weymouth and could find the *Fortitude*. He agreed to continue funding this expedition up to one hundred million dollars. I have spent every last penny."

"So what happens to you if you can't deliver?" Avery said.

Noah shrugged. "From what I know about the man, I imagine something less than pleasant."

"Are you a master scuba diver?" Carter's eyebrows went up and Avery wondered if he'd even heard anything else.

"Recreational only." Noah winced. "That's why I reached out to the two of you. After reading about your discovery of the General's Gold and listening to Avery's speech, I knew you'd be able to help me."

"Does anyone else on board know any of this?" Avery said.

"No. And I'd be appreciative if it stayed that way."

Collectively, they turned to watch as Bertha was hoisted from the moon pool.

"What do you think?" Avery asked Carter.

"I'll need a day to think about it. I've got a deep dive expert who I trust to help with the research."

"You can't tell anyone about what you're diving for," Noah said, clearly alarmed at the prospect of bringing an outsider into the fold.

"You're hardly in a position to make demands, Noah," Avery said.

"Don't worry, Doc," Carter said. "I won't do anything to screw this up. Now that we've located the *Fortitude*, I'd like a peek inside her, too—treasure or no, as long as I come back."

28

Avery and Carter returned to her stateroom, where they found Harrison on the sat phone. Harrison ended the call as they walked in.

"Who were you talking to, Harry?" Carter said.

Avery whirled on Carter. "I think the more important question is what the heck are you thinking?"

"Huh?"

"How can you even consider diving here after everything that just happened? I don't like any of this. Noah flat-out lied to us to get us here, and pretty much the entire time we've been here, too. We can't possibly trust him at this point. She pointed to his laptop. The email you wrote MaryAnn the other day didn't send at the time, but I sent it earlier and she replied almost immediately. She heard some unflattering things about Noah and did some digging."

"That's how you knew all that stuff you said in there?"

"What stuff?" Harry asked.

"I don't like this, Carter."

"So, what do you want to do, leave?" Carter asked.

Harrison put his hands up and whistled. "What did I miss?" He glanced at Carter. "Not that I think she's wrong. There's thrill seeking and then there's just stupid, kid."

"Noah is related to the captain of the *Fortitude*," Avery announced. "And he dragged us here under false pretenses."

"So I was right?"

"Not in practice maybe, but in theory, yes." Avery perched on the bed. "I didn't want to believe you, Harry."

"Hang on a second," Carter said. "While I agree with you that he's been less than forthcoming with us from the start, I think Wyndham's motives are pure."

"Oh, I gotta hear this," Harrison said with a smirk.

"I'm serious, Avery," Carter said. "I'm convinced that the research they've been conducting here is important. You've been saying so all week, and nothing he said just now negates any of that. He wants the treasure so he can fund his own work. It's a little twisted, but there are worse motives for treasure hunting. We've seen them."

Avery tipped her head to one side, thinking. She was mad. And her mother always said making emotional decisions was a fool's mistake.

"I suppose you have a point," she said slowly.

"I think I can do this dive, Avery. You know there's no one more method-ical at checking gear, and my research guy is ex-navy. At least let me talk to him. More than half of the safety in a dive is proper preparation, and nobody is better than I am there."

"I'm confused," Harrison said. "Are we leaving or not?"

"Not," Carter said.

"And you get to decide that on your own, do you?" Avery snapped.

"Of course not. I'm hoping you'll stay with me."

"Why would I stay in a place under the sole control of an admitted liar?"

"Because we're this close to finding another one of the world's most famous lost ships—maybe one of the most famous lost treasures, too. And because in addition to finding these lost artifacts, maybe we help advance the science of ice repair. That's why you wanted to come here. Nothing about your reasons for getting on that crazy plane ride the other day have changed. There's just some new baggage around them, that's all."

Avery kept her arms crossed tightly and tapped her foot. She had liter-ally jumped at the chance to fly down here to help Noah locate the

Fortitude, hoping to further important climate research. A front row seat to a technology vs. nature fight with a sideshow of maritime legend that might save the planet.

Now that they had accomplished that unlikely feat with the help of the DiveNav, the next logical step did seem to be to try to find the lost treasure of Nidaros if Noah really thought it was here.

"We've come all this way," Carter said. "Do you really want to quit when we're this close? Without even letting me see if I can try?"

"Of course I don't," Avery said, scuffing the toe of her sneaker on the worn carpet.

"So, we're staying?" Harrison didn't bother to try to cover his disappointment.

"For now," Avery said. "But it has to be safe. And before the sun sets."

"You won't regret this, Avery," Carter said.

"I half regret it already, but I'll regret it if we leave too, and we're already here, so I'm erring on the side of adventure." Avery turned to Harrison. "Now, who were you talking to on the sat phone, Harry?"

Harrison's face betrayed his guilt as he looked from one of them to the other.

"Well?" Avery said.

"The pilot who brought us here."

"Rollie Fingers?" Carter said. "Why?"

"Because I was hoping he could come get us the hell out of here. Why else?"

"So?" Avery said. "Did you get a hold of him?"

"I did. Said he can't get down here for at least a week."

"So, we couldn't have left anyway," Avery said.

"My mom used to say everything happens for a reason," Carter said. "I really want a shot at this, Avery. If there is a way to do this dive safely in a week's time, which is about all we have left before winter and darkness run us off the shelf, then I want to go for it."

The ship shuddered, cutting back through the ice to port, the floor shifting and lights flickering.

Carter picked up the sat phone and put it to his ear. "Was this working before?"

Harrison nodded.

Carter jiggled the connection button and shook his head. "It's not now. Avery, what do you know about safety and deep-water dives if I can't get in touch with my buddy back home?"

"From the limited research I've done for the DiveNav on diving one hundred fifty meters or more, it's a difficult beast and very much dependent on the conditions of the diver and the environment."

"Look around you," Harrison said. "You couldn't have picked a worse environment to try this."

"Well, I'm in tip-top condition," Carter said.

"Weeeelll." Harrison quirked one eyebrow up and Carter tossed a pillow at him.

"You'd need special tanks," Avery continued, ignoring him. "Different gases for the different depth fields."

"Noah said they either have those things on board or can get them from Halley Station," Carter said.

"There's still a very high risk of not only decompression illness but blacking out down there. And who knows how the Antarctic water temperatures will affect that."

"I already know temperature plays a role in DCI, but my knowledge pertains to the warm water side. Nitrogen uptake is higher during the descent, and in bottom work because my body temperature is higher, but that balances out when ascending because the higher surface temperature causes a quicker release of harmful gases. I'm completely healthy, Avery. If some guy dove eleven hundred feet to get into the Guinness book, I know I can do this."

"And if you're wrong?" Avery stared at him. "I don't want you to get hurt, Carter." Or dead, but she didn't want to say that part out loud because Carter believed in bad luck.

"Do you have faith in me or not?" he asked.

"Faith has nothing to do with it."

"That's funny, because I have faith in you, Avery. And I'm confident that if I need you to, you will figure out a way for me to make this dive safely."

29

Avery kicked Carter and Harrison out of her room. She needed time to think. Time to research exactly what they'd be getting into with Carter's dive in case he couldn't reach his expert with the unreliability of anything with a cord or a chip out here.

Diving safety was largely a numbers game, and Avery wasn't an expert naval diver, but very few people could make computers run numbers better than she could.

Following a quick review of the features contained in commercially available diving software, Avery was convinced they were all woefully inadequate for something as dangerous as an extreme deep-water dive in Antarctica. None of the featured algorithms covered all the variables Carter would likely encounter. She would need to write a program specifically tailored for him and the environment. In a matter of days. Nothing like a little deadline pressure.

Avery created a file on her laptop, and after entering several pages of detailed notes, she headed back up to the now sparsely populated bridge.

Owen was busy at one of the control panels.

"Hey," Avery said. "Owen, right?"

"Good memory." Owen greeted her with a warm smile. "Congratulations on the discovery. That was exciting. We don't get too many moments like that aboard—well, in a lifetime, I guess, really."

"Thanks," Avery said. "I haven't seen much of you since we arrived."

"That's because I travel back and forth between here and Halley. A lot to keep tabs on down here in the land of snow and ice."

"I'll bet," Avery said. "When we first met, you mentioned being Dr. Wyndham's chief research assistant. Mind if I ask what exactly that entails?"

"Not at all. I compile data on anything and everything pertaining to Antarctica's external environment."

"Then you are exactly the person I'm looking for."

"Oh?" Owen raised a brow.

Avery proceeded to pepper Owen with detailed questions about every scientific measurement he'd taken since first boarding the *Weddell*.

"I need information about currents, water temperatures at various depths, as well as seasonal variability, visibility, viscosity, marine life—"

"Whoa," Owen cut her off. "I can answer some of your questions now, but that's a long list. You'll have to give me a little time to compile the data you're looking for on the rest of it."

"How much time?"

"This is about Carter diving the wreck, isn't it?"

"It is," Avery said, noting Owen's sour look of disapproval. "You don't think this is a good idea either?"

"It doesn't really matter what I think."

"It matters to me. Let's have it."

"Our mission here is supposed to be about science research. I don't understand why that isn't enough. What does finding the *Fortitude* have to do with anything?"

It was a fair question, Avery thought. But one for which she didn't have a good answer. She opted for the hard truth.

"Like it or not, Owen, research funding always comes with strings attached. Your funds here are tethered to the *Fortitude*."

Owen nodded. "Money makes the world go 'round."

"Indeed, it does."

"There you are," Noah said as he approached Avery and Owen. "I see you two have gotten better acquainted."

"Owen was just filling me in on what he does around here." Avery exchanged a knowing glance with Owen.

"So he told you he does everything?" Noah clapped Owen on the back. "Our research would be nowhere without Owen."

"Speaking of research," Avery said. "I'd like to take a look at the dive site access and the equipment you have, if you can point me in the right direction."

"I can do you one better," Noah said. "I'll take you out there myself."

"I don't suppose you've seen Carter," Avery said.

"He and Erin are studying the drone video. Would you like me to snag him on our way out?"

"No, that's okay. You and I can handle this."

The Sno-Cat lumbered across the ice shelf toward a spot directly above the wreck of the *Fortitude*. Avery and Noah were safe and warm as frigid winds whipped outside. Avery had to raise her voice to be heard above the engine noise.

"If anything happens to Carter, Dr. Wyndham, I will ruin you."

"I really do believe he can complete the dive safely and that he will benefit handsomely from the video," Noah said. "But I understand you."

"I'm more than a little disappointed. And angry," Avery said. "Just because I'm taking advantage of your offer to show me the site doesn't mean I'm happy with you."

"I can't blame you. I hope you understand that my research is much too important to leave to chance."

"Environmental research or your search for your great-grandfather's ship?"

"Both. Look, I saw an opportunity and I took it. You and Carter were my last hope to keep these projects alive. What would you do if you were in my shoes?"

Avery wasn't sure, but she understood the desire for answers. Hadn't she herself risked everything to uncover the truth about Mark's death?

"And don't worry, both you and Carter will get credit in the history books for your part in the discovery, whether we are successful getting inside the *Fortitude* or not."

"We might get a footnote, but you're the expedition leader."

"Perhaps, but the two of you are more fun to read about than stuffy old Dr. Wyndham."

Despite the dishonesty and the ruse Noah played to get them here, Avery found herself having a difficult time staying mad at him. He was an engaging and brilliant man, and though she hated to admit it, they weren't all that different.

"Do I understand correctly that you think finding the lost treasure will fund your research?" Avery said. "Assuming it's down there, I mean. Won't the person backing you want the finder's fee?"

"It's more about what I'll lose," Noah said almost under his breath.

"I'm sorry?" Avery said.

"Nothing," Noah said. "It's just—yes, but even a split of the finder's fee will return us to the Weddell in October, and with any luck, the find will drum up enough additional funding for our team to see this through. You've seen both stations. A lot of people have given up time with their families, sleep, limbs, we even had one lose his life, all to help me chase my dream. This is on me, Avery—if we fail, I have wasted their time, their efforts, their very lives. I can't have that."

"I'm sorry, did you say someone died?"

"Our assistant mechanical engineer. Heart attack while working on the device, at least, as much as Jillian was able to tell with her equipment here."

Avery shuddered despite the coat. "What did you . . . How do you . . . Where is he now?"

"In a locked room on the mechanical floor. We shut off the heat and created a sort of morgue locker. I will return him to his family in the coming weeks." Noah blinked rapidly and Avery stared quietly out the window, thinking about that locked door.

"Here we are," Noah said as he brought the Sno-Cat to an abrupt stop.

"The *Fortitude* lies approximately six hundred feet beneath where we are sitting right now."

Noah had stopped near the edge of the shelf. A literal sea of ice bobbed directly in front of them, each piece jostling and scraping against the next like hulls of passing ships as the ocean peeked out from between them. Avery spotted a small colony of penguins gathering in the distance and pointed them out to Noah.

"Adélie penguins," Noah said. "They live all along the Antarctic coast."

"Diet?"

"Mostly fish and krill."

"So cool seeing them here in their natural habitat."

"It's the only place you'll find them. Okay, back to the business at hand. This will be the dive command site. We'll set up a remote station here to monitor everything, provide onsite assistance and communication with the *Weddell*. Basically, any support you and Carter deem necessary."

Avery and Noah slid their goggles into place, then stepped out onto the ice.

The drastic change in temperature between the warmth of the Sno-Cat's cockpit and the subzero air was so shocking even in the gear that it took Avery a moment to catch her breath. Every inch of Avery's outer layer crinkled like newsprint as she moved.

Standing at the edge of nothing in the frigid cold of Antarctica, Avery truly realized for the first time exactly how treacherous this dive would be. None of the algorithms, tank mixtures, or water temperature readings even remotely prepared her for the reality of what Carter was about to try. The cruel and hard truth was this dive would be unlike anything he had ever attempted. Maybe unlike anything anyone had ever attempted. Still, there was an undeniable feeling of excitement building up inside of her. The siren call of discovery was impossible to deny.

Avery watched as Noah produced a long, telescoping pole from the back of the Sno-Cat and began to prod at the ice floes.

"What are you doing?" Avery said.

"Just checking to see if the ice is mobile enough for us to utilize a rigid inflatable boat in here. We have several RIBs stored nearby."

"And?"

"At this point we probably can. But conditions change rapidly out here."

Avery held up the DiveNav and after several seconds the air temperature and wind speed were displayed. Kneeling at the edge of the shelf, Avery submerged the device, recording the temperature of the water.

"It gets warmer the deeper you dive," Noah said.

"How much warmer?"

"Where Carter will be going? As much as six degrees Fahrenheit."

Avery glanced back at the ocean temperature displayed on the DiveNav. At these extreme temperatures, six degrees might actually be enough to keep Carter alive.

30

Avery and Noah returned to the *Weddell*. They checked in with Owen on the bridge regarding the upcoming weather forecast.

"Conditions will be most favorable for diving the day after tomorrow," Owen said. "It probably won't matter to Carter, as he'll be underwater, but for the team supporting him, the day after tomorrow is your best window of opportunity."

"Can he prep for the dive that quickly?" Noah asked Avery.

"We've done it before," Carter said, studying the drone video alone now.

"This is new territory, even for me," Avery said. She turned back to Owen. "Assuming I need more time, when would the next good weather window be?"

"About twenty-seven days from now."

Carter looked up wide-eyed from the drone video. "Twenty-seven days?"

Noah shook his head. "That's much too far into the winter season. Conditions will have worsened considerably by then, even with a window of fair weather. And our daylight will be gone."

Avery could feel all eyes upon her. Either she could calculate a safe diving plan, or the search for the treasure, and likely the continued environmental research funding, would come to an abrupt halt.

"Then let's plan for the day after tomorrow," Avery said.

"Is that really smart?" Harrison said. "He's growing on me. I don't want him to drown."

"We'll be ready," Avery said.

"I'll prep the equipment as soon as you tell me what I need." Carter returned to studying the drone video of the *Fortitude*.

Avery and Carter availed themselves of a conference room that Noah had cleared out to prepare for the dive. While Avery continued to research similar dives and their numerous requirements, Carter scrutinized every frame of the drone video, attempting to develop the best plan of attack. Which was slightly more difficult with Erin hanging on his arm, firing a constant barrage of questions.

"You folks have everything you need?" Noah said as he popped his head in.

"Think so," Avery said.

"Actually, I do have a question," Carter said. "What exactly is it we are hoping to find down there? The term *lost jewels* is a little vague. Don't suppose you can be a bit more specific?"

"I can do better than a little," Noah said. "Be right back."

Noah returned in less than five minutes with a thin three-ring binder. Clipped inside were several plastic document shields. Noah set the binder on the table between Avery and Carter, then opened the cover.

"This is what we're looking for."

The protective sleeves held drawings—really old drawings, from the crumpled edges of the paper and faded ink. There were three illustrations in all: a heavily bejeweled gold crown, a golden sword with emeralds embedded along the center of the hilt and Norwegian writing carved into the side of the blade, and a gold Catholic cross with a large ruby at its center.

"Where did these sketches come from?" Avery asked.

"I located them in museum archives," Noah said.

"And they just handed them over to you?" Carter asked.

Noah ignored the question. "To my knowledge these are the only true representations of the missing jewels. The entire treasure stolen from Nidaros is believed to be much larger."

"And if it really is hidden inside the *Fortitude*, where would such a treasure be kept?"

"In the belly of the ship, I'd wager."

Carter pulled out his cell phone and held it up as if he intended to photograph the images. Avery couldn't help but notice Noah flinching at the sight of the phone.

"May I?" Carter said. "Just for my own use."

"Certainly," Noah said after a moment's hesitation. "Please don't share them with anyone."

"Of course," Carter said.

"You're going to retrieve these for me, aren't you?" Noah asked.

Avery couldn't help but notice Noah's use of the singular pronoun. Odd, considering he claimed to be searching at the behest of another.

"I'll do my best," Carter said.

Erin barely contained a squeal of excitement as she tugged on Carter's arm. Avery watched as he flashed her his most confident grin.

After dinner, Avery retired to her cabin to work on her own. She didn't need any distractions from her dive research. But she just couldn't escape the Carter and Erin show.

Avery heard the noisy couple enter his room next door. Not wanting to hear what might come next through the practically cardboard wall, she scrambled for her noise-canceling headphones and got down to work. Her intent was to create an app which, if followed precisely, would allow Carter to dive to the calculated depth safely, spend the maximum amount of time searching, then return to the surface using the proper mixtures of gases to minimize decompression illness—and hopefully, with his lungs free of blood and his eardrums intact. Over a ridiculously slow satellite internet connection, Avery double- and triple-checked the known effects of frigid and deep-water dives and how exactly the fitness of the diver corresponded to DCI. As she worked, she began creating her very own dive parameter algorithms: one tailored specifically to Carter Mosley and one to her. For research purposes.

Several hours later, totally lost in her work, Avery heard a crash followed by a woman's scream. She snatched the headphones off her head and listened for a beat. The next thing she heard was laughter and the sound of Carter's cabin door opening and closing.

Thank God, she thought. *They're leaving.*

Avery rubbed her tired eyes before surveying all the work she had done. She had compiled pages of calculations, and the numbers didn't lie: Carter was right. The dive would be doable, assuming everything went according to plan, and Carter followed her directions to the letter. The best possible sequence for Carter to follow would be to remain cold while alternating gas mixtures during the descent, then warm up while switching back during the ascent.

The equipment list she had compiled included a high-end rebreather along with specialized oxygen, helium, and nitrogen mixtures from multiple different tank configurations. Sitting on the bed cross-legged, Avery leaned back against the wall and wondered how in the world she would ever finish the DiveNav programming for the *Fortitude* dive with so little time left.

31

Avery had passed exhaustion hours before and was racing for full-on delirium by the time she looked up from her computer again. She wasn't sure which part of her hurt the most: her back from sitting on the bed or her brain from inventing a whole computer program in a matter of hours. She had no idea of the time, and peering out the tiny window of her cabin was of little use as the sun barely moved at this far-flung corner of the world.

She scrolled through the program on her laptop. It wasn't quite finished, but she knew it was close. The last key bits would have to come from Carter. She needed the results of his most recent physical because medical research showed the uptake and expression of blood gases depend largely upon VO_2 max and cholesterol levels. She got up and stretched, then headed out into the hall in her stocking feet. Stopping at Carter's cabin, she rapped lightly on the door.

No answer. As she stood there alone in the hallway, she checked her watch and was shocked to find it was nearly five a.m. No wonder she was exhausted. She hadn't pulled an all-nighter since . . . maybe college. Yawning, Avery returned to her cabin and dropped off her laptop. She slipped on her wind pants and boots, then retrieved her coat. She was in dire need of two things: fresh air and coffee. The order didn't particularly matter.

On the main deck of the *Weddell* everything was peaceful and quiet. The sunlight was nothing more than a pale orange ball hovering at the edge of the Antarctic late-summer sky, ticking off their days there as it crept toward the horizon. In the distance, low gray clouds hung ominously over the stark white landscape, but they weren't close. The frigid air was invigorating but far too cold for more than a minute without her goggles and mask: every exhaled breath condensed into a frosty plume of white smoke and her nose hurt even without the wind. Thinking about the drone tech and his missing fingers, Avery turned to head back inside for some badly needed caffeine when she noticed a shadowy figure moving toward the gangway. Hoping she'd found Carter, she hurried in that direction, clapping a thickly gloved hand over her nose. Drawing closer, Avery realized it wasn't Carter, but Seamus, and he was carrying a paper-wrapped bundle about the size of a large bag of flour. Avery couldn't tell what it was, but it appeared heavy from his hunched posture and tight shoulders. She didn't think Seamus saw her as he disappeared down the gangway.

Avery jumped when a hand landed on her shoulder. She spun around, bringing her fists up defensively and coming face-to-face with Harrison.

"Oh my God, Harry. You nearly scared me to death."

"Oops. Sorry. What are you doing up so early?"

"I never went to bed. I was up all night working on Carter's dive program."

"With Carter?"

Avery shook her head. "No. I think he was occupied."

"His new groupie, I'm sure. Wanna grab a coffee? My treat."

"Thought you'd never ask."

Though breakfast wouldn't be served for another few hours, the galley was already warm and inviting and the enticing aroma of fresh coffee filled the deserted space. Avery and Harrison each filled a mug from one of the tall chrome coffee dispensers in the corner, then grabbed a seat at a nearby table. They spoke in hushed tones as the bare metal walls made every sound echo, an acoustical nightmare.

"What's up?" Avery said after taking a sip of the strong dark brew. "You look like you've got something on your mind."

"What makes you say that?"

Avery gestured at the fingers of Harrison's right hand nervously drumming atop the table. "Because you're doing that thing you do whenever you've got something on your mind."

"Guess I'm still not comfortable about this whole setup. We don't really even know these people. And now that the ship has been found, thanks to you, there is a valuable treasure in play. Again. A treasure some of these folks might not be inclined to share, even its discovery. I've seen greed make people do some pretty horrible things, Ave."

"Not you, too." The blurted words were followed by a huff, and Avery spun toward the pantry, where the assistant chef they'd seen the other night was juggling an armload of what looked like baking ingredients while she tried to pull the door shut.

"I can get that." Avery jumped up to work the door and waved the girl toward the counter.

"Not us too, what?" Harry asked.

The cook dumped the bags and boxes on the counter and retrieved a large metal mixing bowl from a shelf.

"I cannot hear one more word about treasure or curses or history or that bloody, blasted sunken ship." Her British accent was even more delightful than Noah's. "It's why I'm up getting my part of breakfast done before Tuva is awake. I didn't realize when I came here how isolating it would be, and her prattle about this legend is driving me right-on batty. The least you can do is go discuss it in the mess hall."

"Tuva really talks about it that much?"

"She's recording a podcast." The girl rolled her eyes, measuring out flour and sugar. "The recovery of the *Fortitude* and justice for her great whatever relative."

"And the treasure," Avery said, intrigued that Tuva had made herself sound befuddled and helpless when talking to them—and she hadn't mentioned the podcast, either.

"Right." She grabbed a whisk and some milk. "She yakked for weeks about getting Carter Mosley here. She thinks he's like some sort of superhero in a scuba suit."

"Did she convince Dr. Wyndham to invite us here?" Avery asked.

"I don't know, I don't hear her talk except to her recorder and on the phone."

"Do you know who she's talking to on the phone?" Harrison asked.

The whisk paused for a moment. "I don't think I've ever heard her say a name, come to think of it. But hang around enough and you'll catch her on a call. At least three a week since I got here."

"And when was that?" Harrison asked.

"In December. Right after Christmas. I replaced the guy who died."

"Someone died?" Harrison stood up.

"Hypothermia, they said." She retrieved a bread pan and poured in the batter, moving to the stove and scooping butter into a saucepan. "I guess it happens here more often than people think. That's why I stay inside. I wanted to see the world and build my resume, and working with Tuva was too good an opportunity to pass up—she's bloody well looney, but people don't know that and she's a respected chef."

Harrison started to say something else and Avery laid a hand on his arm and shook her head slightly.

"We didn't mean to disturb you," she said. "We'll take our coffee to the mess hall." She refilled her cup and motioned for Harrison to follow her.

At a table in the far corner of the empty hall, he leaned in, eyes wide. "You're not bothered that she said someone died?"

"I'm more bothered that Noah told me yesterday that weird cold door down below is a storage room for a dead body, except he said it was the assistant engineer, not a cook."

"Avery, this is bad. Like it just jumped from not good to bad, right there."

"Maybe it slipped his mind," Avery said.

"A dead body he's sharing space with in a remote location slipped his mind?" Harrison put up a skeptical eyebrow.

"It's not like he doesn't have a lot going on, and it was a cook, and months ago. I'm not saying I'm convinced, but I am saying it's possible that one, the engineer guy was the one he interacted more with, and two, he didn't see it as particularly important information that there were two dead people—for the conversation we were having, the one guy he specifically mentioned was enough to make a person feel as guilt-ridden as he sounded."

"I don't trust this guy as far as I could throw this whole damn ship, Avery."

"I don't trust him at all. The longer we're here, the more apparent it becomes that this place is a frozen vipers' nest of folks with their own agendas, and Noah is king cobra, it seems. But I don't think he's dangerous. Greedy, sure. Lying, absolutely. But he's not trying to hurt anyone, and now that the ship has been found, we stand to gain by sticking around, so I see nothing wrong with furthering our agenda on his dime. Well—someone's dime."

"We should go home. That's what I see nothing wrong with."

"You sound like my mother, Harry."

The pained expression on Harrison's face reminded her that he still missed his former partner in a way Avery would never truly understand.

"God, I miss her sometimes," he said softly.

Avery reached across the table and patted his hand. "Me too."

Harrison and Valerie had worked together as homicide detectives in New York City. They had depended on each other, trusted each other, finished each other's thoughts, had each other's backs for nearly twenty years, before cancer had taken Valerie from both of them. Avery remembered Val calling Harry her work husband—she'd always said that was enough, she didn't need a home one, too.

"I guess being back in New York, helping work a case, kind of dredged it all up again," Harrison said.

"The job or working with my mom?"

"Both. I miss the thrill of the chase, bringing order to a chaotic world, trying to find some justice."

"Well, the cook thinks this treasure might be part of a very old murder. Maybe finding it will bring a measure of justice."

"Not sure I can help with that. Statute of limitations and all."

Their brief moment of solitude was broken as Tuva approached their table.

"Good morning, Tuva," Avery said.

"Good morning," Harrison said, raising his mug in salute. Avery could tell he was less than excited, but no one else would've known.

"I'm sorry we didn't get the chance to talk more the other night, and then the excitement of the drone launch scuttled our plans to meet yesterday," Avery said. "Your Gigi sounds like a fascinating lady."

"Thank you for saying so, Ms. Avery. I am troubled."

"What about?" Avery said.

"Now the *Fortitude* has been found, there will be more danger. Maybe for Mr. Carter. They say he will dive to the wreck."

That didn't jibe with what the assistant said about her wanting Carter here, but Avery didn't want to let on that they knew that, so she furrowed her brow.

"Don't tell me you believe in curses," Harrison said before Avery could speak.

"You do not have to be superstitious for bad things to happen, Mr. Harry. It doesn't take magic. Sometimes people and circumstances just bend to them. Like my great-grandfather when the ship killed him."

"From what you told us, it sounded like there was someone responsible for your great-grandfather's death," Harrison said.

"Because of the ship," Tuva said. "A killer who was never brought to justice."

"Or maybe it was just an accident," Avery said.

"Or a coincidence," Harrison said.

"Are the two of you willing to gamble with your friend's life?" Tuva asked.

Avery opened her mouth, then closed it. What if she was right? What if someone had killed her great-grandfather over the treasure? If there was one lesson Avery had learned by hunting treasure, it was that greed tended to thread its way through generations, as it evidently had with Noah's family. What if someone did murder Tuva's grandfather over the lost treasure of Nidaros? Maybe discovering the person responsible could assist them in figuring out who might be trying to sabotage their efforts to find it now.

Tuva continued. "People who touch this treasure—even search for it— have met bad ends, Ms. Avery. I am terribly worried for Mr. Carter."

"Why do you think your great-grandfather was murdered?" Harrison said.

"Because he found the treasure, Mr. Harry. My Gigi told me all about it. Johann, my great-grandfather, kept a journal. He was very faithful about it. But after his death, they went through his things at the ship-works. My Gigi swore there were pages missing from his journal. Among the missing pages were detailed sketches showing how he discovered the lost treasure. My Gigi was convinced the person responsible for murdering him took those pages."

Tuva looked directly at Harrison before speaking again. "Mr. Harry, I know you were a police detective. Do you think you might be able to help me find out who was responsible for killing my great-grandfather?"

Harrison looked to Avery for help, but she just sat there giving him a smug look. Avery knew he wouldn't be able to dismiss Tuva's request as easily as he had hers.

"It doesn't work like that," Harrison said. "You're asking me to solve a century-old murder with one arm tied behind my back. I've got nobody to interview. No photos of the scene. No clear motive even."

"Please, Mr. Harry."

"I can't promise anything, Tuva. But I'll see what I can find out."

They followed Tuva into the kitchen. True to her word, the assistant was gone, the coffee cake baking, filling the room with a delicious spicy-sweet scent. As Tuva cooked bacon and sausage, Harrison peppered her with questions about her great-grandfather, his life, his work, and his death. Avery couldn't help wondering if he would ask about the podcast.

He didn't.

"Is anyone in your family searching for the missing treasure?" Avery said.

"I am," Tuva said. "So I can destroy it."

Avery exchanged a glance with Harrison. Judging by the look on his face, Harrison didn't believe Tuva any more than Avery did.

Following an uneventful breakfast, Avery returned to her stateroom to work. She'd been hoping to run into Carter, but he was nowhere to be found. Back in her room she typed up a quick email to MaryAnn, asking her to have Brady check Carter's desktop computer for an email from

Carter's doctor. She needed the results from his last physical to run through the new program and to finish programming the DiveNav with the schematics of the *Fortitude*.

Avery sent the email and turned her attention to the DiveNav itself. She froze. When she'd left the room in search of coffee, she had placed it on the left side of the desk facing her laptop. Now it was facing the other direction. Could her memory be off due to exhaustion? Or had someone been inside her room?

Avery picked up the device, then checked its settings. No, she was positive. Someone had been messing about with the DiveNav. But who? As she considered the question, it occurred to her that on a ship full of tech nerds and scientists, there were probably any number of people who could have figured out how to get inside the device. But to what end?

Avery reconnected her laptop to the DiveNav, then ran a comprehensive search for malware. Nothing. There was no indication that any new software of any kind had been installed. Why then had they bothered poking around in the device? Why risk getting caught inside her cabin? Avery's eyes slowly scanned the room for anything else out of place. Before she could get up to open the small closet, the floor pitched and rolled under her, and the screech of tearing metal made her throw her hands up to cover her ears. Avery grabbed for the desk too late, thrown from her chair onto a floor that suddenly seemed far less solid than it had only a moment before.

32

Plymouth, England
August 1914

A lone shipwright stood dockside, watching men scurry about. The screech of gulls and whir of heavy machinery filled the air. The Royal Navy Port of Plymouth was abuzz with activity as a large ship was loaded and last-minute preparations were made.

The Norwegian adventure ship *Fortitude* had been sold to the British Royal Navy forces. Originally constructed for the sole purpose of transporting wealthy passengers on pleasure excursions to the Antarctic, the ship was found to be impractical due to its lack of speed. At least until renowned British explorer and well-to-do entrepreneur Rigby Weymouth stepped in. Realizing the ship's potential as an exploration vessel, Weymouth was given command of a project to repurpose the ship for use in Antarctic exploration. British Parliament had hoped, given Weymouth's vast experience, he might be the first person to find a way across the frozen continent, thereby providing the Royal Navy a much-needed shortcut and huge advantage as war had erupted across Europe.

As he witnessed the orderly mayhem taking place on the dock, the shipwright couldn't help but recall a tragedy he had witnessed years before, when he'd been a lowly shipbuilder's apprentice in Norway. It was a day not unlike the current one, when a massive timber came crashing down from a scaffolding, crushing one of the principal owners of the *Fortitude*. A superstitious man by nature, the passing years had done little to assuage the fear he'd felt as he witnessed the man's horrific death.

The shipwright couldn't help but admire the ship and her transformation. She was truly a well-built and seaworthy craft. He hoped the legend of Rigby Weymouth's cunning were true. If so, the *Fortitude* might well help the British in the war effort.

The shipwright noticed an unkempt man struggling with a large and apparently heavy wooden trunk. The man appeared bound and determined to carry his load on board the ship. The shipwright stepped forward.

"Like a bit of help with that, mate?" the shipwright said.

The man turned to him with a look of pure hatred. "I don't need your help," he snarled. "I can handle it just fine on my own, *mate*."

The shipwright recoiled at the man's fury. There was something familiar about him, but the shipwright couldn't immediately place where he had seen him before. Peering closely at the man's face as he continued to struggle with his load, the shipwright finally placed him. The recognition hit him like a thunderbolt, causing him to shiver. The grubby trunk-bearer had once been a servant to the man he'd seen crushed on the docks in Norway all those years ago. In fact, he'd been with him on that fateful day, unable to save his employer and nearly crushed himself.

The shipwright stumbled back from the man, repulsed. Making the sign of the cross, the shipwright said a prayer: "Lord, bless this ship and crew as they set sail with a curse upon them."

33

Present Day

The ear-piercing, repeating *arroogah* sound of a klaxon blasted throughout the ship. The *Weddell* pitched and rocked as if navigating a hurricane. Avery sat stunned on the floor of her stateroom, wondering if they'd been torpedoed. She realized how unlikely it was given that they were on a ship in the middle of quite literally nowhere, but one too many spy novels meant it was the first thing to pop into her mind. She struggled to her feet, using the room's furniture for handholds, and made her way to the door. Avery stepped out into the hallway just as the lights went out, plunging everything into darkness. Someone screamed.

Unable to see, Avery stood glued to one spot, waiting for her eyes to adjust, her heart racing as she stood there wondering what was going on and where Harrison and Carter were. Moments later, red emergency lights flickered to life, bathing the ship's interior in a bloody glow. The first tendrils of smoke began to fill the corridor, and the acrid smell of burning rubber finally reached her nose. *Electrical fire*, she thought as she hurried to Carter's door and began pounding on it.

"Carter," she yelled. "Are you in there?" There was no answer.

She tried the handle, but the door was locked. She found Harrison's door locked as well. She saw the confusion on the faces of her shipmates as the hallway filled with people who left their cabin doors open in a mad rush for the stairwells.

The smoke thickening around her, Avery covered her mouth and nose with the sleeve of her sweater. She lurched forward, trying doors and looking inside each cabin as she passed. On the floor of one room, Avery spotted bits of wire, electrical boards, and tools. Inside the next she noticed a red satin comforter hanging off the bed, partially covering the floor. The flame from an overturned candle raced across the carpet toward the comforter. She hurried inside, snatching a heavy wool blanket from under the comforter, then quickly smothering the fire. Before she could retreat into the hallway, the ship pitched again, knocking her off-balance and onto the floor. As she fought to regain her footing, the door to the cabin slammed shut. She crawled toward it and yanked on the handle, but it wouldn't budge. The metal was bent from the force of the slam, the latch jammed.

Smoke from the hallway seeped under the cabin door, growing thicker with each passing moment. Avery coughed and lifted the collar of her sweater over her mouth and nose and searched the room for anything to block the draft. She settled on the blanket, dragging it away from the bed, then tucking it up against the foot of the door. No longer able to hear people shouting as they ran down the corridor, Avery realized for the first time she was alone. Alone and locked in a stateroom at the center of a ship that was on fire. Surely Carter and Harrison would come looking for her, wouldn't they? Of course they would. They were probably searching for her right now. Assuming they weren't injured by the blast.

Avery pounded on the door. "Help! I'm in here!"

34

Avery did her best to keep her growing panic at bay, even as smoke continued to creep past the blanket and into the stateroom. As seconds ticked by, she began to wonder if anyone would come to her rescue. For all she knew, Carter and Harrison might be dealing with their own issues. As much as she didn't want to consider it, the possibility existed that one or both could've been hurt in the blast.

Her eyes darted about the room as she searched for anything heavy enough to break through a door. The night table and bed, like most of the larger items, were bolted to the floor. The only furniture that seemed to move freely were the two metal chairs bookending a bistro-style table in the far corner. Avery snatched up one of the chairs, then swung it as hard as she could into the door. But the chair was only lightweight aluminum and one of its legs crumpled upon impact with the solid metal door.

Tossing the ruined chair aside, Avery spotted a small storage locker mounted to the wall. Reaching inside, she yanked the contents out onto the cabin floor. There was nothing inside but a heavy coat, several sweaters and four rolled canvases that appeared to be old oil paintings of a seaside town. Nothing she recognized. Her eyes darted back to the closet, where she spotted a small fire safe tucked into the back corner. The metal safe was slightly larger than a shoebox and very solid. Avery grabbed it and headed for the door. Lifting the safe above her head, she brought it down forcefully on the stuck handle. She watched helplessly as the handle snapped off flush with the bezel and bounced off the carpet. The door was still stuck. But the metal was as thin as everything else on board. Avery changed tactics—dropping to her knees, she used the sharp corner of the safe to punch through the bottom panel of the door, nearly losing her grip as the metal gave way, a decently wide section rolling out and down, allowing thick black smoke to pour into the room. Coughing and gasping for air, Avery worked her way around the panel until the hole was big enough to crawl through.

On her hands and knees, Avery pulled herself out into the smoke-filled corridor and staggered to her feet. She turned toward the stairwell and ran straight into someone large. Avery let out a scream.

"Ave, it's me," Harrison said between coughs. "Come on."

The two of them hurried down the hallway and up the stairs.

Up on the main deck Avery and Harrison gulped lungfuls of frigid Antarctic air. Initially the smoke-free air was a welcome change, but Avery quickly realized she could feel her throat closing. To slow her breathing with warmer air, she drew breath through the sleeve of her sweater, wondering how long they could stay outside before frostbite became a problem for more than just one of the *Weddell*'s crew.

All around them milled scientists, chefs, Dr. Jill, the technicians, and engineers. Each face wore a confused expression; a few had smudges of soot.

"What the hell happened?" Harrison yelled to a nearby person, trying to be heard above the klaxon.

"I don't know," the young man said. "I just heard the blast and ran up here."

Noah bellowed just then, waiting to address the crew from atop a bulkhead. "Everyone, please remain calm."

"What happened, Dr. Wyndham?" someone shouted from within the crowd.

"We're working to find that out."

"Did someone target the ship?" another crewmember asked.

"I assure you the ship was not a target."

"How do you know that?" another voice called.

Avery was wondering the same thing.

Noah ignored the question and continued. "The *Weddell* did sustain some minor damage to the hull as a result of an explosion and resulting electrical fire on board, but the fire has been extinguished and there is no need to evacuate the ship."

Harrison turned to Avery. "We're in the middle of nowhere on a floating research vessel. Is there any such thing as minor hull damage?"

Avery turned her attention from Noah's canned speech, her eyes racing through the crowd of frightened faces, hoping for a glimpse of Carter's tall athletic frame or even Erin's red hair. But they were nowhere to be found.

She grabbed Harrison by the arm. "Harry, I can't find—"

"I know, I know," he said, cutting her off midsentence. "I'm looking for him too."

As Avery pushed through the crowd, with Harrison right on her heels, she nearly ran into Noah.

"Have you seen Carter?" Avery asked.

"I haven't," Noah said. "I'm still trying to figure out what happened. Where did you see him last?"

Tuva pulled on Avery's arm to get her attention. "I saw Mr. Mosley and Erin just before the explosion."

"Where did you see them?" Harrison said.

Tuva pointed in the direction of the stern. "They were entering one of the ship's holds on the way to her room."

"That isn't the way to her room." Noah shook his head. "I think I know where they went."

"Show me," Avery said.

35

Avery practically shoved Noah down narrow stairways and dimly lit hallways. He wasn't moving quickly enough for her liking. Not with Carter and Erin still unaccounted for.

The smoke was less dense now, but the emergency lighting was still active, the klaxon still barking.

"Any chance one of your people knows how to shut that damn thing off?" Harrison barked.

"Everything is automatic," Noah said. "Once the fire is out and the smoke has cleared, we'll be able to reset it."

"What happened anyway?" Harrison said.

"I meant what I said to the crew. I don't know."

"Can we just focus on finding Carter?" Avery said. "Where is this hold Tuva was talking about?"

"Here," Noah said as he stopped at a bulkhead door. He pulled up on the latch and the door swung open. "After you, Ms. Turner."

Avery didn't particularly trust Noah, or anyone aboard the ship at this point, but her concern for Carter overruled common sense and she brushed past him into the hold.

"Carter!" Avery yelled. "Are you in here?"

"Erin!" Noah called, earning a dirty look from Avery. "Carter!" he hollered out in response.

"Carter," Harrison bellowed, his deep baritone echoing. "Where are you?"

An image of Carter half-naked curled up in some private corner had been forming in Avery's mind. She had decided if they found the two of them in that condition, and if they were unharmed, she would kill them herself.

The hold was cluttered with rows of plastic totes and metal trunks, each stacked to the ceiling. The passageways in between were narrow to the point that Avery could barely squeeze between them. The room looked more like a hoarder's paradise than anything that belonged on a research ship. Some of the stacks had tumbled over due to the violent rocking of the hull, blocking the way.

With assistance from Harrison and Noah, Avery was able to clear away the cartons and continue forward. They continued to holler for Carter and Erin but got no response through most of the right side of the hold.

"What's in these boxes anyway?" Avery said, pausing a moment to catch her breath.

"Too many things to count," Noah said. "Spare parts for the equipment, personal belongings, you name it."

Avery turned toward the back left corner. "Let's check down here."

Noah grabbed onto Avery's upper arm. "There's a lot of heavy equipment down there and it's dangerous. Why don't I check that area?"

"You know what else is dangerous, friend?" Harrison moved into Noah's personal space. "Grabbing onto her arm."

Noah immediately released his grip on Avery. "I meant no offense. There's no need to threaten me, Harry."

"It wasn't a threat, Doc," Harrison said as he nodded in Avery's direction. "It was a warning."

Noah chuckled nervously as he turned to regard Avery. "Really?" he said.

"Yeah," Avery said as she fixed him with a cold stare. "Really."

"You don't sound like you trust me," Noah said.

"I don't," Avery said. "Carter may be in danger and for all I know it's your fault. If there's one thing I've learned about treasure hunting, it's that the world has no shortage of ruthless, greedy people willing to do almost anything to get their hands on valuable baubles. If Carter is hurt and I find out you had something to do with it, I'll make you regret ever hearing my name."

Noah opened his mouth to speak, but before he could, Harrison pointed behind Avery.

"Look."

Avery and Noah spun around to see Erin's red curls protruding from under a toppled crate the size of Avery's body.

36

Avery yelled Carter's name as she shoved boxes out of her way and moved toward Erin's motionless body. The panic in her voice was clear. Upon reaching the woman, Avery knelt at her side and checked her carotid artery for a pulse. Erin's skin was warm, her pulse strong and regular, but she had sustained a laceration to her head that was bleeding slightly.

"Is she alive?" Noah said.

"Yes, but unconscious," Avery said. "She may be concussed."

Avery gently shook Erin by the shoulders and called her name. At last Erin's eyes fluttered open.

"Avery," she said as she reached up to the wound on her head, wincing. "What happened?"

"That's what we'd like to know," Harrison said, fixing Noah with an accusatory glare.

"We can't find Carter," Avery said. "Was he with you?"

Erin nodded as Avery helped her to a sitting position.

"He was right here," Erin said as she looked around. "He wanted to check out some of the diving gear and tanks."

"Were you able to locate them?" Harrison said.

"Yeah, they were right—here." Erin furrowed her brow and winced as she pointed to several empty crates. "There was an earthquake and then . . . I don't know."

"*Were* is the operative word," Noah said, looking around. "The equipment is gone."

"What exactly is missing?" Avery said as she examined the spilled contents of the crates.

"Two mixed gas rigs, two custom rebreathers, and two specialized cold-water dive suits," Noah said, looking over her shoulder.

"We have to find him." Avery turned back for the door, hoping Carter had taken the equipment to keep it safe or check it out, but an uneasy twist in her gut wasn't so sure.

"Why would Mr. Mosley make off with the equipment unless he was going to attempt to steal the treasure by doing the dive himself?"

"Carter is a lot of things, but stupid isn't one of them," Avery snapped. "No adrenaline rush is worth being your last, he says. Attempting that dive alone and uninformed would be suicide, and Carter enjoys life far too much to be suicidal."

"Whatever his reason, even if he's not planning to dive, I'm simply saying he should have asked." Noah raised both hands in mock surrender.

"Carter isn't a thief," Avery said. "If he took the gear, he had a good reason. But since you've been lying to us since the start of this trip, I'm not inclined to believe anything you say before we find Carter and hear his side of the story."

"I'm not a liar, Ms. Turner."

"Could've fooled me," Avery said.

"Me too. Starting with luring us here under false pretenses," Harrison said.

Noah ignored Harrison's comment. "So what are you saying? That someone took Carter Mosley and all of this dive gear off the ship without his consent?"

"I have no idea, Dr. Wyndham, but I suggest you ready a search party, because I'm going to look for him." Avery paused to look at Erin. "You coming?"

Erin's eyes widened as she shrunk back into the corner. "I-I've got a head injury. There's concussion protocol to consider."

Avery had to bite her tongue to keep from calling her a fair-weather friend to Carter. She turned to Harrison. "Ready, Harry?"

"Right behind you."

Avery hurried down the corridor, past the door she had destroyed while escaping the fire, and into her stateroom. The locker at the foot of her bed was standing open and empty.

Hand going to her throat, Avery scanned the room. The DiveNav was gone.

37

"You sure Carter didn't take it?" Harrison said, earning a *you've got to be kidding me* glare from Avery. "I mean, who else even knows how to use it?"

"He wouldn't, Harry," Avery said. "Carter isn't like that, and you know it. There's something else happening here. And it isn't some silly ancient curse."

"What's the plan?" Harrison said as Avery opened her laptop and began typing furiously.

"I'm sending a message to MaryAnn, telling her that Carter is missing and requesting she find out everything she can about the *Weddell* and her crew, past and present, as well as any wealthy art collectors with ties to Wyndham. We need to find out who is financing this expedition, Harry."

Harrison pointed at the top corner of her screen. "No internet access," he said. "Looks like we're on our own. Grab your gear and let's see what we can do."

"So that's what caused all this trouble," Harrison said. He stood beside Avery on the deck of the *Weddell*, looking down at the ruined Sno-Cats they had ridden in on. "Noah was right when he told us the ship wasn't the target. It was simply collateral damage."

"Looks that way, but that means whoever did this wanted badly enough to take the Sno-Cats out of commission that they didn't care if they sank the ship," Avery said.

"Which means they aren't planning on coming back."

"Carter isn't behind this, Harry."

He nodded, pointing down to the ice. "How bad is the ship damaged?"

Avery shrugged, and a voice came from behind them: "No cause for further alarm," Owen said. "Debris from the explosions damaged the hull, but not catastrophically."

"We're not taking on water, are we?" Harrison said, eyes widening.

"The damage is just above the waterline. The ship isn't in any danger of sinking, at the moment."

"What do you mean 'at the moment'?" Harrison said.

"Well, rising or rough seas could change that quickly."

"Doesn't that mean we need to get out of here?"

Owen shook his head. "We're watching a storm forming off the coast of Australia, but for now the water is calm, our land transports are damaged or missing, and we're safer staying put given the distance from the ship to Halley VI."

"What do you mean, damaged or missing?" Avery asked.

"It appears that one of the vehicles may have been spared, but it's gone," Owen said. "Though it's difficult to tell with confidence when there are so many scattered pieces, Ms. Turner. All I can say for sure is we are the safest here for the moment." He patted Avery's shoulder and walked off toward the mess hall.

Avery turned back to the rail. The blackened and burning husks below them on the ice were all that remained of the Sno-Cats. Bits of the ruined vehicles were scattered around the ice over several hundred feet.

Avery knew in her bones with a certainty that was frightening in its absoluteness that if she found the other Sno-Cat, she'd find Carter.

"I'm going to find Carter." Avery whirled on Harrison. "You coming with me?"

"You're not serious," Harrison said.

"I am deadly serious," Avery said as she grabbed onto the sleeve of his jacket. "He's not here, Harry, he'd have found us if he was. And whatever is going on here, I have a really bad feeling he's in trouble."

"It isn't safe out there, Ave."

Avery spun around to face him. "I wouldn't say it's all that safe here either." She looked up at him and softened her tone. "Something is wrong, and time is ticking. Please. I think I might know where to look. I can't explain why I'm so sure, I just am."

"Your mom called it women's intuition." Harrison sighed.

"Was she ever wrong?"

"Not that I can recall." He pointed to the expanse of ice between them and the shore. "How do you plan to navigate across that?"

"We've got the snowshoes Noah sent. And I have an idea."

They stood at the top of the steel gangway leading down to the ice and stared out across the frozen shelf.

"You know it won't do Carter any good if we both die looking for him," Harrison said.

"Carter wouldn't abandon us out here," Avery said as she snapped a Guru frostbite prevention mask and goggles over her face, muffling her reply.

"*Only* Carter would get himself into a mess like this, Ave. He's a risk-taker who thinks there's a guardian angel riding on his shoulder twenty-four hours a day."

"If he's out there without us, someone forced him off the ship, Harry. And he needs our help. If you don't come with me, I'll go on my own."

"Avery Turner, you're the most stubborn woman I have ever met."

"Are you forgetting my mother?"

Harrison smiled. "Okay, the second-most stubborn woman."

Avery adjusted Harrison's goggles for him, then shoved his snowshoes into his hand. "Let's go, grumpy."

Once out on the ice, Avery examined the wreckage of the Sno-Cats and the debris field left behind by the explosion. The fuel had largely burned off, leaving only charred and twisted hunks of metal scattered about the ice.

"Owen is right," she said. "There are four vehicles and this is definitely not more than three."

Which meant someone else had to be missing. Closing her eyes, she ran back through the crowd she'd seen on the deck right after the fire.

"Seamus!" Avery blurted as she opened her eyes and turned to Harrison.

"Excuse me?"

"Have you seen him since the explosion? On board or anywhere else?"

Harrison paused. "Now you mention it, no. I haven't."

"I saw him this morning, headed down the gangway with something smallish and heavy before anyone else should have been up. How much plastic explosive would somebody need?" Avery said. "I mean, to cause all this?"

"Not really my wheelhouse, Ave. But I wouldn't think someone would need all that much to blow up a few of these things. There's a lot of glass on them. As it is, this feels like overkill. Either whoever did it didn't want to risk there being any chance of them being repaired, or . . ."

Avery waited, lifting her eyebrows. "Or?"

"Or they didn't know what they were doing."

Avery couldn't argue with his logic.

"Let's say you're right," Harrison said. "Why would Seamus want to damage his own ship?"

"Like you said, he has no intention of returning," Avery said. "Perhaps he intends to recover the treasure and escape, now he knows where the *Fortitude* is located."

"So he took Carter along to help?" Harrison mused.

"Forced him, you mean," Avery said. "No way Carter would be involved in any of this willingly, Harry."

Avery and Harrison walked around inside the debris field. Other members of the crew had joined them on the ice, but they seemed solely focused on the damaged hull of the *Weddell*.

Avery stopped suddenly, nearly causing Harrison to collide with her.

"What is it?" Harrison said.

"I just had a thought," Avery said.

"Jeez, Ave. You scared me. I was picturing a landmine or something."

"Get real, Harry. Erin told us about Seamus finding Noah off the ship a few weeks ago. Said he was blown off by a strong wind. What if there was more to the story?"

"Like what?"

"Maybe Seamus shoved him off, or something, then they both cooked up a story to provide cover for what they were up to. Maybe Noah is right in the middle of whatever is happening here."

"Some kind of power struggle, you mean?"

"Why not? Do the math. They are running out of time to find the *Fortitude*. They bring Carter and me in to help them find the ship. Except there's serious money at play that Noah's not super forthcoming about. Seamus discovers that, maybe by talking to Tuva, maybe by eavesdropping on Noah . . . now there's some kind of power struggle between Seamus and Noah and each one is trying to get to the treasure before the other."

"Maybe this treasure really is cursed," Harrison said as he surveyed the nearby ground. "But if you're right, Seamus appears to be leading the charge to it now. I still don't see how any of this helps us, though. If Seamus does have Carter, and all the dive gear, he also has a Sno-Cat and an hour's head start."

"But they went over land. We don't have to. Noah said something about storage on the shelf when we were out the other day. Come on."

Harry followed her, his long legs barely keeping pace with her urgent strides. "Can they dive the wreck without your help?"

"If they've stolen the DiveNav they can."

38

The *Weddell* growing smaller in the distance by the step, Avery and Harrison trudged over the ice along what constituted the shoreline at the base of several very tall rock pinnacles. Though technically daytime, the sun had sunk lower still. Peeking just above the horizon, it provided only the dimmest of filtered light.

"How much farther are you planning to go?" Harrison said.

"Not much, Harry," Avery said as she pointed up ahead. "If I'm right, what we're looking for is just around the next bend."

"I hope so, Ave. If not, we need to think about turning back. There's no way we can get to the dive location from here in time to stop Carter from being sent underwater."

"I think we can. The fastest way out there is directly across the water. We can bisect the arc of the shelf."

"Were you thinking of skipping across those ice floes?"

"Of course not, Harry. Noah said they have a small boat-storage unit when we were riding out to see the dive site. I figure the cliffs would provide shelter for such a thing. And . . . it looks like I'm right." She pointed to a white metal outbuilding so well camouflaged a person would walk right past if they weren't looking for it.

They trekked to the metal building, finding four storage lifts holding four RIBs in all, each with its own motor.

"All the boats are here and accounted for," Harrison said. "And there's no sign of the remaining Sno-Cat having come by here. Now what?"

"Now we get one of these into the water, then motor across to the dive site, hopefully shaving off a lot of their head start by cutting across the water."

They wrestled with one of the lower inflatables, sliding it out of its bay until it was sitting freely on the ice, then pushing it toward the shoreline and the open water.

"Whatever you do, Harry, don't fall in."

"Appreciate the safety tip, Ave."

Once they were both safely inside the craft, Avery lowered the prop into the water and fired up the motor.

"You sure we won't get caught in between the ice floes?" Harrison said, shouting to be heard above the motor. "This thing isn't all that big, Ave. But some of these ice chunks are. What if we get stuck?"

Avery wasn't sure of anything, but she had no intention of abandoning Carter.

"We won't." She said it because it was the only option.

Carter struggled to remove the dive equipment from the back of the Sno-Cat while Seamus stood nearby with a gun trained on him. He hadn't said much of anything, opting instead to let his gun do most of the talking. Carter would bet he was about to be forced to dive the wreck of the *Fortitude*, a dive for which he was realistically probably too ill-prepared right then to survive.

He'd found himself in some scrapes before, chasing the adrenaline rush that came with taking risks, but somehow this felt different. Standing in one of the most remote locations on the planet while a gun-toting treasure hunter forced his hand wouldn't bode well for his future plans. He needed to find a way to disarm Seamus and get back to the ship.

"So, how long have you been searching for the *Fortitude*?" Carter said, trying desperately to buy more time by making conversation. He'd only gone along on what he was pretty sure would be nearly a suicide mission because the gun meant refusing was immediate suicide, and at least if he was still breathing, he had hope of getting himself out of this. But now that they were at the edge of the shelf, time was running out.

Seamus opened his mouth to speak before closing it again.

Carter gestured toward the gun. "You know, if you kill me, there is nobody else on board who can make this dive."

"Conversely, if you refuse to make the dive, or try and run, you'll be of little use to me, and I'll be forced to shoot you. It's better if you just cooperate, Mr. Mosley."

"How do I know you won't just shoot me when I resurface?"

"You don't. But I hear you enjoy risk-taking, so try and think of this as an adventure."

"You need to tell me everything you know about where the treasure might be," Carter said as he leaned into the Sno-Cat and removed one of the dive tanks, checking gauges slowly. "The *Fortitude* is a big ship, and whatever is on board is likely well hidden. I might run out of time before I can find it."

"There is no treasure on board," Seamus said.

"But I thought—" Carter looked up at Seamus.

"Noah Wyndham is a fool," Seamus snarled. "He has bungled this entire project, gambled away his family's fortune. Now he's grasping at the edge of a cliff the loan sharks are about to kick him off."

"If the treasure isn't on the *Fortitude*, then why are you doing this?"

"I want full credit for the discovery. Which I'll get, assuming you survive the dive. Unlike Noah, I am a serious scientist. I didn't come from money, and I don't have Noah's connections. I've had to make my own luck to get here, Mr. Mosley, and will continue to do so. Now, climb into the Cat and suit up before yours runs out."

Avery spotted the Sno-Cat before Harrison did and pointed it out from the water. They could clearly see Carter and Seamus standing beside it.

"I'll be damned," Harrison muttered.

Carter had already donned the dive suit, and Seamus held something . . . Avery squinted. "Jesus, is that a gun?" she blurted.

Harrison nodded. "Sure is," he said grimly.

Seamus was pointing a gun at Carter, and Carter was getting ready to go into the water. It had taken them longer to get here by water than Avery had imagined. Dodging ice floes had added substantial time to their trip.

"There's no way we're going to be able to sneak up on them, Ave," Harrison said.

As if in answer to Harrison's comment, Seamus spun around and fired twice in their direction. One of the bullets ricocheted off a nearby ice floe before passing so closely over their heads that they both heard the whine as the projectile split the air.

Avery turned the boat hard to starboard, attempting to increase their distance from Seamus, but collided with a large chunk of jagged ice.

"Careful, Ave!" Harrison shouted as he grabbed for a handhold.

The sudden jolt nearly capsized the RIB, which would have thrown both of them into the frigid water, where they would have frozen to death almost immediately.

Avery straightened their course before turning back to look at Seamus and Carter. She was just in time to see Carter shuck his air tank so fast it blurred as he slammed it down on the arm holding Seamus's gun. The weapon skittered across the ice, Seamus scrambling after it. As Seamus bent to retrieve the gun, Carter struck him again, this time in the side of the head, knocking the rogue engineer unconscious.

Avery's attention returned to the water as she attempted to bring the boat around.

"Get on it, Ave!" Harrison shouted again. "We're sinking."

Avery could see for herself that the RIB was beginning to take on water. The ice floe she had struck must have ripped a hole in the side of the inflatable craft. Waves splashed up over the gunwale, and they were still at least forty feet from shore, with several ice floes in between.

"Hang on, Harry," Avery called over the whine as she opened the throttle all the way.

The RIB shot forward. They sliced through the water, every bit of

Avery's formidable brainpower focused on dodging the moving chunks of ice. She'd never been so thankful for her hand-to-hand training, the reflexes she'd honed likely saving them from a deadly impact.

Even the small waves in the relatively calm water sloshed up and over the bow, sending more icy ocean water onto the floor of the boat and wetting their boots. Despite the motor operating at full capacity, Avery felt the RIB begin to slow. The weight of the seawater added to their own was more than the little motor could handle. They were less than ten feet from the shoreline where Carter stood waiting for them, but Avery's plan to pull alongside the shore and climb out was rendered useless by how quickly they were sinking. She stared across the ice floes and water, meeting Carter's gaze.

"Come on, Avery," he shouted. "You can do this."

Avery nodded once, narrowing her eyes. She was not dying out here six steps from relative safety. There had to be a way to cross it without falling in. She studied the front of her sinking craft and the ice floes and shoreline, physics equations and geometry zipping quickly through her thoughts.

"Climb back here with me, Harry!" Avery yelled. "We've gotta get the nose up. I'm only gonna have one shot at this."

Harrison scrambled toward the stern as Avery aimed straight in toward the shore and gave the sputtering motor everything it could muster with a final rev. The bow of the RIB bounced up and over the bank, sliding forward on the ice until all forward momentum was gone. The RIB was caught on the edge, with the bow up and the motor nearly underwater.

"Go, Harry!" Avery gave him a light push. "I'm right behind you."

"I'm not leaving you, Ave," Harrison said.

"We don't have time to argue," Avery snapped. "You're heavier than me. Go!"

"Come on, come on," Carter screamed, holding out a hand.

Harrison scrambled as quickly as he could toward the front of the unstable craft. He looked like a big kid trying to navigate a moon bounce. Carter grabbed Harrison's outstretched hands just as the RIB's motor went under, stalling immediately. Avery shrieked as Harrison leapt to the ice, landing slightly awkwardly, but safe.

Half a second later, she dove into Carter's arms, knocking him backward onto the ice.

The three of them lay on the shore, watching as the RIB slid off the icy shelf and disappeared beneath the waves.

Carter climbed to his feet, then helped Avery up.

"Thanks," she said, brushing snow off her pants.

"What a day," Carter said, turning to offer Harrison a hand.

"Is your knee okay?" Avery asked.

Harrison tested his weight on it and nodded.

"What do we do with him?" Avery asked, pointing at Seamus. He was moving, but slowly.

"I say we leave him right there," Harrison said.

"We can't do that, Harry, and you know it," Avery said.

"We give him snowshoes then. Make him walk back."

"Come on, Harry," Carter said. "At the very least he's got a concussion. If we leave him here he'll die, and I don't want that on my conscience. Do you?"

"He had no problem trying to kill us," Harrison said.

Both Avery and Carter stared wordlessly at Harrison. Avery placed her hands on her hips.

Harrison sighed deeply, fogging up his goggles in the process. "Oh, all right. Come on, I'll help you restrain him. Just remember this is what always happens in the movies just before everything goes to hell."

The three of them bound Seamus with nylon straps before loading him and the remaining gear into the Sno-Cat. Harrison held the gun and kept an eye on Seamus while Carter, still in the dive suit, drove them back to the *Weddell*.

39

"Is that a . . . person?" Avery asked, pointing out the windshield of the Sno-Cat about halfway back to the *Weddell*. Carter nodded, and Harrison leaned forward from his post guarding a half-conscious Seamus.

"I don't immediately recognize that coat," he said. "Does anyone on our ship have black-and-orange gear?"

Avery shook her head. "It looks like they're drilling a hole in the shelf. That won't break part of it off or anything, will it?"

"You're asking us?" Carter glanced at Harrison in the rearview mirror. Harrison shrugged.

"Not really," Avery said. "Just trying to figure out what the heck is going to go wrong out here now."

Carter veered just slightly so they'd get close enough to take a look.

As the Sno-Cat rumbled forward, the Stay-Puft-outfitted figure turned and watched, then waved at them. Avery put a hand on Carter's arm. "Let's go see what's up."

"Half the people we've met here, like, escaped from the villains cast in a forties movie," Carter said. "You want to stop out here and talk to a stranger?"

"Harry has a gun, and it's not like everyone's a suspect—Erin and Owen are both fine. Right?"

"I vouch for Erin," Carter said.

"And I can for Noah."

Carter sighed and pulled even with the prospector, letting in the cold when he opened the door.

"First time I've run into someone out on the shelf," a deep, booming voice said. "I'm Jonas Gurley, first assistant at the US NOAA outpost."

"A fellow American," Harrison exclaimed, and Carter laughed.

"Don't mind Harrison, he's easily excited. I'm Carter Mosley, this is Avery Turner, and that's Harrison."

Harry, holding the gun down behind the seat out of sight, nodded.

Jonas tipped his head to Seamus. "He okay? We have an onsite medic."

"He's fine," Harry said. "Just struggling with this constant sun like all of us, and exhausted."

Jonas chuckled. "I can relate. But in a few days it'll be so dark nobody will want to do anything but sleep for the next two months. I've been on-continent for twenty-seven months, and the cycle never fails."

"Twenty-seven months!" Avery's jaw fell open. "How do you take the isolation for so long?"

"We have a small but tight group at our station here," Jonas said. "Between my friends, my work, and a decent internet connection, it's not intolerable. Most of the time." He turned back to Carter. "So, what kind of adrenaline rush have you chased to Antarctica, Mr. Mosley? And am I on camera?"

"I'm not at liberty to say, and no," Carter said. "You follow my channel?"

"I'm a marine biologist by background and a climate researcher by happenstance," Jonas said. "I love your dive videos." He blinked, giving Carter a once-over. "You're not trying to dive here?"

"Not today," Carter said.

"This place can be awfully treacherous, man," Jonas said. "And there are about three dozen international treaties governing different things about the water and the marine life, just so you know. In case you're tempted."

Seamus stirred. "He's going tomorrow."

Avery rolled her eyes and shook her head. "He talks in his sleep. Before we stopped, there was a horse running away with his puppy."

Jonas looked from Carter to Seamus to Avery slowly.

"What're you doing out in this weather?" Avery asked.

"Before winter arrives, we'd like to have all our seasonal research stations set up. We're studying the formation of the sea ice here and how the shelf thickens in the winter months to see if it's possible to artificially replicate that to rebuild the shelf. I'm drilling a hole to place a sensor in this area that should send data back to us through a satellite linkup. If it doesn't glitch out in the cold. A lot of things do that here."

"We've noticed," Carter said.

Avery was glad Carter could talk, because she was at a complete loss for words, which may have been a first for her. The NOAA was doing nearly identical research to Noah's. Without project specifications, she couldn't be sure how close, but it was close enough. So had one of them stolen the other's idea, or did they just both think of the same thing? No way to know, but one thing was for sure: if Noah found out his grant funding or profits were in jeopardy because of this, she wasn't sure what he'd do.

During the remainder of the trip back to the *Weddell*, Seamus regained consciousness. He was belligerent and refusing to talk, but conscious.

"You realize Noah will see you as a traitor," Avery said.

"Probably send you packing," Harrison added. "Might be a good time to save your own skin, Slick, and tell us why you were out there and who else is involved in this. I don't buy for a minute that you knocked Erin out and kidnapped Carter here at gunpoint over a credit line in some science journal."

Seamus stared straight ahead, barely blinking.

"Erin!" Carter shook his head. "I'm a jerk, I didn't even ask about her. Is she okay?"

"She's got a cut on her head, but she'll live," Avery said.

"Teach me to make out in storerooms like a teenager. From now on I'll stick to her satin bedding and candlelight."

"Satin?" Avery asked incredulously. "The cold is actively trying to kill her and she sleeps on satin?"

"Red satin." Carter shrugged. "She likes the finer things. Like doors that lock." Carter pulled up as close to the *Weddell*'s gangplank as he dared, careful to avoid the debris from the ruined Sno-Cats.

"Well, Seamus, my lad, we're home," Harrison said as he climbed down from the Sno-Cat. "I wonder how comfy the brig is on this ship?"

Carter and Harrison removed the straps from around Seamus's boots before helping him down from the rear of the Sno-Cat. They each grabbed an arm and led him up the gangway. Avery followed.

As they reached the ship's side entrance, a small contingent of their shipmates hurried toward them.

"They're back," someone yelled.

"Man, we thought you had gone overboard," another said.

"Seamus saved the day again," someone shouted.

Avery's mouth hung agape. It was clear from some of the comments that there was confusion among the crew about what exactly had occurred. Avery realized Seamus still had friends on board and that the winter gear was camouflaging the bindings on his wrists.

Noah pushed his way to the center of the crowd. It was clear from the excited expression on his face he didn't comprehend what had happened either.

Avery leaned in close. "We need to talk." She moved to one side, allowing Noah to see the restraints on Seamus. Noah's eyes widened.

"In private," Carter added.

"Okay, everyone," Noah said. "We've all got jobs to do. I suggest we get back at it."

Noah's attention returned to Avery and the others. "Follow me."

Avery brought Noah up to speed, watching his eyes get wider as she talked.

"Do you mean to say Seamus is responsible for blowing up my Sno-Cats?" Noah asked. "And my ship?"

Harrison and Carter nodded.

"But why?" Noah asked, looking directly at Seamus. "Why would you intentionally sabotage everything we've worked for?"

Seamus only returned a blank look.

"He said he wanted credit for the discovery of the ship," Carter offered.

"I don't buy that for a minute," Harrison said.

"I'm not sure I do, either," Noah said. "He was slated to be credited." He turned to Carter. "Is the dive equipment intact? Was that tank damaged?"

"Not that I could tell, but I pride myself on my thorough predate routine. I'll be sure before it goes in the water." Carter gestured to the suit. "This fits great and is surprisingly warm."

Noah turned a glare on Seamus. The pronounced lump on the side of his head, from being struck with the air tank by Carter, had ceased bleeding. Aside from the fact that he wasn't speaking, Seamus appeared fine physically.

"We need a secure place to hold him," Avery said.

"Do you have any security on board?" Harrison said.

Noah shook his head and laughed weakly. "Budget concerns, remember? This is a ship full of scientists in one of the most remote locations on the planet. We have a doctor. Who needs security?"

"You do," Carter said.

"Looks like you've just been hired, Harry," Avery said.

"What about benefits?" Harrison said. "I must have paid vacations."

"Your life is a paid vacation," Carter said.

Avery turned her attention back to Noah. "Is there a room with an outside lock somewhere on the ship?"

"Do you really think that's necessary?"

"Yeah, Doc, we do," Avery said.

"He kidnapped me at gunpoint," Carter said.

"And shot at us," Harrison added.

"So, do you have any such rooms?" Avery said.

"All we have is the walk-in freezer and the dry goods storeroom."

Harrison moved in closer to Seamus. "I vote for the freezer. How about you, Slick?"

"We can't keep him in the freezer, Harry," Avery said.

"What a shame," Harrison said as he pulled Seamus to his feet. "Okay, dry storage it is. Come on."

After Harrison and Seamus departed, Avery rounded on Noah. "We need answers, Noah. And if Seamus won't talk, you'll have to."

"Answers about what?"

"What happened with you and Seamus recently? We heard something from one of the crew about you being blown off the ship in a gust of wind, which sounded a little far-fetched if I'm being honest. That isn't what happened, is it?"

Noah hung his head. "No, it isn't."

"Well?" Carter said. "Spill it."

"The truth is I wanted to try and use the portable onboard sonar unit myself to locate the *Fortitude*. I'd been looking for a way to transport it off the *Weddell* without raising suspicion."

"And?" Avery said as she grew more impatient.

"And the whale attack on our ship provided me with good cover. I mean, there wasn't as much chaos as there was today, but it was considerable. I set out from the *Weddell* with the sonar, looking to take one of the RIBs out to search. It wasn't long before I realized I was being followed—by Seamus. When I asked what he was doing, he told me he was concerned about my safety. We concocted the story about the wind gust and the fall when Tuva saw us coming back aboard together, hunched over and tired from lugging the equipment through the cold."

"You don't really believe he was worried about you?" Carter said.

"After today? No."

"Could it be that the person funding this search has decided you're not up to the task at hand?" Avery asked.

"What would that have to do with Seamus?"

"Maybe your collector put him on the payroll," Carter said. "Turned him against you. Sort of a winner takes all."

"Is the donor you're protecting capable of double dealing on you?" Avery asked.

"I don't know even who it is." Noah raised both hands. "Honestly. I borrowed the last of the money I could scrape up from a shady character with offices in Hackney, and three days later I got a box with a note, a weird phone, and some fancy VR goggles. It was an offer to make up the difference in my funding if I could find the *Fortitude*—and the treasure. No names, just a wire transfer and an innocuous email address. I'm not protecting anyone."

"Then who were you texting when we found the *Fortitude*?" Avery said. "And don't deny it. I saw you."

"I won't deny it, but I honestly don't know who it is."

"You expect us to believe that after we've seen what a good liar you are?" Carter said.

"Believe it or don't, it's the truth. I received a package just like you did. It's where I got the idea. The contact phone was included in mine."

"And it just happens to get a signal?" Avery said. "None of ours will function here."

"It's not a normal phone. And I can only communicate with one number. Here, see for yourself."

Noah handed the phone to Avery. She and Carter looked at the number Noah had been sending texts to.

"Where are all the text messages?" Avery said. "It looks like you wiped the history on this."

"I haven't deleted anything. Whomever is on the other end of this phone controls everything."

"Have you tried calling it?" Carter said.

"It only functions as a text messenger."

"And this is how you communicate with your benefactor?" Carter said.

"I don't think the person I'm texting with is the person with the money. Just by the responses I get. Feels like they need to report back before I get further instructions."

"Who do you think it is then?" Avery said.

"It has to be an employee."

Avery snapped a photo of the number showing on the phone before handing it back to Noah. She knew Harrison still had contacts in the law enforcement and intelligence communities. If they couldn't figure out who was behind the number, no one could.

"And what kind of information have you been sharing with your mysterious text buddy?" Carter said.

"I keep them apprised of what's happening here, per the agreement I made when I came here. One message a day, more for major developments."

"You told them about the discovery of the *Fortitude*," Avery said.

"Of course I did."

Avery watched Noah's expression shift. Just slightly, but the tell was unmistakable. He was lying. He hadn't shared the discovery at all.

"No, you didn't," Avery said. "You stalled them, didn't you?"

Noah said nothing.

"You're making a big mistake if you think Seamus won't rat you out," Avery said. "Or maybe he already has. Seems to me he's after the treasure too."

"I don't think he is, Avery." Carter tapped his chin.

"What are you talking about? He nearly killed you to try and get to the ship first."

"But the more I think about what he said, the more I believe him," Carter said. "He insisted he wanted full credit for the discovery, but only proof that the *Fortitude* had been located. He said there is no treasure and called Noah a fool."

"No treasure?" Noah said. "I assure you I'm not the fool in this situation."

"I don't know enough of the history to take sides," Carter said. "But he thinks you're wasting all your time and money chasing the jewels. He doesn't even believe they are down there. I really think maybe he's just after the recognition as an explorer."

"That's why he's never risen to my station," Noah said. "Seamus is short-sighted in more ways than one."

"He's not a big fan of yours either," Carter said.

"How do you mean?"

"Something about your connections and rich friends. Gambling your family fortune away? He appears to have nothing but disdain for you."

"I have never gambled in my life," Noah said.

"I think Seamus meant this trip," Carter said.

Noah sighed. "I never would have guessed it. Seamus has always been so quiet and reserved."

Carter looked at Avery. "That's what they said about Jeffrey Dahmer."

"I wondered where you had all gotten off to," Erin said as she entered the office with a freshly applied bandage on her head.

Avery noticed Erin's focus was squarely on Carter.

"Do you need something, Erin?" Noah asked.

"Yes, Dr. Wyndham. I thought you'd like to know there's a chopper approaching."

Noah's brow rose.

"Are you expecting anyone?" Avery asked.

"No," Noah said as he pushed himself out of his seat. "I'm not."

40

Avery and Carter followed Noah to the bridge. The approaching gray-and-black chopper looked to be military, the rhythmic *wup wup* of its rotors pounding through the desolate Antarctic stillness.

"Fool—he's going to crack the shelf landing so close to the edge!" Noah swore under his breath, waving his arms in a *go away* gesture.

"You really have no idea who that is?" Avery asked.

"Why would I lie?" Noah huffed. "We aren't expecting any emergency supplies either."

"How did a helicopter get all the way out here?" Carter said. "I wouldn't think there would be enough fuel."

"And you'd be correct," Noah said. "A chopper couldn't fly all the way across the Weddell Sea. It had to have taken off from a ship."

As the chopper's main rotor began to power down, a lone, heavily bundled figure jumped down onto the ice, toting a large pack. It was impossible to tell anything about identity with the outerwear and distance.

"I suppose we have company whether we like it or not," Noah said. "Let's go meet our mystery guest."

Avery and Carter exchanged an uneasy glance as they waited with several other members of the crew at the top of the gangway while Noah descended the ramp to greet their unannounced visitor. In her limited treasure hunting experience, someone showing up unannounced via what had to be an expensive trip never portended anything good. It made her doubly glad Harrison was now armed with Seamus's gun.

Avery watched as Noah engaged in a brief interaction with their mystery guest before turning to head up the ramp.

"They must be welcome," Avery said.

"Welcome or not, here they come," the equipment tech who'd lost the fingers said.

There was a moment of unease as Avery watched their visitor untangle themselves from the cold-weather attire. Her unease multiplied when she immediately recognized the interloper: NOAA Agent Allison Miranda.

"Agent Miranda," Carter blurted, making no attempt to hide his surprise.

"You folks know each other?" Noah said, equally surprised.

"Not well," Avery said. "But we have met once before. Nice to see you again, Agent Miranda."

"Time will tell, Ms. Turner," Miranda said.

"Why exactly have you come here?" Noah asked. "You weren't invited, and I don't remember receiving any requests. This is a privately funded expedition."

"Precisely why I'm here, Doctor. My superiors are concerned about what may be happening here from a science standpoint. And they'd like a full report on the discovery of the *Fortitude* before word leaks to the public."

"How could you even know about that?" Carter asked.

"Good question," Noah said. "We haven't told anyone."

"We're the United States government. We know everything, Dr. Wyndham." She waved a dismissive hand. "Now, is there somewhere I can stow my gear? Maybe get a cup of coffee?"

"I'm not sure on what authority you think you can just waltz in here and start ordering us around, Ms. Miranda," Noah said.

"It's Agent Miranda, and as I've said, my authority comes from the government of the United States, as well as the Antarctic Treaty of 1959 and the Antarctic Conservation Act. I have full authority on behalf of the

United States government to inspect your operations and to enforce civil and international criminal penalties on you and your crew for any chemical discharges into these protected waters." She gave Carter a once-over. "Which includes but is not limited to the use of some certain mixed deepwater diving gases. You're more than welcome to check with my superiors. I'm sure they'd be very interested in your lack of cooperation. Perhaps you're hiding something?"

"I'm not hiding anything," Noah said.

"I'm glad to hear it."

"It's just so typical of you Americans to think you can force your way into the middle of our research." Noah looked at Avery. "I guess it doesn't matter all that much now anyway."

"Oh?" Miranda said. "And why is that?"

"Because, Agent Miranda, we've been sabotaged by our chief mechanical engineer, Seamus O'Leary. Perhaps you noticed the damage to our ship and Sno-Cats on the way in? My ship is a wreck, winter is coming, the sea ice will multiply quicker, and we're about to lose the sun. It seems the signs are all pointing to the exit."

"Nobody's going anywhere anytime soon," Miranda said.

"Why is that?" Avery said.

"Because, Ms. Turner," Miranda said, "there's a storm coming."

Miranda turned her attention back to Noah. "Now, Doctor, about that cabin. Oh, and I'll need to speak with this chief engineer. Seamus, wasn't it?"

"What the hell is she doing here?" Harrison said from his post outside Seamus's temporary detention storeroom.

"It seems pretty clear that she talked to Jonas," Avery said. "But she also already knew about the discovery of the *Fortitude*."

"Jonas, the guy we met like three hours ago?"

"Yes—she was prattling about how the dive gases would pollute the water and she needed to monitor our activities for things that are bad for the environment. Like we're not trying to save it or something."

"And how in the world could she have known about the *Fortitude*?" Harry asked.

"She wouldn't say," Avery said.

"I knew someone on board was leaking information." Harrison shook his head. "Trust me when I tell you nothing good will come from her being here. Nothing good ever comes from the feds showing up."

"Good to see you too, Mr. Harrison," Miranda said from behind him.

"It's Detective," Harrison said.

"Retired though, right? Means you're a civilian now. Zero authority. Not that you'd have any out here anyway."

"It doesn't seem to me that we have any evidence of your authority either," Harrison said. "Forgive me if I'm skeptical of your word."

"I am here as a federal agent on behalf of the United States," Miranda huffed. "A local police officer's reach is much more limited."

Avery watched Harrison's face redden. She knew he was at a tipping point when it came to Miranda. Avery made eye contact with him and gave the slightest shake of her head.

"Now, if you'd kindly step aside, I'd like to speak with Mr. O'Leary," Miranda said.

"You do know he shot at us," Harrison said. "Kidnapped Carter at gunpoint."

"My understanding is he's been disarmed," Miranda said. "So, unless you're concerned he might hit me over the head with a can of tuna, I need you to let me pass."

Harrison took a step back, muttering about bigger cans than tuna.

"Thank you," Miranda said as she brushed past him.

"I'm still coming with you," Harrison said.

"Suit yourself," Miranda said.

Harrison leaned into Avery as he passed, muttering, "God, I hate that woman."

41

Avery made a beeline for her laptop and checked the connection, hoping to send the email she'd written to MaryAnn earlier along with a postscript asking for records on Allison. A certified genius, Avery didn't need nearly all her brainpower to know there was something off about Agent Miranda's sudden arrival. This was the second time she had shown up out of the blue, butting into something that really shouldn't have been her concern.

Red box, blinking stop sign. No service. Avery stared at it for a few seconds and had to restrain herself from slamming the computer shut.

"Whatcha doing?" Carter said as he gave a quick knock before opening the door to Avery's cabin.

"I'm trying to sic MaryAnn on our international trespasser, but nothing here works most of the time."

Carter walked to the wall, unplugged the cable, waited, and plugged it back in. Avery's screen cleared, a small green connection dot appearing in the top corner. "It does feel like there's more going on with Miranda than meets the eye."

"I agree. And if you say I should've unplugged that cord before you thought of it, I'll punch you." She pushed Send quickly on the email and watched the progress bar: 31 percent, 47, 68.

It stopped and flashed the red error box again and Avery shrieked.

"I don't know what else to try, and I don't want to get hit." Carter ducked backward like he was evading a swing.

"Why does everything here hate me?" Avery asked.

"I don't think that's true."

"The internet has been out for days, and it comes back for ten seconds with your 1995 Wi-Fi trick, only to go right back off? That can't be random."

"This place is full of things that seem random on the surface but also seem impossibly calculated," Carter said. "Like it can't be a coincidence, this same chick who clearly doesn't like us showing up to the last two searches we've been involved in. You really think NOAA gives a damn about a sunken ship in Antarctica, other than maybe for the news coverage?"

"I have no idea," Avery said. "They have an outpost here that's well funded and constantly staffed, which I didn't know until today."

"But you could disappear into potholes on the interstate in Miami," Carter said. "Nice use of taxpayer money."

"One crisis at a time," Avery said. "The most frustrating thing right now is that I could check Miranda's story myself if this thing would work for ten minutes. She said she was from the Boston NOAA post. I've got a contact up in Boston that my mother used to work with."

"You know what would explain all the seemingly not random but also random bad luck?"

"Do not say a curse."

"I didn't have to. You just did."

"Are you still planning to attempt the dive?" Avery asked, changing the subject.

"Of course," Carter said. "Why wouldn't I?"

"Because we are having the worst luck of anything that's not a cartoon cat trying to eat a bird or a mouse, and I don't want you to die."

"I've done deep-water dives before, Avery," Carter said. "Believe me, I'm not keen on the idea of spending eternity here as food for the seals. No one is better at checking equipment than me, and no one is better at numbers than you. You said yourself this is possible to do and survive. I'm telling you, we got this from both sides. If anyone can do it, we can."

"But what if someone sabotages something? I'm not inclined to trust anyone at this point."

"Your concern is duly noted, but I think we've flushed out the problem. Seamus isn't an issue any longer."

"You can't assume he's the only problem."

"How many saboteurs do you think there are aboard this ship?"

"At least one more," Avery said. "Someone broke into my room and stole the DiveNav, I think after you and Seamus were off the ship. He didn't have it, did he?"

"What? No, I didn't see it."

"But it's gone."

"Can I do the dive without it?"

Avery nodded. "The program I wrote for the dive is on my laptop, and so is my prototype of the DiveNav software. It would be easier if you could take the handheld, but it's not impossible without it. But someone is still targeting us."

"Any ideas?" Carter asked, tipping his head when Avery bit her lip. He watched her for three beats before his eyes narrowed. "Do not say Erin."

"Okay I won't. You just did," Avery muttered.

"Why don't you like her?"

"I couldn't care less about Erin," Avery corrected. "I'm worried about you, Carter."

"I appreciate it, and I get it, I really do—but I'm not saying we've got this lightly. You've run the numbers. You wrote a new computer program in a day, for crying out loud. I will quadruple-check the gear to the last pin and nozzle. You saw those underwater drone shots of the ship. People have been searching for this wreck for more than a hundred years. It's our generation's *Titanic*, and I can be the first person to see it. Do you have any idea what kind of boost to my fanbase a dive video of the *Fortitude* will have?"

"That's what this is about, Carter? Your stupid followers?"

"My followers are not stupid, Avery. In case you've forgotten, those followers are how I make my living. Followers mean advertising dollars. Besides, assuming you still care about finding the lost jewels, I have to make this dive. Tell me you're not excited about recovering another treasure."

As much as she hated to admit it, Carter was right. Avery was still excited about the prospect, and the possibility they might find out what happened to Tuva's great-grandfather.

"What about Noah?" Avery asked.

"What about him?" Carter replied with a smirk. "I don't have to turn over anything I find. Noah's not making this dive. I am."

"In case you've forgotten, you'll be wearing a live video camera. Noah will be able to see everything you see."

"Trust me. I know how to keep things off camera. Which reminds me, have you finished the dive calculations?"

Avery pointed to her screen. "All I lack is your most recent cholesterol level and VO2 max."

"I have that saved in my phone." He went to his cabin and came back, flipping the screen so she could copy the numbers.

The computer spit out a long list of letters and numbers and Avery sat back and clapped. "Assuming all my calculations are correct, you should be good to go."

"Then I need to start examining gear, because if Agent Miranda was right, we'll have to move quickly."

"Right about what?"

Before Carter could answer, someone knocked on the door. Carter answered it. It was Noah.

"What's up?" Avery asked.

"I just received confirmation," Noah said. "Agent Miranda was right. There is a squall coming. And we've got less than twenty hours before it arrives."

Carter turned to Avery. "Looks like it's now or never."

42

Avery examined the air tanks Carter would be using, while Noah helped Carter into the dry suit. All the equipment appeared to match what her research required for him to make this dive safely. *Or at least as safely as a dive could be made under an ice shelf at the edge of Antarctica*, she thought.

"How do we know Seamus didn't sabotage the equipment?" Noah asked.

Avery's stomach dropped at the suggestion.

"Because I was with him the entire time," Carter said. "He never had the chance. Besides, I've checked and rechecked every piece of gear. Everything is tip-top."

Carter looked at Avery, apparently sensing her lack of confidence.

"Seriously, Avery. It's all good. What's next?"

She took a deep breath and continued her speech. "Your next gas mixture switch will need to happen at three hundred feet."

"My dive watch is only rated to a depth of two fifty. It'll never survive this dive."

"Then maybe that's an indicator you shouldn't go," Avery said.

"I'm tougher than a bit of plastic and microchips."

"Is that so?" Avery said as she reached out and punched him in the arm.

"Ouch," Carter said unconvincingly.

Avery knew the research she had conducted for this dive was solid. Her numbers were correct. But she couldn't help but worry. And Carter was right about his own intelligence and skill with the equipment. But it still felt like there were too many variables to contend with. Too many things that could go horribly wrong in a place where so much already had.

"What's this?" Carter asked as Noah handed him a small, banded device.

"*That* is one of the many expensive toys our benefactor supplied for this search," Noah said. "It's rudimentary but it has everything you'll need."

"Depth, time, mixture switches," Avery said, taking it from Carter.

"It also monitors his heart rate and feeds it back to this within a thousand-foot range." Noah held up a rectangular monitor that looked like a first-generation smartphone.

Carter pressed on the rubberized coating surrounding the bezel. "And this thing is rated deeper than my watch?"

"The manufacturer's recommended depth is 750 feet," Noah said. "Beyond that, it would require reinforcing."

"Let's hope I won't need to go deeper than that," Carter said with a nervous chuckle. "Have you done any independent testing on this thing?"

"It was strapped to the drone yesterday," Noah said. "As you can see, it's still intact and functioning."

"This is some radical equipment," Carter said. "And you've got a backup set for everything? Suits, tanks, regulators?"

"Redundancy is the key to successful research, Mr. Mosley," Noah said. "Without it we wouldn't have lasted a week in these conditions."

Avery ran down the requirements again, for Carter's benefit as well as her own. "You'll dive with two twenty-liter side-mounted cylinders. The first is a trimix: 18 percent oxygen, 45 percent helium, and 37 percent nitrogen. That will give you enough time to make the dive, then spend twenty minutes or so inside the wreck."

She paused when she noticed Carter was preoccupied with the dive computer Noah had just handed him. "Are you getting all of this?"

"Yeah. Got it. I know it looks like I'm not listening, but I heard everything you said. Trimix on the descent, twenty minutes inside the *Fortitude*, and then?"

"On the way up, you'll need to switch to nitrox 50 percent at seventy feet."

"Fifty at seventy," Carter said. "Got it."

"Your last change will be the most important. At twenty feet you need to be sure to switch to pure oxygen."

"Pure oxygen. Check."

Noah attached what appeared to be a tiny camera to the right shoulder of Carter's dry suit.

"What is that?" Carter said.

"It's a waterproof camera with a satellite relay," Noah said. "It will feed directly back to the *Weddell*. Everything you see, we'll see."

Avery exchanged a quick glance with Carter. Neither said a word.

"And this was tested at depth too?" Carter said to Noah.

"Of course. We'll also be using short-range radios to keep track of where you are on the dive."

Carter pointed to a red tab on the front of the suit. "What is this?"

"That activates your heating element," Noah said. "Once you begin your ascent, you'll need to turn it on."

"But not before?" Carter said.

"No," Avery said. "During your descent you'll want to remain colder. The lower body temperature will help slow your system's uptake of dangerous gases to the blood."

"Besides, you won't need the heat at that point," Noah said.

"Why not?" Carter said.

"Because the water at the wreck will likely be as much as six degrees warmer than the surface temperature," Avery said.

"A veritable heat wave." Carter laughed.

"Don't joke about this, Carter," Avery said. "A lot can go wrong down there, and that six degrees is a lot in these conditions."

"I get it, Avery. Just trying to lighten things up."

Avery wasn't in the mood for jokes. But she was confident in the research she had done. Using water temperature data, air supply type, Carter's respiratory and pulse rates both resting and under stress, and his most recent blood cholesterol levels, her new program had calculated every aspect of this dive using his biometrics as a guide. If Carter followed her every step, he should be fine. It was the unknowns that troubled her.

"You'll need to be sure to keep your rate of descent below forty feet per minute," she said. "That will give your body time to adjust to the trimix."

"Got it," Carter said.

"Ascending, you'll need a total of nine decompression stops beginning at four hundred feet. Twenty-two minutes each. On your last decompression stop, at twenty feet, you'll need to flatten yourself out horizontally and switch the tank to pure oxygen for twenty minutes. That position will allow for the most even release of gases possible."

"And if I start to feel lightheaded at any point?" Carter said.

"Then you'll need to start your ascent immediately. And be sure to follow my protocol no matter what."

Carter gave her a wink.

"You shouldn't be doing this alone." Avery twisted her fingers together. "I don't want you getting hurt, Carter. It isn't worth it."

"You said it yourself, if I follow your instructions to the letter, I'll be fine."

"*Should* be fine, I said."

"Notice anything about the numbers you gave me?" Carter said.

"What?"

"All twos," Carter said. "My lucky number. Why do you think I named my dive boat back home *The Deuce*?"

Avery wished she shared his confidence.

"I'll be just fine," Carter said. "But I do appreciate your concern."

Avery locked eyes with Carter. He'd made the last comment almost wistfully, totally out of character for him. She leaned in and hugged him, perhaps a little tighter than necessary.

After Carter left with one of the crew, Avery turned to Noah. "Help me into this dry suit, and hand me the other fancy-pants dive watch."

"But I thought—"

"You thought what? I'd let him go down there without backup standing by? No way."

"He's going to see what you're up to, and he'll never let you take the same risk he allows for himself."

Avery was slightly surprised Noah was watching closely enough for such an astute observation. She knew Carter wouldn't want her in that water, especially not without him alongside her. But being ready just in case something happened would help her stay sane. "Not after you help me camouflage the dive suit with outdoor gear, he won't. Grab the spare tanks and regulator too."

"But I thought you said the dive instructions you gave him were designed around his biometrics."

"They are," Avery said, holding up the list of her own. "You said it yourself, Doc, redundancy is the key."

43

The interior of the Sno-Cat was already warm as they rolled toward the dive site. Too warm, given the amount of clothing Avery had donned over the specialized wetsuit. Avery and Noah rode in one of the Cats, while Carter and Erin occupied the one Noah and Owen had retrieved from Halley Station while Carter checked his gear repeatedly back on the *Weddell*.

Avery understood she wasn't nearly experienced enough to make this technical dive, but she also knew there was no way she could live with the knowledge that she'd left Carter stranded should something go wrong.

Harrison had balked at remaining behind, but Avery had insisted.

"I don't like the idea of you being out there alone, Ave," Harrison had said.

"You'll be able to monitor everything from the ship, Harry. And I won't be alone. Who else can I trust to stay with the *Weddell*?"

"Tell me again why we aren't moving the *Weddell* closer to the dive site?" Avery asked Noah. "I know you said something earlier but I barely heard you and I've been a little preoccupied. I wish Carter could make a more controlled dive from the moon pool."

"No doubt it would be the preferred method," Noah said. "But as you remember, I was forced to shut down after one of the engines began overheating during our last ice-cutting run. I don't dare to push it and risk taxing the other. We'll need both to get out of here."

Avery knew Noah was right, but she couldn't help but wonder, given the recent sabotage by the chief engineer, if the engine problem might also have been intentional. As they approached the designated dive site, she could only hope that Seamus had acted alone. If there were others actively engaged in sabotaging the mission, they could be anywhere among the crew.

Carter knelt on the floor of the inflatable boat, staring down into the crystal-blue depths of the Weddell Sea. Hundreds of feet below him lay a legendary ship not seen in more than a century. Ten years ago, he'd have given his left arm for a shot at a discovery like this one. Then came Instagram and a happenstance repost by a fashion celebrity and fame and money—and Avery and Harrison and the General's Gold. Today he'd probably still give his left arm for this, but he was sure glad he didn't have to. A dolphin glided by about thirty feet below, as if punctuating his thought: Everything he'd chased in his life had led him here.

"Go time," he said. He'd checked the equipment until his eyes crossed, and Avery had calculated dive parameters specific to him. Nothing left to do but jump.

Avery put one hand on his shoulder as he turned to perch carefully on the edge of the boat with his back to the water, settling his rebreather in place.

"Please be careful," she said. "Nothing is more important than you coming back up alive, okay?"

Carter nodded and gave her a thumbs-up as he pushed off with his legs.

And then he was gone.

Avery's thickly gloved hand went to her mouth as the water closed over Carter's head, a hunk of sea ice floating past as he began his descent. She used a pole to push it out of the way, noting that several of the ice floes had close to doubled in size since she'd been here with Noah just yesterday. They had to keep the area clear for Carter to resurface safely.

She could do that. She watched him shrink away under the water, pretty sure he was sticking to the maximum rate of descent she'd recommended. He would be fine. They'd run the numbers thirty times. He'd studied the ship's schematics and checked his equipment.

He disappeared into the dark below, and Avery took a seat to wait with Noah and Erin, focusing on the little monitor that showed Carter's heart rate strong and steady at ninety-one beats per minute.

He'd be okay.

He had to be.

Carter felt the frigid chill from the nearly frozen seawater radiating through the suit as he descended into the unknown. It was much like sitting next to a picture window on a subzero winter's day: uncomfortable, but nowhere near as bad as he had imagined. He was careful to follow Avery's instructions to the letter, descending just below the forty-feet-per-minute cap that she had set.

The diffused light filtering beneath the ice was an odd inky mixture of pool-liner blue and black depending upon where he focused his gaze. The sea life was plentiful. Curious penguins and seals darted about playfully nearby, while looming silhouettes of orcas glided past in the distance. The whales were remarkably graceful creatures, but after the story Noah had told them about the attack on the ship, Carter was appreciative that the creatures were giving him a wide berth.

Unable to penetrate beyond two hundred feet, the ambient light from above slowly disappeared, until Carter was left in total darkness. The light from his headlamp gave him only the occasional flash of a seal or dolphin. The lurking presence of the whales was a bit more unnerving now he could no longer see them. Even an unintentional swipe of the tail from something that large could pulverize bones, stranding him here to die.

As he approached four hundred feet, the deepest dive he had ever attempted, Carter thought he felt the water warm slightly. Truthfully, it was impossible to tell if the temperature really had risen or if it was just the power of suggestion put into his head by Avery and Noah. A glance at Noah's wrist-mounted device confirmed the water had indeed warmed by six degrees and that the device was still functioning. As he passed the four-hundred-foot mark, he knew the real test for all his equipment began now.

Carter's excitement increased as the beam of his headlamp caught something clearly man-made. It was the top of the ship's mast and crow's nest still towering above the *Fortitude*'s main deck. His pulse quickened as the realization of what he was witnessing sank in. He was the first person to look upon the *Fortitude* since she had sunk more than a century ago. Not just in drone footage, but actual wreckage he could reach out and touch.

The wooden vessel was in remarkable condition, unlike anything Carter had ever seen. Most of the shipwreck sites he'd visited were in the temperate waters of the Caribbean and Southern Atlantic where micro-scopic sea life, combined with warmer ocean temperatures, hastened decay, reducing them to nothing more than rubble and coral-encrusted mausoleums after only a few decades. It looked as though the passage of time had simply ceased for the *Fortitude*, while the rest of the planet continued to age and change at a normal rate.

A ripple in the water caused Carter to notice three seals gliding nearby as he continued his careful descent. He was trying to stay focused on every-thing Avery had warned him might happen. He felt good—surprisingly so —but he knew at this depth things could change in a heartbeat.

As he passed five hundred feet, his vision began to change, darkness encroaching from the sides. It was like looking through binoculars, or the tunnel vision a race car driver might experience on the track at two hundred miles per hour. The symptom was unnerving but not unexpected. He slowed the pace of his descent but continued.

As his headlamp provided the first glimpse of the *Fortitude*'s main deck, Carter's head began to ache. He willed the symptom into the background and pressed on. He had come too far to stop now. Swimming just above the deck, he turned in a slow circle, trying to give the video feed something to see while orienting himself to the ship. The timer on the dive watch confirmed he was still right on schedule. He had exactly twenty minutes to search the ship and locate what he came for or leave empty-handed, forever.

As he entered the wreck, the headache pounded, constant and pervasive, much like a bad hangover. The condition of the ship's interior was no less remarkable than the exterior. Recalling the detailed blueprints of the vessel, Carter slowly and carefully swam through the hull, beginning with the cargo hold. There wasn't much noteworthy left behind, the exception being a stack of empty food crates and several empty sailing trunks.

Carter moved on through the captain's quarters, bridge, galley, and crew quarters, peeking into lockers and examining furniture wherever he found them. It was clear the crew had taken most everything as they abandoned the ship. As he glided over some debris on the floor of the galley, his headlamp caught a bright piece of metal. Upon closer examination he discovered it was the brass top to a compass binnacle. Carefully he retrieved the item from the detritus on the deck. Though somewhat heavier, the compass and base were no larger than a handheld coffee grinder. Its miniature size made it clear that the compass must have been used to augment a much larger one usually located at the ship's helm. He wondered if it had belonged to the captain. Despite the cracked glass and the rusted steel balls protruding from either side of the bezel, Carter deemed it worthy of recovery and slid it into his dive bag.

He wondered how someone could have successfully hidden an entire treasure aboard this ship. Smuggling it on board was one thing but concealing it from fellow travelers for an extended voyage was an altogether different matter, especially as they salvaged whatever remained on board before fleeing for their lives. The last area he searched looked to be a small storage compartment into which someone had created a makeshift bunk. It was an odd space to bunk down with so many other options. Methodically he searched the room, then disassembled the bed. As he turned to leave, a piece of the wall paneling caught his eye. It was askew. Had it come loose when the ship sank, or had someone used it as a hiding place?

Carter deliberately turned his body away from the panel. Whoever was monitoring the live feed from his shoulder-mounted camera to the *Weddell* wasn't going to have a view of anything he found. Not if he could help it. It took a bit of effort to pull the wedged panel free, but eventually he succeeded in removing it.

The hollow, like everything else about the *Fortitude*, was as smooth and unblemished as the day the ship set sail. Carter felt around, trying to keep his shoulder turned back but reach every corner and crevice inside the wall.

On the last pass across the front part of the lower wall, his glove hit something solid that didn't feel like the softened wood.

Using one hand, Carter worked his fingers behind the object, careful not to let it slip farther into the wall, and lifted it slowly. Pulling it free of the wall, he kept his torso turned perpendicular to the bunk, laying the cloth-wrapped bundle on the bed.

Trying to control his breath to avoid a heart rate spike that would scare Avery, he pulled the cloth away one quarter at a time, revealing the missing Cross of Nidaros. It looked exactly like Noah's sketch.

His pulse picked up anyway, intensifying his headache, as the head-lamp beam illuminated the gleaming treasure. Sticking his hand back into the wall for good measure, he found something else, though he didn't know what to make of it: lying at the bottom of the cavity was a small lens that appeared to be a jeweler's loupe. Carter turned, careful to keep the camera pointed away from the find, and placed both items into his waist-mounted artifact bag alongside the compass.

As he cinched the bag closed, the dive computer buzzed his wrist. His twenty minutes were up. He swam out of the hull and back up to the deck for one last look. The crow's nest was approximately two hundred feet above the deck. It would mark the first of his decompression stops and be a perfect spot to check the accuracy of Noah's wrist-mounted dive computer.

As he followed the mast upward, Carter kept tabs on the device, watching as it marked off his depth at intervals of five feet. An upward glance gifted him with a close-up view of the crow's nest, his four-hundred-foot marker. A sudden halt to his progress, as if someone had grabbed onto his dive suit, sent him crashing headfirst into the mast. Stunned, he took a moment to regain his bearings. He struggled to push himself away from the mast, but he was stuck, his suit hung up on something unseen somewhere just below his left gluteal muscle. His attempts at contorting into a position that would allow him to free himself were unsuccessful. Whatever he'd gotten caught on couldn't have been in a worse location.

The only good thing was that the suit wasn't punctured, at least not yet. Cutting himself free wasn't an option here like it had been in New York. If he tore the suit, he would die of hypothermia long before reaching the surface.

Avery had told him her calculations were accurate, and he had no reason to doubt it. The problem was it meant he didn't have time to waste stuck on a pole four hundred feet and change below the surface. They had planned for every possible contingency—except this one. The last time he'd gotten stuck, in the Hudson Canyon, Avery had come to his rescue. This time there would be no cavalry. Carter was all alone.

His headache had lessened in intensity but thundered back as the first wave of panic set in. Barring a miracle, he would run out of air. Trapped in the dark, with his recovered cross, he would die among the seals.

Maybe the treasure really was cursed.

44

At the surface, Avery was cold and growing more worried by the breath. She and Noah had taken shelter inside Erin's Sno-Cat for warmth after securing their inflatable craft at water's edge. Her attention alternated between the timer on her watch, the gizmo monitoring Carter's heart rate, which after two spikes had settled back to normal, and the occasional radio updates from Harrison as he monitored Carter's progress by video link from the *Weddell*.

"Any update, Harry?" Avery asked as she pressed the transmit button on her portable.

"No," Harrison said, barely audible amid the static. "He started up but now it looks like the camera feed isn't moving."

"Can you see anything at all?" Avery asked.

"Ah, yeah," Harrison said. "It looks like the top of the ship's mast."

"The feed might be frozen," Noah suggested.

Ignoring him, Avery responded to Harrison. "How long has it been since his camera moved?" she asked.

"Hang on," Harrison said. "They said he's been there for almost twenty-five minutes."

"What is his depth reading?" Avery asked, working hard to keep the panic from her voice.

One of the ship's crew cut in on the conversation. "Mosley's holding steady at 405 feet."

"He's supposed to be decompressing," Erin offered.

"That's three minutes too long for a decompression stop," Avery said. "Carter knows exactly how long each one should be."

"Aye, the camera appears to shake every couple of minutes," Harrison said.

"Shake?" Avery heard the alarm creep into her voice.

"Like he's writhing or something."

"Good Lord, what if he has the bends?" She put the radio down and jumped out of the Sno-Cat, Noah clambering after her.

"I've got to get down there." Avery shed coats on her way to the water.

"Look, Avery, you have no idea what you're doing," Erin said. "If something goes wrong—"

"*If* something goes wrong?" Avery shouted. "It already has, Erin. Now help me get ready or get the hell out of the way."

With the assistance of Noah and a reluctant Erin, Avery was ready in less than five minutes, complete with tanks, mixing valve, mask, and rebreather. But it felt like an eternity. Her last communication with Harrison confirmed Carter was maintaining his depth of 405 feet. She knew this dive prep had to be exacting or she'd never make it to Carter to help him, but she felt like she might come right out of her skin as Noah finished fitting the specialized eyewear tight to her face.

"You're sure?" he asked again as she prepared to flip into the water.

Avery gave a thumbs-up and disappeared.

Cold wasn't really an adequate word for the water that shocked her still for a few slow beats, but it wasn't painful—just shy of it, really.

As she descended, the seals surrounded her and began frolicking around as if performing for a new audience, gliding in graceful arcs and sliding past each other like they had a choreographer in the group. Ordinarily, she would have been enchanted, but Avery was on a mission. Carter was in trouble, and she was his only hope. What had they even been thinking? This dive was way too dangerous, both beneath the ice and above, where predators and ulterior motives seemed in plentiful supply.

The dimly lit ocean surrounding her was beautiful, but the view below was ominous and pitch black. And Carter was down there somewhere, directly below her. Boy, he had been spot-on when he'd told her how far four hundred feet—barely more than a football field—could seem when measured vertically.

Avery worked hard to maintain her control despite her panic rising. According to the wrist-mounted computer Noah had provided, her rate of descent was an average of forty-three feet per minute. She had warned Carter about staying below forty feet per minute, but given the circumstances, she reasoned the more rapid rate was necessary.

Sickness began to overtake her around the two-hundred-foot mark, far too soon considering how much farther she needed to go. Avery knew she could combat the feeling by slowing her rate of descent, but she pressed on and the nausea subsided slightly.

The sudden onset of tunnel vision surprised her. One moment she had a clear field of vision and the next it was reduced to a narrow vertical band directly in front of her. The loss of peripheral vision would make locating Carter more difficult, but it wouldn't stop her. Nothing would.

She knew her combined symptoms likely meant she was very near Carter's depth. But what if she missed him? What if she passed right by him on her way to the *Fortitude*'s deck? Or missed the wreck completely? It was so dark. Her diving light revealed nothing but a dark abyss everywhere she looked. Fighting to maintain focus, she shoved her fear into the background, straining to read the depth gauge on her wrist. Her vision was blurred, making that difficult. The one thing she was positive of was the first number—and it was a three. It meant she hadn't passed Carter yet. He was still somewhere below her holding steady at 405.

Could she make it down that far without passing out?

Not far behind that terrifying thought came another: What if Carter had solved his problem? What if he had gotten himself free and resumed his ascent? She had been cut off from any communication with Harrison since she entered the water. She might be down here on a fool's errand searching for someone who was already gone. And with Carter's tanks fully depleted, there would be no one coming to save her.

Avery struggled to maintain focus. It wasn't only her vision that was affected. Her brain had muddled too, and she knew it. She closed her eyes and tried to focus only on her breathing.

"Calm down, Ave." She heard the soothing sound of her mother's voice. "Calm down and concentrate. You can do this."

When she opened her eyes again, Avery noticed what appeared to be a faint grayish patch below her in the black water. Was it an optical illusion? Or was it really a light?

She swam toward the smudge of light in the inky blackness. The illumination intensified as she drew nearer. It was a light. The light from Carter's headlamp.

Thank God. And Mom, too. She kicked harder.

As Carter's form came into view, so did the mast and crow's nest of *Fortitude*. Carter waved his arms. He was alive, and he saw her.

With something to focus on, Avery's mind grew sharper, her thoughts clearer. Swimming hard toward him, she felt the first twinges of a cramp beginning in her left calf muscle. *This is how it must happen*, she thought: the crushing depths of the ocean reminding them that humans were never meant to thrive down here.

As she neared Carter, she realized for the first time he wasn't waving at her but struggling to free himself from the mast. Twisted into a pretzel, Carter appeared to be trying to wriggle free from his tanks. Avery grabbed onto one of his arms to try to stop him. Carter yanked his arm free from her grasp, then spun to face her, his eyes wild behind the glasses, fist balled up and ready to swing. She drifted back, holding up both hands in surrender, watching as both recognition and relief spread across his face.

Carter waved one hand behind him to show her how he was stuck. Avery placed a hand on his arm to calm him, then signaled that she would have a look.

A quick inspection revealed he had gotten his dive suit caught on a splintered piece of the mast, and a folded section had worked its way into a crack and wedged there, getting pinched tighter every time Carter moved. The suit was stretched but remarkably had not torn.

Avery put a hand on his shoulder and signaled their baseball call for hold. He went still, and she silently cursed the thick fingers of her gloves as she attempted to work the twisted material free. She paused to take another look, horrified to see the material had wedged farther into the broken timber. The gloves simply wouldn't allow her the flexibility to perform such delicate work. Carter gestured to his dive knife. Avery shook her head. She didn't dare risk using the sharp blade for fear of slicing his suit accidentally. If she cut the suit, Carter would freeze to death before they got halfway to the surface. But Carter was adamant. He drew the knife, then he handed it to her, handle first. Reluctantly, Avery took it.

She swam around behind him again, then attempted to figure out the best way to use the knife. The blade was strong, but it wasn't designed for use as a timber-prying tool. She inserted the tip of the blade into the wood at the base of the broken protrusion intending to use the knife like a screwdriver. As she began to twist the blade, her vision failed her again. This time, in addition to the tunnel vision, everything blurred. She backed off on the pressure she was exerting on the knife.

The helplessness was unbearable as she waited for her vision to clear. It seemed she was thwarted at every turn. *Perhaps the* Fortitude *is cursed*, she thought, immediately chiding herself for even allowing such a superstitious notion to creep inside her head. There was no such thing as a curse. And thinking that way did nothing to solve their immediate problem.

She willed herself to remain calm. Her blurred vision improved, but only slightly. She took another long look at the section of the ship's mast holding Carter tightly in its grasp, her logical mind going to work: this was simply a problem to overcome. The fact that Carter was trapped in freezing water four hundred feet below an Antarctic ice shelf while the precious minutes slipped away changed nothing—those facts were merely the parameters of the problem. And Avery Turner could solve problems.

She needed to change her plan of attack. Focus on the wood, where it was weakest. Pulling on the suit only exacerbated the problem and increased the risk of a tear. She needed to find a way to take the pressure off. Which meant pushing toward the wood while simultaneously untwisting the material. Pulling on the material had caused this mess, the reverse might solve it.

Avery swam around to face Carter, then handed him the knife. She signaled that she had an idea. He reseated the knife on his belt and nodded his understanding. Avery pantomimed letting her whole body go limp. She needed him to relax, not simply hold still. He nodded understanding.

She returned to the stuck material and went to work. This time she could tell she and the ship were no longer working against each other. Carter's body was fully relaxed, and the material of his dive suit was far easier to manage. After three pressed-in wriggles, it slid free.

Carter turned to face her, clasping her hand tightly in a brief thank-you before he pulled the red tabs on both of their suits, activating the heating element, and gave her the thumbs-up sign, the universal signal for surfacing.

Avery nodded as her muddled brain raced to plot a new solution for their ascent. She knew she had plenty of gas remaining to safely reach the surface, but Carter did not. There was nothing to be done about that, so she quickly calculated a way they might be able to avail themselves of shorter decompression stops without dying.

At three hundred feet they would pause for twenty minutes instead of the previously scheduled twenty-two. At one fifty they would do the same. The shallower stops would provide the most benefit for off-gassing, so they needed to focus on those. As they ascended, Avery signaled her intent to Carter. He nodded his understanding, but there was something resigned about his expression. Avery knew Carter had likely done the math too. She had to keep him from giving up. Get him to stay focused. They were both going to come out of this alive.

Halfway through their decompression stop at seventy feet, Carter's trimix tank ran out. He reached to switch to the 50 percent nitrox mixture, but the valve was frozen in place. The two of them attempted to force the valve open, but it wouldn't budge. Carter's eyes widened as he struggled to pull air from an empty tank. Quickly, Avery switched the supply on her own tanks, then shoved the pony regulator from her tank at him, allowing them to share the mixture.

Avery knew this temporary fix wouldn't last, because they were sharing the nitrox mixture meant for one.

Surface light returned to their underwater world as Avery and Carter continued their ascent. They killed time during their fifty-foot decompression stop watching several seals that were definitely following them. As Avery lifted her hand to signal Carter the time remaining, the shared tank of nitrox ran dry. Anticipating this, Avery switched over to her O2 tank, only to find it empty. She grabbed Carter's rebreather and his pony and tried his O2 tank. Nothing.

Her eyes popping wide behind her mask, Avery kicked for the surface, Carter following.

They both knew the last safety decompression stop was the most important, but they were out of options. Avery prayed the combination of heat and gas switching had been enough as they broke for the surface.

They were almost there when Avery realized it was too dark—much darker than it had been when she went into the water. According to their depth gauges, they were only ten feet down. Something was wrong.

Lungs burning and completely exhausted, Avery realized too late they had come up directly below a wide, thick ice floe.

45

Carter swam just below the ice ceiling, his lungs burning so badly it was hard to believe they weren't melting the floe as he and Avery searched for an opening.

Avery's gloved fingers mimicked his as they desperately searched for any weak points or cracks in the massive ice floe. Having no clear sense how big this one impediment might be, Carter kept trying to locate an edge. He glanced at Avery after noticing she had faltered. Her hands fell away from the ice, her body limp. Crap. She had succumbed to the lack of air and passed out.

He grabbed hold of her arm and pulled her along as he continued to hunt a way out with increasing desperation. He knew Avery would sustain brain damage from lack of oxygen if he couldn't get them out of the water in the next few minutes. Assuming he didn't pass out alongside her.

The water stirred beneath them and it took effort for Carter to turn to see why.

A pair of seals shot toward Carter and Avery from the depths, practically flying thanks to their large size and fully inflated lungs. Tracking their trajectory, Carter saw they were headed toward a small opening he hadn't noticed in the surface ice about twenty feet away. He swam that way with Avery in tow, watching as a third seal overtook the first two, appendages flying and teeth flashing in the dim light as they battled for space under the hole. Blood drifted in reddish clouds, dissipating in the water, as the animals bit and slashed at one another.

Like Carter and Avery, the seals were fighting for air.

Carter's strength waned with every passing second. He looped an arm around Avery's torso and kicked hard toward the seals. Challenging three eight-hundred-pound creatures for a small air hole in the ice was dangerous, but it was their only chance.

Carter knew seals weren't afraid of humans, and these three appeared entirely focused on their struggle with each other. A careless swipe with a tail and Carter and Avery would die, but since they were going to die if he didn't get past the animals, he stayed the course.

As he approached, a random thought passed through his muddled brain—something Avery had said she'd read about these seals using light to guide them to the surface.

With possibly the last of his strength, he tore the diving light from Avery's mask, then swung it in the direction of the seals. As it floated past them, one of the seals broke off from the others to give chase, much like a dog spotting a squirrel. The two remaining seals followed the first, clearing the small air hole. Carter poked his head through and drew a long breath before yelling out for help. Resubmerging himself, Carter ripped the rebreather from Avery's face, then pushed her head up through the hole. With his right arm he squeezed her chest in and out, attempting to perform compressions as best he could.

Ten agonizing seconds later, Avery's chest heaved.

Carter felt her draw a huge lungful of air and begin to kick her feet, and he squeezed up beside her to share the small opening. While there was enough room for their heads, the hole was much too small to allow either of them to crawl through onto the ice. They took turns breathing deeply and shouting as loud as they could for Noah and Erin.

Once again, Carter felt movement in the water below them. Drawing another deep breath, he plunged his head underwater. The seals had returned and were swimming directly for them. Carter knew they would be hungry for air and would have no problem displacing a couple of comparatively small humans.

The time had come to fight or die trying.

The sound of an approaching motor caught Carter's attention. He turned and saw the shallow hull of one of the inflatable crafts approaching from behind. A look back toward the seals confirmed they had seen it too. They scattered. Carter and Avery withdrew from the ice hole as Noah and Erin began to widen it with ice axes, breaking to allow Carter and Avery to breathe every three strikes.

Avery was lethargic, and as Carter held her in his arms, they heard a second RIB approaching, no doubt carrying several other members of the *Weddell* crew. The cavalry had arrived. Hopefully in the nick of time.

In minutes, the hole was wide enough to utilize as an escape hatch. With the little strength Carter had remaining he pushed Avery up through it, taking one last look around underwater before being pulled up to the ice himself.

Carter fought nausea, wincing at severe muscle cramps coupled with an extreme headache, each symptom the result of the hurried resurfacing. Sprawled on the ice floe, he couldn't muster a care about the cold permeating his suit as he watched their rescuers strip off Avery's gear, then carry her to one of the RIBs. She didn't appear to be faring any better than he was. He couldn't help but feel this was all his fault. His hubris about his skill in and out of the water, his generous push of the envelope to be the first person to reach the *Fortitude*—Avery was sick, or hurt, or both, because of him. If she didn't fully recover from this, he would never be able to live with himself.

Carter saw Erin wrapping Avery in a foil thermal blanket as Dr. Jill placed an oxygen mask over her face. Noah and two other members of the crew returned for Carter. He tried to stand but needed their help to do it. As they guided him toward the second inflatable, Noah badgered him for details.

"What was it like, Carter? Did you find anything?"

Carter shook his head in response. The nausea made a verbal response impossible. He glanced down at his dive bag, confirming it was still attached to his suit and cinched tightly. Despite the debilitating symptoms of decompression sickness, he would do whatever it took to hide the find from Noah.

"Hey, Noah," Dr. Jill said. "This isn't the time for that. We need to get them back to the ship."

"Of course," Noah said.

As soon as Carter and Avery were loaded onto the RIBs, they raced through the ice floes to the shoreline where the Sno-Cats and several snowmobiles awaited them.

The Sno-Cat's heater fans blasted, keeping the interior warm, but both divers were chilled to the bone. Carter kept a protective arm around Avery as they slouched together in the back. Avery appeared to be drifting in and out of consciousness and Carter was pretty sure he wasn't far behind her. As the Cat bounced over the frozen tundra, his thoughts kept returning to Noah's mysterious benefactor and what the cross might lead to.

Why had they run out of gas so soon? Those oxygen tanks were meant to supply the air necessary for their last decompression stop on the way to the surface, but both had been empty, and Carter had checked the pressure gauges himself—it took skill and patience to empty a tank and rig the gauge to show it full. What he couldn't say for sure since it was both of them: Was it a fluke accident or bad design? Had the tanks been tampered with? Or was Tuva right?

Carter didn't believe in curses, though he had toyed with the notion when he was trapped four hundred feet below the surface. It was like the *Fortitude* had reached out and grabbed ahold of his dive suit. Were it not for Avery's courage, he likely would have spent the rest of eternity locked in the evil embrace of a possibly cursed shipwreck.

His thoughts grew fuzzy, but he kept trying to work out what had happened. If the tanks were tampered with, had the plan been for him not to return at all? Or were they planning to have another diver intercept Carter on his way to the surface? Relieving him of the cross and whatever treasure he might have recovered? Had Avery's rescue foiled the plan? And if Seamus wasn't the only pirate aboard the *Weddell*, who else was behind this? And why did Agent Miranda keep showing up like a bad penny? There were just too many questions for his weary brain.

One thing was certain, he had to conceal the cross from the rest of the crew. After what he and Avery had been through, nobody was going to get their hands on the treasure but them.

This, here, today, made it personal.

He would find someplace to stash the cross as soon as the opportunity presented itself. Assuming he could still move.

He glanced up and noticed Noah looking at them in the Sno-Cat's rearview mirror. The two men locked eyes for a moment before Noah looked away.

Carter felt another muscle spasm ripple through Avery's torso. He tightened his embrace. A groan escaped her lips. *Hang on, Avery. I'll get us out of this mess.*

46

Harrison and several members of the research team stood waiting at the bottom of the gangway. In the distance two Sno-Cats and three accompanying snowmobiles raced toward the *Weddell*. Between sporadic squawks and bursts of information coming by way of radio transmissions, he had picked up enough information to know both Avery and Carter had returned from their dive, and neither was in good shape. His emotions were a heady mixture of worry, for both, and anger at Carter for making the dive in the first place, putting both himself and Avery in danger.

His first indication Avery had gone into the water was when her face appeared on the ship's video screen as they monitored Carter's dive camera. He'd been shocked, as Avery had never so much as hinted that she was planning to join him on the dive. But he shouldn't have been the least bit surprised that she would attempt to rescue Carter.

Harrison and the others ran to meet the Sno-Cats as Noah and Erin bailed out of the front of one and hurried toward the cargo bay. As the rear doors swung open, Harrison's heart dropped. Avery's unconscious head was cradled in Carter's lap. He was about to read the riot act to Carter until he realized that he, too, was barely conscious.

"Mr. Harrison, Dr. Wyndham, Tony, you're strong enough to help," Dr. Jill yelled over the wind. "We have to get them inside."

Harrison assisted the doctor, the man she called Tony, and another crewman in securing Avery onto a backboard. After strapping her down, the crewmen hurried back toward the ship and ascended the gangway, leaving Harrison to help Noah move Carter.

They attempted another backboard, but Carter waved them off.

"I can walk," Carter said. "I don't need that."

"You sure?" Dr. Jill asked.

"You don't look so good," Noah said, turning toward the ship when Carter dismissed him again.

Harrison accompanied Carter up the gangway. When they were halfway up the ramp and out of earshot of the others, Harrison leaned in close and whispered, "If you come out of this in one piece and Avery doesn't, you will regret the day you met me, Mosley."

Carter just nodded.

Noah waited for them at the top of the ramp.

"Well?" Noah said.

"Well, what?" Harrison asked.

"I want whatever you found, Mosley," Noah demanded.

Carter exchanged a glance with Harrison.

"You need to back off a bit, Doc," Harrison said as he took hold of Carter's arm and led him away. "He needs to rest."

"He's here because of me." Noah ran ahead of them and blocked their way forward. "This is my expedition, my equipment, and my vessel. Anything they recovered belongs to me. I demand to see whatever he has in that dive bag."

Harrison took a deep breath, then turned to Carter. "He's right, Carter. Give him whatever you have in the bag."

His face falling, Carter opened the sack.

Harrison watched pure unadulterated lust and greed bloom across Noah's face. Whatever lofty environmental goals he might have possessed had evaporated—only avarice remained.

Carter removed his hand from the dive bag, holding what appeared to be an antique ship's compass binnacle. The brass top mounted above a wooden base looked more like a pepper grinder from a high-end restaurant than a navigation instrument. The instrumentation bezel was broken, and one of the handle knobs was missing, likely why it had been left behind in the first place. Carter turned the bag upside down, his brow furrowing momentarily, but it was clearly empty. Harrison read the confusion on Carter's face and the disappointment on Noah's.

"What the hell is this?" Noah demanded as he snatched the compass away from Carter. "You were sent down there specifically to locate anything connected to the missing jewels of Nidaros. A cross, a crown, a sword, anything of value. This is nothing but a broken ship's compass. Worthless junk."

Carter shook his head, his shoulders drooping, his eyes still fixed on the bag.

"Sorry, Doc," Harrison said. "Sometimes that's just the way things go. Maybe you could clean it up and sell it on eBay or *Antiques Roadshow*."

Noah stood frozen and red-faced for several moments before storming off down the hallway.

"I don't understand," Carter muttered.

"Come on," Harrison said. "We should check on Avery."

Carter was no longer sure about anything that had occurred during the dive. He'd been positive he'd recovered a cross and a jeweler's loupe in the hidden compartment aboard the *Fortitude*, the same cross depicted in the drawing Noah had shown them. But the ship's compass was the only thing that made it back. His memory of retrieving the compass was just as vivid as it was of the cross and loupe. Had the decompression sickness altered his memory somehow? Or had the bag somehow opened as he struggled to free himself from the ship's mast? Was the cross now lying at the bottom of the Weddell Sea?

With all that had gone wrong today, maybe that was just as well. His knees threatened to buckle as they shuffled down the hallway.

Harrison looped one arm around Carter's torso and half carried him to Avery's cabin. Avery was curled up on the bed, looking smaller than Harrison had seen her in years. Her dive suit had been stripped off and replaced by a sweatsuit, thermal socks, and a pile of heated blankets as Dr. Jill tried to bring her core temperature back to normal.

"How's she doing?" Carter asked.

"Well, she's—" the doctor began.

"Hey, Carter," Avery croaked as she removed the oxygen mask from her face. "You look horrible."

"That's his normal look as far as I'm concerned," Harrison said.

"How are you feeling?" Carter asked.

"Like I came down with the world's worst case of the flu. My head aches, my body aches, and I have like zero strength."

"Yeah, that's the decompression sickness," Carter said.

"You must be suffering from it too, Mr. Mosley," Dr. Jill said.

"I've felt better," Carter said.

"How soon will it pass, Doc?" Harrison said.

"Not sure," she said. "Too many variables here. They may not be out of the woods yet." Dr. Jill prodded Avery to return the oxygen mask to her face. "I'll be right back, Ms. Turner. Don't go running off now."

"I'll try not to," Avery mumbled through the mask.

Carter didn't want to worry them any more than they likely were, but he had no idea how bad the effects of the sickness might get. The mixed gases and the shortened decompression stops were a recipe for disaster. He felt much worse than he was letting on, and he was more than a little worried about Avery.

"Are you going to tell him or am I?" Avery asked Harrison after the doctor had departed.

"Tell me what?" Carter asked.

Harrison walked over to the corner where Avery's discarded dive suit lay in a heap and retrieved her dive bag. He returned and handed it to Carter.

"Open it," Avery said.

Carter uncinched the bag, then looked inside. It was the cardinal's cross he had recovered from the *Fortitude*. The jeweler's loupe was lying at the bottom. He hadn't imagined them. Or lost them.

"But how?" Carter said.

"I switched the bags," Avery said. "And stuck the broken compass in yours."

"When? I was with you all the way to the ship."

"It wasn't as hard as you think, slick," Harrison said. "You weren't doing all that well coming back from the dive either."

Carter just stared at the cross. "I thought maybe I hallucinated the whole thing."

"Might have been better if you had," Harrison grumbled. "I think that stuff really might be cursed."

"Come on, Harry," Avery said. "There's no such thing. Objects are just objects. And we still need to find the rest of the missing treasure."

"Why?" Harrison said. "This hunt nearly killed both of you."

"Not the hunt," Carter said. "Someone aboard this ship didn't want us coming back from that dive. I know my gauges were all pegged at full—I think someone bled those tanks and rigged the gauge. I just can't figure out why. What good does it do anyone for me to get the treasure within seventy feet of the surface?"

"Someone who could dive could have taken the second suit and gone in to get it from you," Avery mused, batting at the mask again. "Rigging both tanks would have ensured it didn't matter which you took."

"But then you took the other dive setup," Harrison said. "If this is true, you foiled an attempted murder. Which probably means you're not the killer's favorite person."

"But if people are being killed because of the treasure, wouldn't it be better if we found it and stopped the killing?" Avery asked as her eyes drifted shut again. "Can you guys get some pictures of that thing from different angles and send them to MaryAnn from my laptop, quick as you can."

"Assuming that's possible with their crap internet connection," Harrison said.

"I had an idea about that, but I can't remember," Avery said. "We need more information."

"You need more rest," Carter said.

"That too," Avery said.

47

Carter retreated to his own cabin with an oxygen tank, plus Avery's dive bag and computer after Avery supplied him with the password. He knew what a big step that had to have been. So far as he knew, even Harrison didn't know her password.

After changing into black sweats and a black watch cap, Carter crawled under the heated blankets Dr. Jill brought in and had his vitals taken and recorded. Once she left, he unlocked the computer, connected to the sat link, then logged into Avery's email account. There were two new messages from MaryAnn.

The intro to the first message was short and sweet. As Carter knew too well, MaryAnn liked to get right to the point. Through an old contact in the UK, MaryAnn had managed to obtain several photographs taken when the ship launched on her ill-fated journey to Antarctica. MaryAnn had compared the images to the ship's manifest and discovered there was an extra person on board, not accounted for in any of the available documentation. Her email stated she would continue her attempts to identify the unknown member of the crew.

He clicked to the second message, finding a history of the curse and a list of treasure the cardinal guy had looted from the church on his way out when he got the boot. Not quite the same as swiping a stapler or a computer mouse.

Carter leaned his head against the wall and closed his eyes. Reading from the computer screen was causing his headache to worsen. He could finish this one later. He had the gist.

A knock on the door startled Carter. He got up slowly, hid the dive bag and its contents underneath his bed, then crossed the room and opened the door.

"Jeepers, Carter," Harrison said. "You look twice as bad as you did a minute ago."

"Thanks," Carter said as he returned to the bed.

"Nice outfit. You look like one of Hogan's Heroes about to go on a night mission."

"Who's Hogan?"

Harrison shook his head. "Never mind. Let me see the cross."

"It's under the bed."

"Great hiding place, Ace," Harrison said. "No one would look for it there. How about we just leave it outside in the hallway?"

"How's Avery?" Carter didn't have the energy for sarcasm.

"She's fallen asleep, but the doc is still with her. Kicked me out, if you can believe it." Harrison looked over Carter's shoulder at the laptop. "Anything new from MaryAnn?"

"She's located some old photos that show an unidentified member of the original crew not listed on the *Fortitude*'s manifest."

"Interesting. Anything else?"

"Yeah," Carter said as he continued to read. "She confirmed the story Noah and Tuva told us about the lost crown jewels of Norway, stolen by some cardinal named Olav Engelbrektsson who wanted to be king."

"Sounds like there were a lot of those guys back in the day," Harrison said as he picked up the cross and examined it closely. "Anything else?"

"Yeah, there's a lot more missing than just a cross and a crown," Carter said. "There are priceless church artifacts and bejeweled ceremonial pieces too. Though she's still checking on the veracity of that because legends tend to grow over time."

"Like me," Harrison said as he patted his stomach and walked toward the bed. "Well, this cross isn't an exaggeration. Maybe the rest of this treasure she's talking about is still down there somewhere."

"Maybe," Carter said weakly as he clicked into a reply box to update MaryAnn on the day's events without alarming her too much and to try to send the photos Avery had asked him to send. "But if it is, it's staying there."

"What's this thing?" Harrison said as he picked up the loupe.

"Don't know. It looks like a jeweler's loupe."

Harrison held it up to one eye and looked at the cross. "I thought they were supposed to magnify stuff. This one doesn't do anything. In fact, the lens is half red and half blue. You think being underwater for a century might have ruined it?"

"I don't know, but I do know I need to snap a few pictures of the cross and loupe for MaryAnn. Hold them up, will ya?"

Harrison posed with both items while Carter snapped several photos.

After attaching the pictures to the email, Carter clicked Send with crossed fingers and watched until the computer said it had gone, then closed the laptop and slid down onto his back under the covers.

"You okay?" Harrison said as he retrieved the laptop to return it to Avery's cabin.

"I just need to close my eyes for a minute," Carter said. As he drifted off, Carter thought he heard Harrison mention something about Noah's financial records and Marco. He was unable to make sense of the statement.

Harrison was halfway down the hallway from Carter's room when he was accosted by Agent Allison Miranda.

"Where is he?" Miranda demanded. "I want a full debriefing from him about what he did down there."

"He's resting," Harrison said. "And he's not to be disturbed. Those kids have been through a lot, and they don't need you in their face."

"That's what the doctor said when she refused to let me see Avery."

"I knew there was something about that doctor I liked," Harrison said as he brushed past her.

"Look, I've got a job to do," Miranda said as she followed him toward the stairs. "Mucking around in a protected area and taking huge risks underwater just to satisfy some unhealthy urge to hunt lost treasure is reckless beyond measure."

"You're telling me," Harrison said, ascending the steps two at a time to try to leave her behind.

"I'm serious, Mr. Harrison."

He stopped as he reached the landing and turned to face her. "Harry. It's Harry, okay? And I need a coffee. You want to talk to me about this, we do it over coffee. From one former government official to another?"

Miranda sighed.

"What do you say?" Harrison said.

"Fine," Miranda said.

48

Avery felt slightly better after a few hours of sleep, but she was a long way from fully recovered as she sat up in her bed, reading the latest email from MaryAnn.

"At least the sunspots or whatever are letting us talk to the outside world," Carter said from the spot in the corner where he sat on the floor with his eyes closed, propped up against the wall. "She come up with anything new?"

"She identified the extra person on board as a painter named Arlo Olsen."

Carter opened one eye. "Is he someone important?"

"Not sure. MaryAnn says he once worked as an indentured servant for the shipyard's lead designer."

"That has to be Tuva's great-grandfather, right?"

"I would say so," Avery said. "The designer died in an accident, resulting in Olsen being freed from his obligations. It says here he began painting landscapes right around the time the *Fortitude* was being constructed."

"I don't see what that has to do with the missing treasure," Carter said.

"Me neither," Avery said as her mind drifted back to the rolled paintings she'd found in the other cabin during the fire.

"What else?" Carter said.

"MaryAnn said Olsen is the guy standing right at the outer edges of several of these photos. But she's not sure how easy it would be for Olsen to sneak aboard a ship with a crew of only sixty-three men."

"Wouldn't really matter once they were at sea," Carter said. "If he did stow away, even if they figured him out, assuming he wasn't dangerous, they would have put him to work doing something. You said he was a servant for the shipyard guy, maybe he had a skill set beyond painting landscapes." Carter opened his eyes wide.

"What is it?" Avery said.

"It makes a lot of sense when you factor in where I found the cross," Carter said. "The space wasn't part of the *Fortitude*'s crew quarters. It looked like a converted storage berth where someone had stuck a makeshift bed. Maybe that's what they did with Olsen after they found him on board the ship. While he was in there, he loosened one of the wall panels and secreted away the cross and the loupe, and then couldn't get it off the ship for some reason when they abandoned it."

The door to the cabin opened after a halfhearted knock. "Everybody decent?" Harrison asked as he stepped inside holding a tray of coffee and sandwiches.

"God does that coffee smell good," Avery said.

"Sounds like you're feeling better," Harrison said before turning to Carter. "How about you, sport?"

"I'll live, but I still feel like death warmed over. Don't know that I can eat anything yet."

"Maybe this will help," Harrison said as he handed him a cup of coffee.

"Where did you get off to, Harry?" Avery asked. "I've been out of it for hours."

"Me too," Carter said.

"I thought I'd let you two get some sleep while I had a nice chat with Agent Miranda."

Avery paused midsip. "Seriously?"

"She's almost human once you get to know her."

"What did y'all talk about?" Carter said.

"I'm afraid that's strictly on a need-to-know basis," Harrison said.

"Let me guess, two government agents come to a truce," Avery said.

"Not sure we're at a truce yet, but I think she's warming to me. So, what's the latest? Any word from MaryAnn?"

"Yeah," Avery said. "She may have identified the *Fortitude*'s mystery man. Looks like he may have been a landscape painter named Arlo Olsen."

"Speaking of the *Fortitude*'s extra man," Harrison said as he sat on the edge of the bed and passed the tray of ham salad sandwiches to Avery, who thanked him. "One of the things I was talking to Agent Miranda about—"

"Harry! You didn't tell her about this when we've only just learned it!"

"I didn't tell her about this guy," Harrison said. "I did tell her about the fact that I noticed when we were watching the drone feed and then again during the fire that accounting for Carter, Erin, and Seamus, there are twenty-four people on this ship."

Carter's left eye popped open again. "Noah said twenty-three when I asked."

"He did. And to me when I asked again yesterday. Yet we do in fact have twenty-four."

"You think he's lying?" Avery asked, picking at a sandwich.

"I can't see why he would," Harrison said. "But I'd give my left arm to see a crew list, because I can see how they might have a stowaway here."

"You what?"

"Sure, think about it. How hard would it be for someone interested in sunken treasure to get on the crew delivering this thing and then just blend in and never leave? MaryAnn said the internet has message boards about this treasure and this ship."

"Wow, Harry," Avery said as she lifted her sandwich and took a healthy bite.

"You might want to go easy on the food," Carter said. "Your nausea could come back."

"Whatever, I'm starving," Avery said, barely intelligible around a mouthful of food. After washing the sandwich down with a swig of coffee, she continued. "So we might have another treasure hunter on board, we should be careful of that. But I wonder if Olsen might be the key to this whole treasure thing. Carter thinks it might have been Olsen who hid the cross on board the *Fortitude*."

"It seems likely that the makeshift sleeping space where I found it hidden in the wall was his bed," Carter explained.

"What about this loupe thing, which isn't a loupe at all?" Harrison asked as he picked it up off the bedcovers.

"Carter's brother thinks it might be a code breaker of some sort," Avery said, pointing to her computer screen.

"Brady and I used to have one we fought over as kids," Carter said.

"Well, this is one super-fancy decoder ring, if that's what it is," Harrison said as he held it up to the light. "So the question becomes, what exactly is it supposed to decode?"

All three of them turned to look at the cross, which Harrison had cleaned up a bit while Avery and Carter slept.

They spent the next several minutes examining every inch of the cross, looking for a hidden clue, but came up empty. The only writing on the cross was visible to the naked eye and didn't need decoding.

"It says 'Odium Dei,'" Carter said.

"What does that mean?" Harrison said.

Avery swallowed another bite of her sandwich before answering. "Well, according to these search results, it means hatred of God."

"That makes no sense," Harrison said. "Why would someone engrave that on a church cross?"

"I never said the translation made sense," Avery said. "I'm only telling you what Google said."

"And you guys wonder why I don't trust this whole internet craze," Harrison said.

"Hey, I've got a message from Marco here," Avery said. "Did one of you reach out to him?"

"I did," Harrison said.

"But how—"

"You gave the password to Carter, remember?" Harrison said. "I memorized it in case I needed to contact anyone."

"You emailed Marco and told him to come get us when he said he couldn't fly here?"

"Given our rather extraordinary circumstances and his friend Rollie's lack of availability, he got a tutorial and he's coming," Harrison said. "You both need a hospital to check you out properly."

"We can't fly so soon after diving, Harry," Carter said. "It would be dangerous."

"Marco said he can fly us out at a low altitude, as there is nothing out there but ocean," Harrison countered.

"I don't know, Harry," Avery said.

"This isn't up for debate," Harrison said. "You both need real medical attention, not some sleep-deprived witch doctor on a research vessel. There's one hell of a storm coming, and we're in a den of murderous greedy thieves. We've got to get out of here before we can't, Ave."

A knock on the cabin door punctuated the brief silence that followed Harrison's outburst.

Avery quickly wrapped the cross and loupe in a towel, then stashed them in the suitcase on the floor beside her bed.

"I'll get it," Harrison said.

"Good evening, Mr. Harrison," Owen said. "I've come to check up on Avery. How is she?"

Harrison blocked the open doorway, intentionally obstructing Owen's view.

"It's okay, Harry," Avery said. "You can let him in."

Harrison stepped back, then opened the door the rest of the way, allowing Owen into the room.

"I'm feeling much better, Owen," Avery said. "Thank you for checking on me."

"I'm fine too," Carter said with a wave. "Thanks for asking."

"I was worried," Owen said.

"Don't be," Harrison said. "We're heading out of here shortly. These two need to get checked out by a real doctor."

"I can understand your impulse, Mr. Harrison," Owen said. "But I read up on decompression sickness, and they really should remain on the ship for at least another forty-eight hours. Just to be safe."

"I understand your concern, Owen," Harrison said. "But it's not really your decision to make, is it? There is a storm on the way and we're getting the hell off this ship while we still can."

"I'm afraid I really must insist." Owen reached under his sweater, pulled out a handgun, and pointed it at Harrison.

"You've got to be kidding." Carter struggled to his feet.

"None of you are going anywhere until the treasure is found," Owen said, his voice calm and conversational. He pulled the DiveNav from his back pocket with his free hand. "This thing is either too smart for the masses, Ms. Turner, or totally worthless. For your sake, I hope it's the former."

This isn't happening, Avery thought. Owen? Sweet, helpful, nerdy Owen couldn't be trusted either?

"What are you doing, Owen?" Avery said, exchanging a quick glance with Carter. "If you watched the video feed, you already know we didn't recover anything from the *Fortitude*."

"That's because you were looking in the wrong place," Owen said as he removed a piece of paper from his pants pocket, shook it open, and handed it to Harrison.

"What's that?" Avery said. Harrison passed her what looked to be a hand-drawn map.

"That, Ms. Turner, is a copy of a map which will lead us to the treasure. You didn't really think that anyone would let the crown jewels sink to the bottom of the Weddell Sea, did you? The treasure is hidden inside an ice cave. Except even with this detailed data, your device says there's a 98 percent chance it's on Maui." He tossed it onto the bed.

"Where did you get that map?" Carter said.

"I have my sources, Mosley," Owen said.

"What makes you so sure it leads to anything?" Harrison said. "Anybody could have drawn that and told you what you wanted to hear."

"I don't think so," Owen said as he retrieved a photograph from another pocket and held it up for them to see.

The black-and-white photo appeared to be roughly the same vintage as the ones MaryAnn had emailed. It depicted a young man standing at the entrance to an ice cave, holding what appeared to be the same cross secreted in Avery's suitcase on the far side of the bed. More shocking was that Avery recognized the man in the photo. It was Arlo Olsen, the landscape painter who had been a stowaway aboard the *Fortitude*.

"Suit up," Owen said. "We're all going for a nice long walk."

49

Carter put himself between Avery and Owen. As he did, Owen caught the sudden movement of Harrison reaching for the gun he'd taken from Seamus and last laid atop Avery's desk.

"Uh-uh, Mr. Harrison." Owen stepped to one side and pointed his gun directly at Avery. "Let's not have any more drama today, shall we?" Owen dropped the photograph on the cabin floor, then held out his hand. "Why don't you pass that to me, grip first? That way no one will get hurt."

Eyes on Avery, Harrison complied. Owen stuffed the extra weapon into the back of his jeans.

Using the barrel of his own gun, Owen waved Carter and Harrison away from the door, then refocused his attention on Avery. "Now, Ms. Turner, if you'd be so kind as to get dressed for our little excursion. Wouldn't want you to catch your death from a cold."

Avery would have loved nothing more than to put an end to Owen's shenanigans by showing him a couple of her best disarming moves, but in her weakened condition she wouldn't have won a boxing match against a puppy, let alone this deranged man who towered over her. Slowly, she climbed out of bed and began to collect her outdoor gear.

"What are you doing, Avery?" Carter said. "You aren't really considering going anywhere with this lunatic, are you? Just show him how to set the DiveNav and go back to bed."

"Nice try, Mr. Mosley, but you know too much now," Owen said. "Besides, I'm afraid God intended these arms for computer keys and small tools—I'm not swinging an ice axe."

"Don't see where we have much of a choice." Avery pointed to the gun. "Didn't you do the same thing with Seamus yesterday? Besides, he's got a map. We did just say we were going to find the treasure, didn't we?"

Carter opened his mouth to speak, then closed it.

"Now, get out so I can get dressed," Avery said.

"You heard the lady," Owen said to Harrison and Carter. "Move."

"All of you," Avery said.

"And if I don't?" Owen gestured with the gun.

Avery crossed her arms. "Then you'll be searching for the treasure by yourself. Best of luck."

Owen's eyes darted back and forth between them. It was clear to Avery he hadn't considered the possibility they might not follow his orders or be petrified by the sight of a gun.

"We'll be right outside," he said at last. "Try anything stupid, and your friends will find out how serious I am."

Avery, Carter, and Harrison led the way through the ship while Owen followed with the gun hidden in the pocket of his jacket. Most of the crew were in the dining hall enjoying dinner, leaving the rest of the ship relatively empty. Owen was able to coerce them out to the ice without incident —or even notice, apparently.

Avery had quietly rebooted and reset the DiveNav, and it showed an inland location near the cliffs.

"So there is another treasure hunter on board," Harrison said.

"But this guy came with Noah, he's not a stowaway," Carter whispered, shooting Avery a look. "I can't believe you didn't even try to disarm him."

"I couldn't disarm a kitten right now," Avery hissed. "And I don't remember seeing you doing anything to help our cause back there."

"I still can't believe we're actually doing this," Carter said.

"If Marco is coming to get us, I want to see if the treasure really is in that cave."

She paused to catch her breath.

"He's been lying about everything else," Harrison said. "What makes you think this is legit?"

"Seems there's an epidemic of lying around here." Avery cast a glance at Carter.

"You're talking about Erin, aren't you?" Carter said defensively. "You think she's just pretending to like me?"

"Did I say anything about Erin?" Avery asked.

"I'm sure she's completely sincere," Harrison said. "I mean, who could resist your charms?"

"Shut up and keep moving," Owen said.

Upon reaching the deck, they paused at the top of the gangway to don their face masks and goggles. The winds had kicked up since earlier in the day, a precursor to the approaching storm.

"How long before Marco arrives?" Carter said as they reached the ice shelf at the bottom of the ramp.

"Two hours." Avery faltered as a cramp hit her right leg.

"Move," Owen growled as he herded them toward the Sno-Cat. He tossed the keys to Harrison. "You drive."

Owen climbed in back beside Avery, while Carter sat in front next to Harrison.

Harrison fired up the engine, then cranked the heater.

"Well, this is cozy," Carter said as he removed his gloves and held his hands in front of the vent.

"I'm glad you think so," Owen said. "Try not to be a hero."

"Who tries?" Carter said. "It just happens."

Avery laughed, despite herself.

"I'm glad you all think this is so funny," Owen said as he jammed the barrel of the semiautomatic into the back of the driver's seat. "Try anything stupid and I'll give ol' Harry here a permanent bypass."

Harrison scowled at Owen in the rearview before putting the Sno-Cat in gear.

Harrison followed Owen's directions and before long the *Weddell* was out of sight. The gloom of twilight had increased steadily over the last several days, and now with the storm nearly upon them, the sky had darkened to an ominous purple, requiring the use of the Cat's headlamps.

"How far away is this cave?" Avery said after they had traveled along the shelf for several miles.

"Just a little farther."

The ice cliffs, which had been visible from the deck of the Weddell, now towered above them. Harrison did his best to navigate through the cols in the dark, but the lower ridge was strewn with icy debris and protruding rocks.

Another ten minutes passed, the DiveNav beeped, and Owen jabbed the gun into the back of the seat. "That's far enough."

"I don't see a cave," Harrison said as he brought the Sno-Cat to a sudden stop.

"Yeah, you sure you're reading that map correctly?" Carter said.

"Shut it off and hand me the keys," Owen said. "We walk from here."

50

Owen had packed everything they would need for the trip into the back of the Sno-Cat before coming to Avery's room. There were adjustable boot spikes, ice axes, pry bars, and headlamps. Avery struggled as she bent down to fasten the crampons to her boots. Bending over was like trying to perform jumping jacks with a hangover. Her head felt like it might split in two. Carter helped her while Owen kept the gun trained on all of them.

"Let's go already," Owen said. "Enough of your games."

"Yes, we're faking life-threatening illness to inconvenience you, man." Carter rolled his eyes, leading their small procession up the rise toward . . . whatever awaited them. Harrison stayed close behind Avery, while Owen hung a few yards back. The wind howled and whipped, blowing snow around them and obscuring visibility. Several times, Avery nearly tripped over protruding pieces of ice. Their pace slowed even more as they trekked up a particularly steep incline.

"This is it," Owen shouted from the rear.

At first Avery couldn't see anything remotely resembling a cave, but as she slowly scanned the ice-covered rock formations surrounding them, her gaze fell on a nearly hidden crevasse. Despite their current situation, and her condition, Avery's heart began to beat faster at the thought of what might lie ahead.

"Let's go," Owen said.

They moved forward single file through the icy maw of the cave and into a strange new world.

The interior of the cave was breathtaking, with walls rising to unfathomable heights, reminding Avery of a wintery cathedral. Every surface was either coated in layers of rime or encased in ice as translucent as glass. The footing was unforgiving, both steep and slippery.

"How far are we supposed to go?" Carter said.

"Don't worry," Owen said. "I'll let you know when you can stop."

The four of them trudged deeper into the Earth for what felt to Avery like a quarter of a mile. She moved slowly, as the occasional muscle spasm continued to jolt her.

Carter moved closer to her. "How are you holding up?"

"I'm holding. You?"

"About the same. Do me a favor?"

"What's that?" Avery said.

"The next time someone invites us on an Antarctic treasure hunt, remind me to say no thank you."

Avery laughed despite the cramps rippling through her torso.

"No talking," Owen barked.

"He is not my favorite person," Carter said. "Zero stars, do not recommend."

Avery's abs ached when she laughed, but it was worth it.

Several minutes later, they reached an antechamber, the DiveNav beeped again, and Owen ordered them to stop.

Avery watched as he removed the map from the pocket of his coat and studied it under the headlamp, then looked at the screen on the DiveNav.

"Is this it?" Harrison asked. "I don't see any treasure."

"That's where you come in, Mr. Harrison," Owen said as he tossed an axe at Harry's feet. "Since you are the only one not suffering from decompression sickness, you can dig."

Avery watched as Harrison picked up the axe and Owen took a step back, raising the gun.

"Don't get any stupid ideas," Owen said.

"Don't worry," Harrison said. "I'd say that market has already been cornered."

"Dig." Owen pointed with the gun to a spot about a third of the way up the back wall of the smaller cavern. "There."

As they watched Harrison toil away on the wall, knocking small chunks of ice onto the cave floor, Avery tried to engage Owen in conversation.

"Why would anyone hide the treasure here?" she asked. "I would have thought selling it would make more sense."

"I spent most of my college years researching the lost Nidaros treasure, Ms. Turner. I managed to compile a fair amount of data no one else had. I build chains of information, like DNA coding. But there were gaps. One of those gaps was a young stowaway on the ill-fated voyage of the *Fortitude*. A young painter named Arlo Olsen. Well, shortly after I arrived here and began working for Dr. Wyndham, I found an old photograph in which young Mr. Olsen was depicted."

It was all Avery could do to keep from blurting out that they already knew thanks to MaryAnn, who hadn't needed years to find the information.

Avery noticed Harrison beginning to tire. The thin, frigid air combined with the physical exertion were taking a toll on him. Carter had noticed as well—as sick as he was, he picked up a second axe and began to chip away at the wall beside Harrison.

"What does this Arlo character have to do with the treasure?" Avery asked.

"I'm glad you asked, Ms. Turner. Arlo Olsen grew up the son of a poor farmer. When his father became unable to pay his debts, the man sold his son into servitude. Arlo was taken to a port city where he was made a servant in the house of a prominent shipbuilder. One day, Arlo overheard his master say he had found a great treasure. Not long after, Arlo was standing right there when the man was killed in a shipbuilding accident. He decided to make it his mission to locate the treasure. And he must have succeeded, because shortly thereafter he bought his way out of servitude to the man's heirs."

"How do you know any of that is true?" Avery said.

"Because, Ms. Turner, I've done my homework. I have access to journals few have ever seen. The family records show they received a windfall months after the shipbuilder's death."

Avery caught Carter's eye upon hearing the comment. She knew he was thinking the same thing she was. The man killed must have been Tuva's great-grandfather. Owen's story begged the question: Did Arlo kill Johann to get his hands on the treasure? Or was he simply in the right place when it happened?

Owen looked over to ensure Harrison and Carter were still doing what he'd ordered. Avery could see both were gassed and in dire need of rest.

"Don't quit now, gentlemen," Owen mocked. "If you can't dig, you're of no use to me and you can probably guess what that means."

After fixing Owen with deadly stares, Carter and Harrison resumed chipping away at the wall of ice and rock.

"So where did the legend of a curse begin?" Avery asked.

"Where do any superstitions begin, Ms. Turner? After stealing the treasure from the dead man's family, Arlo fell on a run of bad luck, losing people close to him. His brother died during the war. Then his new bride fell victim to the Spanish flu pandemic. Following her death, Arlo read an article in the local paper about a ship called the *Fortitude* that was bound for Antarctica. The same ship that was being constructed when his master was killed. He took it as a sign, deciding to steal on board the ship with the remaining treasure. His plan was to hide the treasure at the literal ends of the earth so it could never harm anyone again."

"So naturally you thought it would be a good idea to dig it out," Harrison said as he stood upright to rest.

"Don't tell me you believe in curses, Mr. Harrison," Owen said.

Harrison shrugged. "I was a cop for long enough to believe in karma."

"Well, I don't. Arlo's bad luck was nothing but coincidence. But I do believe in wealth. And thanks to Dr. Wyndham's connections, I already have a buyer lined up when I recover the treasure."

"How much is this buyer paying you, assuming you find anything?" Carter said as he lowered his axe for a moment.

"Oh, we'll find it alright, Mr. Mosley," Owen said. "You can bet your life on it. As far as what I'm getting, while it's really none of your business, let's just say I'll never need to work again and I'm only thirty-two."

Harrison's axe made an odd, ringing *thump* as it connected with something clearly not ice.

"Stop," Owen shouted as he moved closer to examine the wall. "Move back."

"What is it?" Avery said.

"Looks like old Arlo's luck went from bad to worse," Harrison said.

"It's a human skull." Carter winced.

"Proof is what it is, Mr. Mosley," Owen said. "Validation of all my hard work."

After examining the ice surrounding the skull, Owen ordered them to continue to excavate the area. "Carefully," he cautioned. "If any of the treasure is damaged, you'll join Arlo in the wall."

"I've got one foot in at this point already," Harrison growled. "Speaking of which, how long do you think it will be until someone comes looking for us? It's not like the Sno-Cat tracks will be hard to follow."

"That's true," Carter said. "I mean even if they had dessert and coffee after dinner, they'd have to be done by now."

"Shut up," Owen said as he moved closer with the gun, pointing it alternately at each one of them. "Shut up and keep digging. Nobody is coming to save you. And nobody knows about this map."

"We do," Harrison said.

"That's right," Carter said. "Counting Avery, that makes four people who know."

"Nothing is truly a secret if more than one person knows," Harrison said.

Owen backed up several paces and swung the barrel of the gun toward Avery. "I know a quick way to reduce that number to three. One more word from either of you and Ms. Turner won't ever have to worry about decompressing again."

The guys resumed digging, revealing the rest of a preserved skeleton a bit at a time.

"I don't see how that could be Arlo," Avery said. "I mean, everyone on the *Fortitude* survived the voyage, right? It was a highly publicized miracle."

"Arlo wasn't listed on the ship's manifest," Owen reminded her.

"This guy didn't freeze to death," Harrison said.

"How can you tell?" Avery asked.

"Because there's a hole in his temple. A bullet hole."

"Funny how history repeats itself," Owen said.

Carter's next swing with the axe resulted in the sound of splintering wood.

"What was that?" Owen asked.

"Looks like a trunk frozen in the ice," Carter said as he swung the axe again.

"Stop!" Owen said as he rushed toward Carter.

Ignoring him, Carter swung again.

"I said stop," Owen screamed. As he charged, Harrison flipped his axe to the blunt side and swung it down against Owen's gun-wielding arm. The bone made a sickening crunch and the gun dropped to the cave floor and slid downhill.

Carter dropped his axe and scrambled after the gun.

51

Most of the fight went out of Owen while he was thrashing about on the ground screaming. There was little doubt his right forearm was broken. Avery kept the gun trained on him while Carter and Harrison returned to trying to free the wooden trunk from the ice.

"You'll never get away with this," Owen challenged. "The people I work for will kill you when they find out what you've done."

"You're assuming you'll ever make it out of here to tell anyone," Carter said. "You could stay right here with Arlo and become the newest casualty of that curse you don't believe in."

Avery made the most fearsome face she could manage as Owen looked up at her with pleading eyes.

"You wouldn't leave me here to die," Owen said. "You don't have it in you."

"Wanna bet?" Carter asked.

"Carter's right." Harrison shook his head, sticking his tongue out like the words tasted bitter. "If he moves, shoot him, Ave."

"You got it, Harry," Avery said without missing a beat.

"Why wait for him to move?" Carter said.

As Owen looked to Harrison for sympathy, Avery snuck Harrison a wink.

It took another ten minutes of chipping at the ice before the chest was loose enough to pull free of its confines.

Avery watched as Harrison and Carter lifted it out of the hole in the wall and carefully set it on the cave floor. Using the ice axes as pry tools, they broke the lock hasp and opened the lid.

"What's in it?" Owen said as he scrambled toward the chest while holding his wounded arm up with his left hand.

"Get back, geek boy," Harrison said. "Unless you're looking to get shot."

Avery hid a grin as Owen shrank away from them.

At first glance the container appeared to be empty, but upon closer examination Carter noticed what appeared to be three silver coins lying in one corner. He picked them up slowly and turned them over for all to see.

"What are they?" Harrison asked.

"The one is a Saint Brendan medallion," Carter said as he handed it to Avery.

"Makes sense," Avery said as she examined it.

"Because?" Harrison asked.

"He was the patron saint of explorers," Avery said.

"What are those others?" Harrison asked.

"I'm not positive," Carter said. "If I had to make a guess I'd say old Olav minted himself some silver coins."

"Let me see," Avery said. "Yup, that sure looks like a man wearing a crown sitting on a throne. Some ego, huh?"

"That does mean these coins are almost seven hundred years old," Carter said.

"Ought to be worth a mint," Harrison said, earning a groan from Avery.

"That's all that was in there?" Owen screamed as he practically threw himself at the chest. "This is what I've risked my life for, an empty sea chest?"

"Actually, no, you little worm," Carter said. "You risked our lives while you were at it."

"What should we do with all this stuff, Ave?" Harrison said.

"We'll take the coins, the medallion, and the trunk with us," Avery said as she pocketed the trinkets. If there was one thing Avery and Carter had learned during their brief treasure hunting life, it was that the containers often held the most important clues toward finding the actual treasure. A fact which Owen, based solely on his reaction, seemed completely unaware of.

"I'm probably going to prison now, right?" Owen said as he kicked at the trunk. "And for what? A couple of stupid coins."

"That's two stupid coins and a medallion, actually," Carter said.

"I hate to break up this icy little soirée," Harrison said, "but we've got a plane to catch."

They placed the empty chest into the Sno-Cat, then secured their prisoner in the back. Avery sat next to Owen, keeping the gun trained on him. Carter sat up front and Harrison climbed behind the controls. The snow had already begun to fall. Nearly thumb-sized flakes combined with the gusty wind to erode their visibility until it was near zero.

"Be careful, Harry," Avery said from the back seat.

"What?" Harrison asked. "You don't think I can drive one of these?"

"It's not that," Carter shouted as he braced himself for impact. "You're right next to the edge."

"The edge of what?" Harrison asked.

"The ocean," Owen screamed.

Harrison's eyes widened and he made a hard maneuver to the right, then backed off on the accelerator. "That was a little close for comfort." He chuckled.

"A lot. It was a lot close," Carter said.

As they continued toward the *Weddell*, they heard plane engines overhead. Avery looked out her side of the Cat, but it was impossible to see anything through the falling snow. If Marco was up there, she hoped he had better visibility than they did.

Harrison pulled up close to the ship and parked. As they marched up the gangplank onto the ship, Harrison said, "Who are we going to turn Owen over to?"

"What do you mean?" Avery asked as she held the gun on her prisoner and walked him onto the deck.

"I mean, I don't trust anyone aboard this entire ship, Ave."

"We'll turn him over to Erin," Carter said.

"Oh, please." Avery rolled her eyes.

"What reason would you have for trusting her?" Harrison said.

Carter opened his mouth to respond but Harrison stopped him. "Never mind. I don't want to know."

"I don't get it," Carter said, turning back to Owen. "How did you even know how to sabotage the tanks? I mean, doing something like that where I couldn't tell before I went under requires a great deal of dive knowledge. How did you do it?"

Owen looked confused. "I don't know what you're talking about."

"There you are," Noah said as he and Erin confronted them on deck. "Where the hell have you been?"

"Long story," Avery said. "This man needs medical attention and a spot in the pantry with Seamus."

Erin and two of the other crew members led Owen away. Avery handed Owen's gun to Harrison for safekeeping.

"You know, I've been thinking, and your story doesn't add up. I believe you people knew about the treasure all along, and I don't appreciate you coming here under false pretenses," Noah said. "You've been meddling in the search since you got here."

"You've got great big stones accusing us of anything, Doc," Harrison said. "Your entire crew are nothing but a bunch of pirates. You're the one who lied to us, about the entire purpose of your expedition, remember? What happened to your lofty humanitarian goals?"

"I don't feel so good, Harry," Avery said as she dropped to one knee.

"That makes two of us," Carter said, leaning back against the hallway wall.

"I've got to get these two out of here," Harrison said to Noah.

"And just where do you plan to take them, Mr. Harrison?"

"We've got a plane inbound for Halley." Harrison didn't wait for an answer before he turned to gather their belongings.

Harrison quickly emptied each of their staterooms, shoving everything he found willy-nilly into suitcases and duffel bags.

"You know, as the leader of this expedition, there are about a dozen reasons I could keep you here," Noah said from the doorway.

"Is that a fact?" Harrison said as he patted the gun in the pocket of his windbreaker. "Because I can think of one reason you can't."

Avery, in her weakened state, smiled as Noah backed off.

Harrison had a bag slung over each shoulder as he pushed past Noah. "You know this whole thing is like that movie they made about *Clue*."

"What are you talking about?" Noah said.

"You know, the board game. Guess who broke the dweeb's arm, in the cave, with an axe? There was a movie. With Tim Curry."

"You're crazy, mate," Noah said.

"Like a fox. And I'm not your mate. But I do think if we stayed here long enough, we'd figure out that everyone did it. What I haven't quite got yet is whose side you're on, Doc." Harrison turned to Avery and Carter. "Can you walk?"

"Barely," Carter said as he shoved himself off the wall.

"You've only got to get to the Cat. We can wait for Marco back at Halley. Hopefully there are fewer criminals there."

"We can make it," Avery said, shuffling into the hall.

Noah followed them, continuing his protestations all the way off the ship, but made no additional threats about keeping them aboard.

Harrison helped Avery and Carter into the rear of the Sno-Cat, where they could lie down, then fired up the engine before stowing their gear in the passenger seat. He turned back to Noah before climbing inside. "I wouldn't say it's exactly been a pleasure, Doc. But it's a pleasure to be leaving. Sayonara."

52

With the storm intensifying it took Harrison nearly forty-five minutes to reach the runway at Halley Station, the Sno-Cat practically crawling when he wasn't stopped because the front edges of the blizzard winds were blowing the existing snow up and around, making it impossible to see.

At Halley, he saw no sign of Marco or Avery's Gulfstream, and the Cat was running too low on fuel for them to wait outside. He helped Avery and Carter to the sofa in the conference room they'd seen their first night in Antarctica—hard to believe it had been less than a week when it felt like a decade in that moment. Harrison had never wanted to see the stars—or his own bed—so badly in his life.

Not wanting to leave the cross and loupe unguarded for more than a moment, Harrison went back out to retrieve their bags and found the socially awkward climate lady with the spiky gray hair talking to Avery when he returned.

"Dr. Abbott, right?" he asked when she'd finished explaining that while storms over the poles are unpredictable to a large extent, she thought they could still get off the shelf safely with a decent pilot, but it should be soon.

She nodded, turning to him. "Ms. Turner says you spoke to her pilot?"

"No, I emailed him. The internet relay out at the Weddell is terrible, but I think the message went through." Harrison checked his watch. "He should've been here by now. Is there a better connection here? Could we use a phone and call our cockpit phone?"

"I'm afraid our comms went down entirely about an hour ago."

"My God, I want to go home," Harrison said.

"You and me both. At least your transport is coming. Mine got bumped yesterday because the king decided he needed a full entourage to attend a polo match in Italy and both of the pilots who can fly this route are with him."

"You can come with us," Avery croaked. "We're going . . . to somewhere you could get a ticket home from."

Courtney Abbott's face lit up. "Are you sure, miss?" She glanced out the window. "Though you're going to have some trouble if he doesn't get here shortly."

"Get your bags. Maybe you can help Marco navigate the storm."

"I certainly can. I have all manner of monitors that are designed to withstand the magnetic fields here." She hurried off.

"Where are you, Marco?" Harry went to the window.

"Get me the DiveNav and someone's cell," Avery said.

"You need rest."

"We need to call Marco. You have the number of the flight deck phone in your cell, right? Give me your phone, a charger, and the DiveNav." She struggled to sit up.

He did as she asked, watching to see what the heck she was up to.

When the distinct sound of ringing trilled through the phone's speaker, Harrison pumped a fist in the air. "You're a magician," he said.

"No, I'm a scientist who knows how to steal other people's satellite signals." Avery tapped the DiveNav. "And who put a port for a charger in this to allow for battery transfer. I realized day before yesterday that I could probably use the DiveNav's software to ping off any satellite, not just the British ones the comms here rely on, and turn any cell phone into a reliable satellite phone . . ." Her head fell back onto the cushion as Marco answered.

"Harry? I'm nearing you, I can see the station, but this weather, man. I don't know."

"We're waiting and we've got a genius climate expert to talk you through it." Harry kept his voice even and his eyes on Avery's face, which looked way more gray than could possibly be healthy. "She doesn't look good, Marco. We have to go. Now."

"Gear down, Harry. Hang on, Miss Avery."

Dr. Abbot bustled back in just as Harrison heard the jet's engine over the wind. "I've got a crew out clearing the runway."

"Perfect. There's our ride," Carter said without opening his eyes.

"In the nick of time if I've ever seen it," Courtney said, leaning down to help Avery to her feet. "You help Mr. Mosley, and get your bags and let's get the hell out of Dodge, as you yanks say."

"Amen to that, Doc." Harrison half lifted Carter, swearing under his breath when Carter's head lolled forward before he pulled it up with some effort. "Please God, don't let us be too late."

53

Marco had already landed and was hurriedly refueling by the time they half dragged Carter and Avery across the frozen ground through the stiff wind to Avery's plane. Several of the Halley Station crew raced back and forth in two larger Sno-Cats fitted with plows trying to keep the icy runway clear, but the weather was beginning to outpace their efforts.

Avery and Carter, both in rough shape, had to be helped aboard the plane and strapped into their seats.

"I'll stay with them," Courtney said. "Get us off the ground."

Harrison looked between her and Marco, undecided and reluctant to leave Avery with someone he didn't really know after the week they'd had of unscrupulous people.

"Mr. Harrison, I've wanted to work at Halley since it was Halley I and I was seven years old. I'm leaving because I know Noah Wyndham is a brilliant man, but I cannot be party to the increasingly questionable things he's doing in the name of discovery and fame. He abandoned science as a driving ambition long ago. I will sit with them. You help them get us out of here before it's too late."

"Thank you."

Harrison and Marco hurried to load the gear and ready the plane for takeoff.

Once the door was secured, Courtney dug two gadgets out of a bag and offered them to Marco. "If you know how to work your onboard meters, you can work these. But they won't be affected by the magnetic fields here."

"Outstanding." Marco turned the monitors on and touched the screens, nodding. "This just may be enough to get us back to the real world in one piece."

Harrison settled another blanket over Avery and tucked Carter's around his feet.

"Thanks for coming to get us," Harrison said as he squeezed into the cockpit and buckled in next to Marco. "I'm not a pilot but I can follow directions if I can help."

"I made it here, and with these pole-proof instruments, I should be able to make it back out," Marco said as he fired up the engines and began his preflight checks.

Harrison stared at nothing but blowing snow through the windshield.

Marco taxied the plane into position.

"Level with me, Marco—are we being stupid?" Harrison asked.

"I don't know, man. That's the truth. I agree that Miss Avery looks like she needs a hospital. The issue is that we'll have to fly out a different way than I came in because of the storm. We need to get around this weather and come at New Zealand from a more difficult angle."

"But you can do that, right?"

"Well, it's inherently dangerous and ill-advised because of the strong magnetic fields surrounding the South Pole, no matter how well-equipped the aircraft is. These instruments will help, but the fields have shaken planes right out of the sky. And of course, there is low visibility due to the storm and the coming winter darkness. Plus, we'll have to stay below eight thousand feet because of the decompression risk to Avery and Carter. Flying at a higher altitude will put them in greater danger."

"I get all of that, Marco," Harry shouted to be heard above the roar of the engines. "But before we leave the ground, you are up to the task, right?"

"Guess we'll know soon enough, Harry," Marco said with a sigh.

Harrison groaned and held on to the seat tightly as they shot down the runway.

The turbulence was like nothing Harrison had ever experienced, a hundred times worse than the time he took a cheapo deal to Puerto Vallarta and wound up on a plane whose pilot was drunk. The shaking and sudden drops in altitude shot his nerves in minutes, and he worried that he'd chosen poorly, leaving Avery alone with someone they didn't know when she was so sick, but he couldn't get up to go back to her after takeoff. This was a seatbelts-only flight. Even worse was the feeling that at any moment the plane might simply tear apart at the seams.

"That's not good," Marco said about twenty minutes into the flight.

"What's not good?" Harrison said, his voice cracking with fear.

"The magnetic fields are wreaking havoc on my gauges." Marco tapped several of them with his fingers.

"But you expected that, right? I mean, you've got it in hand, right?"

"For the most part. The altimeter is acting up, as is the directional compass."

"Meaning?"

"It's hard to know how high we're flying or which direction we are going."

"What about the thingamabobs Dr. Abbott gave you?" Harrison reached for the bigger one.

"Those are good for weather and icing information, which is important, but no help here, I'm afraid."

"But you can make an educated guess though, right?"

"Might have to," Marco said as he tapped the gauges again. "Don't worry yet—I don't want to die even more than I don't want to fail Miss Avery."

"What's the worst thing that could happen?" Harrison said.

The plane convulsed like it was suffering a seizure before Marco could reply.

Harrison slapped a hand over his own mouth, attempting to keep the nausea at bay. "Never mind. I got it."

"Oh, that's just a little bounce." Marco winked.

"Funny guy. And he flies, too," Harrison said between clenched teeth.

"I guess the good news is I can probably hold our altitude without too much trouble."

"And the bad?"

"If we veer off course too much, there's always a chance we end up flying near the Vinson Massif."

"But we're eight thousand feet up," Harrison said. "We'll fly right over it."

"Mount Vinson is sixteen thousand feet up, Harry. We could fly right into it."

"Let's try to avoid that."

Hours later, after the plane exited the weather front, their flight smoothed out enough so that Harrison could go back and check on Avery and Carter. They both looked exhausted. Harrison didn't imagine the rough start to their flight had helped much.

Courtney Abbott was curled up asleep on a recliner, her short legs bent under her and covered with a blanket. Harrison remembered her talking about being tired and figured as soon as the plane crossed into darkness, she'd fallen out like a light.

"Hey, Ave," Harrison said as he gently pushed Avery's hair from her face with one hand. "How are you holding up?"

"Hey, Harry," Avery said. "I'm hanging in there."

"How much farther?" Carter croaked.

"A while yet," Harrison said. "You guys need anything?"

"You mean besides a decompression chamber?" Carter said. "Nope. That'll do it, thanks."

"How about you, Ave?" Harrison said.

"I just want to feel better, Harry."

"I know you do. Hang in there a little longer, okay?"

"Okay, Harry," Avery said as she closed her eyes again.

They touched down smoothly at the Queenstown Airport in New Zealand. Marco had radioed ahead for assistance, and there were two ambulances and a black SUV with a driver awaiting them as they taxied up to the gate. Harrison, Courtney, and Marco helped the emergency medical technicians shepherd Avery and Carter into the back of the rescue units. After shaking Marco's hand for longer than he'd ever shaken anyone's before and clapping the pilot on the back in an awkward hug, Harrison gave him a credit card for a nice hotel room.

Courtney handed Harrison a piece of paper with her number and address outside London and told him to let her know if they ever needed anything, before disappearing into the customs line, trying to figure out whether she wanted a hotel room or a flight home.

Harrison and Marco checked in with a private air customs officer and loaded up the SUV, where Harrison instructed the driver to take him directly to the hospital and then drop Marco at the Villa del Lago.

As luck would have it, the Lakes District Hospital, less than three minutes away from the airport, was equipped with a state-of-the-art hyperbaric chamber.

Harrison scurried inside and, after sweet-talking a nurse, found Carter lying in an observation room.

"Where's Avery?" Harrison said, nearly breathless.

"No, really, Harry, I'm fine," Carter said. "No reason to make a fuss over me."

"Sorry, kid. How are you feeling?"

"Crappy. Thanks for asking. I told them to take Avery first. I can wait."

"Maybe I was wrong about you after all," Harrison said.

"I knew that already."

"Who are you and how did you get back here?" a tall woman in a lab coat asked. The name badge identified her as Dr. Ainsley.

"My name is Harrison, Doc. I brought Mr. Mosley here and Avery Turner in for treatment."

"Follow me, Mr. Harrison."

"Call me Harry, please."

"Follow me, Harry."

In the hall, and out of earshot of Carter, the doctor asked for details on how Avery and Carter had come by their decompression sickness.

"That's a long story, Doc," Harrison said.

"How long have they been without proper treatment?"

"Quite a while," Harrison said. "We flew here from Antarctica."

"Antarctica?" she asked with raised brows.

"Like I said, it's a long story."

He did his best to keep it short and sweet, leaving out the part about nearly being killed twice by crazy people with guns, never mind once by an explosion.

"You look like you could use some medical care yourself," Ainsley said. "Want us to take a look at you?"

Harrison shook his head. "Honestly, I'm just overtired."

"Well, there is nothing more you can do here, Harry. I suggest you find a nice hotel nearby and get yourself a few hours of sleep. Your friends are in good hands. Don't worry, they will feel markedly better once they've received proper treatment."

"I can wait here—"

"Get some rest, Harry," Ainsley said firmly as she pointed down the hall. "Doctor's orders. Just leave your number with the front desk."

54

"Any good hotels around here?" Harrison asked the driver after finding the SUV waiting outside, Marco safely dropped off.

"I imagine you're not looking for a budget place."

"You imagine right, friend. What's the top of the line nearby?"

"That would probably be Eichardt's Private Hotel."

"Nice?"

"Oh, yes, sir. Has a wine bar, piano player, and sits right on Lake Wakatipu."

"Sounds perfect. Let's go."

"Yes, sir."

Harrison went to the front desk and rented three of the hotel's best rooms, each overlooking the water. After checking in and stowing the bags in the respective rooms with help from the driver, Harrison signed the car service bill, making sure to include a hefty tip.

"Thanks a lot," the man said. "Here's my card, in case you need transportation while you're here."

Harrison looked at the plain white business card. "Thanks, Jack. Might just take you up on that."

Harrison locked the door to his room, ordered room service, then made himself comfortable on the bed. It was time to do a bit of his own sleuthing.

It took him the better part of fifteen minutes to figure out how to navigate an international call to New York.

"Do you have any idea what time it is, Harry?" the groggy voice on the other end of the line asked.

"Hell, Rog, I don't even know what time it is here," Harrison said as he glanced at the bedside clock.

"It's late, Harry," Roger Antonin said. "That's what time it is. Where are you?"

"Queenstown."

"Where the hell is Queenstown?"

"New Zealand."

"Sure, that makes perfect sense. What are you doing in New Zealand, Harry?"

"Long story. Any word on Maggio?"

"You first."

Harrison proceeded to tell Antonin what they had been up to since leaving the Big Apple, holding little back as he went.

"And this is what you call retirement?" Antonin said. "Jeez, Harry. The NYPD sounds infinitely safer than this treasure hunting jazz."

"Any luck on my intel, Rog?"

"Yup. Hang on a minute. I gotta go into the other room. Wife's giving me the stink eye."

"Tell her I said hello."

"Maybe later. Might be more receptive after she's had her coffee."

Harrison listened to the sound of shuffling papers as he opened the door for room service, taking his plate to the bed just before Roger came back on the line.

"Okay, that Wyndham guy you asked about, looks like his research project is being funded by a whole bunch of shell corporations. I've got a trace out on an account where two very large payments originated. It's offshore and belongs to yet another shell company. It's a literal maze of corporate entities with no real ties to anyone. This thing smacks of shady dealings, Harry."

As Harrison worked his way through a slice of pizza, he considered how lucky they all were to have made it off the *Weddell* alive.

"Don't suppose you've got a contact at Interpol?" Harrison asked.

"Let me guess, downtown Queenstown?"

"Doesn't have to be close by, Rog. Anywhere in New Zealand is fine. Now, tell me about Maggio."

"You're lucky you and Val were such good detectives, you know that, Harry?"

"Indeed I do."

Avery sprang up from her hospital bed and gave Harrison a bear hug as soon as he entered the room she was sharing with Carter.

"Man, you look a thousand times better," Harrison said.

"I feel ten thousand times better, Harry."

"What about me?" Carter asked from the other bed.

"Nope, you're still homely," Harrison said after regarding him for a moment. "Maybe some more time in the hyperbaric chamber."

Carter flashed his middle finger up, grinning. "It's so nice to have things back to normal, I'll cheerfully trade barbs with you, Harrison."

"Did you find us a nice place to stay?" Avery asked.

"Very nice. It overlooks some lake I can't pronounce, and they've got room service with great pizza."

"Sounds perfect," Avery said. "What about our luggage?"

"All safe and sound."

"All of it?" Carter asked.

"Every last item," Harrison said as he held up the medallion they had found in the cave. "Even that stupid bindle thingy."

"It's a compass binnacle, Harry."

"Binnacle shminnacle. How soon before I can bust you two out of here?"

"Not until I say so," a nurse said from the doorway.

"Aw, come on," Carter said.

"Young man, you must be suffering from short-term memory loss," the nurse said as she entered the room. "Do you remember what kind of shape you were in when you got here?"

"Not too good as I recall," Harrison said. "He still looks a little bit peaked. Maybe he should stay here for some additional tests, and I'll take Avery with me."

"They're both staying put until the doctor says so," the nurse said. "They need more rest."

Avery shrugged. "You heard the woman, Harry."

"Sounds like you're in good hands," Harrison said as he gave Avery a quick kiss on the top of her head, then walked toward the door. "I'll check in with you both later."

Harrison was halfway to the parking lot when a dark-haired man dressed in an expensive suit approached him.

"Are you Mr. Harrison?"

"I guess that depends on who you are."

"I'm Oliver Clark, from the Wellington office of Interpol."

"Then I'm Harrison."

The two men walked to the hospital cafeteria and grabbed an empty table. Over the course of the next ten minutes, Harrison filled the man in on the cast of shady characters associated with the search for the *Fortitude* and the missing crown jewels of Norway.

"Sounds like quite a crew," Clark said. "So, you want me to check out Dr. Noah Wyndham, Seamus, and Owen. Anyone else?"

Harrison thought about it for a moment. "Why don't you add Allison Miranda to the list."

"Who is she?"

"She's an agent with the National Oceanic and Atmospheric Administration. Bit of a pit bull. Keeps showing up at our dives. First in New York, then in Antarctica. It's almost like she's following us."

"That is interesting," Clark said, raising a brow. "I'll see what I can find."

"It's getting hard to know who to trust anymore," Harrison said.

"Amen to that. Anything else?"

"Nope, that about does it."

"I'll be in touch."

55

The following day Avery and Carter felt almost normal again. The hyperbaric chamber treatments and plenty of sleep had worked wonders. They both ate a sizable breakfast and were more than ready to depart the hospital. After breakfast they pulled out Avery's laptop and set up an impromptu video chat with MaryAnn from their hospital room.

"Welcome back to the land of sunrise and sunset," MaryAnn said.

"And decent internet," Carter said. "Though . . . do I remember something about you MacGyvering the DiveNav into a sat phone before we left back there? Or did I dream that?"

"I liked that show—*MacGyver*, and you were not dreaming." Avery turned back to MaryAnn. "Any luck translating the inscription on the cross?" Avery asked. "Carter thinks it says something about the hatred of God."

MaryAnn laughed. "You got the God part right, Carter. I ran the inscription past a friend of mine who studies ancient languages. According to her, it means 'seek not the riches of the earth, for the selfish man will be rebuked by the vengeful hand of God.'"

"Now I know why the treasure is believed to be cursed," Carter said. "That is literally the same as posting a sign that says trespassers will be shot."

MaryAnn laughed again. "It's more likely that because the cross is a symbol of religious significance and most of the Nidaros congregation wouldn't have been able to read the inscription anyway, the exception being the word *God*, they likely would have seen it as a lucky or blessed artifact."

"And the curse we keep hearing about?" Avery said.

"Seems to be a story told to them down through generations," MaryAnn said. "Add to that a few tragic events loosely connected to the treasure, and you've got yourself a bona fide Cardinal's Curse."

"Anything else you can tell us about it?" Carter said.

"Yeah, my friend also confirmed that the Nidaros cross is in fact part of the original crown jewels believed stolen from the cathedral by Olav. Not only is it extremely valuable, but I imagine the Church of Norway would love to get their hands on it, along with the rest of the treasure if you can find it."

"I'll bet they would," Avery said. "Along with everyone else we've met."

"My friend also has access to a few of Olav's personal papers and those of his most trusted bishop, who legend says made a deathbed confession about his involvement in the theft of the jewels. She told me you're more than welcome to view the papers."

"What's the catch?" Carter said.

"The papers are in Norway," MaryAnn said.

"Did I hear something about travel plans?" Harrison said as he walked into their room, holding a bouquet of flowers and a get-well card.

"For me?" Carter said.

"You wish," Harrison said as he set the flowers on the table beside Avery's bed.

"Thank you, Harry," Avery said. "They're beautiful."

"Hello, Harry," MaryAnn said through the computer.

"Good morning, MaryAnn," Harrison said. "Or whatever time it is back home."

"It's later than you think. I was just telling Avery and Carter that Olav's personal papers are available to view if you'd like to see them. You'll just need to fly to Norway."

"Well now," Harrison said. "Isn't that fortuitous?"

"What do you mean?" Avery said.

"I mean Marco is still here, enjoying a hard-earned weekend in the lap of luxury. And while you two have been enjoying a little R and R here at New Zealand General, I've been busy getting all our ducks in a row. Figured you'd want to take this treasure hunt to the next level."

"Wow, Harry," Avery said. "Since when did you decide to go all in on this hunt?"

"Since someone tried to kill me in Antarctica. Twice."

"Tried to kill us, you mean," Carter said.

"Indeed," Harrison said.

Avery's attention returned to MaryAnn. "Is there any way to date the loupe we found on the Fortitude? Maybe it was part of the treasure or could be used to locate more of it."

"Way ahead of you," MaryAnn said. "We've been doing some research on the Nidaros Cathedral dating back to Olav's time there. Inside the cathedral there is a tile mosaic that depicts a scholar seated at a table, writing while holding a similar object to the one Carter found aboard the *Fortitude*. My friend didn't know the origin or the meaning of the mosaic, but she's willing to bet the symbolism refers to someone coding secrets for Cardinal Olav."

"How fast do you think we can get to Norway?" Avery asked.

"Marco can probably have you there in a day, with a refueling stop in India," MaryAnn said.

"Then let's go," Carter said as he swung his legs out of bed and stood up wearing only his hospital gown and socks.

"Aren't you forgetting something important, Ace?" Harrison said.

"The doctor's blessing?"

"I was thinking more like pants."

"Which reminds me, Carter," MaryAnn said. "Your agent is looking for you. He's called Brady twice."

"Guess it's a good thing my phone was dead, then, huh?" Carter said. "If he calls again, tell him I'll get him back when I'm not running from guns or trying to drown."

"Will do. Anything else I should be working on before I let you go?" MaryAnn said.

"One more thing," Avery said. "Could you check photos from the ship sent to rescue the stranded crew of the *Fortitude*? See if you can locate Arlo. I want to confirm he didn't make it off the continent with Weymouth's men."

"You think it's Arlo's body you found in the cave?"

"Let's call it an educated guess."

"And see if you can find a link to someone Arlo may have befriended among the *Fortitude*'s crew," Harrison added. "Someone followed him to the cave."

"Or forced him there, intending to steal the treasure," Avery agreed.

"You found nothing else inside the cave?" MaryAnn said.

"Nothing besides a skeleton, an empty wooden chest, a medallion, and a couple of coins," Harrison said.

"This medallion," Avery said, holding it up to the laptop's camera.

"I'll see if I can find anyone wearing it in any of the photos," MaryAnn said.

"You're the best," Avery said.

"Don't forget it," MaryAnn said with a wink. "And feel better."

Avery closed the lid to the laptop. "Okay, now I want to get out of here."

"I'll go find the doc." Harrison headed for the door.

56

Five hours later, after the doctor cleared them for flight, Avery, Carter, and Harrison were back on board the Gulfstream with Marco at the controls. The familiar purr and luxury of Avery's jet was like coming home.

"I will never make fun of this plane again." Harrison petted the plush leather seat beside his as if it were a cat.

"I thought you didn't care for all this jet-setting, Harry," Avery teased.

"After sitting in that flying sheet metal deathtrap of Rollie's, I'm a convert. Besides, this old girl earned her keep and then some getting us out of Antarctica."

"The sun set just after midnight last night," Avery said. "So not a minute too soon. I will say this flight is far more pleasant than our last."

Carter laughed. "Something to be said for functional instruments."

"And not feeling like one of us is about to die," Harrison added. "Though I'm still not clear on why we're going all the way to Norway. Aren't we sure the treasure was in Antarctica years after it was taken from Norway?"

"The only thing we're sure of is that the cross was in Antarctica," Avery said as she continued to examine the religious artifact. "Besides, we can investigate the history of the treasure firsthand while MaryAnn checks out other leads."

"That's true," Carter said. "For all we know, the cross may have been the only piece of the original crown jewels to reach Antarctica. Maybe the whole legend of Arlo and the *Fortitude* was made up."

"Except he was in the photos," Harrison said.

"That only means he was on the ship," Carter said.

"What we do know is that Olav stole the crown jewels from Norway, along with a heap of other stuff, before winding up dead," Avery said. "The treasure could have been found and relocated many times over the years."

"Since all we have is the cross," Carter said, "it's conceivable the treasure was split up."

"I'm convinced we'll find additional clues in Norway," Avery said. "We've got the loupe, the mosaic inside the cathedral, and personal papers belonging to Olav and his right-hand man."

"One thing's for sure," Carter said.

"What's that?" Harrison said.

"Neither Owen nor Seamus will be there to stop us."

"Let's hope the same holds true for whoever it is they are working for," Avery said before yawning loudly. "Man, I'm exhausted."

"You should be after what you went through," Harrison said. "Why don't you both try and get some shut-eye?"

"Where are you going?" Avery said as Harrison left his seat and headed toward the cockpit.

"Thought I'd keep Marco company."

"Tell him war stories, you mean," Carter said.

"Nothing better than a captive audience," Harrison said with a wink.

The refueling stop in India was so brief, neither Avery nor Carter bothered to deplane, opting instead to continue dozing in their fully reclined seats. They awoke as the jet touched down at the Trondheim Airport in Vaernes, Norway, home of the Royal Norwegian Air Force.

MaryAnn had taken care of hiring a car and a driver knowledgeable about the area. Both were waiting for them as they stepped off the Gulfstream. MaryAnn had also procured them rooms at the Britannia Hotel, less than a mile from Nidaros Cathedral.

The Britannia was grand, with high ceilings and sumptuous furniture that carried subtle touches of traditional Nordic flair in fabrics and molding accents. They quickly checked into their rooms and stowed their belongings, including the remains of the wooden trunk they'd removed from the cave in Antarctica, camouflaged in a large, zippered canvas tote.

"I really hope there is some kind of clue somewhere inside this thing," Harrison said as he and Carter struggled with the awkward bag.

"Think of it as a replacement for your golf clubs," Avery said.

"My golf clubs might at least come in handy."

Avery knew finding a hidden clue somewhere on the trunk was a long shot, but experience had taught her not to take anything for granted. Clues to hidden treasure were often concealed in the least likely of places.

After showering and changing into fresh clothing, they returned to the car, where their driver was waiting.

"Where are we going first?" Carter asked. "The cathedral?"

"No," Avery said as she turned to the driver. "Our first stop is the Sverresborg Trondelag Folk Museum."

"Very good, Ms. Turner," the driver said.

"What is at the whatever you just said folk museum?" Harrison said.

"MaryAnn's local contact," Avery said.

"What the heck is this?" Harrison asked when the car stopped. "It looks like a thousand-year-old version of colonial Williamsburg."

"You're not far off," the driver said. "This museum was constructed around the ruins of King Sverre's castle, dating back to around 1200 AD."

"So right around the last time you updated your wardrobe, Harry," Carter said.

"So very glad you're feeling better, kid."

"Let's go see if anyone's home," Avery said as she climbed out of the car.

MaryAnn's contact turned out to be the museum curator, Erik Larsen.

"Wonderful to finally meet you in person," Larsen said, his eyes lingering a bit too long on Avery.

Sporting blond hair, blue eyes, and rugged good looks, Larsen looked like he might have just stepped off the cover of a romance novel. Given MaryAnn's history of chasing Carter, Avery had no trouble imagining how she might know Larsen.

"MaryAnn has told me a bit about what you are looking for," Larsen said. "Would you like a tour of the museum first? Or perhaps you'd like to start at the cathedral? I called ahead. Bishop Westergaard is expecting us."

"I'd like to start at Nidaros," Avery said. "If that works for you."

"Of course. Let's get going."

57

"Pictures do not do this place justice." Avery stepped out of the car with her mouth agape, staring up at the soaring architecture and intricate stone and glasswork of the cathedral. It was far more breathtaking than the photographs she had studied online. Flanked on both sides by massive spire towers, the blue-gray stone façade channeled the Roman aqueducts, but more grandiose. Scores of stone carvings in the historic West Front of the cathedral surrounded an enormous stained-glass rose window.

"It's incredible," Avery said.

"Makes the church I grew up in in New York look like it got beaten with an ugly stick," Harrison said.

"It took them more than a hundred years to restore," Larsen said.

"Seriously?" Carter said.

"Yes. It has undergone many restorations during its existence. The most recent was completed in 2001, but the work started in the second half of the nineteenth century. The West Front alone took nearly eighty years to complete."

"I can see why," Avery said.

"Now there's a reality show that would give your social media thing a run for its money," Harrison told Carter. "Extreme church makeovers, anyone?"

"Shall we go inside?" Larsen asked.

The interior of Nidaros Cathedral was even more striking. The vaulted, beamed ceiling seemed impossibly high, as if the soaring interior couldn't exist within the confines of the structure they had seen outside.

"Is that a pipe organ?" Harrison said, pointing to the far end of the hall directly under the rose window.

"Indeed, it is," Larsen said.

"I'm a sucker for those," Harrison said. "Something about those deep bass notes. Man, oh man."

"I'd love a complete tour sometime," Avery said. "But I'm particularly interested in seeing the mosaic today."

"Of course," Larsen said. "I'll introduce you to the bishop. I've actually only met him once myself."

Larsen led them behind the altar to a small space that looked more like an office than Avery had expected. Seated at a small writing desk was a slim gray-haired man wearing a black robe and white collar.

"Bishop Harald Westergaard, so nice to see you again. I'd like to introduce you to some friends of mine," Larsen said. "This is Avery Turner, Carter Mosley, and Mr. Harrison."

Westergaard rose and approached them with a warm smile and an outstretched hand. "Very pleased to make your acquaintance," he said as he firmly gripped each of their hands.

Avery liked him immediately.

Westergaard paused as he greeted Harrison. "Should I refer to you as Mr. Harrison?"

"Harry's fine, Bishop."

"Harry it is."

Westergaard's salt-and-pepper hair extended to his bushy eyebrows and the well-trimmed mustache and goatee he wore.

"Your cathedral is breathtaking," Avery said.

"I appreciate your kindness," Westergaard said as he bowed slightly at the compliment. "But the Nidaros Cathedral is not mine. It belongs to the people of God. It is also the final resting place of Saint Olav, the patron saint of Norway."

"Bishop Westergaard recently transferred from his parish in Denmark," Larsen said. "He is very knowledgeable in Norwegian history."

"Is this a Catholic church?" Harrison asked as he pointed to the gleaming brass crucifix hanging around Westergaard's neck.

"Formerly," Westergaard said. "It is now evangelical Lutheran."

Harrison nodded.

Westergaard turned his attention to Avery. "Ms. Turner, I understand from speaking with Erik that you and your friends are interested in viewing our famed mosaic."

"We would like that very much," Avery said, attempting to suppress the eagerness in her voice but failing miserably.

"Then I suggest we head down to the basement."

They followed Westergaard down several flights of spiraling stone stairs, past a crypt and along several narrow passageways before entering a cavernous room. The mosaic, which covered nearly an entire wall, was illuminated at the far end of the space.

"My heavens, it's beautiful," Avery breathed.

"And much larger than I imagined," Carter said.

Harrison opened his mouth to say something inappropriate, but a warning glare from Avery stopped the words before they hit the air.

"May we take a closer look?" Avery said.

"By all means," Westergaard said, gesturing with one hand for them to approach the mosaic.

"The tiles are in remarkably good condition considering how long this has been here," Larsen said.

"How long is that?" Harrison said.

"Nearly seven hundred years," Larsen said.

Carter whistled. "I would think something as delicate as this wouldn't do well in a damp environment like a church basement."

"It is a struggle to maintain works of art like this one," Westgaard admitted. "They need constant care, and perhaps a bit of divine intervention."

Avery studied each individual tile, paying particular attention to the one depicting the loupe.

"I understand from Erik you may have found a similar loupe," Westergaard said. "May I see it?"

Avery paused a moment before reaching into her pocket and handing it over to the bishop. "I'm not sure of its provenance, but it certainly looks old."

"Indeed, it does." Larsen peered over the bishop's shoulder.

Avery studied Westergaard's face as he examined the loupe and compared it to the mosaic. There was the slightest hitch in his breathing.

"As a student of history, it is always such a pleasure to touch something from the past," Westergaard said as he handed it back. "Might I ask where you acquired it?"

"You can ask," Avery said.

"Touché, Ms. Turner," Westergaard said.

"I told them they might be able to view some of the documents believed to have belonged to Cardinal Olav," Larsen said.

Avery's stomach coiled into knots as Westergaard appeared to ponder the request.

"No photographs," Westergaard said. "And it goes without saying, nothing leaves the cathedral."

"You have our word," Avery said.

58

Westergaard led them to another chamber located on an even lower level of the basement. Avery felt like they were wandering through a subterranean maze. She wondered how they would ever find their way out of this place without a guide.

After keying them into the cathedral's secret library and offering another admonishment about the sanctity of the records, Westergaard left with Larsen. "I'll be upstairs when you've finished."

"We might be a while," Carter said.

"Take all the time you need," Westergaard said. "But we close at six sharp."

"And I'll be returning to the museum, should you need me," Larsen said.

"Thank you," Avery said. "We'll be in touch."

The room was climate controlled and dimly lit, presumably to keep the ancient ink and paper from degrading further. Lining the space on three sides were floor-to-ceiling wooden bookcases, each of which was crammed to capacity with ancient leather-bound tomes. At the center of the room were several rows of lighted metal display cabinets showcasing individual pages of handwritten notes. The papers had been preserved under glass. Looking at the documents reminded Avery of a trip she had once taken to the National Archives in Washington, DC, where she viewed the original Declaration of Independence and the Emancipation Proclamation. The documents contained in these cases were far older.

Each sheet of paper had long yellowed with age. The cramped, slanted script appeared to be Old Norse.

"I'm not sure how these are going to help us," Harrison said. "Unless one of you knows how to decode Norse."

"I know someone who can," Carter said as he dug out his phone.

"You don't honestly think you'll get a signal down here, do you?" Avery said.

Carter showed her the phone. "Two bars."

"I'll be damned," Harrison said.

"You will be if you keep talking like that in here," Avery said.

Carter put the phone on speaker, then explained that they had made it to what passed for the cathedral records room. Avery and Carter both described the space in detail.

"That sounds so cool," MaryAnn said. "I wish I could see it for myself."

"FaceTime is probably pushing it for the available connection here," Avery said. "So, where do we start?"

"I would start with the individual pages. Watch for Olav's name—I'm texting you the Old Norse spelling just to be safe. Use the loupe to examine the margins and backs of the paper."

"What are we looking for?" Harrison said. "Invisible ink?"

"For your information, Harry," MaryAnn said, "last year these researchers I know located some very important invisible ink dating back to the eighteenth century."

"That's all well and good," Carter said, "but unless we've got an X-ray loupe, we'll have to stick to the front of each page. They're all locked inside cases."

"And it's a good bet the cases are alarmed," Harrison said as he examined the edges.

Avery checked MaryAnn's text, showing the spelling, Óláfr, to Carter and Harrison before she went to work scanning each page with the loupe.

"Anything more on Arlo, MaryAnn?" Carter asked.

"Actually, yes," MaryAnn said. "He is not in any of the photos taken on

Easter Island or in Argentina following the trip to rescue the crew of the *Fortitude*. And there was one other person on board the *Fortitude*, named Walter Smyth, who according to records never made it back to jolly old England."

"That's interesting," Avery said. "Perhaps he went spelunking with Arlo."

"But then, which one did we find in the cave?" Carter said.

"That's a great question," MaryAnn said.

"Find out all you can about Smyth," Avery said.

"Already on it."

"What about the medallion and the coins?" Harrison said.

"I can't find any such medallion in any of the photos. Though there may well be other photos I don't have. As for the coins, you were correct. Olav did have silver coins minted in his image. Thousands of them. Casting the silver into coins may have been how much of the lost treasure was taken."

"Easy way to transport treasure," Avery said as she thought back to the General's Gold.

"Imagine what those are worth today?" Harrison said.

"What about all these books?" Carter asked. "Do we need to search through these too?"

"I don't think we should assume the only clues could be found in the displayed papers," MaryAnn said.

"Easy for you to say. You're not looking at just how many not-displayed papers these people have," Carter said. "I thought scribes were rare way back when."

Avery stood up and stretched her back. "You heard the lady. Get cracking."

They ended the call, then spent the next several hours carefully examining anything that looked even remotely promising.

"Damage one of these and I'll bet they'll do more than revoke your library card, Harry," Carter said.

"Damage one of those and I'll see that you both walk home," Avery said.

"Even me?" Harrison said, pretending to pout.

"Especially you."

The air inside the room was becoming stuffy. Avery peeled off her jacket.

"This might be worth a look," Carter said as he lifted a Bible from the shelf and held it up. "It says it belonged to Bishop Óláfr."

"Let's take a gander at that," Harrison said as he slid over next to him.

"Find anything?" Avery asked after several minutes.

"Maybe," Carter said.

"What does that mean?" Avery said.

"It's more like what we didn't find," Carter said. "There are pages sewn into the back of this book with nothing on them."

"Blank pages are nothing new," Harrison said. "I read books like that all the time."

"It wasn't done back when these were made, Harry," Avery said. "Paper was a luxury item. Nothing was wasted. Let me see that when you have a minute."

"I'll bring it over," Carter said. "Need to stretch my legs anyway."

Avery examined the pages using the loupe, but nothing appeared on any of them, blank or otherwise.

"I'm starting to get a headache," Carter said as he rubbed his temples.

"It's probably staring at this ancient text," Harrison said.

"More likely it's the glare from these lights," Carter said.

"Wait a minute," Avery said. "That's it."

"What's it?" Harrison said.

"The lights," Avery said.

"Pretend I've got no idea what you're talking about," Harrison said.

"Who's pretending?" Carter said.

"We're trying to find a clue that may have been left hundreds of years before electric lighting was even invented. These guys worked by candlelight."

"You're not suggesting we bring a candle down here, are you, Ave?" Harrison asked.

"I'm pretty sure the bishop might have something to say about that," Carter agreed.

"Not an actual flame," Avery said as she walked toward the light control plate on the wall. "But I may have something just as good."

Avery retrieved her jacket, pulled out her cell phone, and activated the candlelight app, then turned out the lights.

"Voilà," she said.

"Why would someone need a candle app on their phone?" Harrison mused, shaking his head.

"And here I thought you were a true romantic, Harry," Avery said.

She bent down and examined the blank pages of Olav's Bible through the loupe. "Oh, God."

"What?" Harrison and Carter said simultaneously.

"It actually works," Avery said. "There's a map and writing."

"What does it say?" Harrison said.

"Not a clue," Avery said. "Get out your phone and type down the letters as I recite them."

"Ready whenever you are," Harrison said.

Avery read off each letter, making sure to articulate clearly. If she had learned anything about hunting for lost treasure, it was that details were crucial, and not everything was as it seemed. Ever. Interpretations mattered.

When they had finished, Harrison held up his phone and looked at what he had written.

"Well?" Carter said. "Any clue as to what it means?"

"It all looks Greek to me," Harrison said with a chuckle.

"Funny," Carter said before turning to Avery. "What about the map?"

"It looks like a lakeshore but it's faint. We might be able to photograph it with one phone if I hold mine close enough to illuminate it."

It took them several attempts, using the low-light setting on Carter's phone and the loupe as a lens before they captured an image worth saving.

"What about the other blank pages?" Harrison said. "Anything on those?"

Avery examined both sides of the remaining pages but found nothing on any of them. To be thorough, she rechecked the margins of the protected pages under glass but came up empty.

"Okay," Carter said. "Looks like we may have found what we came for. Now we need to figure out what the writing means and where the map leads."

Harrison looked at the words he had typed on his phone again. "Maybe we can ask Bishop Westergaard to translate this."

A sudden flash of light illuminated the entire room, making them all squint.

"Translate what?" Westergaard said from the doorway, one hand on the light switch and the other wrapped around the handle of a gun.

59

"Even the priest is trying to kill us?" Harry threw his hands up. "Twenty-seven years on the job and I've been held at gunpoint more in the past three days than in my entire career."

"You're not a real bishop at all, are you?" Avery clutched the Bible to her chest like it might sprout wings and fly away.

"God, I hope not," Harrison said. "My faith is on shaky ground as it is, Padre."

Westergaard laughed but there was no humor in his expression. "Then you'll be happy to know I am not a priest at all, Mr. Harrison. That should do wonders for your faith."

"What are you then?" Avery said.

"I guess you might call me a contract mercenary."

"And the real bishop of Nidaros?" Carter said. "Where is he?"

"I'm afraid he's gone to meet his maker," Westergaard said as he turned his attention to Avery. "You had asked before about the maze of tunnels running beneath this cathedral. Now you'll have to satisfy your curiosity, Ms. Turner. Up close and personal."

Westergaard stepped into the room, then used the gun to wave them toward the doorway.

"Who hired you?" Harrison said as he moved slowly around the left side of the room toward Westergaard.

"I'm afraid the kind of money I've been paid also buys anonymity," Westergaard said. "Let's just say my client is a very powerful man who wants the lost treasure of Nidaros quite badly."

"Why would someone who has enough wealth to hire mercenaries care about some old religious artifacts?" Harrison said.

"For some people, enough is never enough."

"I assume you're planning on killing us too," Carter said as he approached the doorway from the right side of the room.

"Spoiler alert, I'm afraid so."

"Then what difference would it make if you told us who hired you?" Avery said.

"Breaking a promise is dishonorable," Westergaard said as he ushered them out into the corridor. "Besides, it seems a few other folks have tried to kill you people, yet here you are. Now move."

They advanced down the dank, narrow corridor as a group, with Westergaard and his gun bringing up the rear. At the far end was yet another circular stone staircase descending to yet another tunnel. Every footfall echoed; every sound distorted. Avery found navigating the dimly lit passageway with eyes that hadn't fully adjusted difficult, stumbling. Harrison's fingers closed around her biceps as he caught her from behind.

"You okay, Ave?" Harrison said.

"Having a hard time seeing, Harry."

"Don't worry, Ms. Turner," Westergaard mocked. "You'll all get used to the darkness, eventually."

The passageways continued, as did the steps leading them farther beneath the ground. Avery did her best to keep track of the number of left- and right-hand turns, but eventually she lost count.

"I don't suppose you've got a plan," Harrison whispered to Carter.

"I'm working on it," Carter whispered back.

"Work faster."

"No talking," Westergaard barked.

Something large scurried directly in front of Avery's feet, causing her to let out a yelp and stop short. Harrison tripped over her, sending them both to the tunnel floor.

"Ouch," Avery shrieked.

"Now what?" Westergaard said.

"I'm so sorry, Ave," Harrison said as he regained his feet and attempted to help her up. "Are you okay?"

"My ankle," Avery said.

"Can you stand?" Carter said.

"I don't think I can put any weight on it."

"Out of the way," Westergaard said, ordering Carter and Harrison past the spot where Avery lay on the floor.

"Is this some kind of trick?" Westergaard said.

"No," Avery said. "I saw a rat and twisted my ankle."

Westergaard huffed and stepped back. "Get her up," he said, pointing the gun at Carter.

Carter did as he was instructed, leaning in close and wrapping his arms around Avery, whispering, "Is this part of a plan?"

"I couldn't very well wait for the two of you," she whispered back.

Avery regained her feet and her grip on the Bible and began limping forward, pretending to need Carter's assistance.

"Congratulations, Mr. Harrison," Westergaard said. "You just earned rodent duty. You take the lead. Now move."

Avery's limping slowed their pace significantly.

"What are you thinking?" Carter said.

"I'm thinking even if we overpower this guy, I'm not sure we'll be able to find our way out of here," Avery said.

"I have faith in your directional capabilities," Carter said. "As for the fake priest, he looks old. How spry can he really be?"

"Looks can be deceiving, Carter. Look at Harry."

"Good point."

"That's far enough," Westergaard said as they reached a confluence of two separate passages.

The ground beneath their feet had softened considerably to a dark mixture of earth and gravel.

"What are we supposed to do here?" Harrison said as he looked around.

"Dig," Westergaard said as he grabbed one of two spades leaning against the wall. He tossed one to Harrison and the other to Carter.

Harrison laughed as he caught the shovel by the handle, then threw it down. "You really must be stupid if you think we're going to dig our own graves."

"Yeah," Carter said. "If you're planning to shoot us, the least you can do is bury us yourself."

"What about the noise?" Avery said. "Someone in the cathedral will likely hear the sound of a gunshot."

"Oh, I wouldn't worry about that, Ms. Turner," Westergaard said as he approached her and ripped the Bible from her hand. "You obviously have no idea how far underground we've come. No one but the rats will hear a thing."

Carter and Harrison moved toward Westergaard.

"Back up, heroes," Westergaard said as he alternated pointing the gun at each of them.

They stopped in their tracks; Carter still held the spade in one hand.

"Tell me what you found in the book," he said.

"Why in the world would we do that?" Avery asked. "I figure the fact that you didn't see enough upstairs to know is the only reason we're still breathing now."

"People on the street would've heard the shots up there, too."

"A murderer with a brain," Harrison said.

Westergaard held Avery's gaze for five beats before putting his hand out. "Have it your way, I'll figure it out if you did. And now, I'll take the loupe, if you please."

Avery fished the loupe from her pocket. She reached out as if to drop it into Westergaard's outstretched hand, instead tossing it to the tunnel floor.

"I would have expected more from you, Ms. Turner," Westergaard said.

Avery shrugged.

"Pick it up," Westergaard said as he turned the gun on her.

Avery stared at the barrel of the firearm as she slowly bent down to retrieve the loupe along with a handful of earth.

Carter charged Westergaard at the same moment Avery tossed the dirt in the fake bishop's face, momentarily blinding him. Carter tackled Westergaard high on his torso, trying to wrap him up, just as the deafening sound of a gunshot rang out, echoing off the stone walls.

Harrison grabbed Avery by the hand and yanked her away, shielding her from Westergaard with his own body as another shot rang out. The bullet punched into the already-crumbling wall, causing several of the rocks to tumble onto the tunnel floor.

"Carter," Avery shouted as she wrestled free from Harrison and hurried toward Mosley.

Carter groaned as he staggered to his feet with the gun dangling from his hand.

"You okay?" Avery said.

"I think so," Carter said as he checked himself for holes.

Avery looked down at Westergaard's motionless body as Harrison checked him for a pulse. "Is he dead?"

"Unconscious," Harrison said.

"Told you he wasn't spry," Carter said.

A low rumble began somewhere farther down the tunnel.

"What was that?" Harrison asked.

"I don't know." Avery strained to listen. Everything went quiet again.

"Whatever it was, it stopped," Carter said as he handed the Bible back to Avery.

The rumbling returned, louder and closer this time, like an approaching freight train.

"No, it hasn't," Harrison said, wide-eyed.

The ground seemed to ripple beneath their feet, and the wall beside Westergaard collapsed, squashing his face like a rotting pumpkin.

"Run!" Avery yelled. "That way!"

Carter led the way, with Avery and Harrison hot on his heels.

"Left," Avery yelled as they reached another intersection. "Right," she said as they came to a T.

They ran until their lungs burned. Avery continued shouting out directions. Neither Carter nor Harrison even thought about questioning her instincts. The rumbling seemed to be emanating from everywhere. Like a mirage, the entire tunnel wavered before their eyes, the formerly solid stone collapsing all around them now.

As they ascended the final stairwell to the tombs, the last of the subterranean passageways collapsed directly beneath them, sending a cloud of stone dust up from below.

The three of them stood hunched over, hands on their thighs, gasping for breath.

Carter turned to Avery. "Have I ever told you how awesome it is to be friends with a mapping genius?"

"I got lucky," Avery said.

"I'll take that kind of luck any day," Harrison said as he brushed the soot from his clothes.

It was at that moment they noticed a small group of sightseers gaping at them.

"Um, we look like chimney sweeps," Carter said.

"Speak for yourself," Harrison said.

"Come on," Avery said.

"What happened to you guys?" one of the tourists asked as they passed.

Harrison leaned in to answer. "Are you folks signed up to take the tunnel tour?"

"No," a wide-eyed woman said.

"Don't," Harrison said. "Total rip-off."

They reached the ground floor of the cathedral, then hurried past the curious stares of tourists to the outside.

"Now what?" Harrison asked as they stood on the sidewalk.

"We need a ride," Carter said.

"No, I meant who do we notify? We left a dead fake priest down there. And a caved-in church."

"A fake bishop," Carter corrected. "And he's dead because he tried to kill us. As for the church, it looks fine to me, I don't think the tunnels were part of the foundation."

"Carter's right," Avery said. "We need a ride."

Carter turned toward the street and raised his arm. "Taxi."

60

"Say, what happened to you folks?" the taxi driver asked. "You look like you've been cleaning out fireboxes."

"Ever hear the one about the cop, the priest, and the billionaire who walk into a tunnel?" Harrison said.

"It's a long story," Avery said.

"I can't believe the place is still standing," Carter said. "I see it, but I don't believe it."

"It has a lot to do with how those cathedrals were constructed," Harrison said. "The buildings were built on foundations separate from the tunnel structures beneath. That way, should the tunnels fail over time, it wouldn't have any effect on the building above."

"You know a lot of weird stuff for a retired homicide detective," Carter said.

"How *do* you know so much about ancient cathedrals, Harry?" Avery said.

"Saw it on the History Channel. Or maybe in one of those BritBox mysteries."

Avery stared out the window in silence as the taxi driver navigated them back toward the museum.

"What are you thinking, Avery?" Carter said.

"I'm thinking our fake bishop went through a lot of trouble to get here before we did."

"Meaning?"

"Meaning, it speaks to the power wielded by whoever is funding these bad guys."

"That's true," Harrison said. "Even that Westergaard guy wouldn't give him up."

"We've got a bigger problem," Avery said.

"What's that?" Harrison said.

"Assuming that guy was working for Noah's mystery benefactor, besting Owen and Seamus meant nothing. If he sent a fake bishop to head us off before we even arrived in Norway, you can bet there will be others."

"Hopefully, Larsen will have some answers," Carter said.

"As long as he's who he says he is," Avery said. "Carter, have MaryAnn text us a photo of her friend Erik Larsen. We can't afford to make any more assumptions."

MaryAnn responded almost immediately with a photograph of her and Larsen, taken the previous year. Her friend in Norway was in fact the same man who had introduced them to Westergaard.

"I had no idea he wasn't the real bishop," Larsen said after leading them to his private office inside the museum. "I met him for the first time only a few days ago, right after MaryAnn said you might come here."

"Having a bishop pull a gun was definitely a first for me," Harrison said.

"Hopefully a last, too," Carter said.

"No harm done," Avery added to minimize Larsen's guilt.

"I'm so sorry I led you into that situation," Larsen continued. "I can't believe it. He was so convincing. Where is this Westergaard, or whoever he is, now?"

"I'm afraid he died in the cave-in," Harrison said.

"Cave-in?" Larsen said with a shocked look on his face. "Did part of the cathedral cave in?"

"No, no, nothing like that," Carter said. "Just the catacombs underneath the cathedral."

"But we did manage to find what we were looking for," Harrison added proudly. "Show him the bishop's Bible, Ave."

As Avery pulled out the leather-bound Bible, removed from the church library, she watched Larsen's face turn ashen.

"You stole a Bible from the Nidaros Cathedral?" Larsen said.

"More like borrowed," Carter said.

"It is a library, after all," Harrison said.

"We were hoping you could translate some writing we found on these blank pages at the back," Avery said.

Larsen stood up and pointed toward the door of his office. "I think you need to leave now."

"But if you could just take a look at the writing," Avery persisted.

Larsen shook his head. "Stolen books, cave-ins, dead bishops—"

"Phony bishop," Harrison corrected.

"I want absolutely no part of this, Ms. Turner," Larsen said. "Now please take your friends and leave."

They heard the door to the museum lock behind them as they walked toward the parking lot.

"That went well," Carter said.

"In hindsight, maybe I shouldn't have mentioned the cave-in," Harrison said sheepishly.

"I don't think it was that, Harry," Avery said. "I think he's just afraid of whoever is behind all of this."

"Now what?" Carter said.

Avery held up the Bible. "We still need this text translated."

———

At Harrison's suggestion, they caught another taxi and headed straight for the closest university—which turned out to be the Norwegian University of Science and Technology.

The taxi dropped them off in front of the administration building, where Avery located a campus directory board.

"What are you looking for?" one of the students passing by said.

"The language department," Avery said.

After obtaining directions, they hustled across campus to the brick-and-glass structure. They entered the lobby and realized that they were still drawing stares from curious onlookers regarding their disheveled appearance.

"Maybe we'd better clean up a bit first," Avery said.

"Good idea," Carter said. "Meet you back here in five?"

Avery checked herself using the camera app on her cell phone. "Better make it ten."

They headed off toward their respective restrooms. It took Avery a bit of scrubbing with wet paper towels and the reapplication of makeup before she looked nearly presentable.

"What do you think?" Avery asked as they reconnected in the lobby.

"You look great," Carter said. "What about me and Harry?"

She studied them for a moment before responding. "Truthfully, you look like a couple of escaped convicts, but it will have to do."

"We can go back and try again," Harrison said.

"I want to take advantage of the time we have," Avery said as she hurried them toward the library. "Nobody knows our phony bishop is dead yet. We've got the upper hand now, but it won't last long. Come on."

61

They met a young bespectacled library intern named Britt who, after learning what they needed, seemed eager to assist them. After Larsen's harsh reaction to the stolen Bible, Avery decided to show only the photos of the writing on her phone and not the actual Bible itself.

"Well, what do you think?" Avery said.

"You've definitely come to the right place," Britt said. "Did you know we have an original letter penned by the pope in the twelfth century in our collection?"

"Man, I'd love to see that," Harrison said.

Britt stopped short. "I could show you the letter right now," she said.

Avery knew Harrison was being facetious and shot him an angry glare. "Maybe after we decode this writing," she said.

"Oh, okay."

Britt led them to her professor, Dr. Aakre.

Aakre seemed far less eager than Britt had to assist them. Suspicion registered in his eyes immediately.

"And where did you come by these writings, Mrs. Turner?"

"Ms. Turner," Avery said. "And I'd rather not disclose the source, if you don't mind. I'm sure you can appreciate how hard it is to keep this kind of research from leaking out to the public."

"Indeed, I can, Ms. Turner. Do you have these writings? May I see them?"

"Certainly, I have several images of them here on my phone." Avery pulled up a photo and passed the device across the desk.

"A photo?" Aakre said, making no attempt to hide his scowl. "How high-tech of you."

Dr. Aakre donned a pair of bifocals and began to try to decipher the text.

Avery and the others spent the next several minutes trying to keep quiet, watching the professor's lips move as he read the text in silence. At last, he handed the phone back to Avery and removed his glasses.

"Well?" Avery said. "Were you able to decipher what it says?"

"Yes," Aakre said. "It appears to be a warning of some kind. Not a curse exactly, but it speculates that selfish motives invite the wrath of God."

Avery thought of the engraving on the cross.

"Whose motives?" Harrison said.

"I have no idea, Mr. Harrison. It seems whoever wrote this was making a very broad statement. A generalization if you will. Was there anything else accompanying this text, Ms. Turner?"

"Actually, there was." Avery pulled up the map photo and passed the phone back to Aakre. "This map."

Aakre slid his glasses back into place, then studied the photo.

"I apologize for the poor quality of the image," Avery said. "We were interrupted before we could record a clearer picture."

"I'll say," Carter said, earning a curious over-the-glasses glance from Aakre.

"I don't suppose you recognize any of the landmarks shown on the map?" Avery said.

"I don't, unfortunately. As you said, it's difficult to discern some of the details due to the poor quality of the photo. May I ask what it is you are all working on?"

"It's a project for an international supernatural festival," Avery said.

Aakre's forehead creased. "You came all the way from the United States for that?"

"It's a very big deal in some places," Carter said.

Aakre raised a brow, then looked to Harrison for confirmation.

"Very big," Harrison said. "Sometimes it's even hard for me to believe it."

Aakre shook his head as his attention returned to Avery. "I am sorry I couldn't offer you more information, Ms. Turner. Hopefully, my translation will be of some benefit."

"I'm not sure how it helps us, Avery," Carter said as they climbed inside another taxi to head back to the hotel.

"Yet again, I agree with Carter." Harrison shuddered. "My takeaway is that some moldy, old, long-deceased bishop thinks we should stay out of this. Maybe we should consider listening to him."

"We don't know if that passage was even written by the bishop," Carter said. "Could have been some lower-level priest doing the bidding of ol' Olav."

"Regardless, nothing good has ever come from this treasure," Harrison said. "People have died over it. And in case one of you missed it, there are people actively trying to kill us over it."

"Only part of the treasure is lost, Harry," Avery said, undeterred. "We've still got the cross, the loupe, and now this map."

"A map that doesn't appear to point to anything, Ave."

"That's because we haven't entered it into the DiveNav yet," Avery said.

Back at the hotel, Avery reformatted her photo of the map from the Bible, then uploaded the image first to her laptop and then into the DiveNav. Knowing the analysis might take some time, she stripped off her soiled clothing and spent the next twenty minutes scrubbing off the grime and musty smell of the Nidaros tunnels, luxuriating in the hot water wall jets of the hotel shower.

After drying her hair and wrapping up in a fleece robe, Avery returned to the laptop to see what, if anything, the DiveNav had come up with for a location. She was frustrated to find it was still in thinking mode. The long wait combined with the glitches were unacceptable and had to be resolved before they went to market—the average diver or hiker looking for a reef, wreck, or cave would expect the device to just work without the need for rebooting or other tinkering. She needed to check on her second-generation prototype DiveNav device—a quick phone call to her manufacturer confirmed a prototype of the new, improved model was just barely ready. She arranged to have it shipped overnight to her home in the Florida Keys, then sent a text to her housekeeper to be on the lookout for it.

Avery had just finished dressing in jeans and a comfortable pullover when there was a knock at the door. Carter and Harrison came in with a pizza box and a bottle of soda.

"It's like you read my mind. Where did you find pizza around here?"

"Everyone loves pizza," Carter said.

"You want plates?" Harrison asked from the small kitchen.

"Heck no," Avery said as she opened the lid of one of the boxes and inhaled the luscious scents of basil, oregano, melted mozzarella, and a thick yeasty crust. "I'll eat mine out of the box."

"Me too," Carter said.

"Savages," Harrison teased.

While they ate, they discussed the progress they'd made so far.

"I really thought the language professor would be helpful," Harrison said around a mouthful of pepperoni pizza.

"I'm not sure that guy could have translated what you just said, Harry," Carter said.

Harrison rolled his eyes at Carter and swallowed his food. "You two are still all in on this, I assume."

"We're not dead yet, and I'm not about to quit," Avery said. "You know how much I hate to lose."

"I may have picked up on that," Carter said.

"What's our next move?" Harrison said.

"I'm waiting on data from the map I uploaded into the DiveNav," Avery said. "Once we have that, I'll have a better answer to your question. I'm slightly frustrated that it isn't working better and faster, but this is why field tests are an important part of invention."

"Isn't your manufacturer building a newer version?" Harrison asked.

"They just finished it. The new and improved DiveNav 2.0 is being overnighted to Florida."

"Sweet," Carter said. "A better, faster, stronger DiveNav."

"You should call it Steve," Harrison said, prompting Avery and Carter to laugh out loud. "So these loons chasing us won't know what you're talking about."

As Carter reached for another piece of pizza, his cell rang with an incoming call from MaryAnn. He answered and put the phone on speaker.

"How are you guys making out?" MaryAnn said. "Anything shake loose?"

"Only the ground beneath the cathedral," Harrison muttered.

"What was that, Harry?" MaryAnn said.

"We'll fill you in later," Avery said. "How about you? Any luck with Arlo's connection?"

"I think so," MaryAnn said. "According to the records I found, Walter Smyth oversaw all the inventory aboard the *Fortitude*, including the hold. There's a lone reference in Smyth's log about a heavy wooden chest secured with a chain."

"Were the contents listed?" Carter said.

"No, but get this, the chest wasn't listed as belonging to any of the crew members."

"That's odd," Harrison said.

"Right?" MaryAnn said. "It's not like they were delivering it to Antarctica."

"Assuming for a moment the remains we found in the cave were Arlo's," Avery said, "what happened to Smyth?"

"That's another interesting part of this story. It looks like after being rescued, Smyth never returned to England. Instead, he ended up in Argentina of all places, where he lost a leg to gangrene shortly after arriving there in 1915."

"That's a little too perfect," Harrison said. "After stealing priceless treasure, this guy became a peg-leg pirate?"

"Not quite," MaryAnn said. "He became a peg-leg priest and changed his name to Father Carhill."

"Where in Argentina did he settle?" Avery said.

"A town called Rio Gallegos. I've managed to find a librarian there and we're working through their archives. I'll keep you posted."

"Thanks, MaryAnn," Carter said.

"Anytime. Any idea where you're going next?"

"I'm thinking home," Avery said as she picked up her phone and typed a quick text message to Marco.

"What?" Carter put his pizza down.

"Didn't you just say you don't like losing?" Harrison asked.

"Of course I did. But I need some clean clothes, and my new DiveNav. And Florida is on the way to Rio Gallegos."

62

They touched down in the Keys at eleven p.m., each exhausted from all the travel but more than ready to get back into the hunt. During the flight Avery had compiled a timeline of what they had discovered so far, including the most recent information about Walter Smyth, who'd become Father Carhill. Just the fact that the guy had changed his identity and never returned home made her want to look into his story, and something about seeing things written in chronological order had always helped her to process the next logical steps and revealed anything she'd overlooked.

A car was waiting for them as they deplaned. They had the driver drop Carter off at his beachfront house before continuing around the shore to Avery's.

She was pleasantly surprised to find a package waiting for her on the kitchen island and tore into it like a kid on Christmas morning. It was the new DiveNav, and love at first sight: the casing was sleeker, and lighter, though still virtually indestructible, and the internal CPU and AI software were up-to-the-minute state of the art. After linking the new device to her laptop, she uploaded the map they'd found in the ancient Bible and all the pertinent information she had about it, including the location of the church and the letters she'd written down that surrounded the map on the original page. The onboard software would process all of that through the artificial intelligence to tell her where she had the best chance of finding the area the map depicted. While the new DiveNav searched, she sat up in bed, taking care of a few remaining items for their trip to Argentina. Marco had told them the closest airport to Rio Gallegos was the Aeropuerto Internacional Norberto Fernandez, so Avery wanted to research the area. Before she had done much more than locate the airport's website, she fell asleep.

Marco was already waiting when they pulled up to the Gulfstream at 8:05 the next morning, and helped them load their gear into the cargo hold of the jet.

"You still have the chest and the cross?" Avery asked as she climbed the steps to the cabin.

"Safe and sound, Ms. Avery," Marco replied.

Twenty minutes later they were in the air, headed for Argentina, enjoying mimosas and some homemade breakfast sandwiches Dorothy had whipped up for their trip and wrapped in foil.

"I know you didn't go to bed without checking out the new computer," Harrison said to Avery.

"You got the new DiveNav?" Carter said. "How is it?"

"It's awesome," Avery said as she removed the device from her bag and handed it over.

"Any luck with the map from the Bible?" Harrison said.

Avery grinned. "It returned the results about five minutes after I fell asleep."

"High probability on location?"

"Ninety-eight-point-four percent," Avery said.

"Super," Harrison said. "Where is it?"

"About two hundred miles from Trondheim, Norway," Avery said.

Carter's jaw dropped. "You're kidding."

"Nope. A place called Skagens Odde."

"Shouldn't we be heading back to Norway, then?" Harrison asked.

Avery shook her head. "I think Argentina might be a better lead for now. It's more recent intel, and we can always return to Norway later if this doesn't pan out."

"Speaking of things not adding up," Harrison said. "I heard back from one of Roger Antonin's Interpol contacts last night. According to Interpol, Allison Miranda hasn't worked for NOAA for the past five months."

"What?" Carter dropped his sandwich in his lap and Harry laughed.

"I don't know why I'm even surprised when someone is lying at this point. According to one of her former colleagues, she said something about finding a lead on sunken treasure in the North Atlantic before quitting her job."

"Then what was she doing in Antarctica?" Avery said.

"Or New York?" Carter said.

"Those are excellent questions," Harrison said.

Carter held up the new DiveNav. "I wonder if it had anything to do with this."

63

The southern Argentinian city of Rio Gallegos spread out before them like a picture postcard. Avery, Carter, and Harrison stared through the windows of the Gulfstream on approach to the Piloto Civil Norberto Fernandez International Airport. A cerulean sky, dotted with caramel-tinged cumulus clouds, framed the oceanside city all the way to the horizon.

"Man, I wish we were here on vacation," Carter said.

"You ready to settle down?" Harrison asked.

"Not really. I'd just like a few days in a beautiful place without people trying to kill me."

"Don't even pretend escaping from those collapsing tunnels under Nidaros Cathedral wouldn't have made awesome online video content," Avery said.

"I still can't believe I didn't think to turn on my phone's camera."

"You were busy trying not to get squished," Avery said.

"True. And the occasional break is nice, but this life rocks."

"There's the Carter Mosley I know and love," Avery said. "As the cliché goes."

After landing, Avery tucked the cross and the Bible into a concealed pocket in the back of her bag before throwing the strap over her shoulder. After clearing customs, she phoned MaryAnn, who provided all the contact information she had for the librarian and offered to find them a hotel.

"Camila Sanchez has been extremely helpful," MaryAnn said. "She has a wealth of historical knowledge of the local parish because her grandfather was once the caretaker."

"Thank you, MaryAnn," Avery said. "I can't wait to meet her. We'll text in a while if we need a room—I'm not sure yet how long we'll be here, but we have our bags just in case we don't find what we're looking for today."

"Sounds good. Oh—I'm also sending you photographs of Arlo and Father Carhill from the *Fortitude*, in case the collection there has photos for comparison."

Harrison made no attempt to hide his displeasure at Avery's decision to take a horse-drawn carriage into town instead of a more modern mode of transportation.

"Come on, Harry," Avery said as she climbed into the coach. "Where's your sense of adventure?"

"I can tell you where it isn't. Behind the ass end of a horse."

Avery's Spanish was rusty but Carter, who had spent his whole life in south Florida, was fluent. Avery stared in awe as he carried on an animated conversation with their driver.

"Did you know he could speak Spanish?" Harrison asked.

"I did," Avery said. "I've just never heard him use it."

"I learned Spanish before I learned English," Carter said as he leaned back in the seat beside Avery.

"It shows," Harrison said.

"My mother insisted on it."

"A wise woman," Avery said as she waved to a group of pedestrians. "I love it here already. Everyone's so friendly."

"So was Westergaard," Harrison growled. "Right before he tried to kill us."

The Juan Hilarion Lenzi Biblioteca Publica Provincial prided itself on being the largest and most important reference library in all of Santa Cruz. Located at 60 Jose Ingenieros, the salmon-colored structure occupied most of a single block.

"That thing looks more like a warehouse or a converted school than a library," Harrison said. "You sure this is the right place?"

Their carriage driver, who apparently at least understood English better than he had let on, nodded and pointed at the sign. "Si. La Biblioteca Juan Lenzi."

"Have I ever steered you wrong before, Harry?" Carter asked.

"Where would you like me to begin?" Harrison retorted.

"Gracias," their driver said enthusiastically as Avery paid him in pesos.

"How much was that?" Harrison said.

"Seventeen thousand five hundred pesos."

"Are you kidding me?"

"It converts to about fifty dollars."

"Nice tip. No wonder he's smiling."

"Come on, Scrooge." Avery took him by the arm and led them inside.

Camila Sanchez looked much younger than Avery would have guessed. Her shoulder-length hair framed a beautiful face with glowing skin. And her umber eyes kept drifting toward Carter as she spoke.

"What is it with you?" Harrison whispered.

"What can I say?" Carter chuckled. "It's a burden being irresistible."

"I'd like to introduce my friends," Avery said as she gestured back to them. "This is Harrison, and Carter Mosley."

Sanchez shook each of their hands before turning back to look at Avery. "Buceador?"

Not understanding the word, Avery looked to Carter for help.

"She asked if I was a scuba diver," Carter said. "Si, buceador."

Harrison rolled his eyes. "Here we go again."

Sanchez blushed. "I did not know you spoke Spanish, Mr. Mosley."

"Even better than he speaks English," Harrison said.

Sanchez led them to her office at the back of the library and poured four cups of the best-smelling coffee Avery had ever shared a room with.

Sipping it and smiling, Avery explained that MaryAnn had sent them.

"We do have a limited collection of Argentinian religious reference material here at the library, but I haven't found anything regarding Father Carhill specifically. May I ask why you are so interested in a priest from such a small remote town?"

"Don't tell anyone," Avery said. "But we are working on a historical article about little-known priests for the *Catholic Times*."

Sanchez raised a brow. "Forgive me, Ms. Turner, but three reporters to research a single article? And an assistant who called ahead. Twice. You must have expense accounts too."

Carter and Harrison turned toward Avery and said nothing. If she was looking for help, she was on her own.

Avery sighed. "I guess I need to learn to lie better."

"Si," Sanchez said. "Perhaps the truth might be better for everyone."

"The truth is we believe Father Carhill may have stolen something from a shipmate during a voyage from England," Avery said.

"This was very long ago, no?" Sanchez said. "What could he have stolen that someone stills cares about?"

Carter stepped in. "Family heirlooms. I'm sure you can understand how important items passed down from family are."

Sanchez's smile lit her entire face as she appeared to study Carter.

"It is as you say, Mr. Mosley. I am sure MaryAnn told you my grandfather once worked for Father Carhill. He used to say Carhill had the worst luck of anyone he ever knew."

"A vengeful God," Harrison muttered, earning a curious glance from Sanchez.

"What about any papers belonging to parish priests either directly before or after Carhill's tenure?" Avery said.

"I'm not sure," Sanchez said.

"May we look?" Carter said.

"Certainly, I'll show you where we keep them." She waved for them to follow her and led them to a long, narrow room lined with shelves, lit only by high rectangular windows and a dim overhead fixture.

"May I refill your coffee?" Sanchez asked after showing them where the religious materials were kept.

"I will almost never turn down coffee," Harrison said.

"I'll make a fresh pot. It won't take but a minute," Sanchez said. "If you would like to start without me, they are all in order by date."

"Thank you," Carter said, flashing his best on-camera smile.

"Laying it on a little thick, aren't you?" Harrison said following Sanchez's departure.

"I'm just a poor buceador, Harry."

"This may take a while, guys," Avery said, sizing up the shelves, many of which were visibly sagging under the weight of the records they needed to search through.

"Why am I getting a feeling of déjà vu?" Harrison said.

"What do you mean, Harry?" Avery asked.

"I mean the last time someone left us to go through their records, we were nearly murdered."

"You think Sanchez is a phony librarian?" Carter laughed.

"Come on, Harry," Avery said. "You've been watching too many BritBox mysteries."

Sanchez returned with their coffees on a small tin tray. "I brought an assortment of cookies, too, in case you were hungry."

"Thanks," Harrison said as he dug in.

"Beware the phony librarian," Carter whispered.

"Whatever," Harrison said through a mouthful of sugar.

Sanchez helped Carter search through the tomes, removing any that appeared promising and setting them on a table for Avery and Harrison to leaf through.

The carafe was nearly empty and the cookies long gone before Avery found something in one of the journals.

"I think this could be helpful," Avery said.

"What is it?" Carter said as he came and stood behind her.

"It's a journal belonging to the parish priest who directly followed Father Carhill. There's a reference here to his predecessor fleeing home to England like a man possessed."

"Does he say why?" Harrison said before yawning loudly.

"Apparently, Carhill fled right after the church burned to the ground after being hit by lightning. The priest opines here that Carhill came to the church later in life looking to cleanse his sins but never quite outran his demons."

"Sounds like he knew him well," Sanchez said.

Avery continued, "It looks like there was a scandal because Carhill was believed to have absconded with a sizeable donation he had previously gifted to the church after his arrival in Argentina."

"Does he say what kind of donation?" Harrison said.

"He does not," Avery said.

"It would have to be the treasure, wouldn't it?" Carter said as he drained his coffee, then set the empty mug on the table. "Does this mean we're going to England?"

"What treasure?" Sanchez furrowed her brow.

As Avery turned to glare at Carter, he grabbed onto the corner of the table, then slid down to the floor.

"I've never seen a look actually knock someone out," Harrison took a step toward Carter.

"There's something wrong with him, Harry." Avery shoved her chair back and hurried to Carter's side. "He's passed out. Do you think it's something lingering from the decompression sickness?"

Harrison didn't answer.

"Harry?" Avery said as she looked up in time to see him slump against the shelves, then drop to the floor.

Avery's wide eyes turned to the empty coffee mugs on the table. The guys had finished theirs, while her mug was still half-full. Before she could speak or stand, something heavy hit the back of her head.

Avery collapsed on top of Carter.

64

The light hurt Avery's eyes when she dragged them open, and she tried to bring one arm up to block it. Her arm didn't want to move, and the light was everywhere—it didn't take long for her to give up on avoiding it, forcing her eyes wide like ripping a Band-Aid off, then slowly pushing herself up and off the floor. The back of her head throbbed, making her glad she'd packed some Advil. She had no idea how much time had elapsed since she'd been knocked unconscious, but she could see Carter and Harrison were both still out. Harrison, as usual, was snoring.

Using the table as a crutch, Avery staggered to her feet and saw Camila Sanchez taped to a chair. The librarian sobbed quietly. The tears had caused a piece of duct tape to come loose from across her mouth, flapping from her cheek as she shook her head at Avery.

"*Lo siento*, Miss Turner. I didn't want to help those men, but they threatened to harm me and my family if I didn't serve you the coffee."

"You drugged us?"

"They forced me to."

"Who hit me?" Avery said as she gently pressed the knot growing on her head.

"The taller man. The one with the broken arm."

Owen, Avery thought. *He beat us to Rio Gallegos, but how? Even if he knew about Father Carhill from his own research, he was locked up on the ship just days ago.*

The storm. Avery sighed. Noah probably cleared out and let Owen go when the storm cleared—winter had arrived there this week.

"How many men were there?" Avery asked.

"Two." Camila sniffled.

So assuming they didn't have another villain with a broken arm, was the other man Seamus, or someone they hadn't yet met?

Avery took a moment to collect herself. She didn't know for sure if Sanchez was telling the truth. It was impossible to know who to trust anymore. In the short time she'd been hunting lost treasure, she had met shotgun-toting old ladies, phony bishops, and now a sweet little librarian who served cookies and drugged coffee. Greed certainly was a powerful drug.

First things first, Avery thought. *I need water and some painkillers.*

Avery left the room to fetch some factory-sealed, drug-free bottled water. When she returned a moment later, she noticed for the first time that their bags were gone.

"The men took them," Sanchez said as she watched Avery search around the room.

"Great," Avery said. "No cross, no Bible, and no pain medicine." Not to mention that now Owen had her laptop and the new improved DiveNav.

"I have something you can take for your headache," Sanchez said.

Avery held up a hand. "No offense, Camila, but I think I'll pass."

Carter and Harrison began to stir. Avery helped them to their feet.

"What happened?" Carter asked.

"Somebody drugged us," Harrison said.

"Who would want to do that?" Carter asked.

"Her," Avery said, pointing at Sanchez and evoking fresh sobs from the woman.

"But why?" Carter asked.

"Hey, my bag is gone," Harrison said.

"They're all gone," Avery said. "Owen was here. He had a partner, but I don't know who."

"Looks like this chase just got a little more dangerous," Carter said.

"I'd be cool with you people choosing less danger from here on out," Harrison said.

The guys untied the librarian while Avery brought her some water, sitting down across the table to question her.

"Did you hear them say anything else?" Avery said. "Particularly any names?"

"One of them mentioned Heathrow as they were leaving."

"Damn," Harrison said. "They must know Carhill went home, too."

"Owen is a smart guy, and he'd clearly done his homework on this subject." Avery turned back to Sanchez. "Did they happen to mention how they would get there?"

Sanchez cocked her head to one side.

"Maybe a private jet?" Avery said.

Sanchez shook her head. "I don't think so. The one who taped me to the chair asked how to get to the airport, and the one with the broken arm was complaining about a long flight in cheap seats."

"That ought to slow them down," Harrison said.

"Can you describe the man who tied you up?" Carter said.

"Gray hair, tan, British accent," she said. "He was very . . . how do you say . . . condescending. Very condescending when he spoke to others."

"That could be Seamus," Carter said.

"Could also be Noah," Harrison added.

"It might even be some random British villain we haven't yet met," Avery said.

"How did they evade Interpol?" Carter said. "The guy in New Zealand put out a warrant for Owen and Seamus, didn't he?"

Harrison nodded.

"They must be using fake travel documents," Avery said.

"Great," Harrison said. "So how do we find them?"

"We may not have to," Avery said. "Come on. I have an idea."

"At least they didn't think to swipe our phones from our pockets," Avery said as she ended the call to the local police. "Which means we still have the map."

"Could that be how they managed to find us?" Carter said. "Like someone tracked us before, when we were hunting the General's Gold?"

"Malware." Avery snapped her fingers. "I should have thought of that. Owen is Mr. Tech. He would have known how to install that kind of software."

"But how would he have gotten access?" Harrison said.

"Someone had been in my stateroom before we left. Ten bucks says it was Owen."

"You can keep your money," Harrison said. "If we ever catch up to that little weasel, I'll break his other arm."

65

Marco was already waiting for them when they reached the airfield.

"I was beginning to worry," he said. "You were gone longer than I thought. Where are your bags?"

"It's a long story, Marco," Avery said.

"At least we got some rest," Harrison said, earning a look of confusion from Marco.

"I'll fill you in as we go," Avery said as she hurried up the steps into the Gulfstream.

"Where are we going?"

"London," Carter said.

"And step on it," Harrison said.

After freshening up and changing clothes, Avery gathered with the others in the main cabin.

"Here," Carter said, handing her an ice pack. "Thought you could use this."

"Thanks," Avery said.

"Guess you should have had more coffee," he said. "Then they wouldn't have had to knock you out."

"I can't wait to meet Owen again," Harrison said, punching a fist into his other palm.

"Whatcha doing?" Avery asked, noticing Carter working on his laptop.

"Probably counting his groupies on social media."

"They're called followers, Harry, and I'm doing no such thing," Carter said. "I'm checking all commercial flights departing from this area to London to see if I can figure out where those two knuckleheads might be."

"Good idea," Avery said.

"So, what are your thoughts after seeing the library notes from Father Carhill's replacement?" Harrison said to Avery.

"I think it's clear Carhill likely killed Arlo, then left him to rot in the cave," Avery said. "Arlo wasn't on the *Fortitude*'s manifest, so he probably assumed nobody would miss him."

"Doesn't seem like anybody has but us," Harrison said. "A hundred years later. Kind of sad."

"Why not return to England with the others?" Carter said.

"Somebody might start talking or asking the wrong questions," Avery said. "It was a lot easier to disappear in 1915."

"Plus, he had a chest full of stolen treasure," Harrison said. "Which reminds me, we still have the empty chest. How did Carhill get the treasure out of Antarctica?"

"He may well have smuggled it in his own baggage," Avery said. "Left some of his belongings behind."

"Okay, so say he makes his way to Rio Gallegos with the crown jewels," Carter said. "How does his leg become infected?"

"The curse?" Harrison raised his eyebrows.

"Puh-lease." Avery shot him a look of disapproval. "Who knows how he got the infection? Suppose Arlo took a swipe at him as they fought over the treasure in the cave. By the time he crossed the sea to South America, the leg was infected."

"And he thinks it's because of the curse, so he rids himself of the treasure by donating it to the church," Carter said.

"Makes sense," Avery said. "Cleansing himself of the theft and murder in an attempt to stop what he believed was a real curse."

"Wrath of God stuff, that is," Harrison said. "Nothing more Old Testament than believing God will strike you down from the heavens with a lightning bolt."

"Or gangrene. Whatever's handy," Carter said.

"I might've run halfway across the world too," Harrison said.

Avery stared at him wordlessly.

"Okay, maybe more of a slow jog," Harrison said.

Carter looked up from his computer. "Think I might have something."

"Another follower?" Harrison said.

Carter ignored the jab. "I've checked every flight leaving Rio Gallegos today for London or anywhere near London where they might catch a connecting flight."

"And?" Avery said.

"And, assuming Marco's estimate of our arrival time is accurate, the soonest Goofus and Gallant could possibly land at Heathrow is about four hours after us."

"That doesn't give us a lot of lead time," Avery said. "But it's something."

Avery pulled out her phone and fired off a text message to MaryAnn, asking her to research where in London Father Carhill's family might have resided. When she finished, she looked over to see both of her companions sound asleep in their seats.

Collecting their phones, she set out to find and destroy whatever tracking malware Owen was using, but to her surprise, a thorough search revealed nothing amiss with any of their phones.

So how was he tracking them, then? She pulled her jacket off and the sleeves of her T-shirt up, searching her arms for blemishes or cuts in case he'd slipped something under her skin while she was out in Argentina. Nothing visible, and a chip insertion would be big enough to see. Going with the more likely low-tech option, if Owen had stashed a LoJack into one of their bags, he was tracking himself after stealing them.

Avery smiled and closed her eyes.

Avery was awakened several hours later by the vibration of her cell phone. It was a response from MaryAnn.

Call me.

Avery sat up and rubbed the sleep from her eyes. Her head still ached slightly but it was better. *The ice must have helped*, she thought. Seeing Carter was still asleep and Harrison was nowhere to be found, which usually meant he was up in the cockpit regaling Marco with war stories from his homicide cop days, Avery walked to the rear of the spacious cabin to make the call.

"Any luck?" Avery said as she gazed out the window at the darkened surface of the Atlantic Ocean far below them.

"A bit," MaryAnn said. "I managed to find a quaint little village just outside of London where Carhill lived, called Great Missenden. It's in Buckinghamshire about forty-five miles from London."

"But?"

"But there doesn't seem to be any record of any Carhills living there now."

"What about his real last name?" Avery said. "Walter Smyth."

"No joy on that name either. You might want to start poking around in the village when the sun comes up."

"It'll have to be before that, I'm afraid," Avery said absently.

"You sound exhausted," MaryAnn said. "Did something happen?"

"You could say that," Avery said with a laugh as she gently touched the back of her head. "Let's just say there are two bad guys hot on the same trail."

"Are you behind or in the lead?"

"Got about a four-hour head start, we think. But these guys are resourceful and smart. On second thought, make that resourceful and persistent."

"Not smart?"

"Jury's still out."

"Well, if the clock is ticking, you might start at a small abbey I located right in Great Missenden proper. I'll text you the deets. Someone there may be able to help you. The abbey's been there for three hundred years. And church is always open, right?"

Avery hoped MaryAnn was right. The last thing they needed was to bump into any more phony men of the cloth.

"We'll need a car," Avery said.

"Way ahead of you, boss. It will be waiting."

"Thanks, MaryAnn. What would we do without you?"

66

It was overcast and drizzling when they touched down at Heathrow. Given the early hour, the airport was nearly deserted, and they had no trouble finding their car. MaryAnn had rented them a roomy four-door sedan for the trip. Carter volunteered to drive while Harrison rode shotgun and Avery commandeered the back seat.

"I take the A40, right?" Carter said.

"Yes," Avery said as she studied the GPS on her cell phone. "From there you'll eventually turn onto the A355 toward Amersham. Then the A413 all the way to Great Missenden."

"Whoa, whoa," Carter said. "One route at a time."

"Have you really thought this through, Ave?" Harrison asked.

"Thought what through, Harry?"

"Letting him drive. I get nervous enough when Evel Knievel drives on the right side of the road."

"Ha, ha," Carter said.

"Also, I know we're on a tight schedule," Harrison said, "but if I don't get a coffee and something to eat soon, I'll die."

"Me too," Carter said.

"Okay," Avery said. "But it'll have to be a road stop. We're operating on a clock, remember? Four hours isn't much time."

After crossing the Waterloo Bridge, they pulled over at a coffee shop that Avery located just off the Kingsway.

Avery and Carter purchased extra-large coffees and bagels, while Harrison ordered coffee and two five-cheese toasties before carting everything back to the car.

"I can't believe I flew all the way to London just to go to a Starbucks," Harrison grumbled between bites of his first toastie.

"Hey, you got a toastie," Carter said. "What could be more British than that?"

"Eyes on the road, Junior G-man."

Avery sipped her latte in silence, keeping an eye on the GPS.

A text popped up from MaryAnn with a quick overview about the abbey and the village of Great Missenden. According to what MaryAnn had found, the Abbey was known as Uptown Abbey, and it had been serving the village for several hundred years.

"Who is that?" Carter asked.

"MaryAnn," Avery said. She rechecked her GPS. "Don't forget to turn onto the A355 toward Amersham."

"Does that woman ever sleep?" Harrison asked.

"No," Carter said. "No, she doesn't."

It was barely five thirty in the morning when they pulled up in front of Uptown Abbey. Low cloud cover and drizzle cast everything in gloom.

"Why do you think they say half five?" Harrison said as they walked toward the entrance. "What does that even mean?"

"I suppose it's easier than saying five thirty," Carter said.

"I don't see how," Harrison said. "Our way definitely makes more sense."

Avery shook her head. "You two need more sleep. Come on. I need you to be charming. We're about to wake up a priest at half five in the morning."

It took several attempts at knocking on the door before Avery was able to rouse someone.

A disheveled middle-aged man in a plaid bathrobe pulled open the door. "May I help you?"

"I sure hope so." Avery painted on the most contrite expression she could muster. "I am so sorry to bother you at this hour, Father, but we're in a bit of a jam."

"And you are?"

"Oh, where are my manners? I'm Avery Turner, and this is Harrison and Carter Mosley."

The priest looked at each of them before his attention returned to Avery. "Are you looking to elope?"

"No, nothing like that." Avery laughed. "And no one is pregnant."

"Although, I do confess to feeling a bit bloated," Harrison said. "Think it might be the extra toastie."

The priest wrinkled his brow, thoroughly confused. "I have precious little tolerance for shenanigans, young lady."

"Understood. Is there any chance we could get out of the rain, Father?" Avery said. "I'll explain everything."

The priest sighed, then took a step back, opening the door wider. "I suppose you'd better come inside."

They followed him into the rectory kitchen, where he gestured for them to sit, then immediately put a kettle on for tea.

"I'm Father Moore," he said after joining them at the table. "Now, what is it that is so urgent you couldn't wait until a respectable hour of the morning?"

Avery explained they were looking for information about a priest named Father Carhill and it was a matter of some urgency, as dangerous men were searching for the same thing.

"Well, if it is the same Father Carhill I'm thinking of, I can't imagine any urgency. He's been dead one hundred years odd. Returned to England after serving as a priest in Argentina."

"That would be the one," Carter said.

Moore gave Carter a look most people received for bugs crawling across the floor. Carter sat back and got quiet.

"Might there be anyone connected to him still living nearby?" Avery said.

"There is a man living in town named Mason, who happens to be the son of a young apprentice who departed from the church around the time Father Carhill returned from South America.

"Departed from the church?" Harrison asked.

"Yes, Mr. Harrison. He was afraid to attend church for years after Carhill's return."

"Do you have any idea why?" Avery asked.

"I am not in the business of speculating, Ms. Turner."

"Would you happen to know if Father Carhill might have made a substantial donation to the church before he died? Or maybe to the town of Great Missenden?"

"Not that I've ever heard."

"It wouldn't have necessarily been money," Carter pressed, earning another look of disdain.

"Young man, while one hundred years may seem a long time to an American, it is far shorter here where history is longer."

Moore's comment gave Avery pause. She was almost positive the cook aboard the *Weddell* had made the exact same comment. Or at least very similar. Avery wondered if it might have been a phrase taken from a book or movie, or perhaps a common European colloquialism. Either that or she was becoming paranoid.

"I don't suppose you'd be willing to tell us where we might find this apprentice's son?" Avery said.

Moore appeared to consider her request carefully before answering. He got up and crossed the room in his slippers, returning to the table with a piece of notepaper and a pen.

He scribbled down the name and directions, then accompanied them to the door.

"We can't thank you enough," Avery said.

"Allowing me to return to my slumber is sufficient thanks, young lady. I will be around tomorrow, during proper hours, should you have further questions."

67

They returned to the car, then did their best to follow Father Moore's directions, but many of the old homes were missing street numbers. They parked in the general area of the address and continued the search on foot. It began raining steadily as they approached a home that should have matched the number they were looking for.

"It's still very early," Avery said. "I'm not that keen about waking another stranger. Especially when he doesn't live in a church."

"Relax, Ave," Harrison said. "Britain's strict gun laws definitely improve our chances of coming out of this alive."

This time a woman wearing curlers opened the door, wearing displeasure on her face like a mask.

"You want next door," she snapped, cocking a thumb down the street.

"I'm terribly sorry," Avery said as the door slammed shut. "Thanks so much for your help."

"She seemed pleasant enough," Carter said as they walked toward the correct address.

"I'm sure you could have charmed her," Harrison said. "You had such a great rapport with Father Moore."

It took three knocks at the next house before anyone answered the door. At least the homeowner was dressed this time. Judging by the reading glasses and the book he held in his hand, they had finally managed to bother someone who was already up.

"May I help you?" he said.

"I hope so," Avery said. "I'm so sorry to disturb you at this hour. We are trying to find a man whose last name is Mason. We were told he lived here."

"Young woman, if you're looking for a quick wedding, you need to go to the church."

"We get that a lot," Carter said.

"Actually, it's you we are looking for, Mr. Mason," Carter said.

"And none of us are getting married," Harrison said while struggling to maintain a straight face.

"We are looking for information about a friend of your father's," Avery said.

Following a quick round of introductions, Mason invited them in, with a warning about removing their wet belongings.

"You can hang your coats on the wall pegs and leave your shoes by the door. I don't want water tracked all through the house."

They followed him into the parlor, where a small fire was burning in the fireplace. Avery could see he'd been reading in the wingback chair beside the fireplace, as it was directly under the only lamp in the room. Mason gently placed the book on the chair, gesturing for them to sit in any of the others.

"Tea?" Mason said.

"Please," Avery said.

"Can't get enough of the stuff," Carter said.

"Thank you," Harrison said.

Following Mason's departure to the kitchen, Harrison leaned over to Avery and lowered his voice. "Any more tea and I'm going to need a catheter."

Several minutes later Mason was seated beside the fire while Avery occupied the adjacent chair and Carter and Harrison sat across the room at opposite ends of an old, faded plaid sofa.

Avery and Mason spoke at length about their reason for intruding, but she was careful not to overshare. As they spoke, a fluffy butterscotch-colored cat hopped up on the sofa between Harrison and Carter before deciding on Harrison's lap for a morning nap.

"Jinx seems to have taken a shine to you, Mr. Harrison," Mason said. "She's usually a very good judge of character."

"Has she ever been wrong?" Carter asked, earning a chuckle from Mason.

"The short answer to your question, Ms. Turner, is that everyone in the village knows the legend of the Cardinal's Curse," Mason said. "Carhill never kept it a secret. He spoke about the evils of greed constantly."

"Do you know what became of Father Carhill?" Carter asked.

"He died about five years after returning to the parish. By all accounts he had a decent life here. Friends, service projects, and the like."

"I don't suppose you'd know where he was laid to rest?" Avery said.

"Right here in Great Missenden. In a crypt located in the oldest part of the Memorial Park Cemetery. It is said he was entombed in the very box he trapped evil inside."

"But that's just part of the legend, right?" Harrison asked, chuckling nervously.

There was no humor in Mason's face as he turned to Harrison. "See for yourself."

The rain had stopped by the time they left, but the dark ominous clouds above them threatened more precipitation.

"Where are we off to now?" Harrison asked.

"The cemetery," Carter said.

"We're not actually going to visit this guy's crypt, are we, Ave?" Harrison asked as they walked to the car.

"Yes, Harry, we are," Avery said. "Come on. The clock is ticking, remember?"

68

It took them the better part of an hour to locate the tomb. The drizzle had started again, nearly guaranteeing they wouldn't be seen by anyone strolling among the stones.

The tomb was large and macabre-looking, with figures carved into the marble that appeared to be angels and demons locked in battle.

"This monstrosity is the final resting place of one man?" Harrison said as he walked around the exterior.

"Apparently," Avery said as she examined the vault more closely, searching for additional clues.

"What are we hoping to find?" Harrison said.

"Anything that may lead us to the missing crown jewels, Harry," Carter said.

"Outside clues, right?" Harrison said.

Avery and Carter exchanged a glance.

"Oh, come on," Harrison said. "You're not seriously considering breaking into this thing, are you?"

"You worried about a vengeful old priest, Harry?" Avery asked, only half kidding.

"Maybe he thinks we'll be cursed," Carter teased.

"It's the curse of the Bobbies I'm concerned about," Harrison said. "You're talking about grave robbing here."

"Not robbing," Avery said. "Just peeking."

"I suspect the local police will fail to understand the difference," Harrison said.

"We're going to need some kind of pry tool to get this open," Avery said.

"Well, we don't have anything, so I guess it's time to go," Harrison said cheerfully.

"There might be a pry bar in the trunk of the rental car," Carter said. "One of those lug nut wrench pry bar combos. I'll grab it."

Carter returned after a few minutes with the tool in hand. "It's not as good as a crowbar, but it will do."

"I can't believe we're doing this," Harrison said as he watched Avery and Carter work on the crypt door.

"Keep a lookout, Harry," Avery said.

"Oh, good. Now I'm an accomplice to grave robbing. Wonder what they'll say about that in the Old Bailey."

"What's the Old Bailey?" Carter said, grunting with exertion as he jimmied the steel bar into the gap in the vault door.

"Keep prying on that crypt, mister, and you'll find out."

"He's talking about the UK's Central Court."

"Good to know. Thanks, Harry. Very helpful."

"Just keep an eye peeled, Harry," Avery said.

"I think it's starting to budge," Carter said. "Yeah, the crack is definitely getting larger."

"Someone's coming!" Harrison said in a loud whisper as he ducked behind the nearest monument.

Avery and Carter scurried to the rear of the crypt, pressing themselves flat against it.

"Who is it?" Avery whispered back.

"It's a woman out walking her poodle," Harrison said.

"In the pouring rain?" Carter said. "Who does that?"

"Um . . . we are. Except we don't have a dog," Avery said.

"She's nothing like us," Harrison said. "Know why? Because dog walking isn't a crime. Here she comes. Keep quiet."

The woman drew nearer to the crypt. Then when it looked like she would walk right past them, she turned right and headed back toward the cemetery entrance.

"That was close," Harrison said. "Too close."

Avery and Carter resumed their work on the door.

"What if she saw us and she's on the way to phone the police right now?" Harrison said.

"She didn't see us, Harry," Avery said. "Stop being so dramatic. And that wasn't a poodle. They're called Labradoodles."

"I'm gonna Labradoodle if you don't hurry up," Harrison said.

"Got it," Carter said at last as he tugged the stone door open by hand.

Harrison joined them at the opening to the crypt as they peered inside the darkened space.

"Jeez, these things always give me the willies," Harrison said, keeping one eye peeled for other dog walkers. "Can you see anything?"

"Just a minute," Avery said as she dug out her phone and tapped on the flashlight.

"That's better," Carter said. "You hold the light steady, and I'll go inside."

Avery watched as Carter crept inside, almost like he was trying not to wake anyone. He moved slowly along the wall, looking like he was studying something.

"What are you doing?" Avery said.

"Trying to figure out what's in all these vaults if Carhill is the only one buried here."

"Well, hurry up."

"Found it," Carter called back, his voice bouncing off the stone like an echo chamber.

"Can you get it open?"

"I think so. Just give me a—got it."

"Keep watching, Harry," Avery said. "I'm going in with him."

She didn't wait for Harrison's answer. She was pretty sure he wouldn't be excited about it.

Avery found Carter and peered inside the vault, which was decently sized at probably four feet square at the mouth with around ten feet of depth, based on the distant white marble wall Avery could barely see the light bouncing back from. She handed Carter her phone.

"You wait here with the light, and I'll check inside," Avery said.

"Why you?"

"Because if we end up going to the Old Bailey, I want to share in the guilt. Besides, this isn't my first time in a cramped dark space with a skeleton."

Avery crawled through the opening, fighting through a maze of cobwebs.

"What do you see?" Carter said. "Bones?"

"No," Avery said. "Just a dark wooden box."

"A coffin?"

"It's not big enough," Avery said.

The box was hand-finished rosewood, with a carved silver cross covering the top end to end and side to side. *The box he trapped evil in*, Avery remembered Mason saying. *Great*, she thought. *I'm about to become Pandora.*

Carefully, she lifted a corner of the thick wooden lid, attempting to shift it to one side, but it wouldn't budge more than a couple of centimeters. She tried to peer inside, but it was too dark to see anything without a light.

"It smells like flowers," Carter whispered from directly behind her.

Avery jumped, dropping the lid back into place. "Jesus, Carter. You scared the heck out of me."

"Sorry, I just wanted a look."

"Help me slide the top off. FYI, the flower smell is rosewood," Avery said. "It has religious significance to Catholics—my mom had a rosary made out of it, and it smelled amazing. Still does. Lasts forever apparently."

They managed to move the lid partway off the box so Carter could shine the light inside.

"No bones," Carter said.

"You sound disappointed."

The box contained only two items. One appeared to be a very old decorative glass bottle of water so blue it practically glowed. The other item was a large brass skeleton key.

"What's in the bottle?" Carter said.

"Probably holy water."

"Why is it glowing like that? Is it supposed to do that?"

"I don't know," Avery said. "I don't think so. Let's just grab these and get out of here. This place creeps me out."

"Me too."

"Help me with the lid," Avery said.

They slid the heavy wooden top back into position, then scurried from the vault.

Avery stowed both items in her bag as Carter resealed the vault.

They hurried through the entrance to the crypt, nearly colliding with Harrison as he rounded the corner.

"Give the old guy a heart attack, why don't you? Did you find anything?"

"A key," Avery said.

"Help me close this up, Harry," Carter said.

Harrison crossed his arms in defiance.

"Come on, Harry," Avery said. "The sooner you help him, the sooner we can get out of here."

"I must be crazy to let you talk me into this stuff," Harrison growled. "Move over, Junior."

Harrison grabbed onto the stone door and shoved alongside Carter. The door moved back into place much more smoothly than it had opened. After making sure the coast was clear, they double-timed it back to the car and drove away.

69

"I thought we were leaving?" Harrison asked between mouthfuls of chicken soup as they sat near the front window of a local diner. "Crawling around one grave is enough for today, isn't it?"

"Not until we hear back from MaryAnn," Avery said. "She might turn up something that will require us to look further in Great Missenden."

"I'd rather get as far away from here as possible," Harrison said.

"Whatever that key unlocks could be nearby," Carter said. "The guy lived here when he got the idea for the tomb and the box and all. What do you think it opens?"

"I assume it's the *key* to this whole thing." Harrison waggled his eyebrows.

"Oh, that's bad," Avery said, rolling her eyes and laughing anyway.

"It's too big to fit into any modern locks," Harrison said. "It kind of reminds me of one of those padlock keys I used to see in old movies as a kid."

"What should we be looking for then?" Carter said.

Harrison shrugged as he tore off a mouthful of his sandwich.

"After what we've learned about Carhill, I was positive we'd find the remaining treasure in the tomb," Carter said.

Avery's cell rang with an incoming call. MaryAnn's name popped up on the caller ID.

"Speak of the devil," Carter said.

Avery answered the phone. "Tell me you've found something."

"I did. There's a lab not far from the village that can analyze the water sample you found. A new friend of mine named Otto works there. He'll be discreet."

"You are a true miracle worker," Avery said.

"Are you all okay?"

"For now." Avery glanced through the plate glass to the street outside. "No sign of any known mercenaries."

"Or the police," Carter added.

"That's not even remotely funny," Harrison said.

MaryAnn laughed. "Sounds like Carter and Harry are just fine."

"Aside from being a little wet and overtired, we're all good here. Did you get the picture of the key I sent?"

"Got it. I've reached out to an expert, and I'll let you know as soon as I hear something. Do you need anything else? A hotel maybe?"

"I'd rather stay mobile," Avery said. "It will make us harder to find."

"I'd really like to change out of these wet clothes," Carter said, blinking puppy dog eyes at Avery.

"And get a nice long hot shower, and maybe a bit of shut-eye," Harrison added.

"Sounds like you've got a mutiny on your hands, Avery," MaryAnn said.

"Okay, find us something comfortable and close to the lab," Avery said.

"With early check-in," Harrison added.

"You heard that?" Avery said.

"On it," MaryAnn said.

They delivered the water to the lab a bit before noon. Avery provided her cell number and Otto promised to fast track the results.

Better still, he didn't ask any questions about where they got it.

Avery awoke with a start to the ringing of her cell phone. She hadn't realized how sleep deprived she was until she'd wrapped up in the plush hotel robe and laid her head on the pillow. She checked the time before answering the call, surprised to see it was nearly three in the afternoon.

"Hello," she said.

"Ms. Turner, Otto here, from the lab. I've got the results of the analysis you requested."

"Wow, that was fast."

"Nothing but the best for a friend of MaryAnn."

Avery wondered what she would need to do to get that kind of respect instead of having people trying to kill her constantly. And how many friends did MaryAnn have, anyway?

"Did you find this bottle somewhere here in England?" Otto asked.

"We did." Avery kept her tone guarded, signaling that she wasn't willing to say more.

"Interesting," Otto said.

"Why's that?"

"Oh it's—I know why the water glows the way it does, and it couldn't have been sourced anywhere in the UK."

"So that wasn't just my imagination then?"

"Not at all. The water you gave me has an extremely high fluorescence under UV light. It contains a high concentration of scheelite, a mineral combination of calcium and tungsten, which glows blue in the dark."

Not magic at all, Avery thought. Much like the curse. She wondered if Carhill had even believed the tales. Maybe he used superstitions against those he preached to as a way of keeping them from the treasure. A hundred years ago, glowing water would have been a convincing trick.

"So if it isn't from the UK, where would water with these chemical properties come from?"

"Do you have a pen and paper? You'll want to write this down."

Avery rang Carter and Harrison immediately following the call with Otto and told them to meet her out front. She dressed, then hurried downstairs.

Carter and Harrison had already pulled the car around to the hotel entrance and were waiting for her.

"So, where are we headed?" Harrison asked as Avery climbed into the car.

"Back toward London," Avery said.

"Aye, aye," Carter said.

Avery filled them in on what she'd learned.

"Scheelite," Harrison said. "What the heck is that?"

"It's a combination of calcium and tungsten," Avery said. "It's the reason the water was glowing in the dark."

"Where does scheelite come from?" Carter said.

Harrison turned around in his seat to look at Avery. "If you say it's found in Antarctica, I swear to God I'm going back to the force."

"Relax, Harry," Avery said with a laugh. "Otto told me it's mined in California and North Carolina—"

"You hear that, Junior?" Harrison interrupted, turning to Carter. "We're going home."

"Not exactly," Avery said. "Apparently the stuff mined in the US doesn't have a high enough concentration to cause the glow we saw."

"Then where?" Carter said.

"Otto told me there's an Odde—that's a lake—in Denmark, fed by a river that cuts through a mountain riddled with the stuff. Apparently, when the weather is warm enough, the water glows at night for about an hour after the sun goes down. People come out to watch it. According to Otto it's the only known place on the planet with a concentration as high as what we found."

"Tell me we're not going mountain climbing again," Harrison said.

"How do we know Carhill didn't simply have the water from years earlier? Or buy it from a snake oil salesman?" Carter said. "It might not have anything to do with where he hid the crown jewels, right?"

"MaryAnn thinks it does," Avery said. "I called her after I got off the call with Otto. She's been digging further into Olav's exile and she stumbled upon Kristoffer's journal."

"Who is Kristoffer?" Harrison asked with a look at Carter, who shrugged.

"He was Olav's cousin," Avery said. "Admiral Kristoffer Trondson. Also the head of Olav's army."

"You know, Harry," Carter said. "Cousin Kristoffer. Try to keep up, will you?"

Avery continued, "Evidently, according to this journal, Kristoffer was on a journey with one of his soldiers. The soldier claimed to have seen Olav months before his death. The soldier said he'd been given a treasure to sell in Italy. But something went wrong, and then Olav died."

"And?" Harrison said. "What happened to the treasure?"

"Kristoffer doesn't get into specifics, either because he didn't want to write it down or because he didn't know. But the journal does say the soldier mentioned passing right through those exact Danish mountains Otto described, on his way back to Norway."

"But hundreds of years before Carhill's time," Harrison said.

"But Carhill had some of this water. And Mason said he buried the evil, right? What if he took the treasure back to where Tuva's great-grandfather —or whoever else—found it in the first place? The place Olav's lackeys dumped it when he died?"

"Denmark, anyone?" Carter asked.

"Marco needs a raise," Avery said. "And Harry doesn't even know what day it is anymore. But yeah—let's go."

"It's Thursday," Carter said to Harrison.

"Okay, neither of you know," Avery said. "It's Wednesday."

"Speaking of Marco," Harrison said, "we'd better phone and let him know we're leaving."

"I already have," Avery said.

70

The northern port town of Skagen was in Vendsyssel, Denmark, on the Jutland peninsula, parts of which reminded Avery of the sand dunes and lighthouses of Cape Cod. But there were vast differences too. One of those differences was the architecture: everywhere they looked, they saw half-timbered Tudor-style homes and Danish cathedrals with stepped rooflines. It was like a painting.

Known as a fishing village, Skagen was made world famous by an artist colony known as the Skagen Painters. Some of the original plein-air oil paintings, now several hundred years old, were considered priceless by today's art collectors. As Avery wandered through the rental shop while Carter assembled the equipment they'd need, she found herself drawn to a large wall poster of one of the paintings.

"You like that stuff?" Harrison said, twisting up his face to indicate he didn't.

"Um, this says 'that stuff' is a reproduction of a sixteenth-century artwork," Avery said. "By all accounts the original is priceless."

"Not really my taste," Harrison said.

The middle-aged proprietor of the dive shop strolled over. "That's a beauty, isn't it?"

"It certainly is," Avery agreed. "It looks somehow familiar to me. I'm wondering if I saw it in a museum—we've been to several all over the world in the past few months."

"You wouldn't have seen this, I'm afraid. It was stolen from a collector right here in the village fifty-odd years ago during a robbery."

"What a shame," Avery said as the owner went back to assisting Carter.

Harrison leaned in. "Why do we care about this painting? I thought we were looking for Olav's jewelry box."

Avery turned to him and lowered her own voice. "Because I saw what I'm positive was the original painting in a stateroom on board the *Weddell*."

Harrison blinked. "You're kidding me."

"The room I was trapped in after the explosion."

Harrison's face blanched white. "I saw you coming out of that room. The bed had red satin sheets, right?"

Avery nodded.

"Carter mentioned something about Erin having red satin sheets," Harrison said.

"Of course she did," Avery said. "How many more liars and thieves could they have stuffed onto one ship?"

Harrison shook his head in disgust. "Not a straight arrow aboard that entire ship, Ave. Not a one."

"So, what are you folks doing in town?" the owner asked, eyebrows up.

"We're photojournalists," Avery lied. "We're documenting highlights of the village for a national publication."

"You don't say? Well, there's plenty for you to document around here. If you don't mind my asking, why do you need all this equipment? I wouldn't think a photojournalist would have need of canvas straps, ropes, diving salvage float bags, and shovels."

"It's underwater photography," Avery said, earning a perplexed look from the man. "There's still a lot I don't understand about this assignment myself, but I'm figuring it out."

"We're hoping to get some nice shots exploring the Odde," Carter said.

"The lake or the peninsula?"

"Lake," Avery said.

"Oh, it is beautiful. You'll want to be careful, though. It's deep and very cold."

"How deep?" Avery said.

The owner seemed to ponder the question for a moment. "About forty-five meters."

"Um, what's that in American?" Harrison said.

"Roughly one hundred and fifty feet at its deepest point," the merchant said with a scowl. "In American."

"In that case we'll take another two hundred feet of rope." Carter flashed a toothy smile. "Just to be safe."

Avery decided to rent rooms for the night at a local establishment called the Brondums Hotel.

"You sure we can spare the time, Ave?" Harrison asked. "What about Owen?"

"Relax, Harry. Even if he managed to track us to Great Missenden, he wouldn't find a single clue once he reached the tomb. I think we can afford to take a little break and enjoy this quaint village."

"Besides, we're dead in the water until the marina opens in the morning anyway."

"Would you do me a small favor?" Harrison said.

"What's that, Harry?" Carter said.

"Don't use terms like dead in the water."

"This will be nothing like Antarctica," Avery said. "Trust me."

71

Avery, Carter, and Harrison were up with the dawn. Well rested and ravenous, they enjoyed a typical Danish breakfast in the Brondums' restaurant, which was part of the original farmhouse from the 1700s.

"They say breakfast is the most important meal of the day," Harrison said around a mouthful of sausage as he tapped his fork against the stack of cheese Danish residing on his plate. "I don't want to see you kids miss out."

"Okay, Dad," Carter said, rolling his eyes.

"Got to keep your strength up for diving," Harrison said.

Avery laughed, but she knew Harrison was right. The problem was, she was worried about what they might come up against as they moved ever closer to the lost treasure of Nidaros.

She picked away at her rye bread and cream cheese, while pushing the cured meat to one side.

"More coffee?" their waiter asked.

"Yes, please," Avery said as she set the fork down and lifted her mug.

"Anything from MaryAnn about the key we found?" Carter asked Avery.

"No," Avery said. "And I haven't found anything online even remotely resembling it."

"Well, it must be important if it was buried in Carhill's tomb," Harrison opined. "Like safe-deposit-box-key important."

Carter laughed, but Avery wondered if Harrison might be onto something.

After paying their tab, they hurried back to their rooms to collect the rest of their gear and finish packing the car.

They drove toward the Odde, stopping at the marina just as it opened for business.

"Help you folks?" the owner of the marina asked.

"I hope so," Carter said. "We're diving the Odde today and we need to swap out our tanks."

"Of course. Where are yours?"

"In the trunk."

"I'll give you a hand," the owner said. "Actually, there are two different Oddes here. Most people come here to dive at the ocean point they call the Odde. I assume that's where you're heading."

"Nope," Carter said. "We're diving Lake Odde."

"Beautiful spot, Lake Odde. You should see it at night. Quite popular today for some reason, too."

"How's that?" Avery said.

"There was another group in last night just before closing asking about diving it."

Avery and Carter exchanged a glance.

"What did this group look like?" Carter said.

"I say group, but I only saw two men," the owner said. "The older one looked a bit like that actor from *Jurassic Park*. The paleontologist with the smirk."

"Sam Neill?" Harrison said.

"That's the one," the owner said.

Avery's shoulders drooped. "It's Noah."

"I tried to tell you that guy was Dr. No-Good," Harrison said.

"And the other guy?" Avery asked the marina owner.

After hearing him describe Owen to a tee, Avery shook her head. "They got here when we did. Maybe before we did."

"But how?" Carter mused.

"They must have chartered a flight," Avery said. "As for how they knew to come here, I have no idea."

"You folks know these men?"

"Unfortunately, we do," Harrison said. "They are fugitives, probably traveling under false identities. Did you rent them any gear?"

"I didn't. As I said, I was just closing when they arrived."

Carter pulled out a business card, then scribbled his number on the back and handed it to the marina owner. "If those two guys should return, I want you to call the police. And call me, too. We'd like a heads-up."

"Are they dangerous?" The marina guy sounded alarmed as he studied the card.

"Very," Harrison said.

"I'm happy to help, on one condition," the marina owner said.

"What's that?" Carter asked, perplexed. Who didn't want to help catch criminals?

"Any chance I can get you to autograph this card? And allow me to snap a selfie with the famous Carter Mosley?"

Carter laughed. "I see. Sure thing." He put an arm around the man and smiled for the camera.

Harrison rolled his eyes.

The owner walked them back to the car and thanked them for stopping by. "Glad to have you here, Mr. Mosley—should be good for business. Good luck out there today."

"Thanks," Avery said as she took off her ball cap and waved.

The owner's jaw went slack as he recognized her. He began waving his hands for them to come back but Carter pulled away before they had to field any questions about lost treasure.

"That was close," Avery said. "Thanks for saving me."

"Not at all."

"Here, let me give you my business card," Harrison said, mocking Carter with a falsetto voice. "I'm the famous Carter Mosley."

Carter looked at Avery in the rearview. "Nowhere on the card does the word famous appear. He must have just known it instinctively."

Avery laughed.

It was nearly ten thirty by the time they'd reached the shore of Lake Odde. Access was only available by way of a long dirt road which led to a gravel lot adjacent to the lake. The sky was overcast with a light breeze rippling the surface of the lake. It was the perfect day for a dive.

The body of water was large. By Avery's estimate it was at least two hundred yards wide by three hundred yards long. Lit by the chemical anomaly Otto had described, Avery imagined it must have resembled an in-ground swimming pool at night.

"Man, that's beautiful," Harrison said. "Makes me wish I was diving with you."

"How many times you think people have driven up here at dusk to watch the glowing water?" Carter said as he adjusted the waist belt on his dive suit.

"Thousands," Harrison said as he gazed out across the water.

"There have probably been crowds for decades," Avery said. "And families who come every summer, too."

"With no idea what might be lying at the bottom," Carter said with a grin. "Funny, isn't it?"

"Let's not get ahead of ourselves," Avery said, though the butterflies had already begun to take flight in her stomach.

"What do you think?" Carter said as he prepared the high-powered underwater metal detector.

"Since those weasels stole my brand-new DiveNav prototype, I'm just using my own logic here, but if Carhill was trying to return the treasure to the place it was abandoned centuries before, well—MaryAnn said the journal recorded the soldiers coming over the mountains, which are there." She pointed west. "So I say we start on that side. Those soldiers would've been tired and probably freaked out by the idea of a curse. My bet is they didn't carry the trunks around the lake before they sank them."

"West side it is," Carter said. "We'll work in a grid pattern."

"Sounds good to me," Avery said. "And Harry, you know what to do if Tweedle Dee and Dr. Noah should pop up."

"Leave them to me," Harrison said grimly.

The first two hours turned up not so much as a rusty can. Carter and Avery took turns covering each section of the grid, to conserve their energy and their air. Harrison kept an eye peeled for Noah and Owen, but aside from a couple of elderly bird watchers, they were alone.

Avery was beginning to think they should break for some lunch when Carter popped up and began waving madly.

"You got something?" Avery hollered as she swam toward him.

"Oh yeah," Carter said. "It's only about fifty feet down, but I'm gonna need some help uncovering it and getting it to shore."

Carter marked the find using a buoy. Avery dove down beside him, following the nylon rope to the bottom. Excitement made her skin tingle as they descended. There was something sort of magical about this place, science be damned. It had to be here.

The Odde was basically a river-fed reservoir lined with an oceanic sediment and rock, so the water was incredibly clear, nothing like the muck they had found off the eastern seaboard of the US looking for the *Moneymaker*.

As they neared the bottom, Avery got her first glimpse of the wooden trunk. Like with the *Fortitude*, the cold water appeared to have done an awesome job of preserving the wood. The steel bands were heavily rusted, resembling something more akin to sienna-colored coral than hardened steel, but still intact. Only a small portion of the top end of the container was visible above the sand.

They worked in tandem, doing their best to remove the sediment by using their gloved hands and small diving shovels. It was slow going, however, as half of the sediment settled back into the void with each scoop taken.

After about fifteen minutes they had managed to uncover nearly half of the trunk. Carter signaled to Avery that he was going to try to pry the trunk out of the sand using one shovel as a fulcrum and the other as a lever. At first the trunk didn't seem to budge, but as Carter repositioned the shovels, inch by inch it became clear that the entire trunk was beginning to rise.

Once the trunk was completely exposed and resting on the lake bottom, Avery took a long look at the lock built into the side of the container. The keyhole was definitely big enough to accommodate the key they had found in Father Carhill's tomb. Avery pointed to it, and Carter nodded his understanding. She checked the time remaining on her tank. If they were going to attempt to use the inflatable bags to aid in recovery, they needed to work quickly. Once they got the trunk to the surface, they could swim toward the shore, then engage Harrison to help maneuver the trunk out of the water. Avery gave Carter the thumbs-up, then headed toward the surface.

Raising the trunk and moving it to shallow water took far longer than any of them had imagined thanks to two small punctures in the inflatable bags that rendered them quickly useless. It was nearly three in the afternoon by the time the trunk rested near enough to the beach for Harrison to be helpful. He bellowed about having to climb into the lake to his waist, soaking his pants and shoes in the process. Both Avery and Carter were spent, collapsing on their butts in the sand beside the weathered old trunk as the waves lapped against it.

"I can't believe you actually found this thing," Harrison said as he plopped down beside them, shaking his head.

"I told you we'd find it," Avery said.

"Yeah, but you never said anything about flying to multiple continents to do it. You may be the best treasure hunter ever, Ave."

"Hey," Carter said, attempting to look wounded. "What about me?"

"You're the best treasure hunter's assistant ever. Good enough?"

"From you, that's some lofty praise."

Avery glanced at Carter. "Ignore him, partner. We make one heck of a team."

"Come on," Harrison said. "Let's finish dragging this thing onto the beach before we lose it again."

Avery kicked off her fins and trudged across warm sand to the car, retrieving the key while Carter and Harrison used the shovels to pull the trunk across the dry sand toward the parking lot. Avery met them just as a dark sedan slid to a stop not far from them. Owen and Noah jumped out and rushed their way.

"Behind you, Avery," Carter yelled.

Before she could react, a hail of bullets came at them from the hillside above the lake. Everyone dove for cover, the chest momentarily forgotten.

72

Avery heard the bullets whizzing past and saw puffs of sand kicking up from the beach all around her. They split up, Carter scrambling one direction while she and Harrison ran in another, frantically searching the beautiful meadow surrounding the Odde for cover. She ran as fast as her exhausted body would allow, with Harrison practically dragging her behind a rock outcropping.

"Who the hell is shooting at us?" Carter yelled from behind a nearby sand dune.

"I don't know," Harrison hollered back as he drew his semiautomatic handgun from its holster.

"You brought your gun?" Avery said, surprised.

"With the number of them we've been on the wrong end of lately?" Harrison scoffed. "It was the first thing I packed."

Avery peered around the rocks toward the parking lot. Squinting directly into the sun, she saw Noah and Owen had also taken shelter, pinned down behind their vehicle. Someone else was indiscriminately firing at all of them.

"We have more company." Avery pointed.

"They're taking fire too," Harrison said. "Good!"

"But whoever that is, they're shooting at all of us. So not great."

Carter moved to his left trying for more solid rock cover instead of the sand. Just as he dove behind it, a bullet ricocheted off the ledge in front of him. Something struck him in the upper arm and he yelped.

"Are you hit?" Harrison hollered.

"I think I may have caught a piece of the rock," Carter shouted back. "I'm okay."

"You don't look okay," Avery said when she saw the blood running down the side of Carter's bicep from a tear in his suit.

The shots paused.

Noah's head rose over the hood of the sedan after a moment.

Harrison peeked out.

"Did they run out of ammo?" Avery asked.

"That was awfully quick," Harry said, watching for movement.

"Do you see the shooter?" Harrison asked Carter.

"Yeah," Carter said. "Repositioning up on the hillside behind the parking area. Maybe thirty yards out. It's a rifle."

"I can see that," Harrison said. "Looking for a description, a number of people . . . something helpful."

"Single shooter, average size, dressed all in black," Carter yelled back.

She turned to Harrison. "Thirty yards. Can you make that shot from here?"

Harrison peeked over the ledge again. "Once, maybe. But I've been out of the cop game for a while now, Ave. Thirty yards, uphill to boot, is a long way off." He sighed. "Only one way to find out. Stay down."

Avery rolled onto her back and watched as Harrison prepared himself mentally for the shot.

"Hey, Junior Mint," Harrison yelled. "Has he moved?"

"Nope. Setting up on the hillside, I think."

"I need you to distract him for a second."

"How exactly am I going to do that?"

"Give him a target."

"What?"

"You're already bleeding. Let him take another couple of shots at you."

"You can't be serious."

"I only need a second," Harrison said, praying he was right. "Run away from us, back toward the sand dune."

"Fine." Carter crouched. "Tell me when."

"On three. Two. One. Go, go, go!"

Carter took off at a straight-out sprint toward the dune, kicking sand up behind him like it was water. A rapid succession of rifle fire followed him as he ran. The first few shots struck the rock Carter had just left, the next few dusted the sand less than five feet from him.

Avery saw Carter dive headfirst into the sand as he reached the dune at the same instant that she heard a much louder gun discharge nearby. It was Harrison's sidearm. Only one shot. The rifle fell silent for several seconds.

"Did you get him?" Avery said.

Another rifle shot sounded, but it sailed wide of Carter.

Avery heard Harrison's gun fire again. This time no other sounds came from the hillside.

"I think I got him." Harrison sounded far away as Avery stared in horror at Carter's motionless body.

"Carter," she screamed, taking off toward him.

Just as she hit her knees next to him, he moved, crawling up on all fours before he began to spit.

Avery laid one hand over her heart. "Jesus. Are you okay?"

"Other than eating a mouthful of sand, I think so. You sure took your time about it, Harry."

"Just wanted to be sure I didn't miss."

Avery stood, ears ringing, as she tried to get a better look at the hill. She could just make out a prone body lying there. Owen and Noah peeked over the hood of their car, drawing Avery's full attention.

"One down, two to go." Harrison didn't put the gun away, keeping his eyes on their expedition leader and his right hand, who seemed to be discussing their next move.

Minutes passed.

"Should we go on offense?" Carter asked, gesturing up the rise.

As if they'd heard him, Owen and Noah started down the rise toward Avery and Harrison. Both had their handguns out.

"No more games, Ms. Turner," Noah said. "We know you found the key. Hand it over."

"Not gonna work like that, fellas," Harrison said.

"You're right, Mr. Harrison," a familiar voice said from behind Avery and Harrison. "I'll take the key. And no sudden moves or Avery takes the first bullet."

73

"You have got to be kidding me," Carter said just as Harrison tossed his gun to the ground.

Avery glanced over her shoulder to see Erin pointing a rifle at them. She was bleeding but very much in control.

"You're bleeding," Avery said.

"Flesh wound," Erin said. "Thanks to Dirty Harry here." She redirected the business end of the weapon at Noah and Owen. "My command applied to you as well, gentlemen."

They both dropped their guns in the sand.

"But I thought—" Owen began.

"What?" Erin said. "That we were working together? You really must be naive. Do you have any idea how much space-level science I had to learn to garner an invitation to be part of Team *Weddell*'s expedition? Only to have Noah go and ruin everything by inviting Avery and her band of misfits to the party."

"She must be talking about you, Carter," Harrison said.

"Um, I believe she used the plural version of misfit, Dirty Harry," Carter said.

"It was Owen's idea to invite you," Noah grumbled. "Not mine. He watched some video you made where you mentioned diving in Antarctica as something you'd always wanted to try."

"Only they underestimated you," Erin continued. "These two morons figured you'd be able to help them recover the treasure and then they'd take it from you."

"And what, you figured seducing Carter was a better way?" Avery said.

"More fun, anyway." Erin flashed a salacious grin. "Either way, it would have ended the same. A tragic accident on the world's most unforgiving continent claims the life of famed treasure hunters Avery Turner and Carter Mosley."

Erin turned her attention to Noah and Owen. "Why don't you two make yourselves useful and load the trunk into my van?"

Both men looked at each other.

"How are we supposed to lift that thing?" Noah said. "It must weigh a couple of hundred pounds."

"At least," Carter said.

"And I've got a broken arm, remember?" Owen whined.

"Then Carter and Harrison will help you," Erin said. "Won't you, boys?"

Erin used the rifle to herd all five of them toward the lake, where the chest still sat at water's edge.

"I can't believe I got taken in by such a conniving woman," Carter muttered to himself.

"You're just mad that your oversized ego landed you in trouble again," Harrison said.

"How did you get out of Antarctica in the first place?" Avery said.

"I hitched a ride with Allison Miranda on the NOAA chopper," Erin said.

"Don't tell me she's a treasure hunter too," Noah said.

"Okay, I won't," Erin said.

"Allison left her job at NOAA," Avery said. "We checked."

"You think she doesn't have friends there?" Erin said. "Now who's being naive? Who do you think tampered with the tanks you and Carter used on the dive?"

"Of course! Allison is an experienced diver," Carter said. "She would have known how to rig them."

"And where is Allison now?" Harrison said.

"She stayed behind in Argentina," Erin said.

"How did you find us?" Carter said.

"It wasn't that hard. I knew Noah and his lapdog would follow you to the ends of the earth to get the treasure. I followed them."

"I am not a lapdog," Owen snapped.

"Whatever," Erin said. "You're not all that observant either. The tracking device I placed in your bag is how I was able to follow you."

"You didn't check your bag?" Noah stomped his foot.

Avery turned to Noah. "So how did you find us, then? I checked our phones and you have our bags—what kind of high-tech tracking device did I not think to look for?"

"You really think you're so smart," Owen said.

"I know I'm so smart," Avery shot back. "Which is why it's bugging me that you two keep popping up like bad pennies."

"We used the incredibly high-tech and sensitive tracking device known as the human eye," Noah said. "Your plane has a tail number. Your pilot must file flight plans. We just downloaded a simple private flight tracker and watched you skip around the globe."

"Enough talk," Erin said as they reached the surf. "It's time for some action, boys. Hoist that trunk and put your backs into it."

"What a shocker," Avery said.

"What's that?" Erin said.

"That you'd want more action."

"Careful, honey. That smart mouth is likely to get you shot."

Carter released his grip on the trunk and stood up. "And what exactly were you planning to do if we decided not to help you with this trunk?"

"That's a great question," Harrison said. "You can't move it by yourself."

The confidence melted from Erin's expression.

"That's right," Owen said. "You need all of us to load the crate."

Erin began laughing. "Have you looked at yourself in the mirror lately, Owen? Avery can probably lift more weight than you can. Broken arm or not."

Avery could feel her temper boiling at the cruelty exuded by this woman, but she kept a neutral expression.

"How about this," Erin said. "Anyone willing to help put the chest into my van gets to walk away breathing and a percentage of the cut. Small, but better than a bullet, right?"

Nobody moved.

"Or I'll just start shooting people until some of you help me." She scanned the group with the rifle barrel, finally deciding on a target. "Let's start with Avery."

"Stop," Carter said. "We'll help you. Come on, Harry. Give me a hand."

Reluctantly, Avery pitched in and grabbed onto one corner of the trunk beside Carter. Noah and Harrison struggled with the opposite end while Owen pretended to help carry one side with his good arm.

Erin followed closely as they struggled across the sand and over several rock ledges toward the parking lot. Avery kept one eye trained over her shoulder, hoping for an opportunity to turn the tables.

Noah tripped, breaking his hold on the trunk. Harrison lost his own grip, stumbling back out of the way just as the heavy chest crashed down onto the rocks, breaking open.

As soon as Erin's attention shifted to the trunk, Avery sprang at her. She tackled her at the waist, driving her entire body backward onto the sand and knocking the rifle free from her grip with an elbow. Erin struggled, but hours of strength and hand-to-hand combat training meant Avery won the fight easily once the rifle was gone. Leaning on one forearm positioned across Erin's chest, Avery stared down at her. "You're done."

Erin held her gaze with a defiant glare for a few seconds, and Avery leaned harder on her elbow until the glare became a sulk.

"Um. Avery?" Carter sounded puzzled. Or disappointed. Avery twisted around without letting Erin have any wiggle room, her eyes following Carter's gaze to the broken trunk just as Erin did the same.

"Noooo!" Erin wailed as she saw for the first time what she had been willing to kill for. The chest was completely full of rocks.

A decoy. Nothing more.

Harrison scooped up the rifle, then checked to make sure it was ready to fire.

"Are we good?" Avery asked.

"Oh, we're good," Harry said.

"They're getting away," Carter said as Noah and Owen scurried up over the knoll toward their car.

"With nothing," Harrison said. "Let them go. My friends at Interpol will pick them up before they make it out of the country."

74

Avery, Carter, and Harrison spent the next several hours trying to explain the afternoon's events to the local authorities. Erin said nothing except that she wanted to call the embassy. Avery might have felt bad for her if she hadn't tried so hard to kill them.

"The good news is, since she wasn't talking, she didn't say anything about Harry's gun," Carter said as they turned the corner near the police station.

"What gun?" Harrison said, trying for the *I'm innocent* expression with shrug combo, but failing.

"What do you think will happen to her?" Avery asked Harrison as they watched Erin being led away by the police.

"Whatever it is, it won't be nearly enough for all she's done," Carter said.

"Amen," Harrison said. "But at least she didn't end up with a priceless treasure."

Avery regarded Carter for a moment. She was pleased to see he was no longer enamored of the cute femme fatale, but already wondered who the next one would be. Carter wasn't the kind of guy who spent many nights alone, which was fine as long as it didn't interfere with their work.

"I don't get this Carhill fella," Harrison said. "Why go to all the trouble to hide what amounts to nothing more than a lousy decoy?"

Before the authorities had arrived, Avery'd retrieved the key they'd found in Carhill's tomb to see if it would indeed have opened the lock on the smashed trunk. It took some effort, as the metal was corroded, but it eventually turned and disengaged the mechanism.

"I don't get it either," Carter said. "You think Father Carhill kept the treasure after all?"

"I'd be very surprised if he did," Avery said. "No, I think he really believed the treasure was cursed. Maybe he sank the decoy to keep anyone from finding the real thing and unleashing the curse again."

"Then he had to have found another hiding place for the real thing," Harrison mused. "Somewhere that wouldn't be disturbed. But where?"

"Where is the nearest church?" Carter asked absently as he poked at the bandage on his arm.

Avery's eyes widened. "That's brilliant, Carter. Absolutely brilliant."

They didn't have to drive far. A quick call to MaryAnn confirmed the closest church to the Odde was less than five miles away.

"Are you all okay?" MaryAnn asked, clearly concerned.

"We're all good," Avery said.

"Thanks to Avery," Carter said.

"Saved the day again," Harrison said. "Pretty good flying tackle."

"Enough of that," Avery said. "Tell us about this church."

"Well, the first mention I can find was back in 1387. The locals refer to it as the Old Skagen Church but get this: the original Danish name is *Den Tilsandede Kirke*."

"Meaning?" Avery said.

"The literal translation is The Sand-Covered Church or The Buried Church."

"If that isn't irony, I don't know what is," Carter said.

"Sounds to me like Father Carhill may have had something of a sense of humor," MaryAnn said.

Avery felt the excitement building again.

The church was exactly as MaryAnn had described. A tall tower-like structure with a white painted façade and stepped gabled roofline. It seemed oddly placed, so near the ocean, like the remnants of an old castle repurposed into a house of worship. Given the sandy ground around the church, Avery understood why they had needed to battle constant sinking of the structure. The loose soil supporting that much weight would have mimicked quicksand over time.

As Carter swung the rental car into the nearly deserted lot, Avery noticed the property was undergoing a renovation. There was staging, various pieces of construction equipment, and storage trailers scattered about.

"Doesn't look like it's open to visitors, Ave," Harrison said. "There's nobody here."

"Except that guy," Avery said, pointing to the man who had just come around from the rear of the church.

From the first glance it was obvious he was the property's handyman. Late sixties, ruddy complexion, wearing worn blue jeans, black knee-high Wellington boots, and faded maroon suspenders over a tight-fitting tee to show off his sinewy torso.

"There's our man," Avery said. "We win him over and we're in."

"He doesn't exactly look like a pushover to me, Ave," Harrison said, touching the handgun at his hip.

"Harry! He's a caretaker at a church—are you trying to get us cursed? Lock that thing in the glovebox."

"Are you sure that's a good idea?"

"Noah and Owen ran for the hills, and Erin is in police custody," Avery said. "If this guy keeping the grounds at a tiny church is lying in wait for us ... well, maybe the bad guys deserve to win this one."

Harrison shot Avery a look that said he wasn't happy as he did what she'd asked. "We'll need a good story," he said.

"Leave it to me."

"Care to share with the rest of the class?" Carter asked as they climbed out of the car.

"Just follow my lead," Avery said.

75

It took Avery all of three minutes, her camera, and a story about visiting the church where her grandmother got married to turn the brawny caretaker into a sentimental mushball who gave her the run of the place.

"Just be careful, okay?" the man said. "The workers have left a mess all over this place. I don't want any of you getting hurt."

"Thanks again," Avery said with a wave. "Oh, one more thing. Does this church have an onsite tomb?"

The man shot her a perplexed look.

"I just wondered if any of my other relatives might be buried here."

"Ah. No, there's no tomb. Let me know if you need anything else."

The building wasn't that large. Avery and Carter commenced searching while Harrison kept an eye out at the front door.

For the next twenty minutes, Avery pretended to take photographs of everything while she and Carter rummaged through all the places one might hide a fortune in stolen treasure. They poked around in the rafters, the pulpit, even under the floors in the basement, but they found nothing.

"There's nothing here, Avery," Carter said.

"There must be," Avery said. "It's the only thing that makes any sense. Otherwise—"

"Otherwise, this whole trip has been for nothing," Carter said. "That is what you were going to say, right?"

"I'm sorry, Carter," she said. "Of course, it hasn't been for nothing. We found *Fortitude*. You risked your life to find the cross and the loupe."

"And you risked yours to save me."

Avery smiled. "It was a life worth saving."

"I think the cleaning guy is getting antsy," Harrison called. "Looks like he wants to call it a night."

Avery looked at Carter as she gently wrapped her hand around his uninjured arm. "I guess that's it then."

The three of them walked outside to find the caretaker leaning against the side of his truck, waiting for them.

"Find what you were looking for?" he said.

"Just some old ghosts," Carter said.

The caretaker chuckled. "Wouldn't surprise me if you did. I gotta close up and get home for dinner, but you're welcome to explore outside for a bit before you go."

"Thank you," Avery said. "I really appreciate it."

"Not at all."

Avery spotted a building at the far end of the property. "Does that belong to the church?"

"Indeed, it does. They built it about a hundred-odd years ago as a carriage house. Mainly used for storage now."

"May we?" Avery asked.

"By all means. Watch out for ghosts."

They waited until the caretaker left before filing inside the building. The space was dark and musty smelling, with stacks of moldy old cardboard boxes everywhere. Availing themselves of the flashlights on their cell phones, Avery and Carter searched the entire first floor, coming up empty, until she spotted a trap door in the floor with a large, rusted metal ring protruding from it.

"Where do you think that goes?" Carter said.

"I'd say down," Harrison deadpanned.

"Ha, ha," Carter said.

"It's probably access to an old root cellar," Avery said. "Pretty common for that time period."

With Harrison's help they lifted the door, and Avery and Carter descended a set of creaky steps into a fieldstone basement. The moldy smell was more intense than it had been above. Avery caught sight of a large shadow scurrying behind a stack of old wooden boxes.

"Tell me that wasn't a rat," she said.

"Okay, it wasn't a rat," Carter said.

Avery squinted at him. "Did you even see it?"

"Nope."

"Then how do you know it wasn't?"

"Hey, I just said what you told me to," Carter said. "Would you like me to go check?"

"No," Avery said, putting up a hand to stop him. "Let's just stick with the original story."

"I don't think there's anyplace to hide something down here, Avery. If Father Carhill had tried to hide it here, someone would have found it long before now, don't you think?"

Avery sighed. "You're probably right."

"You ready to go?"

"I guess. Wait."

Avery trained her flashlight on a section of the cellar wall directly beneath the wooden plank stairs. Mortar had been added at some point to hold the original fieldstone walls together. But there was something markedly different about the mortar under the stairs.

"Take a look at this, Carter. It's a totally different color than the rest."

"You're right."

They looked around the basement for any kind of tool. After a moment Avery reappeared with a small crowbar, the kind for removing wood trim boards.

"Will this work?" she said.

"Let's see," Carter said as he began to chip away at the mortar.

"Just be careful," Avery said. "I don't want to damage anything for no reason."

"No problem," Carter said. "I'll just remove enough to get this stone out of—"

Before he could finish the thought, a large section of the wall collapsed at their feet, causing them to jump out of the way. A cloud of dust filled the air, reducing the visibility and making them sneeze.

"Oops," Carter said as he waved away the dust from in front of his face.

Avery glared at him, her hands on her hips. "What part of be careful was unclear?"

"It's like that Jenga game."

"The object of Jenga is to leave the wall standing, Carter."

"I was never any good at that game."

"You two okay?" Harrison called from the top of the stairs.

"Yes, Harry," Avery said, making no attempt to hide her annoyance. "Carter's just down here trashing the pl—" Avery froze midsentence. Her flashlight caught the glint of something shiny inside the hollow Carter had made.

Slowly she reached into the cavity and removed a golden chalice wrapped in fabric. Avery held it up for Carter to see as they both shined their lights on it.

"Oh my God. It's beautiful."

"Did you find something?" Harrison asked as he hurried down the stairs.

"Did we ever," Avery said.

She shined her light back into the hole. Almost the entire hollow was filled with precious metals. There were jewel-encrusted chalices, heavy crosses, a crown, and a scepter in gold and silver. Pieces worthy of a king.

"Look at all of that," Avery breathed.

Harrison stood beside them with his own light trained on the hole. His jaw dropped. "I can't believe you did it again."

"We did it, Harry," Avery said. "We did it."

A slow clapping came from the top of the stairs, freezing them where they stood.

"Bravo, Ms. Turner," Noah said as he and Owen descended the steps. "Bravo."

Carter turned to Harrison. "Maybe this stuff is cursed after all."

76

Owen pointed a gun at them as he and Noah descended the steps to the basement of the old carriage house. Avery, Carter, and Harrison moved back from the collapsed wall, doing their best to spread out. Avery swore under her breath, feeling naive for making Harrison secure his weapon inside the rental car.

"A spectacular find," Noah said, still clapping as he stared at the treasure spilling out of the wall. He picked up one of the gold chalices. "Truly remarkable."

"You don't really think you'll get away with this, do you?" Avery said.

For the first time Noah focused his attention directly on Avery. "I have gotten away with it, Ms. Turner. You and your ragtag team of treasure hunters were every bit as good as I hoped. Bringing you down to Antarctica was the best idea I ever had."

"You mean *we*, don't you?" Owen asked. "The best idea *we* ever had, right, Doctor?"

Carter swiveled his head from Noah to Owen. "Sounds like you two have a lot to hash out. Maybe we'll just head for the—"

The gunshot was deafening in the confined space of the basement.

"You won't be heading anywhere, Mr. Mosley," Noah said as he swung the smoking barrel of the gun around and aimed it at Carter.

Avery stood wide-eyed, looking down at Owen's lifeless body as it lay oozing blood rapidly onto the stone floor.

"There've been so many of you from the start of this, I never could quite figure out who was actually in charge," Harrison said.

"I hope I've been able to clear that up for you here at the end, Mr. Harrison," Noah said.

"Indubitably, Doc," Harrison said.

"Indubitably?" Carter said. "Did you really just say that, Harry?"

"What? I read, you know."

"Enough dad jokes," Noah said. "Mr. Harrison I'm afraid I will need your gun."

Harrison raised his arms, pulling back his jacket to show he wasn't armed. "The police confiscated it after you fled."

Noah clicked his tongue against the roof of his mouth. "What a shame. And the rest of you?"

"We were never armed," Avery said as she and Carter followed Harrison's example to prove they weren't carrying.

"Poor planning on your part," Noah said as he fished a set of keys out of his pocket and tossed them on the ground in front of Avery. "There are several canvas duffel bags in the trunk of my rental. Go and fetch them, Ms. Turner."

Avery felt her face redden. "Fetch?"

"Bad idea," Carter said.

"What's this?" Noah kept his attention on Avery. "Not used to having people tell you what to do?"

"Especially not someone like you, Doctor," Avery said. "It must be someone I respect. And that certainly wouldn't be you."

"I do apologize if I haven't properly motivated you," Noah said. "Maybe this will help. Either you fetch the bags as I asked, or you can choose which one of your partners gets to lie down with Owen. Permanently."

Avery glared at Noah for a moment before bending down and snatching the keys off the floor, never taking her eyes off him as she moved toward the steps.

"Oh, and don't think about doing anything stupid," Noah said. "Or I'll just dispense with the choosing and kill both of them."

Avery said nothing as she slowly mounted the steps. He was going to kill them anyway, she was sure. He was just playing with them, reveling in the role of the puppet master. And maybe he was a little lazy, too—all the stuff under the stairs would weigh a ton.

"Hurry back now," Noah called.

Avery ran to the parking lot. The sedan Noah and Owen had been driving was parked perpendicular behind the one she had rented, blocking them in. Prior to grabbing the bags from the trunk of Noah's car, she used her own keys to retrieve Harrison's gun, carefully tucking it into the back of her waistband. She had put them in this defenseless position. It was time to rectify that.

As she hurried back toward the carriage house, a bright light blinded her, stopping her in her tracks.

"Hold it right there, Avery," a familiar voice ordered from the darkness.

"I wonder what could be keeping her?" Noah said as his eyes wandered from Carter to Harrison, then back.

"I wouldn't worry about Avery," Harrison said. "She's got a good head on her shoulders."

"Let's hope so, for both of your sakes, Mr. Harrison."

"What exactly are you planning to do once you've taken the treasure?" Carter said. "I mean, you won't be able to just walk into a bank and pay off your debts with a chalice."

"It isn't the banks you're in debt to, is it?" Harrison said.

"Very good, Detective," Noah said. "Been checking up on me I see."

"I do believe in being thorough."

"If you must know, I already have a buyer waiting."

"Of course you do," Carter said. "The private donor who bankrolled your expedition to Antarctica, right?"

"He hardly bankrolled the entire thing, Mr. Mosley. Only the extension.

Long enough to bring you and Ms. Turner along for the ride. But yes, he is the buyer waiting to take possession of the treasure of Nidaros."

"And what makes you think he won't double-cross you after he gets it?" Harrison said.

Noah's eyes narrowed, then shifted to his watch. "I figure Ms. Turner has about thirty seconds left before she ends up carrying the entire load to the car by herself."

"I'm here," Avery said as she descended the steps.

77

"What took you so long?" Noah barked.

"Relax," Avery said, her voice shaking just the barest bit with nerves. "It's pitch dark out there. I tripped on the lawn coming back to the carriage house and had to find your keys."

Noah eyed the grass stains on Avery's clothing. "I didn't take you for the clumsy type. Give me the keys." He pointed the gun at Harrison and Carter. "You two, start bagging up every piece of that treasure."

Noah turned back to Avery, pulling her new DiveNav out of his pocket. "While they're packing my things, you will show me every secret detail of this thing. Can you load information into it that's not straight mapping data? How often is it wrong? How can you correct a map that was previously entered?"

Avery stared. "This is the other part of your payoff. You're supposed to deliver the treasure—and my prototype."

"This is actually going to auction," Noah said. "It should fund my retirement nicely—a lot of people who have been hunting treasure far longer than you have are willing to pay obscenely for your fancy toy."

Avery took the DiveNav and turned on the screen's backlight so she could see.

"You need the second menu screen to reprogram existing data," Avery said. "Click here." She touched the screen. "And then touch Reset."

"And that will do only one map?" Noah looked skeptical. "How do you choose which one?"

"It'll bring up a menu after you press Reset." Avery clicked the light off and bobbled the DiveNav, dropping it.

As she leaned to pick it up, Harrison moved in close and bent to fuss with a duffel bag, making eye contact. She knew he was thinking about his gun. She gave only the slightest shake of her head to avoid tipping off Noah. The disappointment on Harrison's face was obvious.

"Is that everything?" Noah asked.

"Seems like it," Harrison said, standing.

"Time to get a move on. I've got a plane to catch."

"And us?" Avery asked.

Noah shrugged. "Let's not get ahead of ourselves, Ms. Turner. You still must take all of this to my car. And I want to see that map feature if you can hold yourself together long enough to operate your gizmo."

There were three nearly person-sized bags, each stuffed to capacity with treasure and extremely heavy. Avery led the way as they struggled up the steps with Noah right behind them.

"Now back away from the edge, Ms. Turner," Noah said as he approached the ground level. "We wouldn't want you getting any crazy ideas in that pretty little head of yours."

She did as he asked, but while the idea of incapacitating Noah by throwing all that weight down on top of him had occurred to her, it wasn't worth the risk to Harrison or Carter should she fail.

Noah took up a position opposite Avery around the trapdoor opening, following Carter and Harrison's progress as they hoisted their bags up over the stairs.

"Almost done," Noah mocked as he waved them forward out of the carriage house with the gun.

"Yes, you are, Doctor," Avery whispered to Carter as he walked beside her.

Carter turned his head toward Avery. "What are you—?"

"Everybody on the ground, now!" a voice amplified by a loudspeaker commanded. The entire lawn lit up with spotlights, blinding them.

Avery, Carter, and Harrison immediately complied, dropping their bags in the grass and diving down beside them. Noah, dumbfounded by the ambush, remained standing, spinning slowly with the gun in his hand as if searching for a target. Avery peeked up at his pale face until he finally focused on her.

"Drop the weapon, Dr. Wyndham, and get down, now!" the amplified voice said.

Noah's gaze remained fixed on Avery. She watched as his eyes narrowed and he brought the gun around in her direction. Rifle fire exploded from several different positions within the churchyard. Noah's body appeared to dance for a moment before collapsing to the ground.

Avery hid her face in the grass, staying on the ground with Carter and Harrison until someone told her to stand.

Cold hands pulled Avery to her feet. Turning to say thank you, her jaw fell open and she yanked free, stumbling backward. "Freeze right there!" she blurted. "You guys missed one."

Allison Miranda appeared again.

"That's okay, Avery," Allison said. "The cuffs won't be necessary for this one. He's with me. Officer Young, Miss Turner is free to go."

"Officer?" Avery pointed to the frostbitten drone tech from the *Weddell*. "You were the stowaway?"

He grinned. "You really are as smart as people say," he said. "Nothing gets by you. Glad you folks are okay." He jogged off to help load the treasure bags into an armored car.

Carter and Harrison staggered to their feet with identical expressions, the same one Avery had worn when she first saw Agent Miranda in the churchyard.

"You're a crook," Harrison sputtered. "You left NOAA. You tried to kill Carter and Avery . . ." He looked around at the tactical team, floodlights, and vehicles. "What the bloody hell is happening here?"

Agent Miranda holstered her weapon and patted Harrison's shoulder, leading the way to an SUV where they could sit down. "I did leave NOAA— for Interpol. You all stumbled into the middle of a massive multi-agency investigation that's been going on for more than a year now." She turned to look back at Noah's body, squinting when she spotted Carter still several feet behind them. "Mr. Mosley, are you okay?"

"Just a little knock-kneed," Carter said, walking over on shaky legs. "You were onto Noah, then?"

"We were hoping he'd lead us to the donor he hooked up with last year, actually. We believe his contact is the head of an art theft and trading ring that spans at least three continents and billions in artifacts." She studied each of them. "He didn't say anything to you about this, did he?"

They shook their heads in unison. "No. Not a word," Avery said.

EPILOGUE

The sun shone brightly over the festivities on the lawn of the Miami Medical Center, where more than one hundred fifty people had gathered. Avery caught Carter's eye and tried not to laugh as he made a face while the medical director droned on. Avery knew how much Carter and Harrison hated getting dressed up and attending formal events, even if the event was as important as the groundbreaking and dedication of the new wing of the hospital.

"I would especially like to thank Ms. Avery Turner and Mr. Carter Mosley for their substantial and selfless donation, without which none of this would be possible."

Avery felt her face redden in response to the applause. Carter waved to the crowd like the celebrity he was.

"Good on you, kids," Harrison said.

Mercifully, the director concluded his remarks and gestured for Avery and Carter to come forward to help him cut the ribbon. Avery grinned as she watched Harrison take the hard hat and shovel from one of the board members. They waited for the photographers to capture the moment, then Harrison moved a spadeful of dirt from the ground, spilling some of it down inside the cuffs of his tailored suit pants.

"You can dress him up," Carter said, "but you can't keep him clean."

Avery laughed.

Once the ribbon was cut and the champagne was flowing, Avery, Carter, and Harrison wandered the grounds, holding their crystal flutes and trying to take in all that had happened since they'd found the *Moneymaker*.

"You know, this really was a good idea, Ave," Harrison said.

"Donating our finder's fee to the hospital?" Avery asked.

"Of course," Harrison said. "It's not like you need the money."

"It's never been about the money, Harry," Carter said.

"The thrill of the hunt really gets you," Harrison said.

"It certainly does," Avery said as she raised her glass in salute. "Here's to the best treasure hunting partners a woman could ever hope to have."

"Here, here," Carter and Harrison said simultaneously as they clinked their glasses together.

Avery leaned in closer, pulling her phone out of her sequined clutch. "MaryAnn texted just as we arrived. We've hit another dead end on that phone, Carter."

"Pretty slick, swiping that thing off Noah's body in the middle of a tactical scene without anyone noticing." Harrison's words dripped pure admiration.

"I knew when he started prattling about his buyer that he must have the phone he'd been using to talk to the guy on him," Carter said. "Really frustrating that none of our computer geniuses have been able to trace an ID on who programmed it or recover any of the messages between Noah and his backer. But at least Agent Miranda didn't realize I stole evidence, I guess? Somehow I feel less bad about that knowing it's pretty worthless anyway."

"Speaking of Allison," Harrison said, "I've been working with her to try and bring some closure to the cook on the *Weddell*."

"Tuva?" Carter said.

Harrison nodded. "We culled through a shi—"

"Harry," Avery cautioned.

"Sorry, culled through *many* records and it looks like Tuva's great-grandfather *was* killed by his business partner in their shipbuilding endeavor. Apparently, the other guy paid someone to cut the rope holding the timber, giving him access to the journal pages which led to the lost treasure. And then we know it wound up with Arlo after that, and the rest isn't a mystery anymore."

"The same journal pages Noah showed us," Carter said. "I wish I knew how he got his hands on them."

"They were purchased about ten years ago by a private entity as part of an estate sale. Something to do with relics of Viking history."

"Any leads on who the private entity might be?" Avery said.

"None. The entire transaction was paid for in cash and picked up by a private courier."

"I'd bet on Noah's mystery benefactor," Carter said.

"More than likely, I'd say." Harrison nodded.

"You think they'll ever unravel who was really pulling the strings?" Avery said.

"On the strength of investigative skills? Not likely," Harrison said. "Someone has gone to a lot of trouble and expense to stay hidden, and the feds have a big enough fish with Erin. Noah and Owen are dead—not worth the time and resources." He put his arm around Avery. "My fear is that this person, clearly used to getting what they want, wants your Dive-Nav, and won't stop coming for you until they get it."

"Maybe Seamus will give him up," Carter said. "He needs the leverage."

"I honestly don't think he knows who was funding them," Harrison said. "He was a lower-level employee than he wanted to think. By the way, I spoke to the director of the museum in Norway. They are some kind of tickled to have their lost artifacts back."

"I'll bet," Carter said. "Those babies have been missing for a long time."

"If you could have kept any of the recovered pieces, which one would you have chosen?" Avery asked Carter.

"Guess I'd have to go with the cross," Carter said. "We almost died trying to bring that one back."

Avery looped her arm through his. "That we did, Mr. Mosley."

"Which reminds me," Carter said. "My agent has three TV producers going nuts over the *Fortitude* dive footage. I turned them down on the idea of a series, but a television special is still on the table. Would you guys be interested in being interviewed for the show if I decide to do it?"

"The limelight isn't really my thing," Harrison said. "You two have fun."

"What about you, Avery?" Carter asked. "Surely you must be up for another adventure."

"What do you think, Harry?" Avery asked. "Should I?"

"That's entirely up to you, Ms. Turner," Harrison said. "You know I'll back whatever decision you make."

"That's what I love about you, Harry," she said. "And you're a great bodyguard, too. Okay, Mosley. You're on."

"Seriously?"

Avery squeezed his arm a bit tighter and gazed into his eyes. "Anything for a friend."

The Pirate's Secret
The Turner and Mosley Files Book 3

An ancient secret awakens, beckoning the brave into the shadows of history.

Carter Mosley is thrust into an unexpected adventure when his childhood friend and former dive partner, Jeff Shelton, leaves him a cryptic message. Carter is hesitant given his friend's shadowy past, but loyalty draws him in. Joined by Avery Turner, he heads to England to follow the trail. The quest turns deadly when Jeff is murdered and a link to Captain Ace Mullins, a legendary pirate whose tale conceals a priceless treasure, is unveiled.

From England's ancient reefs to Paris's underground catacombs, their search escalates into a high-stakes race across Europe. As Carter and Avery confront mercenaries and decode the past, the treasure they seek becomes more than just riches; it's a puzzle steeped in history, where each clue could be their last.

Get your copy today at
severnriverbooks.com

ACKNOWLEDGMENTS

So many people had a hand in getting this book into yours, and we are thankful to all of them. Our fantastic team at Severn River Publishing: Cate, Amber, Lisa, and Randall, who helped make the story, the cover, and the pages shine, and pushed us to dig every bit of danger out of Antarctica possible, thank you for all your hard work as always. Since we just had the first book in this series out a couple of months ago, we'd also like to thank the marquee authors and book bloggers who took the time to read Avery and Carter's first adventure and offer kind words about it: thank you all so much for believing in this series and helping get it off the ground. And last but never least, we'd both like to thank our families for keeping us on track and making sure the story got told: Karen Coffin, Justin Walker, and all three littles, you are the talent behind the scenes that we'd be lost without. As always, any mistakes you find are ours.

ABOUT BRUCE ROBERT COFFIN

Bruce Robert Coffin is the award-winning author of the Detective Byron Mysteries. Former detective sergeant with more than twenty-seven years in law enforcement, he is the winner of Killer Nashville's Silver Falchion Awards for Best Procedural, and Best Investigator, and the Maine Literary Award for Best Crime Fiction Novel. Bruce was also a finalist for the Agatha Award for Best Contemporary Novel. His short fiction appears in a number of anthologies, including Best American Mystery Stories 2016.

**Sign up for the Turner and Mosley Files newsletter at
severnriverbooks.com**

brucerobertcoffin@severnriverbooks.com

ABOUT LYNDEE WALKER

LynDee Walker is the national bestselling author of two crime fiction series featuring strong heroines and "twisty, absorbing" mysteries. Her first Nichelle Clarke crime thriller, FRONT PAGE FATALITY, was nominated for the Agatha Award for best first novel and is an Amazon Charts Bestseller. In 2018, she introduced readers to Texas Ranger Faith McClellan in FEAR NO TRUTH. Reviews have praised her work as "well-crafted, compelling, and fast-paced," and "an edge-of-your-seat ride" with "a spider web of twists and turns that will keep you reading until the end."

Before she started writing fiction, LynDee was an award-winning journalist who covered everything from ribbon cuttings to high level police corruption, and worked closely with the various law enforcement agencies that she reported on. Her work has appeared in newspapers and magazines across the U.S.

Aside from books, LynDee loves her family, her readers, travel, and coffee. She lives in Richmond, Virginia, where she is working on her next novel when she's not juggling laundry and children's sports schedules.

Sign up for the Turner and Mosley Files newsletter at
severnriverbooks.com

lyndee@severnriverbooks.com